The Iron Will
of Shoeshine Cats

Hesh Kestin

W F HOWES LTD

This large print edition published in 2012 by
W F Howes Ltd
Unit 4, Rearsby Business Park, Gaddesby Lane,
Rearsby, Leicester LE7 4YH

1 3 5 7 9 10 8 6 4 2

First published in the United Kingdom in 2012
by Mulholland Books

A CIP catalogue record for this book is available
from the British Library

ISBN 978 1 47121 314 4

Typeset by Palimpsest Book Production Limited,
Falkirk, Stirlingshire
Printed and bound in Great Britain
by MPG Books Ltd, Bodmin, Cornwall

MIX
Paper from
responsible sources
FSC
www.fsc.org   FSC® C018575

The Iron Will of Shoeshine Cats

For

Margalit, Ariel, Ross,
Ketura and Alexandra

— with their father's love

And special thanks to Stephen King, that
rarity among scriveners, a gentleman.

AUTHOR'S NOTE

In the time and place in which this story is set it was common to use words like *wop, mick, chink, nigger, spick* and *kike* in normal conversation – sometimes with opprobrium, often not. In order to reflect the spirit of the time I have not bowdlerized its language. Readers who may find this practice vexing are forewarned.

The novel's Bhotke Young Men's Society never existed, though a Bodker Young Men's Aid Association was very much in existence in the last century. My late father, Bernard L. Kestin, was a member. The actual Bodker Association was uninvolved in the events that follow, which are fictional.

So far as the author knows, the details of a vanished era in this book are all correct – but one. Find it if you can. And let me know via heshkestin@gmail.com.

H.K.

CHAPTER 1

The notorious gangster Shushan Cats walked into my life through the doors of the Bhotke Young Men's Society – in 1963 the only truly young man in the group was me – where I had become recording secretary the month before by a vote of 57 to 56 with three abstentions after it had been decided to switch the group's official language to English. In one sense this was foolish, because while most of the members were fluent in Yiddish, Hebrew, Aramaic, Russian and Polish, in English there were few who did not sound like the character on the Jack Benny Show – when television was still mainly black-and-white – called Mr Kitzel, whose voice, inflection and grammar made the average shopkeeper on Sutter Avenue, in Brownsville, the section of Brooklyn where I grew up, sound like Lawrence Olivier chatting airily with Vivian Leigh.

Why did the Bhotke Society make the change from Yiddish? In those days being foreign-born was somehow suspect. The Red Scare was still on, though somewhat evolved. Only a few years before, Ethel and Julius Rosenberg were executed as nuclear spies, and now the US was engaged in, and apparently losing, a space race with the Soviet Union. Among the minorities Jews stood out, marked by a culture, to say nothing of a religion, that would not go away; aside from a few sects in odd corners, Jews were then the only non-Christians. In melting-pot America we were heat-resistant, tempered by several thousand years of being close to, if not in, history's fires. In a largely Protestant nation, even the president, a handsome, charming and intelligent scalawag named John Fitzgerald Kennedy, had almost failed to reach the White House because many voters questioned whether his ultimate loyalty was to the Constitution or to the pope in Rome. While a younger and more affluent generation of native-born Jews felt as American as baseball, Frank Sinatra and Chinese food, the foreign-born, most of whom had escaped the Nazi ovens through pure luck, considered themselves marginal. For their sons the line between newly American and American never existed – many had fought in Korea, or in World War II, or both – but for the so-called greenhorns *American* was not a noun but a verb: you had to work at it. Even the longtime recording secretary, whose Yiddish was not only perfect but perfectly legible, voted himself out of the job in a flurry of nativism that would have given pause to the Ku Klux Klan. Because my late father had been a member, I was drafted: my English was perfect. In fact, it was at the first meeting at which I was in charge of the minutes that the doors opened with a flourish – they were double doors, and they were flung open – and I saw what would be my fate.

The figure who stood there – it seemed for minutes – was one of those small men native to Brooklyn who appeared to have been boiled down from someone twice the size, the kind who when a doctor tries to give him an injection the needle bends. Even in a belted camel-hair coat over a brown suit with sky-blue stripes he looked muscular, intense, dangerous. He may have had a baby-face and a baby-blue hat with a brown silk band, but believe me this customer was neither childish nor comical, though with the election of John F. Kennedy, bareheaded at his inauguration three years before, hats would already seem archaic, like music without a strong back-beat. (Whether as cause or effect, car roofs were growing lower every year, making hats impractical for men and women both.) The man at the rear of our meeting room could get away with it. Shushan Cats could wear a clown costume and cover his face in jam and feathers, but the way he stood there would nonetheless demand respect, if not outright fear. Unlike the Bhotke Society members, who had wives and children, who had jobs or businesses, who had in fact something to lose, this type, known in Yiddish as a *shtarker*, a hard-guy, had nothing to defend, not even his life. If you cut off his fists he would go after you with

3

the stumps of his arms; cut off his legs and he would wriggle like a snake and bite into your femoral artery until you died and he drowned in the blood. Even the Italian gangsters stayed away. There was something in these tough Jews that created a micro-climate of anticipation, if not fear. These were the nothing-to-lose Jews who had fought to the death in the Warsaw Ghetto, the pimps who had run the white-slave trade in Buenos Aires, the Hebrew avengers who had strung up five British soldiers for every Jewish rebel hung in Palestine. In the thirties they had formed Murder Inc. to sell custom-made assassination to the Italian mobs. In boxing they had dominated the ring in the undernourished divisions. In business they had been ruthless. And after the war they had become the smooth operators who managed criminal enterprises for a Mafia that was long on muscle but short on the kind of entrepreneurial skills that would build Havana as the world capital of gambling, and when President Kennedy closed that down with an embargo to punish Fidel Castro, Las Vegas to take its place. It could be seventy degrees in a heated room in the Crown Heights Conservatory on Eastern Parkway, which rented such places to fraternal organizations, political groups and social clubs, but when Shushan Cats walked in he brought with him a chill.

Also he did not close the doors, which did not help.

The president of the Bhotke Society at the time was a dentist named Feivel (Franklin) Rubashkin (Robinson) – he was in the process of Americanizing his name, a popular occurrence in the sixties. Feivel stood six-foot-three, especially tall in those days, and was a health fanatic who lived on nuts and then-exotic items like avocados and artichokes that most people at the time would not even have known you could eat, much less how, and he kept himself in top condition by lifting weights and swimming a hundred laps a day at the Young Men's Hebrew Association on Rockaway Avenue. But I didn't need a microscope to see him give an involuntary shudder when the man in the doorway finally spoke.

'Is this the Bhotke club?'

Addressing over two hundred men this way – all were turned around in their seats, only Feivel and I on the dais facing the door – was as close as anyone could get to asking the perfect rhetorical question. Poor Feivel looked at me as though to ascertain the truth: *Is* it? Is *yes* the right answer? Could someone *else* answer?

Whether because I was naive or simply took my new position as an officer of the Bhotke group seriously, I said in a clear voice: 'It is.'

The *shtarker* stood in the doorway, letting in the cold. 'My name is Cats,' he said. 'My mother was born in Floris, next door to Bhotke. I understand people from Floris can become a member because there is no Floris association.'

5

Again it was left to me. I turned to Feivel, who nodded. 'That's true,' I said with borrowed authority. I had never even heard of Floris. But I knew of Shushan Cats.

'So make me a member.'

'Please come in then.'

'I can be a member?' Cats said, so plaintively he sounded like a child who for the first time was offered love, or perhaps only acceptance.

'You have to fill out a card.'

'Okay.'

'And pay ten dollars initiation. Then it's eighteen a year in dues, including for a cemetery plot.' As with most of the Jewish fraternal organizations, this was the big draw. The Bhotke group had a choice piece of real estate in Beth David Cemetery in Queens, squeezed in on either side between the Gerwitz Association and the Loyal Sons of Bielsk, and facing the huge plot of the Grodno Union.

'Not a problem,' the gangster said. Immediately he pulled a roll of bills the size of a baseball out of his pocket and peeled off a single banknote. 'Ten to start, and another ninety, which takes care of five years. How's my math?'

I don't know where I got the nerve. 'Maybe you'd like to shut the doors and come in,' I said. 'There's a draft.'

He took several steps forward. Behind him a large man in a light grey suit and a hat like a watermelon, both in color and size, appeared out of nowhere and closed the doors behind them both. Probably a bodyguard, he had a thin mustache like a dirty line over his upper lip. 'That's it, that's the whole deal?'

Feivel, the president, looked to me. It appeared I was the designated speaker. 'That's it. Is there something on your mind, Mr . . . ?' Everyone in New York knew who he was.

'Cats,' he said with amused patience. 'Shoeshine Cats.'

Now the entire membership swiveled back to look at me. From the moment the gangster had entered everyone had turned around in their seats, magnetized. The man had been on the front page of the *Daily Mirror* the week before, being pulled along by two huge detectives in a perp walk on his way to an arraignment for a whole menu of crimes, the least impressive of which was racketeering. The headline was typical of the day:

HE'S NO PUSSY
MOBSTER CATS
BELLED BY COPS
SHOESHINE TO DA:
'DROP DEAD, NAZI!'

As he walked down the aisle toward me the gangster stopped to shake hands with those seated at the end of each row. It became a kind of triumphal procession. At each hand he would look the person in the eye and say, 'How ya doin'?' or '*Shalom Aleichem!*' or 'Good to see ya!' By the time he reached the dais even Feivel had relaxed sufficiently to press his hand. 'Are you the boss?' Cats demanded.

'Dr Robinson,' Feivel said to the accompaniment of a soft groan from several of the more unrepentent Yiddishists, who had never forgiven Isser Danielovitch, whose father had been a founding member, for changing his name to Kirk Douglas. 'I'm the president. It's not like a union, for life. My term ends in February.'

'A doctor?'

'Of dentistry,' Feivel said. He started looking for a card in his blue suit.

'A dentist ain't no doctor,' Cats said, waving him off. 'I got one. Fleishberg, on Pitkin Avenue.'

'Fine man,' Feivel said. He was becoming nervous again. There hadn't been so much excitement in the Bhotke Young Men's Society since the time – I was a child then but my father told the story – when Maurice Kuenstler's wife broke in to accuse him of adultery with his secretary, a *shwartzer* at that.

'Yeah, yeah,' Cats said, showing about as much patience as any of us had with Feivel, who had the job because nobody else wanted it. 'Who's the kid with the mouth?'

By this he meant me. 'I'm no kid,' I said. 'I'm the recording secretary.'

'You got a name too?'

'Russell.'

'Russell ain't a name. It's a half of one.'

'Newhouse.' I put out my hand.

Cats took it. His own hand was small, smaller than my own, but seemed to be made of some sort of warm steel, with no fat on it, just sinew. He held mine in his, trapped. 'Russy,' he said. 'I'm going to deal only with you, because you got a set of balls on you could sink a battleship. You're my man in the Bhotke group, okay?'

My hand wasn't going anywhere. 'Okay.'

'I'm a member, right?'

'Yes, Mr Cats. Paid up for five years.' Most members were in arrears. The treasurer complained about it at every meeting.

'So I got a spot?'

I looked down at his hand. A spot? A dot? A freckle? 'A spot?'

'In Queens?'

I still didn't get it.

'Where the dead go.'

'A *cemetery* plot? A spot in the cemetery?' Was this gangster preparing for the next world – would other gangsters or maybe the police burst in with guns blazing to rub him out right here in some settlement of accounts? Like everyone else in New York, I fancied myself an expert on the underworld, not least because the tabloids pushed the Mafia in front of our eyes every morning. For my consternation, my hand was gripped even more tightly.

'What are you, a wise guy?' Cats said. It wasn't a question. 'A minute ago I thought you was smart,

9

now you don't know one thing from the other? Yeah, a *cemetery* plot. What do you think I'm here for, the social life? The booze? The broads?'

'I don't know, sir.'

'*Sir?* How old are you?'

'Twenty-one,' I said, adding only a year.

'Friggin' old enough to vote and you can't tell when a guy is in mourning? My mama died last night. She's laying on a slab in Maimonides Hospital, in a frigerator, because we ain't got nowhere to lay her for her internal rest.'

'Sir, I—'

'Don't call me sir. You call me Shushan, not Shoeshine like in the papers. Shu-shan.' He turned to the rest of the membership. 'Everybody else, you can call me Mr Cats.' He turned back to me. 'You're a smart kid. I got a good feeling about you.'

'Thank you . . . Shushan.'

'Goddamn right,' the gangster said, giving my hand a further squeeze, tenderly now, as though it were a tomato being tested for ripeness. 'So all the details, the arrangements, the hearse, the flowers, the invites, the rabbi, the gravediggers, all that shit, I'm leaving to you. I'm trusting you, Russy.' He released my hand – then grabbed it again, and pumped it like a well-handle. 'You take care of my mama, Shushan Cats'll take care of you.'

CHAPTER 2

y life at this point hardly left a lot of
time for arranging funerals, or anything
else. To put it mildly, I fancied myself
something of a Jewish Casanova, which some
might say was only to be expected, since that's
how Newhouse comes out in Italian. How I myself
came to Italian was simple: English I learned on
the street, Yiddish from my father, Hebrew I
absorbed from after-school religious lessons
I suffered through until I was thirteen, but when I
had a choice of languages at Thomas Jefferson
High School on Pennsylvania Avenue in East New
York, I didn't take French or Spanish or German
but was drawn, if not magnetized, by the language
of Dante Alighieri, Giovanni Boccaccio, Niccolo
Machiavelli, Giussepe di Lampedusa, Luigi
Pirandello and Marie-Antonetta Provenzano. The
writers I knew, more or less, but Marie-Antonetta
I wished to know, intensely, deliriously, repeatedly.
She had thick black hair usually piled on top of
her head in a teased beehive like a crown, tiny
feet, wet brown eyes and nipples so prominent
behind the tight pastel sweaters she wore to school

11

they might have been light switches. She was fifteen. Little wonder that at fourteen I was in love with everything Italian, and even more so in the way of unrequited love when six months later her family moved to Long Island and I never saw her again. All I was left with was Boccaccio and company, in truth not such a bad deal, because when I read the classics, which is pretty much all I read, I neither risked catching a disease nor had second thoughts as I smoked a cigarette and looked up at the ceiling while some female, a perfect stranger in all ways but the flesh, insisted on making conversation; Pirandello never let me down. The fact is, I spent most of my non-reading time with the fair sex, with whom I dealt on a non-exclusive basis. Maybe it was because I lost my mother when I was still little more than a toddler there was a void in my life that literature could not fill: in love for a day, a week, a month, and then on to the next. By the time I was sixteen I was living on my own in a single-room ground-floor apartment on Eastern Parkway in the same building where I had once lived with my father. Sometimes one girl would walk in as another left. On top of this I made my living for a while as a sperm donor, which tied economics to physiology. Condoms were more or less the birth control of the day, and I was usually able to slip one off, pour the contents into a vial, call a cab and send it to a doctor on Park Avenue who paid me for every drop. Even today sometimes I'll spot a young man or woman with a nose that looks too much like mine.

At the time Shushan Cats came into my life I was seeing a girl named Celeste Callinan whom I'd met in advanced-Italian class at Brooklyn College. Celeste was one of those sweet-tempered outer-borough girls Henry Miller liked to write about: pliant of will, strawberry of hair, and so loudly orgasmic she must have frightened the neighbors, Hasidic Jews so modest about things sexual that, despite spawning dozens of kids, husbands and wives never saw each other in the nude. Celeste had no such hang-ups, possibly because unlike the Hasidim she could neutralize her sins at the nearest corner church for the price of a *mea culpa* and three Hail Marys, ten if the priest was gay. Celeste was so active I barely had to do anything but show up, and she had the delightful habit of bringing food, usually pizza or lo mein, Brooklyn's two major food groups. That I was circumcised probably added to her love for me, and love it was. I discovered this, first to my gratification (who doesn't want to inspire love?) and then my outright horror (who wants a woman who won't go away?) when I was ready to move on. I was twenty years old and male, for crying out loud, and half the population of the five boroughs was demonstratively female. It wasn't so much that I wasn't ready to settle down – it was that I wasn't ready for anything but the most extreme variety. Keeping Celeste at bay

13

while I continued my gynecological researches had become a full-time job. At first I found her waiting on my stoop. Then she graduated from Stalking 101: she had stolen a copy of my key, so she could get into my apartment at any time unless I used the iron security bar to double-lock the door when I was home. When I wasn't I kept finding someone waiting for me, which is just what occurred when I walked down Eastern Parkway with a funeral on my mind, and let myself in.

Maybe I was too much involved with figuring out how to arrange for the eternal rest of Shushan Cats' mother. As soon as I closed the door behind me I tried immediately to open it again. A large foot attached to a policeman pushed it shut. I wasn't really afraid of the police, no more than any other white kid in New York at the time, but I had reason to fear this particular cop.

Like the other two men in the room, he had Celeste's strawberry hair, brightly freckled skin and, it turned out, the same enthusiasm for robust physical activity. All of them were big – and bigger together.

The cop didn't speak first. In fact, I don't remember him speaking at all. It was the priest, whose words were soft, unthreatening, understated and cut off by the fireman, who got in the first punch. After that it was every New York Casanova's nightmare: three Irish older brothers taking turns. By the time they left I not only hated myself for having banged their sister, but personally regretted the entire Irish potato famine that had sent the United States of America an emigration that really, really hurt.

CHAPTER 3

By noon the next day I managed to limp to the bathroom, survey the external damage, and piss blood. Standing in the grotty shower for a half hour, I let the hot water do its job while my mind slowly tried to crank like an engine that was all but seized. Little by little I came to realize the problem was not Celeste and her brothers – their work was done – but Shushan Cats, who was expecting a funeral. If he didn't get his, I might very well get mine. It is amazing how fear can energize the exhausted.

But it wasn't just adrenalin that was flowing through me: it was, I was surprised to note, alacrity. By the time I was able to get down a cup of instant coffee with enough sugar in it to float a spoon – and then throw it up: more blood – I had formulated a plan. In the Yellow Pages I chose the largest ad. Even dialing hurt – this was a time when making a phone call was a physical activity. 'I'm calling for Mr Shushan Cats. His mother died yesterday and he wants you to make the arrangements.'

'I'm sorry for your loss,' the man on the other end said. 'Who?'

'Shoeshine Cats, the gangster.'

'The one in the papers?'

'No, the one whose pointy-toe shoe is going to be buried up your ass if you don't pay attention.'

Then I called Feivel.

'Russ,' he said. 'I can't talk to you now. I have a patient.'

'Strangle him,' I said. 'Feivel, Frank, whoever you are today, I need you to call Beth David, arrange for a plot with a sign on it that says *Cats*, and a hole big enough for Shushan's mama, plus bring every member that can show up.'

'I have a patient.'

'Fine,' I said, and as I did noticed that one of my own teeth was a bit wobbly. 'I'll tell our grieving friend you're too busy for his mother's eternal rest, and I'll give him your address.'

'What are you talking, Russ? This is not something for a dentist.'

'I'm not addressing you as a dentist. I'm addressing you as president of the Bhotke Young Men's. You wanted the job?'

'Yes, but—'

'But nothing. You got it. Believe me, Rubashkin or Robinson or whatever, if you fuck with me Shushan Cats and company are going to fuck with you. If you're lucky they'll break your hands so you can't make a living. If you're less lucky you'll have a new career—'

'What kind of—'

17

'As a soprano. You want Shushan to make you into Christine Jorgensen?'

That did it. Christine Jorgensen was the first American male to have a sex change. An icon of the fifties, she was famous as 'The man who went abroad and came back a broad.' Even the *Daily Mirror*, the most sensational tabloid of the day, did not have to exaggerate the headline on its front page: EX-GI BECOMES BLONDE BEAUTY. Instinctively I knew that when you make a threat, it helps to provide a visual. And this hoodlum wisdom was only from shaking Shushan Cats' hand. It was a hell of an intense shake.

By the next day I had stopped pissing blood and managed to hold down soup and toast, though on the subway to Beth David the condition of my face caused strangers to stare. I was now forced to rely on public transportation: not content to bust up my body and apartment, the brothers Callinan had as well played *Erin go bragh* on my car, a big-finned 1957 Plymouth Belvedere convertible that had seen better days but still, before the coming of the Fenians, had a roof, window glass, head and tail lights and unslashed tires. I was however less concerned with property than with body and soul, with emphasis on body. Almost certainly I had a couple of nicely cracked ribs, both on the right – the brothers Callinan were southpaws – where at least bone could not splinter off and puncture my heart. But my ribs were probably damaging something: parts of my body were announcing themselves to which I had never been formally introduced. To make matters worse, it had just begun to rain.

As I walked quickly down the main road of the cemetery a red 1963 Cadillac Eldorado Biarritz convertible, top of the line – in that year the car cost $7500, annual take-home pay for a successful lawyer – braked hard and its four-foot wide door flew open like the wing of some giant cardinal. In the driver's seat was the large man with the pencil mustache, this time in a dark gray suit and a large black hat, and beyond him his employer, who said something I couldn't hear.

'He says get in the car, dummy,' the large man said. This was a nice enough meatball whom, I was to learn, everyone called Ira-Myra's, because of his wife, one of those lush Brooklyn beauties whose body could stop a parade, and whose name was always on Ira's lips: Myra this, Myra that. The big lug was so helplessly in love it was cute, except that he was also maniacally jealous. Maybe a parade would have stopped for Myra, but everyone in Shushan's circle made it a point not even to look in her general direction. For all practical purposes, the combination of her shape and Ira's jealousy made her all but invisible, a striking woman who could enter a room and be totally ignored by every man in it.

Ira-Myra's leaned forward and the front seat canted open for me to climb in. Before I could say thanks I found myself swallowing hard: I was seeing

19

a ghost. There on the back seat was none other than an excellent facsimile of Marie-Antonetta Provenzano, an older version for sure, but from the same maker.

Shushan turned in his vanilla-leather seat. 'It's my sister, Esther.'

That was what he meant to say: I heard 'Smy sista, Esta.' Shushan's English took some getting used to, although even in my dampened, surprised and generally beat-the-shit-out-of state I could make out there was something wrong with it, like a stage-Irish brogue or one of those no-tickee-no-shirtee accents that are too heavy even for Chinatown. Despite my condition I almost wanted to answer him in kind: *Plizd, ahmshore*. Instead I said, 'You look like someone I used to know.'

Shushan turned around again. 'Not if I can help it. Esther, this is Russy the college boy. Knows everything, can't keep his mouth shut but is so far doing okay. He arranged for mama.'

Esther looked intently at me while I looked at her. On closer examination she was not Marie-Antonetta, but might have been if Marie-Antonetta had had something going on behind those liquid brown eyes aside from food, make-up and grindingly slow dancing. This version had the same hair but cut short, pixieish à la Zizi Jeanmaire, the French dancer, not piled on top of her head, a petite face dusted discretely with rust powder over deeply tanned skin and heavily-shadowed eyes that made her seem at once alert and somnolent, and

20

small, rounded lips like fish, one above the other and each facing a different way so that her mouth appeared pursed in silence yet pregnant with some phrase designed to hit me where Celeste's brothers had missed. 'You're just a kid,' she said. From her standpoint that was true: she was younger than her brother, but had a good ten years on me.

'Yeah.' I would have said yes to anything. But I couldn't leave it at that. 'Like you.'

'Yes,' she said. 'Like me.' With that she started to cry so hard it was all I could do to keep from putting my arm around her, and I might have done so, but we were already pulling up to the Bhotke Society subdivision, a barren neighborhood with a few headstones and a lot of discrete markers to indicate room for the inevitable depopulation explosion.

What we had come to wasn't a funeral. It was a collection of crowds. At my father's funeral there couldn't have been more than twenty. Here there seemed to be two hundred, standing in clumps as though representing a broad array of conflicting ideologies in some politically unstable republic. Probably there had not been so many people for a funeral in Beth David since Louis Gelb, the loan shark, died suddenly and his debtors, according to the *Daily Mirror*, showed up to make sure. (I read the *New York Times* and the *Herald Tribune* every day as well, but that was merely citizenship: in the tabloids was all the stuff that would be on the final.) Quickly I ran around the rear of the car and helped

21

Esther out, watching her heel sink into the soft ground like a signet ring into warm wax. She hung on my arm as though we had been friends for a long time, but aside from the heady smell of her – not perfume but some sort of musk rising from her dark helmet of hair – I barely felt the incipient lust that was my companion night and day, and which was neither subtle nor discriminating. Perhaps it was my sore body, or the presence of the dead, or her brother, or all these people.

The main group, standing around the grave with its back to the plot of the American Fellows of Gompitz, were familiar faces from the society, sixty at least, with Feivel/ Franklin standing in front looking athletically despondent, like a sprinter who has once again come in last, and with him a generic rabbi, probably supplied by the funeral home, whose representative stood on his other side, all shiny suit, morose expression and pecuniary interest. Like the rabbi, a small man with a white goatee and a homburg, the mortician was what he was.

I realized instantly that Shushan Cats, like any mourner, probably did not know what to do. With Esther on one arm I collected Shushan as he stepped out of the car on the other side and brought them to where the trio of officials stood before the grave.

'Are these the children?' the rabbi asked. He muttered something in Hebrew and then, out of nowhere, in his hand appeared a blade.

In retrospect it could hardly have taken minutes for what was to transpire, though it seemed to: the birds stopped singing, the wind stopped blowing, even the crisp November sunlight seemed to dim as I saw it all as if in a dream, the unrelentingly slow this-is-happening-but-is-not-happening union of fear and wonder that leaves us all as mute as an audience at a concert where the soloist falls off the stage or like an eyewitness at an accident as one car slowly, inevitably hurtles into another. But in dreams and concert halls and on highways we are never this close: Ira-Myra's stepping forward from behind his boss, his thick arm in a perfect right cross pushing his open hand almost lyrically to seize the rabbi's, the big man's fingers wrapping the rabbi's wrist, pushing it up and then down and around until the rabbi was on his knees, Ira-Myra's's own knee poised over him for the kind of kick that would have buried the rabbis' white goatee in his own teeth.

There they stood, frozen, a tableau waiting for resolution, until someone shouted, 'Whoa – it's just the rending of garments. Let him go!'

Along with everyone else's Ira-Myra's's eyes moved to the speaker. I followed their gaze. They were looking at me.

Me?

How did this happen? Only two days before I was spending my days in happy fornication and my nights too, in between smoking the odd joint, going out with friends to hear jazz in the Village

– for months I was a regular at a dive called The Showplace, where the angrily percussive bassist Charlie Mingus once fired the piano player in mid-set, saying 'We have suffered a diminuendo in personnel' – or drinking irresponsibly with a series of young women whose names and embraces run together like a medley of old songs, and from time to time visiting Brooklyn College where my professors allowed me to skip classes as an honor student so that I could spend time in a carrel at the library researching Milton or Mark Twain or Melville, so that I could deliver papers at term's end and within one more term graduate. And do what? I didn't know. I did know I spent as little time at the library as possible, but somehow delivered A-papers that I wrote a week before the end of the term, tossing in footnotes, a good many fictional, like some mad chef spicing a dish before it went into the oven. Look here, I wanted to say now: this is not my funeral, not my place, not my bodyguard, not my rabbi, not my anything entirely.

At least for the moment, Shushan relieved me of my burden. 'Ira,' he said quietly. 'Let the nice rabbi go. He's supposed to cut my coat, not my throat.' He looked to me. 'Also Esther's?'

This was out of my theological league.

Helped to his feet by Ira-Myra's, the rabbi nodded yes.

Oddly, I seemed to be the only one shook by this pocket violence. Everyone around us merely looked on with the same respectful attention while the

24

rabbi made a cut in Shushan's left lapel as though from time to time it was normal for a rabbi to be wrestled to the ground by a mourner. The rabbi said a prayer in Hebrew, which Shushan clearly did not understand – he said 'Amen' only when the rabbi translated it into English: 'Blessed are Thou, Lord our God, Ruler of the universe, the true Judge.' He then did the same, making a smaller slit, on the very edge of Esther's coat – careful so as not to offend a woman's modesty even in the face of death, a rabbi normally takes pains to make a miniscule tear that threatens to reveal nothing – and then summarized the benediction: 'Blessed be the true Judge.'

Beyond that it was your normal garden-variety funeral, except when Shushan took me aside and pulled a sheaf of typed papers out of his vest pocket. 'You done good,' he said.

'I'm trying, Mr Cats.'

'Shushan. Could be more flowers.'

'Shushan.' What was I supposed to say – next time?

'I want you should read this.'

'Now?'

'Yeah, because otherwise you won't be familiar with the words.'

'I have to be familiar with the words?'

'It's the eulogy.'

Sometimes time passes slowly, sometimes super-fast. Time was now making up for lost time. 'The eulogy?'

25

'I want you should read it.'

It occurred to me that perhaps Shushan was illiterate. Somebody had to read it. He couldn't. So he chose me. Made perfect sense. 'Maybe the rabbi would be a better choice. Or Feivel, the Bhotke president.' Or Walter Cronkite, or John F. Kennedy. Anyone. Just not me.

'You're the man.'

'I never met your mother, Mr Ca – Shushan. I mean, it would be . . . strange.'

'I wrote it,' he said, 'But I can't read it.'

'You wrote it.'

'Sure,' he said. 'It's all true. She was a wonderful mother. She deserves a good reading.'

'Me?'

'Who else, Ira-Myra's?'

I looked at him. 'You?'

'Not me,' he said.

Not him. 'If you don't mind my asking. . . .'

Shushan nodded in the direction of the Gerwitz Association real estate to our right where several groups of individuals hovered in bunches, as carefully arranged as battleground figurines, the sun glinting off their sunglasses and silk suits like so many search lights. A good forty were clearly *goombahs*, the kind Hollywood would shortly be making a stream of movies about, their names ending in vowels and their lives ending, it would seem, in either a bullet to the head or prison. These were not people who died in bed. Several feet away, standing in a clump of their own, were more of the same, thirty or so, but black, each one more elegant than the next in double-breasted black suits, bright white shirts, black ties, and on their heads broad brimmed black hats. The Italians were a mixed group, mostly older men in glasses and given to paunch, along with a sprinkling of muscular youngsters who were either their sons or their soldiers, or both. The blacks were rangy, big men who had gotten to where they were because they were handy with their fists. Further along, several yards separating them, stood a dozen or so Chinese, short, chubby, dressed straight out of Brooks Brothers' window, none of them wearing hats, probably because not one had ever before been to a Jewish funeral. I watched the mortician walk up to them and hand them black skull-caps. Each examined the item, then placed it on his head so gingerly it was as if it might cause some sort of explosion.

'Your people?' I said.

'Professional associates,' Shushan said. 'Also . . .' he nodded in the opposite direction, where three cars were parked separately from the rest, as if they were visiting a grave at the site reserved for the Loyal Sons of Bielsk. From one car three men emerged, one carrying a camera. Only cops could dress that badly. From each of the other two cars a lone photographer emerged. I was wrong: In the matter of *bas couture*, the press actually outdid the police. One of these press photographers – probably from the *Daily Mirror* itself, which covered organized crime the way the *New York Times* covered Congress – stood on his car's rear bumper the better to take in the field. Ira-Myra's came up to us. Shushan shook him off. 'We don't want a scene,' he said. 'Let the vultures lunch.' He turned back to me. 'Russy, if I read it I'm gonna cry. People don't want to see that. You read it. I got confidence.'

CHAPTER 4

For a supposed illiterate, a man whose *deses* and *doses* seemed to scream Brooklyn, it was a hell of a eulogy. Written in a neat hand that probably had not changed since seventh grade, it was clean, clear and grammatical. And organized. I could have used it as a model term paper at Brooklyn College. It began with a topic sentence meant to catch attention – 'Goldie Cats was not a great woman but a good woman, who raised her children with love and was kind to everyone she liked and hell on wheels to those she didn't' – and then proceeded into biography. Born in Eastern Poland, Cats *mère* had come to New York as a young girl, worked in a sweat shop, and lived most of her American years in the same railroad flat in Brownsville, tub in the kitchen, little heat or hot water, and after her husband's passing had been forced to take in piecework from the garment district to support the children she taught to respect their elders, work hard and be good to each other. Her daughter had grown up to be a professional, her son a businessman. That's what it said, businessman. She was semi-literate in English, her ability to write minimal, but she had a good command of her native tongue, and kept diaries in flawless Yiddish on the back of bills and wrapping paper. More than once she was called in to confront her son's exasperated teachers; always she defended him. It was not that either child could do no wrong, but that when it came to the outside world she would defend her children to the end. She lived by a code, and this extended to giving. No matter how little she earned she always set a portion aside for charity. A blue-and-white tin *pushka* from the Jewish National Fund always hung on a nail in the kitchen – every month or so someone came around the neighborhood to collect pennies and nickels from the Jewish hovels. She taught her children right from wrong, how to welcome guests, and never to take an insult. 'When someone hits you, hit him back ten times,' she would say. 'Pound him into the earth. The Nazis never disappeared – they're all around us. Nobody loves the Jews because we didn't accept that a simple rabbi from Galilee is God.' She tried to send her son to Hebrew school in the afternoons, but he was too busy with American things like basketball and, later, 'business.' He did not graduate from high school, but her daughter earned a BA *magna cum laude* in psychology from Hunter College, then the city's institution for women, an MA from Columbia in social work, then a doctorate in clinical psychology from the University of Pennsylvania. She now 'helped people help themselves' as a therapist in private practice on the

Upper East Side. Both her children took care of Goldie, supporting her financially as soon as they could, and always making sure to visit at least once a week. They begged her to move to a more comfortable dwelling, but she preferred to live modestly, to the end of her life in the same cold-water flat. 'Goldie Cats was a good woman all her days,' I read from the neatly handwritten pages. 'She did not set out to be great, to have university degrees or fame or riches. She became great by being good to those who deserved it, defending those she loved from anyone who would threaten them. She was the shining light of pure goodness, and her greatness was in one simple and indisputable fact. She did not know it.'

Getting an audience to start bawling is no great accomplishment at a funeral service, but here even the rabbi and the mortician lost it. An Hispanic looking man standing to Shushan's left began sobbing so heavily the lapels of his light gray suit began to turn as black as his shirt – I watched as he kissed Shushan on the cheek, his tears transferring to the bereaved son. Beyond the few family members and the crowd from the Bhotke Society I could see the Italians wiping their eyes with their white breast-pocket handkerchiefs, and the black hoodlums as well letting tears fall on their black silk suits. Most of the Chinese remained poker faced, possibly because they were as little acquainted with English oratory as its deceased subject – though two younger men

31

in long overcoats turned away so as not to weep publicly.

Over my shoulder I was aware that pictures were being taken. It was not a sound. The clicking of shutters would not be heard over the muted persistent cries of the mourners. The photographers' presence was reflected in the faces of the crowd. Once a camera appears few people are so single-minded not to pose, even if the pose is to feign ignorance of the lens.

The rabbi made a final blessing and gave Shushan a prayer book, out of which he read, haltingly but respectably, the prayer for the dead, which in Jewish practice is a hymn of praise to God. Shushan then picked up a spade and began shoveling dirt into the open grave. One by one – except for the cops and press photographers – all the males present did the same, even the Italians and the blacks and the Chinese. When they were done, I picked up the shovel. I must have been shoveling for a long time – three spadefuls are considered adequate – when I felt a hand on my elbow. When I looked up I saw the cops and the press photographers packing up. The Hispanic-looking individual, having regained his composure, was helping Shushan's sister into a long limousine. Ira-Myra's stood silently by the red Caddy. The show was over.

'You done good, kid,' Shushan said. 'I want you should help out a little more, with the mourning period, and then you're a free man.' Under his

32

reddened eyes he offered a wan smile. 'If you want to be.'

'Whatever you need,' I said. And I meant it. This was possibly the first selfless thing I had ever done, and done well, and despite having been dragooned into it, I did not want it to stop. I let Shushan guide me toward the gangsters who stood in three distinct groups, like separate species, at the far end of the Bhotke Society lot.

'I gave Feivel the dentist some bills to take the Bhotke people to lunch,' he said. 'They were nice to come. My mother—'

'She was a fine woman,' I said. 'You wrote a beautiful eulogy.'

'Yeah, yeah,' he said. 'But you read it good. My mom, she would have been proud to see this crowd, very respectable people.'

At which point we came up to the less respectable. Starting with the Italians each kissed Shushan Cats on the cheek with a warmth it was hard to square with the fear they must have caused every day of their lives. The blacks took Shushan's hand and clasped him tight, not kissing but squeezing the smaller man in a bear hug and clapping him – once, twice, three times – on the back. One of these, who wore mirrored aviator sunglasses so that a third of his face was covered, said: 'Your mama sound just like my mama, Mr Shushan. I got faith they in heaven together.'

'It's got to be, Royce,' Shushan said. 'No bullshit segregation upstairs.'

'Amen,' Royce said, as the entire group of his colleagues joined in.

When he came to the Chinese each made a little bow, not a Japanese deep bow, but a tiny inclination of the chin, and each said something I could not catch it was muttered so low.

Shushan shook their hands, then stepped back, raising his voice and speaking to all of his professional associates, his eyes finding theirs. 'You guys want to join me in something to eat?' Silence. He turned to the *goombahs*. 'There a decent Italian place out here?' The *gavones* shook their heads. One of them, a thin elegant man in his seventies wearing small dark glasses, who might have been their leader, addressed the others in Italian. Again they shook their heads. Shushan then looked at the black guys, but didn't even ask. Who knew what *shvartzers* ate? Ribs probably, and with waffles yet. The Italians wouldn't go along. The negroes nodded yes. 'Okay, then it's us minorities,' he said. He turned to the Chinese. 'You gentlemen know a good place for chinks?'

CHAPTER 5

From what I could see, either Shushan Cats lived in hotel rooms or where he really lived was a secret. Both turned out to be true. For the mourning period he took me to a three-bedroom suite in a residence hotel on East Sixty-Third Street, where the staff seemed to know him.

The Westbury was one of those old fashioned places that have gone the way of cars with fins and family magazines like *Life* and *Look* and the *Saturday Evening Post* – over the next decade all three weeklies would bite the dust. It was the beginning of a period of change in America. Vietnam was a gathering cloud on the horizon, Castro had consolidated his power in Cuba as a Davidian rival to America's Goliath, the threat of nuclear confrontation with the Soviet Union hung in the air like stale smoke, and the Dodgers – having left Brooklyn to stew in its own bitter juice – were in Los Angeles: a footnote to an historical footnote, but a landmark to Brooklynites, who for once were at a loss for words. We had called them Bums when they were in Brooklyn, so it was difficult to think of an epithet. Someone suggested 'the former Bums,' which at least had a finality to it. About the players diehard Dodger fans never faltered. We knew the move was not the fault of the heroes we had rooted for and loved: Carl Furillo, Duke Snyder, Sandy Koufax, Jackie Robinson, Roy Campanella, Peewee Reese. Things were changing, and the Dodgers were just a part of it. The month before the *Saturday Evening Post* trumpeted a story on its cover entitled: *A Distinguished Negro Reporter Asks: ARE MY PEOPLE READY FOR EQUALITY?* That week *Life* ran a photo of Bob Hope on *its* cover, plus headlines of stories to be found inside: *INCOME TAXES – Why they must be cut now, IQ TESTING – A scandal in our schools,* and *HOW THE MOB CONTROLS CHICAGO,* the fourth in a series called *Crime in America.*

If this sounds like another time, it was. In New York most of the West Side was still raffish, downtown down-at-the-heels, and the Upper East Side an island of tranquility. Among the townhouses and high-rises were still residence hotels like the Westbury, where the tiny lobby led to a couple of small elevators opening out to narrow corridors carpeted in beige and rose, which in turn led to rooms of such size, even grandeur in some *haute bourgeois* way, that they might be considered the other side of the telescopic lens from the city's palatial hostelries, where grand lobby flowed into grand lobby, banks of huge elevators standing to one side like brass-lined bank vaults, these letting out to endless broad corridors until the ultimate let-down of tiny rooms, scaled down furniture and bathrooms you could not turn around in without shutting the door. The Westbury later was turned into a condominium. Shushan did well with it.

He had inherited the place by paying the gambling debt of the hotel's owner. For this individual – the father of a much-married and combed-over real estate developer who these days likes to put his name on buildings – this was not a good deal but the only one. With interest on the loan mounting at two percent a week – the lenders in fact may have been at Shushan's mother's funeral – in a year he would lose all of what he owned. When Shushan came in as white knight, both buyer and seller profited. Shushan invested in redoing a couple of floors, and set up a plan for upgrading the rest. Shushan was not a hotelier, but he was a businessman. And he liked having the use of the hotel.

The suite itself was furnished attractively but impersonally, the rooms elegant but neutral. The residents were mostly people from the nearby United Nations or businessmen being rotated in and out of New York for several weeks or months. The furniture was what was then known as Danish modern, inoffensive teak and mahogany, and there were no zebra-skin rugs or outrageous paintings on the walls – though a close look at the only painting, a black-on-black abstract over the fireplace, would have shown that it was by Max Ernst's son Jimmy, in its understated elegance itself a statement about

37

the man who resided here: you could not tell precisely what it was. In the large living room two green-leather sofas faced each other, dominating the room, the carpeting a deeply patterned tan and eggplant wool, the walls putty, and the drapes sheer. When Shushan showed me to where he had chosen to receive guests for the *shiva* period I expected his sister would be installed in the second bedroom, but I learned that Esther – she liked to be called Terri; her brother demurred – preferred staying at her own place ten blocks uptown, where she also maintained her practice.

'She's not what you'd call a traditional girl,' Shushan said. He had taken a seat on a low wooden crate facing both green-leather sofas, the crate a symbol of mourning within what struck me as a stage setting: refined, unostentatious, clearly expensive but quietly so. 'I wanted her to stay here, make a united front. We don't have much family. There were people in Europe but they didn't make it. My mom couldn't get them out. They couldn't get out. Who knows what happened? Well, you're a smart boy. You know what happened.'

'I know.'

'Esther, she's a modern girl. I don't even think she'll get married. Maybe when she's older. I'd like to be an uncle.'

'You're not married either.'

'In my line of work it's not a pleasure for the wife. The dagos they keep their women in the kitchen and spend their nights with all kinds of bimbos, some of them a long time. I mean decades with the same *goomah*. A habit from the old country. A man who didn't have a belly and a mistress he wasn't a man. The black guys and the Chinese I couldn't tell you. They got their ways. You know that Royce. Thirty-six years old and he's a grandfather. Give him credit he takes care of the family. But mostly they're not nesters, you know. Must be some African thing, or from slavery. The Chinese they're a whole puzzle inside a mystery inside a . . .' Here he paused, as though either unsure of the word or unwilling to say it.

'An enigma,' I said.

'Yeah, a enigma.'

'Winston Churchill,' I said. 'You're quoting Winston Churchill.'

'Tough man,' Shushan said. 'Without him Hitler would be sitting in that palace . . .'

'Buckingham Palace.'

'Yeah, but he stood up and got counted.'

Despite my curiosity I restrained myself from asking what a two-bit bum the tabloids liked to call Shoeshine Cats was doing quoting Churchill. I doubted anyone at the funeral, except maybe the more cerebral members of the Bhotke Society, knew enough to quote Churchill. 'If you don't need anything I'd better be going.'

'What's the rush?'

The rush was this: I didn't work for Shushan Cats, had done enough as shanghaied representative of the Bhotke Society, and had a life. I had to clean up what was left of my apartment, decide what to do about my car, which since it was already pretty smashed up on Eastern Parkway was probably stripped of wheels, radio, battery and anything else of value, and I had to be at school the next morning for a conference with the professor who had excused me from class on the basis of a promised paper on *Huckleberry Finn*. Aside from that I was still in bad shape from Celeste's brothers. And aside from that this was getting a little claustrophobic. 'No rush,' I said. 'But I think my work here is done.'

'You hungry?'

'We just ate Chinese.'

'Well, you know what they say,' Shushan said, clearly straining. 'Ten minutes after you eat a Chinese girl you're hungry again. How about a drink? I could use one. There's a bar in the kitchen. Whatever you want, help yourself. I'll have a vodka from the freezer. Just as it comes. You like vodka?'

'I do, sir.'

'Forget sir. *Shushan*. You know it's the name of a city?'

'The capital of Persia at the time of—' For the first time I got it.

'Purim. That's how we got named. For the holiday. I got the city. Esther got the queen's name. My mom and dad, they didn't know much English, but they knew their Jewish stuff. She always said if they ever had another kid he'd be named for Mordecai. That'll make a tough kid in Brooklyn.

40

But the old man was out of the picture before it could happen.'

'My father too.'

'Yeah?'

'Yeah. I mean, he died three years ago. He's actually buried near your mom, my mom too. Practically neighbors.'

'I didn't see you go over to another grave,' Shushan said. 'You're supposed to put a pebble on it, to show you visited.'

'I was busy,' I said. 'And I don't like graves.'

'Me neither.'

We sat in silence for a while, he on the crate, myself on the couch, until I got up and found a bottle of Stolichnaya, then an unknown brand, in the little fridge. I poured a slug into a water glass. It came out half frozen, slow and thick. What the hell. I poured myself one as well.

'It's okay for me to drink,' Shushan said. 'I read up on Jewish mourning. You got to cover mirrors so you won't look at yourself after a death. And you don't greet people. I mean, when they come in you don't say hello. You just take them in stride. You talk with them, about anything. There's no limit. But you don't say hello and goodbye. A greeting is supposed to be joyous. They're supposed to bring food. Also no music. And you're not supposed to change your clothes or wash more than so you don't make people uncomfortable. And someone is supposed to be with you, take care of things like.'

41

I almost choked on the cold vodka as it reached my throat. 'Mr Cats . . .'

'It's just till Wednesday. I'll pay for your time.'

'It's not a matter of money,' I said, though I could have used it. Orders from the Park Avenue urologist had been slowing down. Maybe my sperm were slowing down. Maybe after what the brothers Callinan did to me they'd be slowing down even further. I hadn't thought about sex since it happened, even when I saw Shushan's sister. Well, I'd been busy.

'Like, someone's got to cover the mirror in the bathroom. And when people come in open the door. That kind of thing. Walk in the park for a smart kid like you.'

'Mr Cats . . . Shushan. I really like you. You're a fine man, and I know you're in need. But maybe you'd be better off with Ira-Myra's, or somebody else that's employed by you. I'm just a college kid with a lot to do.'

'Like go after the guys who layed into you?'

I looked at him. His mouth was set in a straight line across his face, his small hard jaw looking like it was made of rock. I noticed for the first time that his nose was somewhat off-kilter, just enough. His eyes, which could sparkle when he wanted you to like him, looked dead, a kind of North Atlantic blue. When he smiled they were light and clear, Caribbean. 'Ah, no,' I said after a while. 'That's not my thing. My thing is forget about it. The only way I could get back at them is with a gun.

Even if I were that kind of guy I'd be dealing with the Archdiocese of New York, the Fire Department and the entire NYPD. There's no percentage in that.'

Shushan pursed his lips, causing his eyes to go even darker. 'That's what the Jews in Europe said. Forgive and forget. Maybe the Nazis will go away. Let me tell you something, kid. They keep coming.'

I finished the vodka in my glass. It burned as it went down, cold at first and then searing. Now that the pressure was off with Shushan's funeral I could feel it again: it was my body but like someone else's, like wearing another man's ill-fitting clothes. Here was too much room, here too tight. I don't remember the brothers hitting my throat, but it was sore. My stomach hurt too. And my lungs, particularly on the right side, where my ribs had cracked. 'They're not Nazis. I fucked around with their baby sister, that's all.'

'You knock her up?'

'No,' I said. I suppose I could have told him about the rubbers and the Park Avenue urologist – the last thing I'd wanted was to lose those sperm. 'She's not pregnant.'

'So let me get this straight, kid. You and this girl have intimate relations. Once?'

'Many, many times.'

'Which tells me maybe she was not exactly forced into it.'

'No, she wasn't forced. She was pissed off I didn't want to continue.'

'Ah,' Shushan said. 'The green-eyed monster.'

'What?'

'I thought you was educated. *O, beware, my lord, of jealousy!/ It is the green-eyed monster which doth mock/The meat it feeds on.*'

'Othello,' I said.

'Act III, Scene III. See that, I was right. You know your stuff.'

'You read Shakespeare, Shushan?'

'Ah, you know, sometimes.' He smiled. I'd seen that smile before. The little boy with a secret. The smile changed, straightened, the lips compressed, his jaw again hard. 'There's also that bit about a woman scorned. Never pleasant. They really worked you over, eh?'

'I'll live.'

'You'll live, eh? You're such a tough guy, Russy. One day you won't.'

'Neither will you,' I said. 'None of us will. That's what cemeteries are for.'

'Yeah, but I don't let nobody do that to me.'

'It was three nobodies. Three big nobodies.'

'So fucking what, kid? You couldn't do something then, but you can now.'

'Now?'

'You got to punish them,' Shushan said. 'Like you read about my mom. Hit them back ten times. Bust them up bad.'

'I got to go,' I said.

'Because you're scared?'

'Because they were only protecting their sister.'

44

'The Nazis were only protecting the fatherland,' Shushan said. 'That's such bullshit it stinks before it hits the floor. She was pissed at you. She sicced them on you. They enjoyed it. Let me ask you, was she raped?'

'I told you. If anybody was raped it was me.'

'So where's the beef? I'll tell you where it is. The beef is they hurt you for the simple Irish pleasure of it. I know these guys. The dagos, at least with them it's business. It's just for money. Same for the rest. The chinks and the niggers, that's not their style. The micks, they just like to do it.'

'One was a priest.'

'Yeah, especially them. Now tell me something. I'm going to ask you once. You stick with me tonight.' A statement, not a question. 'Maybe those bruisers are coming back.'

'I don't think so. They had their fun.'

'Yeah, see what I mean? Fun. But you're right. They're through with you.'

'I guess I can go to school from here, in the morning.'

'Sure you can. You got a whole bedroom for yourself. There's a television in there. Color. I'm not supposed to watch, but you're not in mourning. Just me.'

'I'm sorry for your mother, Shushan.'

'It's nothing. Death, it happens. She had a long run. Maybe she was poor, but she was proud. You gave her a good send-off, all those people. I was proud.'

'Me too,' I said.

'So what I want to know is this.'

'Sure,' I said. 'Anything.'

'You know when Mr Sfangiullo. . . .'

'Who?'

'Sfangiullo, the old *gavone* in the dark glasses.'

'That was Auro Sfangiullo? No wonder the cops and the press were there.'

'Be hard to find a guy as ugly as him for the impersonation, kid. Guy's got pits in his face you could hide bodies in. Of course that was him. Who'd you think, Robert Frost was coming to pay his respects. Bob Wagner?'

Robert F. Wagner Jr. was mayor of New York at the time. 'I had no idea.'

'Just another dago crime boss, Russy. They're interchangeable. One goes, another steps up. They're not dangerous individually, but you want to watch out when they're together.'

'Right,' I said. 'You wanted to know . . .'

'When Sfangiullo was standing there and I was asking if they knew of an Italian place nearby, he said something in their language.'

'I remember.'

'What'd he say?'

'He said—' I cocked my head. 'How did you know I speak Italian?'

'I didn't.'

'Then. . . .'

'But when he was talking I happened to look at you,' Shushan said. 'I could feel you paying attention.

46

Like an animal does when he's concentrating. You ever have a dog, Russy?'

'No.'

'Me neither. But I'm interested in animal behavior. You can walk down the street and there's a dog you can almost understand from the way he stands what he's thinking. You were like that. Concentrating.'

'Their Italian isn't very good. It's thick, and they drop consonants, even syllables. For instance, they would say: *They Ita int v'good.* It's not Sicilian. They must be from Naples.'

'*Napolida,*' Shushan said, smiling. 'That's how they say it.' Now he cocked his own head. We must have been looking at each other that way, half sidewise, like a pair of monkeys. 'So what'd he say, our *dottore?*'

'*Dottore?*'

'They call him that. A sign of respect.'

'He said, "Would you believe this? Not only do we have to come to this Jew's funeral, but now he wants us to break bread with savages."'

'The dagos, they have no respect for other races. What else?'

'"For two cents I'd put bullets in all their heads."'

'Yeah? Sfangiullo said that?'

'Yeah,' I said. 'Then he said, "Except that I like the Jewboy, even if he is a Christ-killer."'

Shushan laughed. It came rumbling up from inside like bile. His mouth was laughing, but not his eyes. 'More?'

'That was it,' I said. 'Not exactly Shakespeare.'

'Not Shakespeare,' Shushan said. 'Not even fuckin' Congreve. Two things I want you to do. Number one. Go to the phone over there and tell the desk clerk to order us some pizza. You like pizza?'

'Sure.'

'Anchovy?'

'Why not?'

'The other thing, whenever you and me we're in the presence of *goombahs*, never but never let on you know what they're saying. Unless you need to. You got that?'

'Sure,' I said, but all I could think was: *Congreve?*

CHAPTER 6

Before I could call the desk the desk called me. The phone rang on the table next to where Shushan was sitting. He looked at me. 'Are you going to pick it up or what?'

'Me?'

It kept ringing. 'I'm in mourning, kid. Do your job.'

I picked it up. 'They got a guy downstairs wants to come up.'

'He has a name?'

I asked. 'Jacky from Texas. They said he's packing.' Abruptly I realized this was not about luggage.

'Jacky,' Shushan said, thinking hard as he did. 'Oh, no.' Then he seemed to reconsider. 'Yeah, it's okay. Tell them it's okay.'

'Who's Jacky?'

'An old friend,' Shushan said. 'Though I use the word loosely.'

Jacky's knock gave him away. A knock on the door is like a handshake – it can speak volumes: Is this a straightforward person, is he cloaked, is he all front, is he afraid, is he unwilling? Jacky's

49

knock was a roll of thunder – never mind that he didn't use the doorbell – an announcement of presence that demanded, with entirely too much force: Take. Me. Seriously.

A fireplug in a short-brimmed gray Stetson and black cowboy boots with eagles stitched in red on the instep, the man was the living obverse of the maxim Shushan liked to quote, 'Dress British, think Yiddish.' Jacky's motto might be 'Dress old trail, talk wholesale.' Jacky was like a cross between a would-be Al Capone and a Jewish Texan with an acute need for attention. For one thing, he was carrying a bouquet of flowers about the size of the King Ranch. He put these down to brush past me and grab Shushan by the ears, pulling him off his low crate like a cocker spaniel. Surprisingly Shushan hardly complained and instead allowed his guest to hug him like a rag doll.

'How long I don't see you, Shu-man, and now it's got to be in a tragic disaster,' Jacky said. 'I'm so sorry for your grief.'

'I thank you for coming,' Shushan said, shaking loose and retreating to the safety of his crate like an unhappy boxer who knows the fight has just begun. 'I didn't know you ever came east.'

'I don't.'

'But you're here.'

'I heard in the grapefruit your mother, bless her memory, she was passed.' He nodded vigorously as if to affirm this. 'So I hopped a flight. The funeral, however, I missed. I mean to say, don't think bad

50

of me for that, but between Texas and New York is even further than Chi. Who's the kid, your son?'

'I'm not married.'

Jacky removed the Stetson to reveal a receding hairline that may or may not have been darkened. He had that peculiar kind of black hair that looks painted on, and the sweat built up under the heavy hat made it look like enamel. He winked. His eyes were set far apart, his face compressed as though it been sat on. Round and a bit too shiny, it was the kind of face that appeared to have been made up of spare parts from other people. Even the deep cleft in his chin looked wrong, each side sagging so that they looked like breasts. His damp eyes glowed. 'You can't have a kid if you're not married? Shu, we're men of the world, ain't it?'

'No wife, no kids,' Shushan said. 'Jack, this is Russell Newhouse. He's kind of looking after me during the *shiva*.' He clarified. 'A friend.'

Jacky now concentrated on me, squinting as though I were a target he was sighting in. 'You with us?' he asked in a way that was hardly conversational – as if the wrong answer might be really wrong. 'You know, with *us*?'

I looked to Shushan.

'Yeah, he's a good Jew kid.'

'You could be either,' Jacky said. 'These days you can't tell the Hebrews from the *goys*. Especially the *shiksas*. Not that I got something against, but for instance I had a girl working – I'm in the entertainment business – a real classy dancer, and

51

one day I tell her "I won't be in the club because it's Yom Kippur," and she says, "Jack, me too." You could have kicked me over with a pickle. This girl, she was like Debbie Reynolds. Usually I don't mess with the talent, but I got to tell you, Shu-man, I fell in love.'

'And . . .'

'What can I tell you? Every time I find a girl or make a friend, it gets to be splitsville. Things happen. So tell me, kid, how long you know my Shushan? Don't answer. I can see you go back a long stretch. But nothing beats my history with Shushan. When he came to work for me he was a real hero, a Marine with the Navy Cross, which I only found out when I did some research with the PD. I always try to keep close friends with the cops. I'm known for being a help when I can, but not – read my mind – if it means *too* much information. Like I comp them at the bar, and every once in a while when I need a favor they help me out. There ain't a police station in town I'm not welcome in. They see me coming it's like they don't even see me, part of the landscape. And always a turkey at Thanksgiving, Christmas presents for the kids. Bring your wife, watch the show, don't even think about paying dime one, except I always tell 'em, take care of the waitress, they're all living foot and mouth, country girls, with bad husbands or maybe walked out, with kids. Oh, the hard-luck stories I could tell you. So what you do, kid? Work in a bank? Me, they wouldn't let me near a bank except to put in money. The Texans, they're so anti-semite you wouldn't believe it's the middle of the twentieth century, to which I say to them, What, it's two thousand years since the Romans killed Christ and the *goys* are still sticking this rap on the Jews, like as if Christ was some sort of Pentecostal Baptist himself. Ain't it, Shu-man?'

'Right as always, Jack.'

'Ain't it, kid?'

I couldn't help myself. 'Ain't it what?'

'Ain't it? *Ain't* it. Like in ain't it *the truth*. Kid, it's a short form. I got a lot of 'em. Like people say Chi for Chicago, I say TX for Texas, and Jack F for the president to extinguish him from me. Like I like to say, TXans they have a problem with Jack F, but not with *their* Jacky, which is me. Though to tell you the God's honest, with his wife also a Jackie, but spelled different, it gets mixed up. Mostly I think the shit-heels don't like him because he's with the pope, which I don't care for either, but he's a good president. That other one, Eisenhower, a great general but only so-so as a president. Too much golf on the brain.'

'This one would do us all a favor if he took up golf, Jack,' Shushan said.

'What, I can't believe it, a guy like you, a Republican?'

'I'm no Republican,' Shushan said. 'I actually voted for Kennedy because I couldn't stand the other guy, but now I'd take Nixon in a heartbeat.'

53

'Between friends politics is a rickety bridge,' Jacky explained to me. 'Wisdom is knowing the difference.'

'Between what and what?'

Jacky laughed, throwing back his short arms so that his suit jacket, a light blue western cut with tan piping on the lapels and pockets, parted like the curtains in a small-town moviehouse. Packing? The man was not exactly discrete. Sticking out of his waistband was a .38 Colt Cobra, a cop's gun, big enough to stop a man but not, as my father used to say, so long or heavy it would make your pants fall down. 'What do you mean?' Jacky said. 'Between *what* what-and-what?'

From his spot on the crate I could see Shushan warning me off with his eyes.

'I see what you mean,' I said to our guest.

'Damn right,' Jacky said. 'You know how long I know this character? Since 1953. I had a club then, the Silver Spur. That hit bad times, but back then it was a gold mine. I should have called it the Golden Garter. Every cop in town used to come by, and even some of the heavy hitters, if you know what I mean.' I could see Shushan roll his eyes. 'Better I shouldn't have to name names, but serious people. Of course they're angry at Jack F, but it's all because of his no-good brother. He has a thing for the mob. But before long, believe me, that Bobby, something will happen to him, the son of a bitch. He's not a classy guy like his brother.'

For some reason Shushan decided to speak up. Maybe it was only to end what was becoming a marathon monologue. 'Jack,' he said. 'You're good to come to New York for my *shiva.*'

'I tried to make the funeral, but the fucking anti-semites at the airport—'

'Russ, this guy gave me my first job out of the service.'

'A hero, a real Jewish hero.'

'Yeah, yeah. But I haven't seen you in what – ten years? – and now you come in, and you're packing, which is not exactly legal in New York City—'

'Legal, shmeegal. You know how many times they had me arrested back home for carrying concealed, and every time they laid me off.' He turned to me. 'I got a night club, for gossake. Every night I got to carry a lot of cash. If I told you the amount a hundred flies could enter your mouth.' He turned back to Shushan. 'Since when are you afraid of the cops, a guy like you?'

'Since I have a trial coming up next week and a visit from you carrying a piece with all the discre-tion of a fucking cowboy, which anyway you're not, could cause me grief.'

'Grief?' Jacky pulled the gun out of his waistband holster and handed it to me. 'Flush this down the toilet, kid. Or keep it. Nobody should think I would cause grief to my old friend Shushan Cats.'

'The kid doesn't want the gun, Jack,' Shushan said. 'Put it back in your pants. I'm just trying to explain how things are in the east. You can't buy cops for a few drinks and a turn with the stripper in the back room against the empties. It's different here.'

'Yeah,' Jacky says. 'It costs more, ain't it?'

Shushan smiled. 'You're just the same as you were, Jacky. Kid, don't you dare say it to his face, but they used to call him Sparky, because he could ignite in a second. Once I had to keep him from beating a guy at the bar half to death because he said something about Israel. I mean, that can't be good for business, right? This man can go off, can't you, Jack?'

'You call me Sparky, it's okay. Somebody else, this kid here, he's dead pizza pie. What can I say – I'm an emotional individual. My feelings, they just come to the top like the head on a glass of Lone Star and I got to follow them to the Alamo. That's why I come to New York. Someone mentions to me your mother, bless her, is gone, and right away I go to the airport. Believe me, not even a change of underwear, which is okay, because I'm going right back. I got a nightclub to run.' He fixed me with his wet eyes, at once spaniel-like and yearning for approval and also threatening in case he did not get it. 'You know what, kid? If you ever have a nightclub, or a restaurant even, watch those bastards like a hawk because they'll steal you blind, especially the broads.' He rose. 'Shushan, ever since you came to work for me my luck changed. You brought me the *mazal*. You showed me I don't have to beat the shit out of people to get respect. You worked like a dog for me and those other four guys I don't even want to mention – you know they're using amateur strippers, just fuckin' hick girls from like Waco, so they won't have to pay for union talent? I was a organizer for the union in Chicago. A union man, that's me right down the line, otherwise the rich bastards they'll ruin this country.' He leaned down and kissed Shushan, who didn't move. 'And think twice about Jack F. He's a good guy.'

Suddenly my hand was in his. Or on it, his fingers so thick and short it was like shaking hands with the end of a four-by-four. 'Take care of my friend,' he said by way of farewell. 'Or so help me I'll put a slug in your gut, Jew or no Jew.'

'What the hell was that?' I asked after the door slammed shut, the man's exit as noisy as his entrance.

Shushan laughed. 'A poor soul,' he said. 'Tell you the truth, it's a miracle he stayed in business this long.'

'You worked for him?'

'I was coming east after the Marines. He and three other bars, they needed a bouncer. They were all on the same street, practically next door to each other. I used to circulate. Jack was impressed I'd been a Marine – from what I can remember he did his time in World War II in like Alabama, guarding planes – and that I'd been a prize-fighter. A guy like that, he grew up in foster homes, his father was a violent son of a bitch and his mother was nuts. So what do you expect?'

'Just to fly in for a short visit like that, he must really respect you.'

'Yeah, well, he probably reads the newspapers in Texas. They got newspapers there too, but with short words. Probably tomorrow morning he'll be telling the strippers in his bar all about his trip to New York to see his pal the big-time gangster. That's the way he is.'

'You're no fan of JFK, is that it?'

'Bullshit guy,' Shushan said. 'Bullshit president. Lets the coloreds get beat up trying to buy a fucking tuna-fish sandwich at a lunch counter in Alabama, so instead he persecutes the hell out of Fidel Castro. What can I say? The guy spends his time fucking starlets, fucking every woman he sees. You think he has the *time* to be a president?'

'I thought Fidel Castro was a communist.'

'Maybe now, but it didn't have to go that way. Fidel, he's a right guy.'

'Fidel?'

'Yeah. Fidel.'

'You know him?'

Shushan sighed. 'I had certain interests in Havana. I mean, that was a great town. Rest in peace. Kennedy did that.'

'You met Castro?'

'When he was up in the hills, the Sierra Maestre it's called, I went to see him.' He took in my skepticism. 'At a certain point it looked good he was going to win it. Some people asked me to go talk to the man, before it was too late, help him out if he needed something—'

'Something?'

'Something, anything. Like a loan, or a pack of Luckies. Whatever. The idea being he would be nice to certain people, or at least not predisposed against, when and if he came to power. I went up there with a guy I knew writing for *Life Magazine*. Spent a week. Sweet guy, Fidel. Or at least he was. Throws a mean fastball.'

'You're telling me you're friends with Fidel Castro?'

'What's the difference, kid?' Shushan said. 'Nobody is going to care one way or another. That son-of-a-bitch Kennedy killed Havana. But he didn't kill us. We're still here.'

'We?'

'Me and you, and a few other people. You know what I think? Somebody is going to take the guy out.'

'Castro?'

'Castro? No, not Castro. He's too fucking clever. Not Castro, kid. Kennedy.'

CHAPTER 7

By the third day it was getting lonely at the Westbury. In the morning Esther/Terri came by, delivered by Ira-Myra's, who brought Myra, who looked like a sack of melons topped by a pouty mouth, tiny nose and enough bouffant champagne-colored hair to qualify for a drag show – clearly a woman who slept in her make-up. After a series of ritualized condolences, both took up seats at the far end of the room by the door in a kind of alcove, like a pair of foo dogs planted at the entrance. Compared to Myra, Terri – I couldn't call her Esther, not to her face; she so thoroughly disapproved of the name – looked like a separate species: a semitic version of Jean Seberg, whom I'd fallen in love with on screen in Jean-Luc Goddard's *Breathless* (for months after seeing this at the Eighth Street Cinema I thought I was Jean-Paul Belmondo, who thought he was Humphrey Bogart – resilient, romantic, doomed). Despite her short hair – according to the style of the time, mine was longer – there was nothing boyish about her. Her look was confrontational: she was one of those women,

60

rare for the sixties, who looked a man up and down. If this was the bright dawn of the feminist era, I needed sunglasses.

'Not too much business yesterday,' Shushan told his sister. 'You should've stayed over. We could've played Scrabble. We still could. The college kid here would probably beat us both.' He said it *bote*, though it was becoming clear Shushan was something of a verbal chameleon. When he talked to me it was almost standard English; with his business associates or someone with roots in the old neighborhood, like Terri, he seemed to descend, maybe consciously, into *deses* and *doses*. 'You play Scrabble, Russy?'

'I have.'

'For money?'

'For money?' I repeated. 'I'm not much of a gambler, Shushan.'

Terri glanced at me with interest. 'Someone my brother knows who isn't a gambler? This is rich.'

'Everyone's a gambler,' Shushan said. 'Gambling is part of human nature. Terri's clients, they're gambling if they talk long enough at so much an hour then they'll be cured. You're probably gambling a college education is going to get you further in life. On which the odds are the same as Terri's losers.'

'Shut up,' she said.

'Yeah, I tease her. That's the old story of brothers and sisters, right? So tell me, doctor. When you look at young Russell here, what do you see? I mean from a few words, body language. First impressions. Would you trust him?'

Terri examined me with her eyes, thankfully stopping at the neck. 'With what?'

'Money.'

'Maybe,' she said. 'Depends how much.'

'Your life?'

'I wouldn't trust anyone with that,' she said. 'You know that.'

Shushan smiled. 'I would.'

From across the room I could see Ira-Myra's perk up. Oblivious, his wife continued studying a day-old copy of the *Daily Mirror*, whose cover had a picture of Shushan, Sfangiullo and others – including me, almost out of the photo – under a headline as unpleasant as it was predictable:

MOB WHO'S WHO
AT CATS MOM RITES

'I wouldn't,' I said.

'You wouldn't if you *was* me, or you wouldn't trust *me* with your life?'

Both, I thought. But copped out. 'I wouldn't trust me with anyone's life,' I said. 'I'm not dependable.'

'You did the funeral.'

'I thought maybe it would be dangerous not to,' I said, at the same time wondering why I was being honest. 'You didn't seem to be in the kind of state that needed opposition. Anyway, everything I did, anything I did, it was just a few phone calls. And showing up.'

'Are you afraid of my brother?' Terri asked in a tone so casually conversational she might have been asking about tomorrow's weather.

'Afraid? Sure. Sometimes. Maybe not now. But at first. He has a reputation. He's in the newspapers. He's one of those guys when I was growing up it was always better to be on the other side of the street.'

'And now you're on the same side of the street,' she said. 'How do you feel about him now?'

'Hey, Esther,' Shushan cut in. 'You doing a psycho-whatchamacall on Russy here? That's not nice. Let the kid alone. He already said it. He's no gambler. So why would he gamble on getting a stranger like me, as unfairly as I'm characterized in the public prints, angry? He's more smart than that. Even if all that isn't much true.'

'Anybody want something to drink?' I said, standing. 'Eat? There's cold cuts. Or I could order in.' From the corner of my eye I caught Terri looking at me, coolly evaluative. I could almost hear her thinking: Flunky. But I didn't feel like a flunky. I felt like I was taking care of Shushan the way no one had bothered taking care of me when my father died. I'd sat through the week-long mourning period alone. Friends came and went, my father's and mine. A few cousins. There weren't more than a few anyway. Several teachers from Thomas Jefferson High School. A neighbor lady looked in from time to time. But that was it. I'd grown up without a mother, so I was used to it. But until I bumped into Shushan I never knew how much I'd missed. Besides, Shushan needed looking after by someone he wasn't paying to do so. He could trust me that far. 'Anybody?'

We were eating when the cops walked in.

Actually they'd been invited. A desk clerk had called from the lobby, 'There's a couple of police officers downstairs who want to come up and pay their respects.'

Ira-Myra's looked alert, a guard dog with someone approaching the gate.

Shushan finished chewing on his corn-beef sandwich. 'Tell 'em yeah, sure.'

The two cops were Cohen and Kennedy, so mismatched a pair they looked like socks a blind man might have picked out of a drawer. Cohen was tall, balding, and given to smiling nervously. He had a face that looked like he was in the wrong job. Probably he should have been a salesman. He had on a blue blazer and tan trousers – a uniform of sorts – and he was one of those guys who had a five o'clock shadow at noon. It was now almost two. The shadow had lengthened. His partner was more my size, just under six foot, with chestnut hair combed straight back off a friendly face. He had bright blue eyes and a nice round nose beginning to show broken blood vessels, and even less sense of how to dress than his partner. Tie askew, his suit, shiny from repeated pressings, was that olive poplin half of New York wore in summer. This was November.

'I'm sorry for your loss, Mr Cats,' Cohen said.

'Me too,' Kennedy said. 'May your mother rest with the angels in heaven.' He looked suddenly uncertain, and turned to Cohen. 'That okay to say?'

'Sure,' Shushan said. 'You can practically say anything that works.'

'I wouldn't mention Jesus Christ,' Cohen said.

'I wasn't going to.'

There was something about them of an old married couple: they must have been together a while. When one moved the other looked. And when one looked the other caught his eye to say, It's nothing – I was just shifting in my seat.

'Russy, give these nice coppers something to eat,' Shushan said. 'And drink.' He winked. 'Or are you guys on duty?'

'It's a condolence call, Mr Cats,' the Irishman said. 'I mean, technically we're on call. I mean, if there was a shooting in the next block or something. But the NYPD isn't that technical about these things. A wake, something like that, it's okay. Ain't that right, Stan?'

Cohen nodded. 'The last thing we'd want you to think is this is a police matter. It's personal, that's all.'

I brought them a mid-level bottle of Scotch and a couple of tumblers with ice. They didn't hesitate.

'This is my sister,' Shushan said. 'Ira you know.' He skipped Myra entirely. 'And this is my protégé, Russell.'

The cops examined me with renewed interest.

I looked at myself with renewed interest. Protégé? Uh, do I get to go to jail now or do we wait until after the mourning period? 'I'm just helping out,' I said weakly. 'For the *shiva*.' I turned to Kennedy. 'The wake.'

'Yeah, well, don't worry, kid,' Cohen said. 'We don't have an interest in you. That is, if we don't have no call to. Anyway Mr Shushan here is a kidder. He's famous for a kidder. You know what he said when we arrested him?'

Kennedy picked it up. 'He said, "What took you so long?" Ain't that something? I got to tell you, Mr Shushan, if every hoodlum in this town was as much a gent as you it would be a pleasure to be a cop. As it is, we got them dagos they'll spit in your eye as soon as say good morning. They're surly bastards is what they are. I'd rather arrest a whorehouse full of niggers' – he looked over to Shushan's sister – 'cat-house I mean, than one of them wops, and their ladies is even worse. You go to search their house they wouldn't offer you a cup of coffee or even a glass of water. It's like they take it personal. Like their husbands ain't what they are, what they know they are.'

'My mother, my late mother,' Shushan said. 'She used to say you shouldn't judge other people, because maybe they didn't have the advantages you did.'

66

Terri shot me a look, and then a wink. She had caught it as well. The cops never would. Ira and Myra had probably never read a book in their lives. It was just Terri and me. She smiled in complicity. I kept quiet. What was I going to say: Shushan, your mother was F. Scott Fitzgerald? Your mother wrote *The Great Gatsby*, on whose opening page Nick Carraway, the narrator, speaks that line? Instead I coughed, hard.

'You okay, kid?' Shushan asked.

I stood, swallowed, and made my way to the kitchen. 'It's nothing. The rye bread. I got a caraway seed stuck in my throat.'

I'm sure Shushan got it. But I wasn't aiming for Shushan. I was aiming for his sister. Maybe I had a chance after all. She was stifling laughter. If you can make a woman laugh, that's a base hit.

When I returned with a glass of water and a grin the cops were growing expansive on the one interest they shared with their host.

'Well, you got a chance,' Cohen was saying. 'The papers like you, Mr Cats. That's something. I don't think the *Daily Mirror* would want to see you go away. Every morning you're on the front page they sell more papers.'

'Unlike the dagos,' Kennedy said. 'Take a guy like Sfangiullo, they put him on the front page and everybody hates him. He's just another bloodsucking *mafio*, know what I mean? And one of them is pretty much like the next. Carbon copies. They don't touch nobody's heart strings because

67

probably themselves they don't got a heart. With you it's like Robin Hood or something.'

'You're saying I rob from the rich to give to the poor?' Shushan said.

'I'm not saying one way or the other, Mr Shushan,' Kennedy said. 'I'm saying how people react. Okay, maybe there's an element of, you know, the man's a hoodlum. But it's like he's *our* hoodlum. Them dagos, they don't have the sympathy of the working man.'

'And the working man, Mr Cats,' Cohen said. 'That's who is going to be your jury.'

'And there's going to *be* a jury because you two working men arrested me, isn't that right?'

'Aw, that is so unfair, Mr Shushan,' Kennedy said. 'We arrested you because it's our job. It's like saying a fisherman has something against an individual striped bass. Or a hunter against a particular deer.'

Terri cleared her throat so vigorously it was like a call to order, then stood. 'If it's all right with Bambi here, I've got patients to see. It was so nice meeting the men who arrested my brother.'

'She's just kidding,' Shushan said. 'She kids too. We kid each other. Nobody is holding any grudges or bad feelings. Isn't that right, Esther?'

Terri nodded. 'I always find it odd how nice some people can be to those who hurt them. I see it every day in my practice. People come in and they've been maimed by the people they love. I guess it's not so much of a stretch to love the people who maim you.'

68

The two cops went white, Kennedy especially, the color draining from his face almost perceptively, like wine out of a clear bottle. 'That's not it at all,' he said. 'You got us wrong.'

'Maybe,' Terri said. 'But all I know is that if my brother goes away it's you two who sent him there.'

'Not at all, miss,' Cohen said. 'That's for the DA and the judge and jury. We're just agents of the . . . of the . . .'

'The system,' Shushan said. 'It's okay. I never expected different. So you two guys, you have another drink. And you, Joe College, you make sure my sister gets to her place. This is a rough town. A person could get mugged on the street. Ain't that right, officers? And with these two dicks up here with me the odds are even worse. So take a walk with my sister, kid.'

'Sure,' I said, standing. 'If that's what you—'

'I want what you want, kid,' Shushan said from his crate on the floor. 'Just make sure you come back. You know what else my mother said?'

'No,' I said. 'I don't.'

'On n'est jamais si malheureux qu'on croit, ni si heureux qu'on espère.'

The accent was queer, but I got it. *One is never as unhappy as one thinks, nor as happy as one hopes.* To the cops it was Greek, or maybe Yiddish.

CHAPTER 8

In the nineteen-sixties the Upper East Side of Manhattan was hardly a dangerous place. It was in fact the best neighborhood in the city, with leafy streets, museums, elegant shops, drugstores with real soda fountains – the amenities of a village with the resources of a major city. Your neighbor might be an Astor or Rockefeller – or a Feinberg, O'Rourke or D'Angelo. On Lexington Avenue you could eat *sole meunière* served by a waiter named Sol at a restaurant called El Sol and right next door get your shoes resoled. Bankers and brokers lived here, but also bartenders and shop-owners and floor-walkers in the midtown department stores. By all odds it was the safest neighborhood in the city, not least because it was the richest, with more cops per resident than anywhere in the five boroughs. It was also the least racially mixed. Germans lived in the eighties, Czechs in the nineties, but the number of resident non-whites was so low the student body of the Upper East Side's public elementary schools – the neighborhood was sprinkled with private academies – had the racial profile of a segregated white grade school in Selma, Alabama. Suspicious doormen seemed to be everywhere, a kind of standing patrol against the disenfranchised. There was little street crime, though this was slowly changing because the nascent civil-rights movement kept pressure on New York's mayor, whose official residence was in the neighborhood, to moderate the NYPD's practice of stopping black male pedestrians and ordering them to pedest elsewhere. From the strictly parochial viewpoint of the police this made sense, because blacks – Negroes then – were unlikely to be residents, so aside from maids and colorfully-attired African diplomats – the United Nations complex anchored the south end of the neighborhood – anyone not white had to be up to mugging, rape, burglary, or just plain trouble. Over time, as restrictive rental laws fell away and wealthy blacks could find apartments in the area, the police gave up the practice entirely. This was a victory for civil rights, but also benefited the residents of Harlem, which began on the north side of Ninety-Sixth Street: instead of preying on their neighbors, Negro criminals drifted south to target the Upper East Side – why mug a black when a white might be carrying a lot more cash?

'Three colored kids tried to snatch my purse last week,' Terri said as we walked. She set a pretty pace. At this rate we might be at her place in ten minutes.

I had been hoping for a half hour, with maybe

71

even a coffee-break on the way. Aside from Little Italy and the Village, this stretch of Lexington Avenue was then one of the few places in the city where you could get a cup of espresso. 'They succeed?' I looked down at her purse, chocolate-brown alligator the size of several volumes of the Encyclopedia Brittanica.

She stopped momentarily to look me in the eye. 'You really think I'd let those cocksuckers rip off an Hermès purse that cost me a hundred-fifty bucks?'

I whistled. In today's prices that would be fifteen hundred, maybe more. 'A high price for modesty,' I said. That was the way it was done. One of the gang would come up, pull a woman's skirt up over her head, a second would knock her down while the third grabbed the purse. That year women were wearing long skirts, very full. It was like an invitation. In a short while New York women would all be in mini-skirts or pants – the incidence of this kind of purse-snatching dropped.

'Clocked the first one before he even got started,' she said, 'Second one I kicked in the nuts.'

'And the third?'

'What third?' she asked, showing a deadpan insouciance that could not be learned other than through growing up in the city. In Paris the women were elegant. Here they were matter-of-fact about a well-placed shoe to the genitals. 'Son-of-a-bitch ran before the second piece of shit hit the ground. Do you know the crap I have to listen to all day to earn that purse? My mother didn't love me. My mother loved me too much. I'm not comfortable with my body. Gimme a break.'

'Isn't that what you wanted, when you got into being a shrink?'

'I wanted to help people with real problems, not fashionably middle-class pseudo-neuroses. You know who has real problems? People who can't afford psychotherapy, who in fact don't even know they have problems.' She smiled wryly as she walked.

I knew exactly how she smiled, because I had one eye on where I was going and the other on her tanned face – she must have been able regularly to get away to the sun, because even in a warmish November there were not enough rays in New York City for a tan like that. 'People like who?'

'Whom,' she said. 'I thought you were some sort of literary whiz-kid.'

'I try to disguise my brilliance when I'm talking to people from Brooklyn.'

'I'm *from* Brooklyn, Russell. No longer *of*.'

Just her saying my name sent a chill down my back, the hairs standing as though called to attention. 'You don't have to be ashamed of Brooklyn,' I said. 'Walt Whitman was from Brooklyn.' I searched my mind. 'Henry Miller. Norman Mailer.'

While I searched for more, she spoke. 'Delusional faggot, talentless nut-job, pathetic self-promoter. In that order. You know what those three have in common? Mistaking noise for achievement. You know how a Brooklyn intellectual commits suicide?'

'Is this going to be personal?'

'He jumps from his ego to his IQ. You, child, are exactly the kind of person who could use a solid dose of psychotherapy. In a year you'd probably discover things about yourself that would make your hair stand on end.'

'It already is.' We had stopped at a corner waiting for the light to change. 'You want to get a cup of joe? There's an espresso place on the next—'

She looked at me with something between disdain and amusement. 'The short answer is no.'

'What's the unexpurgated?'

'No, thank you.'

'Very nice,' I said. 'Did anyone ever tell you it's not polite to be curt with people?'

'Many times,' she said, stepping into the street. Just at that moment a cab came hurtling around the corner from Lexington. I grabbed her arm. 'I saw him,' she said coldly.

'Good,' I said even more so. 'Then I'm sure you can find your way home safely without me. Terri, Esther, whatever, it's been fun.'

Abruptly she took my arm and led me like a blind man across the street. 'Don't be such a pussy,' she said. 'I only rag people I like.'

'Oh, I'm so fucking relieved.'

She continued holding onto my arm when we got to the other side. 'Like who, like whom – it doesn't really matter. I was trying to say, Like *you*. You're fucked up.'

'I'm glad somebody noticed,' I said, so pleased to have the arm of this ravishing woman she could spit at me and I'd be happy. 'Why am I fucked up?'

'How much time do we have?'

'Where do you live?'

'Seventy-third.'

'Then I guess we have four blocks. We could walk slower. Or stop for coffee.'

'Nice try,' she said. 'But I wasn't kidding. I have a patient.'

'I could wait. What is that, an hour?'

'Fifty minutes. Then I have three more. Besides, there's only two ways a kid like you, a nice kid, Russell, but a kid, is going to see the light. The first is really intensive psychotherapy—'

'Because . . .'

'Because you're fucked up. You don't like responsibility because it means commitment, and you won't do that. You give off all the scents and sounds of the critically abandoned. An orphan. It's you against the world, and you don't like either one, you or the world. You want women in your life but not one woman, because if you have only one you're afraid she'll walk out on you. Did your mother walk out on you, emotionally?'

'She died when I was a kid.'

'Bingo. Your father?'

'Passed when I was sixteen.'

75

'Were you close?'

I had never really considered the question. 'We sort of lived in parallel worlds. We shared the space of a life, but there wasn't a lot of contact.'

'In Nazi Germany, Vichy France, Soviet Russia, any autocracy, a guy like you would be easy pickings. You need a hero. You can't get close to a woman except to fuck her, so you do that as a sport. You might as well be riding a horse. With a guy like you there's an empty space where most people have a model for how they should live. Usual stuff: warm family, Thanksgiving dinner, playing catch with the old man, mom forgives your faults, even loves them. Or it could be the opposite. A real mess. Bad family, bad model. Or more usually a mix. Nobody gets the brass ring every time. Some people come out better, some worse. But a kid like you—'

'I'm twenty-one,' I lied.

'But a mature gentleman like you, with nothing in the model department, he's desperate for someone, some thing, to create his life around.' She hung onto my arm as if I were the strong one. 'So what is it like, being alone?'

'It's okay.'

'I wasn't looking for a value judgment – okay, not so good, medium, terrific. I asked for a description.'

'You do this to all your patients?'

'They should be so fucking lucky,' she said. 'Take all the time to answer until we get to Seventy-Third.'

76

I believed her about the patients. I would have believed her if she said she was Sandy Koufax and was just going off to pitch a perfect game. But we were walking at her pace: Seventy-Third was fast approaching – there was no time for evasion or, I realized, need. 'It feels like shit,' I said. 'It feels like I'm my own species, that whatever I do I'll never find anyone who. . . .'

'Go ahead. Say it.'

'Who cares about me and is worth caring for.'

We were at Seventieth, at the corner. Waiting for the light to change.

'Well, I can't say you're unable to articulate. That's a big help.'

'It'd be a bigger help if I had someone to articulate to.' I paused in speech just as the light changed and we continued to walk. 'I've been reading since I was a little kid.'

'Solace.'

'No. Yes. Maybe,' I said. 'But it was more like a search. You open a book you open a life. You try to see if there's a . . . a model there. Something that makes sense for you. For me. You want to see if there's a way. But there isn't any. You know, *The Great Gatsby*, that's my favorite book, but it's not a road map. It's like La Rochefoucauld – a sketchbook. You think your brother knows French, or he just learned the one phrase phonetically?'

'You're changing the subject.'

'Maybe it's the same subject,' I said. 'I got kind of kidnapped into this with your brother.

Shanghaied. Suddenly I wake up and I'm on a ship and it's heading for some strange port and I'm signed on. There's my signature. Whether it is or it isn't, there's not much I can do about it now. So I'm suddenly in someone else's life and, you know what, it's a hell of a lot better than my own. I mean, where was I going? Two days ago I called this guy, a professor at college, who is supposed to supervise my honors program. You know, we meet every month or so and he buys me lunch and we have a beer and bullshit about literature. So I tell him, Professor del Vecchio, I'm so sorry. I won't be able to make it tomorrow. There's a death in the family. And he says, Someone close? You know what I told him?'

'Your mother,' Terri said.

I stopped dead in the street, right there in mid-block in front of an estate-jewelry store and a florist. 'How did you know?'

'Maybe I'm not as stupid as I look.'

'You don't look stupid.'

'No?'

'You look wonderful. You look smart, direct, no-bullshit honest. You look like heaven in bed.'

She smiled, the twin fish of her mouth moving in opposite directions so that the entire bottom of her face seemed to be opening, welcoming me in. 'Right on all counts,' she said. 'Tell me something, Russell. How do feel about vaginas?'

'Vaginas?' We were standing still in the middle of the sidewalk, the entire Upper East Side flowing

78

around us. From somewhere far away I heard a car horn sound, then fade. 'Vaginas?'

'You know,' she said, looking me in the eye. She wore heels, but still had to tilt her chin, almost as though offering her lips.

I was close enough to see a tiny chip of lipstick coating the top of one of her bottom teeth. 'I like them.'

'Do you love them?'

I shrugged, my smile deepening. 'Guilty as charged,' I said. 'Okay, I love them. I love vaginas.'

'How do you love them?'

'There's more than one way?'

'You love how they look, how they feel? How they smell? You like a nice hot smelly vagina, Russell?'

'You know what Napoleon wrote to Josephine from Egypt? "Coming home – don't wash."'

'You really feel that way?'

I felt like the luckiest man alive. 'Yeah. I do. I love vaginas.'

Terri leaned forward and kissed me on the cheek, holding her lips there for what seemed to be forever. Then she took a half-step back and looked me directly in the eye. 'So do I,' she said. Taking my hand, she raised it to her lips, and kissed it. 'You can't grow a vagina, can you, Russell?'

'I can't even try.'

'You know what I said? That there are two ways out for you. The first—'

'Spilling my gut for a year on a couch.'

'The couch is optional, and a little old-fashioned, but yes, a year at least. Maybe ten.'

'And the other way?'

'Do something.'

'I just tried, and got . . . rebuffed. Unmuffed, maybe. Turned down.'

'You tried to make me into another woman who is supposed to give you comfort, solace, direction even. When that doesn't happen according to your needs, your bottomless needs, you go looking for the next. No, I mean *do* something. As a man.'

'And women doesn't count?'

'Not for you,' she said, putting down my hand with such tenderness it was as if it would break if she let it go too abruptly. 'As a man.'

'As a man?'

She stepped away, then as she turned said it so quietly I almost did not hear the words. 'Among men,' she said, and continued down the street, leaving me looking after her, as much unsure of what she meant as sure that she was right.

CHAPTER 9

Eugene del Vecchio, head of the Honors Program at Brooklyn College, was a translator of Macchiavelli and Bembo, and a poet whose work I had read in anthologies when I was still in high school. A tall man with tumbles of prematurely gray hair over a craggy face, half-frame tortoiseshell glasses always slipping down the slope of a seriously Roman nose, he spoke in the same lovely mutated English I had learned on the streets of Brooklyn – his acquired in Bensonhurst, a rather more pleasant area of trim attached single-family homes, each with its own concrete virgin in the postage-stamp front yard. Professor del Vecchio followed professional football, had boxed as a youth, and worshipped Hemingway (whose death by suicide two years earlier caused him much public grief, and provided fodder for a string of poems and a couple of essays). He was in short no one's clichéd idea of an aesthete, a college professor or a homosexual. He was also no one's idea, especially not mine, of someone who might be found sitting on a couch in Shushan Cats' suite at the Westbury. He rose when Ira let me in. Myra was gone.

'I'm so sorry for your loss,' Professor del Vecchio said with that familiar mixture of the wise and the street-wise, each peculiar enunciation coming through clearly, a spoken palimpsest, one sound overlapping the next. *Palimpsest* was in fact one of Professor del Vecchio's favorite terms, along with *villanelle* and *sestina*. He took my hand, pulled me close to him until I could smell the scent he used, some sort of bottled musk, part tobacco, part bay leaf. 'Truly a tragedy.'

I looked to Shushan, seated on his crate as though it were a throne. Whoever had devised this Jewish tradition of ritualized discomfort during mourning never considered the possibilities hidden in the term *hard-ass*. Shushan was thriving. He'd probably gain weight on a diet of grubs and water. The man was even tougher, I thought, than his reputation, which was not saying a little. His dark eyes, aglow with beneficence, seemed to shower blessings. It was hard to believe this Shushan Cats would next week stand trial on a laundry list of felony indictments.

'Mr Cats must have told you it's *his* mother who passed away,' I said after del Vecchio released me. 'Probably a mix-up on the phone.'

'Oh, there wasn't any, Russell,' the professor said. 'I wouldn't take anyone into the Honors Program without knowing his family background, love of animals, if and how much he or she drinks, does dope. That kind of thing. Hell, I interviewed your high-school English teachers. A brilliant orphan, they said. I don't get too many of either brilliant or orphans. So I remembered.'

I was growing tired of this orphan stuff. I had never traded on it, and didn't want to start now. It was cheap. 'How did you. . . .'

'You phoned and left a number. So I rang you back.'

'So. . . .'

'So I thought it a bit strange you were calling from a hotel, though perhaps not so strange because your mother had after all died many years ago. I rang back and asked the desk where the Westbury was. And here I am.'

Shushan was clearly delighted by this. 'And here he is,' he said. 'An unexpected visitor is always nice,' he explained, then revised. 'Usually. And a professor. That's more unexpected than normal. Russy, you keep surprising me to the good. Now I got a new friend in Del. And Del knows his stuff.'

'Del?' I said.

'My friends call me Del,' the professor said. 'You're welcome to as well.'

'Del,' I said. 'I've known you three years and it's been Professor del Vecchio, and you're here what fifteen minutes—'

'Almost an hour,' Shushan said. 'Came in just as you and Esther left. She okay?'

'Oh yeah,' I said, wondering idly what he knew of his sister's sexual orientation. 'Del. Okay, *Del*, how come you're here – I mean, seeing as how you knew I was bullshitting you.'

83

Del shrugged good naturedly. He was drinking Scotch, neat. This was turning out to be a hell of a mourning period. Aside from Ira, who had all the *joie de vivre* of a tire iron, everyone was drinking, laughing, goofing around. I wondered if my own mother's *shiva* had been like this. My father's wasn't. Del – how peculiar it was to call him that – put up his hand as if to stop me from going too far. 'I knew it was *something*, so I came. I don't have too many students like you, Russell. You probably don't know that.'

'You came to catch me in a lie.'

'I figured *somebody* died,' he said. 'And I now learn you delivered the eulogy—'

'Beautiful,' Shushan said. 'Everyone was crying.'

'You wrote it.'

'Yeah, Russy, so I'm Shakespeare and you're Richard Burton. What's the diff? Next time I got a funeral I'll get Del here to write the eulogy and you'll read it and then I won't even be involved. Del's a hell of a poet, did you know that? I have his book.'

'Which one?' Del said.

'*Forms of Remorse*,' Shushan said. 'I like the one that begins "The telephone is an engine of unpassion, reducing . . ."'

'Reducing apocalypse to noise,' Del finished. 'That one I still like. Most of the others, eh.'

'Don't say that,' Shushan said. 'Which one you like, kid?'

Kid didn't like any of them. And he did not like

84

being grilled by a gangster on a poet's work with the poet grinning on the opposite couch. 'They're all . . . great.'

'You ever read any?'

'Shushan, I never read none.'

Shushan laughed. 'Kid's got balls, I'll tell you that. Thinks he can make fun of my English right in front of my face.'

'Better than behind your back,' Del said. 'He's not like that. Though I'm pretty sure he writes his term papers in the last week of the term.'

'What's the difference when I write them? You like them.'

'I like them more than my other students' – but I think you could do better. You're coasting.'

'So?'

'So coast,' Del said. 'But don't expect to get a great education out of it, only the minimum. You finish reading *Huckleberry Finn*?'

'I read it when I was twelve—'

'You're not twelve now. You must have missed a lot.'

'And when I was fourteen. And when I was sixteen, during another *shiva*, as it happens. You're right, professor. It's not the same when you're a kid. *Tom Sawyer*, that's a kid's book you read once. But *Huckleberry Finn* you could keep reading forever.'

'I'm gratified you feel that way.'

'But I do know the book. I mean I know it intimately. I could write a paper right now.'

'You could write a paper now?' Shushan said. 'On *Huckleberry Finn*?'

'Sure.'

'Could you write it on the seventeen fucking accents and dialects in it, or the place of theater, or Nigger Jim's options, or the resolution of sequence, like when . . .' Shushan stopped. 'What'd I do? Russy, shut your mouth a fly will come in.'

Finally I had to speak. 'What is it with you, Shushan? Are you a gangster or what? Every time I look up there's another literary reference fired off, another allusion. Professor del Vecch – *Del*, an hour ago this guy was quoting La Rochefoucauld to a couple of gumshoes—'

'The elder or the son?'

'*Père*,' Shushan said. 'To my mind, the son was nothing.'

'I concur,' Del said.

'*Père?* Would you two just cut it out!' I was livid. 'What kind of bullshit gangster quotes a French aphorist of the seventeenth century – in French? The only good part of this is you both have it wrong. The one you call the son was born in the mid-*eighteenth* century, about seventy years after the original one died.'

'They were both *duc* though,' Shushan said. 'Like Snyder.'

'Probably grandson,' Del added. 'I always assumed . . .'

'You assumed fucking wrong,' I said. 'How can you be the head of an honors program if you don't know La Rochefoucauld? And how can *you* be a fucking gangster if you do?'

Maybe I would have gone off further on them – it was as if everything I'd known was upside down – but the door-buzzer sounded and we all turned to watch in a moment of blessed silence as Ira looked through the peephole and unlocked the door. Like a mastiff with a razor-line mustache, he seemed only to come alive when there was a question of defending his owner. Great, I thought, now we're going to have four members of the Harlem head-bangers who will give us a fucking *a capella* rendition of Handel's *The Trout* while simultaneously proving Fermat's Last Theorem on the opened white handkerchiefs from their breast pockets. Wasn't anything what it seemed, or what it should be?

But Royce Wilmington and the brothers – the three actually were brothers: Ed, Fred and Ted Lincoln or Jefferson, one of those – were not there to prove a point, except that they had been well briefed on what to bring on a *shiva* visit. Carrying in enough food for an army, they looked like the native bearers in the black-and-white Tarzan films I had seen Saturday mornings at the Loew's Premier on Sutter Avenue, except a lot better dressed. 'S'all kosher,' Royce said. 'Y'all know the Second Avenue Delicatessen? Got a certificate right up there on the wall as you come in. Got everything there but the fruit – y'all don't have kosher and not kosher fruit, do you?'

These were big men, and so expensively got up they seemed to present a tableau, a kind of staged negritude that declared in no uncertain terms *We is here*. That was unfair, of course, because transliterating their Southern dialect consistently would call for doing the same for Shushan's, for Del's, for mine. All of us had grown up with a license to torture the mother tongue, each in his own way. Besides, these four had been speaking their particular form of English, if we include their forebears, for hundreds of years. The four white men in the room – though Ira-Myra's rarely spoke and at that only in a rumbling whisper – were all first- or second-generation Americans. If anyone had an American pedigree, it was Royce and the brothers, whose silken patois was on the record in *Huckleberry Finn* itself, and on every blues recording for fifty years.

'Y'all sit on a box, is that it?' Royce said.

'Some Jews sit on the floor,' I said.

Royce looked hard at me, as if to ask, *Who you, boy*? He fingered the knot of his white tie, which pushed out on a collar pin from his pink shirt like a signal flag. His suit, cut long and lean, was charcoal with a soft pink stripe. The others were dressed with similar pizzazz: everything of the highest quality, everything custom, everything matching – though none of this would be found downtown until decades later, when white men felt they too could be peacocks. The uniform of the brotherhood of black gangsters was simply this: if we can't be equal in all other matters, we're going to be a whole lot better dressed.

'It's a sign of mourning,' Del said. He put out his hand and introduced himself.

'Del's a professor,' Shushan said with evident pride. 'Also a poet.'

'No shit,' Royce said, quite as though he had been introduced to a Martian. 'How you get to be that?'

'You bullshit your way through three degrees,' Del said. 'Then you bullshit your way up the ladder in various universities, more or less job-shopping, until you've gone pretty much as far as you can go. Then you keep on doing the same thing, teaching, writing, teaching. Before too long you're dead.'

This speech seemed to hit its mark. The room was silent. Even Ira in his mastiff spot by the door shared our embarrassment and discomfiture. As one all four of the new guests pulled cigarettes out of their pockets, Kool filters to a man, and as one paused to look to Shushan, who said, 'Sure, smoke 'em if you got 'em.'

Little was said while the four lit up, drew deeply and exhaled smoke rings that formed as if eternal, then dissipated into the air until the vapors reformed at the ceiling, creating a kind of proximate heaven, a room-size cloud. The menthol itself must have burned off. All that remained was the familiar stink of cigarettes that, like the exhaust fume of burnt gasoline or the assault of perfume in a crowded elevator or the summer stench of melting asphalt was only another pot-holed item on the city's olfactory menu. Like the clang of the early-morning garbage trucks and the threatening rattle of traffic, the screaming-soprano subway trains, the staccato of approaching high heels, it was part of the sensual symphony in which I had grown up, and which I little understood. There was so much to it, so many pieces, so many individual parts, it was impossible to understand how it all worked, or could. One thing was certain: however the city functioned, these men were what made it work. For the first time I heard Shushan speak more than a few lines at a time. The subject, which somehow had arisen in the time I was examining the cloud on the ceiling, was the Fulton Fish Market, then located on a truly smelly spot where way-downtown met the East River. The market would later be relocated to the Bronx, thus freeing up valuable real estate for the stock brokers and bankers who would be buying condos on the site and dining in restaurants serving fresh fish that had once been sold wholesale on the same blocks.

'The *goombahs* want in,' he said. 'But they'll kill it. Okay, someone has to be in charge. Without someone in charge, every cheap chiseler with a knife in his pocket or a baseball bat under his coat could stop the whole business. You got six hundred vendors in the market. Five thousand people employed. That's directly. But you got to look further. If you consider the truckers who bring the fish to the restaurants, the restaurants themselves, the retail fish markets themselves, the Chinese restaurants that don't serve alleycat, it's gotta be a hundred thousand people easy. Who's gonna protect them? The cops? I pay the cops myself a lot of money. Somebody else might pay them the same to let chaos reign. Hey, and what about the guys on the fishing boats and their families? The market doesn't work they don't. Now we got a situation where we could have chaos just because the *goombahs* don't have enough on their greasy plates – excuse me, Del, we're not talking about all Italians here – but *these* Italians, they like chaos. Chaos is good for their business.'

'Amen,' Royce said in the rumbling bass that through the fifties could be heard on every rhythm-and-blues song recorded in America, and on many street corners as well. He was joined by the brothers, who came in all together, a living doo-wop.

'You're saying a dictator is what America needs?' I said to Shushan. 'We don't need to elect a president, just a Hitler?'

'You're calling me a Hitler?'

'You could be one if you wanted. You could squeeze the fish market until it croaked. If you wanted to.'

'Which would get me exactly what, junior?'

'Okay, maybe the next dictator isn't as smart as

91

you. Hitler destroyed the Jews, who made Germany's economy. Stalin killed off his Jews, and the peasants, and even his own secret police.'

'They knocked their own proposition,' Shushan said. 'If I did that I'd be diselected.'

'By who?'

'By everybody. It wouldn't be tolerated. The mob – the papers call it that because they don't understand it, as if it's this fucking single-minded club, like the Elks or something – is just a lot of guys that *facilitate*. You know that word, college boy? They facilitate. Without us everything would stop.'

'Yeah,' I said. From the beginning I felt total confidence in speaking my mind. Shushan and his kind were ass-kissed day and night. They respected when someone spoke straight. Unless he spoke to the cops. 'Without organized crime there wouldn't be gambling, hookers, drugs.'

'Yeah? So what's wrong with that. Each one of those is just commerce. You know what there'd be? Disorganized crime.'

'But what you do is still crime, right?'

'Exactly. When there was prohibition it was a crime to make, transport, even drink booze. One day in 1933 it was suddenly not a crime. In Russia it's a crime to buy a sack of potatoes for three rubles and sell it for four, even though you took the time and trouble to truck it to Moscow from some farm, then stand in the freezing cold and sell it one fucking potato at a time. In America that's not a crime, it's a requirement. In most places it's a crime to marry more than one broad; in dozens of countries you got an option for four. In some countries if you as much as suspect your wife is stepping out on you it's okay to kill her just like that. In other countries you get the chair. Look, there are certain things that ain't ethical, and maybe we can agree shouldn't be done. You shouldn't rape a broad. It's wrong. But in some countries you do it and they reward you with a wedding with the same dame. There's Albanians in the Bronx, that's how they get married. They been in America fifty years and they're still kidnapping brides, raping them and then there's a ceremony and it's all grins and *l'chaims*. Still, it's a crime. But it's also a crime to kill your old man, right? But what if your old man is beating the shit out of your old lady – what then? All these things, Russy, they're very subjunctive. Me, all I know is I try to play fair, give value and pay my taxes like a good American.'

Much nodding ensued. The brothers were clearly enthused the same way that people get lumps in their throats when they see the flag, or at the movies when the good guy finally overcomes. I looked to my professor for a bit of perspective, if not outright cynicism, but he was busily pouring out more shots and clinking glasses with men who under different circumstances would just as soon cut his throat in the street.

'This has been a public service message,' I said in my best radio announcer tone, 'from the people who gave you Murder Inc., union racketeering and a surcharge on every truck that enters or leaves Manhattan.'

The brothers turned to me. As usual, they let Royce speak. 'You confusing me, little man,' he said. 'First you at the funeral and talking like you be family. Then you sitting down with me and the brothers and the chinks after a funeral and sharing lobster lo-mein and what-not. Now you tight amongst us and being shocked by what you know be just the way of the world. You know it be, don't you?'

'I know it is.'

'Then why you be *pro*-testing it? You got to go along to get some. Where we be if every weekday you got someone talking about busting up the system that took so long to get built up in the first place? Answer me that, young friend?'

'We'd be in fucking Mississippi, and people like you would be trying to ride a bus or sit at a lunch counter, and the cops would have dogs on you.'

Silence. The brothers looked at me, looked at Shushan, glanced at Del, then back to me – in unison.

'Kid's right,' Shushan said quietly. 'On that one he is one hundred ten percent right. Sometimes the system works, sometimes it don't. You gentlemen with Dr King? You believe in the struggle?'

'Hell yes,' Royce said. 'Hell yes we do and amen. But that be happening far away, thank the Lord, and that the reason we here, because we be there we be on the wrong end of that po-lice dog, for sure.'

The brothers grinned at this in self-satisfaction.

Shushan cut them off. 'Frankly, Royce. Fred. Teddy. Ed. I'm not proud to hear you say that.'

'Well, what you want us to do, go down there and fight the entire Ku Klux Klan, including the po-lice. Man, my mama and daddy come up here to be free from that shit, and every morning I in New York I thank the Lord they did.'

'So you're just going to let that happen to your own people?' Shushan said.

'Shee-it, they be my own people like the Africans over in Africa be my own people. Yeah, they look like me, maybe they talk like me, but they ain't me. They just foolish fucking niggers ain't got sense to leave that place and come north.'

'Would a runaway nigger run south?' It was Del.

'Wazzat?'

'I said, *Would a runaway nigger run south?* That's a direct quote from the story of Huckleberry Finn, gentlemen. You ought to read it. It's about a slave who runs away and figures he has a pretty good chance of putting the slavers off his trail if he goes in the wrong direction.'

'You calling me nigger or what?'

Del put down his drink and smiled like a man who had nothing to lose, always a scary moment. 'I'm calling on you to do something about what's happening to your people. *I'm* going down to Mississippi. Half the white students I deal with

95

they're going down to Mississippi. Let me put it to you straight, Mr Royce. Either you march for your people or you march against them.'

From the corner of my eye I could see Ira-Myra's come alert, the dog in him sensing violence. I looked to Shushan, but he maintained the same evenly beatific pose, his face relaxed, his shoulders down, his hands in his lap.

'You hear this dago fool call me a nigger, Mr Cats? You hear this pro-fessor say that?' Royce turned to the brothers. 'Y'all hear that?' As one they nodded. Royce turned back to Shushan. 'Here we come to pay our respects. We bringing enough food for ten funerals. We dress to impress. We sincere friends. And we get this nigger talk. Man, I hope you can put this poetry man in his place, because if you don't there going to be four insulted niggers right here.' He reconsidered. 'Afro-Americans.'

Shushan got up slowly from his crate, walked slowly around the couch the black brothers were seated upon, and stood before their leader. Without a word he bent low and kissed the man on his cheek. Then, soundlessly, he kissed each of the brothers the same way. 'Professor del Vecchio didn't mean an insult,' he said quietly. 'I can vouch for this man. He's good people. All he means is that it's time for all you Afro-American black jiveass nigger jigaboos to hang together, otherwise you are going to hang separately. You know who said that? Benjamin Franklin, that's who. Signed the Declaration of Independence, practically discovered electricity and wasn't a bad writer himself. You and me we all know what's going on down there. Maybe it *is* time you got off your fat black asses and went to the aid of your people. They getting whupped pretty good, as Mark Twain might say – don't you think they could use some *un*whuppin'?'

Through the long evening, as the gangsters swapped stories and Del recited poems and food and drink were indulged in to an extent that could only be called biblical, I understood something that I had missed only hours before: I had fallen for Terri Cats not least because I loved her brother. I loved him more two days later, the last day of the mourning period, when the brothers Callinan reentered my life with a vengeance – not theirs, Shushan's.

CHAPTER 10

This is not the way to Chinatown, I thought from the middle seat of the red Eldorado as Ira-Myra's pointed it uptown. Maybe I had seen too many gangster movies, but when a certain kind of person takes another person for a ride and it is clear they are traveling in the wrong direction, it's just as clear that something untoward may occur. I put this out of my mind. Why would Shushan want to knock me off? Hell, I didn't know why Shushan did anything, though I did suspect there was a reason for everything he did do. But this clearly was not Chinatown. Shushan had been talking all day about getting a decent Chinese meal to close out the mourning period – it was the one thing we had not ordered in because, he said, Chinese places on the Upper East Side were, in his own word, 'deracinated.' How he knew the word was at least as much a mystery as how he knew, a couple of decades before anyone else did, one Chinese cuisine from another, and how he knew enough to determine what was or was not deracinated within it. Seated to my right, Shushan had not said a word since

98

we had entered the car. It was his first day out of the hotel room, his first shave, his first glance in a mirror. For that matter, though I'd gone for a stroll every day to pick up the papers, it was pretty much my first real outing as well. Having shared his mourning, I now shared his relief at its conclusion. On the radio the Four Seasons were blasting out 'Walk Like A Man,' whose macho advice was delivered in a strident falsetto, medium and message perfectly out of whack.

It was the first music I had heard in a week, and I imagined this must be what prison is like: you remain the same while the world changes around you. In a matter of days Shushan's trial would begin. I was wondering if this was on his mind as well when Ira-Myra's deftly pulled the big boat into a parking place in front of a small church on East 132nd Street in Spanish Harlem, right under a sign that read:

CHURCH
NO PARKING

'You ever been in a Roman Catholic church?' Shushan asked as he got out.

'Once or twice.' I realized this was not an idle question. 'I'll wait.'

'Get out of the fucking car, college boy,' was his answer.

I got out of the fucking car. A light rain was falling. Lit by a street lamp, the spray of tiny droplets seemed to be falling only here: beyond the light it was merely a soft November evening, not raining at all. I considered how easily the eye can deceive the mind. 'You changing religion?' I asked brightly.

Shushan rewarded me with the aborted beginnings of a smile. His eyelids scrunched up, his nose creased at the top above where the hook began, and even his ears seemed to draw together as though bowing to one another across the sharp planes of his face. But his mouth remained one solid line. 'You sit where I show you, and you pay attention. If anyone's gonna change his religion, college boy, it'll be you. Look, listen and learn.'

Inside, the church was in semi-darkness. But even in this light it was clear it had seen better times. These streets had once been heavily Italian, an immigrant population so uniformly Roman Catholic that its churches were among the richest in the city, not so much because their parishioners were generous but because there were so many of them. In the past twenty years what had been Italian Harlem had been inherited by impoverished Puerto Ricans and Dominicans – many of whom even in their homelands had defected to Evangelical sects. It was simple economics – there were too many churches for too few clients. In the ensuing years dozens of churches in Spanish Harlem would be closed by the Archdiocese of New York, but in the sixties the empty collection plates in many churches were unable to fund routine maintenance or even regular cleaning. I had only to look up: high above at the top of the nave two pigeons seemed to have made a home. They squawked and dipped. The church had a distinct smell, and not a good one. It was as if small animals had died in its walls. The bench I sat on at the front had not been polished by anything but Catholic behinds for a long time. Behind me Ira-Myra's took a seat. Shushan went right to the confessional, behind whose old-fashioned grills low wattage bulbs burned with little effect.

'*Bienvenidos, mi hijo,*' came a voice in New York-accented Spanish from the left-hand grill.

'Good evening, father,' Shushan said quietly.

'Good evening, my son. We don't often have English-speakers. Are you here to confess your sins?'

'Yes, father.'

'When is the last time you confessed?'

'A long time, father,' Shushan said.

'How long, my son?'

'Maybe never, father.'

'Maybe?'

'Never, father.'

There was a pause. I could not help but imagine what the priest was thinking: never confessed, a stranger who has found a church far from where he lives. Probably it was not uncommon, the sons or daughters of Italian immigrants returning to confess theft, adultery, murder or – infinitely worse – lapse of faith. 'Have you sinned?'

'Oh, yes, father. I have sinned.'

'I am here,' the priest said.

'I have taken the name of the Lord in vain.'

'Is that all, my son?'

'I have stolen.'

'Yes, my son.'

'I have killed.'

A long pause. 'Tell me more, my son. In the eyes of Christ we are all sinners.'

'You know how it is, father. Do I need to tell you the details?'

'In the eyes of Christ all may be forgiven, but only if truly confessed.'

'In Korea, in the war, I shot a man.'

'In war it is necessary to kill.'

'I shot him in the back, father.'

'Was there reason, my son?'

'Oh yeah, father. He was an American officer, running away.'

'And was this the only time you killed, my son?'

'I killed a lot of Koreans. North Koreans. Maybe some were Red Chinese. You couldn't tell. They wore Korean uniforms. It was at the Chosin Reservoir. All the others I shot in front.'

'You were in the army?'

'The Marines, father. First Marine Division. No better friend, no worse enemy.'

'I am sure you fought bravely and did not sin.'

'Also several wops, a mick and two kikes.'

'In the army, my son?'

'No, father, the Marines. Not in the Marines. Just in life.'

'Tell me about this, my son.'

'It was just what happens.'

Pause. 'Tell me.'

'Well, you know, father. It's New York. It's not Iowa or somewhere. It's what happens. Pretty much that's it. What happens. It's the kind of thing where if you don't do it to them they do it to you.'

'Are you a policeman, my son?'

'Hell, no. Excuse me, father. No, far from it.'

'How far, my son?'

'Very far, father.'

A really long pause. I had grown up in the fifties, when radio was still alive, not yet fully replaced by television. I remember staying up late when I was eight listening to *Gunsmoke* and *The Fat Man* in bed: the deep voices, the eerie hyper-realism of the sound effects, the silences that foreshadowed some dramatic high point to come. 'Tell me about the stealing, my son.'

'Ah, that was nothing, father. I mean, I was a kid. Does it count if you're a kid?'

'And taking the name of our Lord—'

'You know, father, just God damn this, God damn that.'

'These are mortal sins, my son.'

'I figured as much, father.'

'Are you prepared to repent, to ask forgiveness of Jesus Christ our Lord?'

Now the silence came from Shushan's side of the confessional. 'Let me think about it, father. To repent, do you have to be a Catholic?'

From behind me Ira rose – in the way of really big men he moved gracefully, though the very bulk of him was a presence, as if the air around him were being pushed back, disturbed. He stepped in front of the priest's side of the confessional, facing it as though to look through the grill. But the grillwork was meant for a seated man. It met Ira's waist.

'Yes?' the priest said.

'I'm just waiting,' Ira said in his hoarse whisper.

'Please take a seat in the rear of the church, my son. I shall be with you shortly.'

Ira didn't move.

'Do I have to be a Catholic?' Shushan repeated.

Pause. 'Are you not a Catholic?'

'No, father.'

'Were you baptized, my son?'

'Uh-uh, father. Though I do like to swim. Sometimes I go out to Jones Beach in the summer. Florida and Mexico every winter. I used to go to Cuba, but since Kennedy went after the guy with the beard. . . .'

'You have no place here, my son,' the priest said.

'Well, yes and no, father. I figured you might want to know who's going to do it to you. You know, that I'm not some amateur.'

At this point the narrow door to the priest's side of the confessional swung open and then was slammed back hard as it met Ira's big shoe, which was then wedged tight against it.

'Be patient, father,' Shushan said.

'I have no money,' the priest said. 'This is a poor church.'

'Hey, there's more money in the Roman Catholic Church than in all the Rockefellers' bank accounts combined,' Shushan said. 'But I'm not interested in money. I got money. You ever read Shakespeare, father?'

'Shakespeare?'

'The Merchant of Venice?'

'What do you want?'

'A pound of flesh, father. You probably have a pound to spare. I mean, if you want to atone for your sins, you might consider parting with a pound or so. Or maybe your two brothers would volunteer in your place. A pound is all I want—'

'Shushan!'

'Shut up, kid,' he said. 'This is between me and Father Bill here. Father Bill, right? You know, father, I don't like to cast asparagus, and unlike you I don't get involved in calling people on their sins, but your sister is something of a hot babe. Did she bother to mention she was the one who—'

'This is a church!' the priest shouted. 'I'll call the police!'

'You can call the fucking pope for all the good it'll do, father. Just stay calm and we'll get through this. Are you going to stay calm or would you prefer that we take you out of this box and nail you to the fucking cross where your parishioners can find you in the morning and maybe venerate your bones. Are you listening to me, father?'

'I'm listening,' the priest said quietly.

'Like I say, I don't want to get into who's right and who's wrong, because even if your sister wasn't getting vengeance on my friend Russell for losing interest – which you probably wouldn't know about, but believe me it seems to be God's plan for men and women – even if your sister, what's her name?'

Silence.

'What's her name, father? You want to cooperate or not? If not just let me know because we got ten-inch spikes and a hammer in the car—'

'Celeste.'

'Nice name,' Shushan said. 'Look, I have a sister too. Hey, she doesn't do what I want all the time. You can't control the whole world. But what you did, that wasn't right.'

'I did nothing.'

'You and your mick brothers beat the shit out of a good friend of mine.'

'I know nothing about it.'

'Ira,' Shushan said in a bigger voice. 'Go to the car and get the Jesus tools.'

'I'm sorry,' the priest said quickly. 'I was overcome with anger. Your . . . friend . . . dishonored our sister.'

'My friend fucked your sister and your sister fucked him right back. Do you want me to bring

106

in the two witnesses to these repeated acts of carnal congress or will you take my word? Because if you don't take my word I'm going to be offended.'

'I take your word.'

'Good,' Shushan said. 'Are you ready therefore to confess your sin?'

'I may confess only to Jesus Christ.'

'He's not in the room?'

'I may confess only to a priest.'

'Ira,' Shushan said, so conversationally it was like a suggestion to go out and pick up a pack of smokes. 'Go out and see if you can't round up a priest.'

'No!' the priest said. 'All right. We were angry. We struck out. We punished your . . . friend.'

'Damn right,' Shushan said. 'Now how about my pound of flesh?'

Silence. This was no radio drama. Still, with every stretch of blank air would come, I knew, another critical point in the narrative. As an old-time radio narrator might have put it, I was riveted to my pew.

'Father Bill, how about it?'

'I don't know what you want. Whoever you are, please. I don't know what you want.'

'Shushan Cats.'

'Shushan Cats,' the priest said. Apparently he read the papers. 'Sir, you have no idea. This is a mistake.'

'A pound of flesh, that's about the weight of an adult hand. I'll take a hand.'

'A hand?'

'Right, left. No matter. Or a foot. No, better a hand. Either from you or from your brothers, or from all of you. How about you sit down and come up with five fingers between you?'

'Five fingers?'

'Technically that's probably going to work out to less than a pound, but what the hell, father. Consider it a sheenie discount. You are familiar with the term sheenie? How about kike? Hebe? Hebe is good. A hebe discount. The regular price is one whole hand, but for you five fingers. Practically half price. What do you say?'

Silence.

'Father? You still with us, father?'

'Your friend attacked us.'

'Yeah, he hit you in the boot with a couple of ribs. Father, we're getting close to cross-time here. Work with me.' He paused. 'Russy!'

'I'm here.'

'You been following this theological conversation?'

'From the beginning.'

'What do you think?'

'Think?' Was I allowed to think? 'I'm sure the father is sorry,' I said.

'You do? Does he repent, do you think? Father, do you repent? I mean, three big micks on one little kike kid, that's probably a sin. It's for sure a crime. If you think about it, more than one actually – aggravated assault, conspiracy, maybe even attempted murder. Do you repent, father?'

108

'I repent,' the priest said quietly.

'Louder, please, father.'

'I repent.'

'You know about the Second Vatican Council? In Rome? Of course you do. They may actually allow the liturgy to be in English. Or Spanish. Very democratic. If you don't mind me saying so, a shrewd move. But probably it won't bring in more clients. People like the mysteries. If you make everything too clear you lose them. It's uncertainty. People are fascinated by uncertainty. But hey, it's your fucking religion, father, not mine. I'm just speaking as an observer. Anyway, in whatever language, did you sin in busting up my friend?'

'I sinned, Mr Cats.'

'So as I understand it, you have to do three things, right? You have to be sorry, deeply sorry. You have to seriously intend never do anything like that again, right?'

'Yes.'

'And you have to do penance according to the decision of the priest. Is that right?'

'Yes.'

'I'm your priest, father. I want that hand.'

'I don't . . . I don't know what. . . .'

'Father, it's like five Our Fathers and ten Hail Marys. It's something you have to do. I suggest you discuss this with your brothers and in a month or so get back to me with your decision. What is it, November? Come back to me January. After Christmas. That's probably a busy season for you, right? January second, say. January second okay with you?'

'January second?'

'What is it with you people? You want it in Latin? Talk to your mick brothers, I mean one cop and one fireman and one priest, that's pretty mick, isn't it, father?'

'Yes. No. I don't know, Mr Cats.'

'The only thing more mick would be a sister who's a nun. But so far there's no sign of that, right?'

'Mr Cats, I—'

'Okay, father. We have an understanding. You talk to your brothers. Work it out on the fingers, the hand, whatever you prefer. You get the sheenie discount. If you want it. Otherwise, one whole hand. And the date you got?'

'January second.'

'Brilliant. Now before I go, I have to absolve you.'

Absolve me?'

'Sure. I'm your priest, right? I got it in my pocket. Just give me a sec. The light in here could be better. You might tell Pope John to do something about that. Okay, here goes: *Dominus noster Jesus Christus te absolvat; et ego auctoritate ipsius te absolvo ab omni vinculo excommunicationis et interdicti in quantum possum et tu indiges.* Now as I understand it the priest is supposed to make the sign of the cross. You do it for me. You doing it? Okay, back to the script. *Deinde, ego te absolvo a peccatis tuis in nomine Patris, et Filii, et Spiritus Sancti. Amen.* I know you know what it means, but we got some unbelievers here. Pay attention, gentlemen. "May our Lord Jesus Christ absolve you; and by His authority I absolve you from every bond of excommunication and interdict, so far as my power allows and your needs require. Thereupon, I absolve you of your sins in the name of the Father, and the Son, and the Holy Ghost. Amen." Pretty good, huh? For a Jew?' A sound like a whimper came from the priest's box. 'I take that as a yes. Oh, one more thing, what they call the post-absolution prayer, but I can't let that one go without your promising me you'll do everything in your power to make sure your brothers don't develop vigilante ideas and try to get back on Russy here, because if they do you are one dead priest, and so is your brother the fireman and especially the cop. Your sister, unlike you, I hold her more or less blameless. Women get pissed off. It's understandable. Now, promise me, father, you'll do everything in your power to let cooler heads prevail.'

'Yes. I will, Mr Cats.'

'Delighted to hear that, father. Okay, here goes. *Passio Domini nostri Jesu Christi, merita Beatae Mariae Virginis et omnium sanctorum, quidquid boni feceris vel mail sustinueris sint tibi in remissionem peccatorum, augmentum gratiae et praemium vitae aeternae.* That's it. Frankly, I hope we all have the reward of everlasting life, though the Jewish idea, and Jesus wasn't exactly an Irishman, is this one counts more. Father, it might be a good thing if you sat in your closet for a while after you hear us leave.' The right-hand door opened. Shushan stepped out, slipping a folded sheet of paper into his inside breast pocket. 'Gentlemen, I believe our work here is done. Anyone for Chinese? I could do with a little Hunan myself right about now.'

CHAPTER 11

On the way downtown the silence in the car echoed the silence going uptown, but this time there was an air of satisfaction that was so thickly palpable I could taste it. I didn't dare speak to Shushan about what had occurred. In my mind I wasn't precisely sure what that was. If Shushan believed intimidating Celeste's brother – for that matter, all of them – would in some way push me further into his debt, at a certain point I would have to make it clear this was not the case. All it got me was further involved in something I could live quite well without. While the radio blasted a song that reminded me I had not so much as looked at a joint for a week – it was 'Puff the Magic Dragon,' pretty much the pot-smoker's anthem – I tried to think my situation through.

For reasons unknown, I seem to have been adopted. That was clear. Maybe it was my fault. Had I been sending out delirious signals that I needed a father or older brother? It was true my old man had died three years before, that I had grown up motherless, and that my father's grief at her loss never seemed to allay itself in an emotional attachment to their only child. A lot of people had it worse. Me, I ate regularly, could depend on the old man if I got in trouble, and from time to time there was even the hint of warmth, maybe not enough to heat up the room but sufficient so that I did not freeze to death. And it wasn't me who had walked into the Bhotke Young Men's Society, it wasn't me who had volunteered to organize Shushan's mother's funeral, or his mourning. It was just something that . . . happened. On the other hand, the idea that dominated the sixties was that nothing happened without complicity: Fidel Castro had taken over in Cuba because the US had long supported a series of brutal dictators; America was locked in a nuclear stalemate with the Soviet Union because neither side was brave enough to come to terms; in Vietnam we were getting deeper into a fight we wouldn't win because we were too vain to understand what had happened there to the French. The ethos of the time was this: our failure – a nation's, a group's, an individual's – was rooted in our own weakness or greed or lust or love or even in our genes. We could not blame someone else: we were our own enemy.

'What the fuck is this stupid gimme-another-joint-and-all-will-be-well shit?' Shushan said suddenly. He had apparently been paying attention to the lyrics; not even pot-smokers did that.

Ira reached forward to punch in another station.

'You know how many great themes there are for songs, kid?'

'Love,' I said. 'Bravery. Loss.'

'Very good. Mostly it's all love songs now. You believe in love?'

'I guess.'

'You ever *been* in love? Ira, what do you think, you're in love, right?'

'Right, boss.'

'And well you should be. So what do you say – as a lover, you see this kid believing in love?'

'I don't know, boss,' Ira said, turning right to head around the Washington Square Arch, where folk singers and junkies were scattered around the fountain in the mostly concrete park like medieval jongleurs, their music blowing in on the wind through the open windows of the convertible. As if to hear them better, Shushan dropped the top, which lifted itself automatically from the roof, seemed to catch the air like a parachute, momentarily buffeting the huge Caddy as it came around the west side of the square, and then settled into itself, the canvass and mechanism hidden as though they had never been.

'I dreamed I saw Joe Hill last night . . .' someone sang from the fountain to the accompaniment of several guitars and a banjo before the verse trailed off as we moved south.

'Heroism, yeah, and sacrifice,' Shushan said. 'In a way it's always about sacrifice. Love, that's sacrifice. Look at Ira here. Big handsome mug like that can get all the pussy in five boroughs, and all he thinks about is taking care of his Myra. Isn't that right, Ira?'

'That's about it, boss.'

'Every great song, when it comes right down to it, it's about sacrifice. Putting yourself in the way of something powerful, standing up to it, standing for it, standing against it. You think those coloreds getting dogs set on them in Alabama they're not sacrificing themselves? That's a wonderful thing. I don't know if it'll work. But I do know they must feel real good about themselves. Even if one of them loses an arm or a leg he'll feel like the subject of a song. You know what I'm saying, kid?'

'That's a very romantic notion, Shushan,' I said, then realized I might be misunderstood. 'By romantic, I don't mean—'

'Shame on you, college boy. I know what romantic in that sense means. Tell me, who's the most romantic modern poet?'

I took a shot. A great one had died just the month before. 'Robert Frost?'

'Shit no,' Shushan said. 'You know Auden?'

'Yeah.'

'What a man. Total pansy and he has more testosterone than everybody together in this car. You know how we can win in Vietnam? Make Wystan Hugh Auden and Allen Ginsberg run the show. Auden could handle the army, Ginsberg could be commandant of Marines. I don't give a damn about the Navy and Air Force. They're just

116

technical. But on the ground those two would clean it up fast.'

'I kind of think they're anti-war,' I said, perhaps snidely.

'Everyone's anti-war, or should be.'

'Were you really a Marine?'

Shushan snorted. 'Was I a Marine? Ira, was I a Marine?'

'You sure was, boss.'

'I was a good Marine. Let me tell you, there was a time I thought I'd make it my life. But circumstances—'

'Korea?'

'Oh, yeah. The Chosin people. That's what they called us. You ever hear about the battle of Chosin Reservoir?'

'Was it bad?'

'It was fucking awful,' Shushan said. 'That's when I pulled the trigger on a guy for the first time. I mean, growing up in Brownsville, there's a kind of Brooklyn thing. You could maybe kill someone, but maximum with a knife if he pulled one and you had to. But usually it was fists. You just beat the shit out of them and that was that. Okay, maximum a baseball bat. A baseball bat, it had a certain finesse, plus not illegal to carry. Better than a gun, actually, up close. But pulling a trigger, that's a whole different dimension. That's why I vote for Wystan Hugh Auden as head of the joint chiefs. Ginsberg, he'd make a great leader of the Corps. These are guys they don't back down in the face of bad news. Although, let me tell you, Wystan is not the kind of guy who'll let on what he thinks. Should be in the Mafia.'

'You can tell that from reading him? How do you know what he thinks other than what's in his—' I stopped. 'Wystan?'

'You want to meet him? Miserable son of a bitch, but like I say, he'd make a fine general. You know what it takes to be a general?'

'A military mind?

'Kid, shut up with the wise cracks for a minute. This is serious. A general and a poet are exactly the same in one thing. What they do they have to do with critical efficiency. Not a word or an action wasted. And the action has to be more important than the man who creates it. You know Yeats?'

'You knew Yeats too?'

'Of course not. Yeats died fucking I don't know forty years ago. I know Auden because he plays poker. You didn't know that, WH fucking Auden plays poker? Badly, let me say. The man gets into dutch from time to time.' In the constraint of the front seat, squeezed between Ira's shoulders rolling as he turned the wheel and Shushan's smaller yet more sinewy frame that seemed to jerk when he jabbed with his left index finger as if lecturing the windshield, I was hammered every time Shushan wished to emphasize a point. 'So what's wrong with that? Everybody gets in trouble once in a while. Look at you, kid. You too, right?' When I didn't answer he simply went on. 'So what did

Yeats say? He said, I'm not quoting exactly, that a poet has to choose between the perfection of his life and the perfection of his work. That's why Wystan would make a hell of a general. A great general, all he cares about is the poem, the battle, each one, one at a time. Kid, do you know what I'm saying?'

I nodded. 'But I don't know why you're saying it.'

'I'm saying Yeats didn't have the whole of it. He didn't go far enough. All a man is *is* what he does.'

'And this applies to. . . .'

'To everybody,' Shushan said. 'There's Justo.' He said it *Yusto*. 'Pull up, Ira.' The big man stopped the car in front of a fire hydrant. Across the narrow street was a police precinct. Neither Ira nor Shushan seemed concerned. 'I'm going to introduce you to someone who is going to be very important in your life.'

I could see a wiry man, hatless, in a light suit, dark shirt, light tie, standing smoking under a streetlamp in front of a restaurant in which small red-painted animals, ducks some of them, others looking mysteriously like unfamiliar mammals, were being turned on a spit in the window. The entire scene was straight out of some cheesy Hollywood film. I hadn't been shanghaied by a gangster – I had been shanghaied by a gangster movie. '*Chinga*! Justo!' He turned back to me. 'So why, you're asking yourself, is Allen Ginsberg a natural to lead the Corps?'

'You know Allen Ginsberg too?'

'Met him once or twice,' Shushan said. 'Not my kind of guy. Too much, you know, *ganj*. But he's a Marine.'

'Allen Ginsberg is a Marine,' I said, following him out of the car. No one bothered to put up the top. The windows were down. On the windshield Shushan carefully tucked a twenty-dollar bill under the sidewalk-side wiper blade, either to take care of the cops or to show the world that no one in his right mind would dare touch it. 'Okay, I give up. Why is Allen Ginsberg a Marine?'

'Because he don't give a shit about anything but getting the job done,' Shushan said. 'Goes to the sound of the guns. That's a real poet.'

Shushan had me by the arm as we came up to the little guy in the gangster-movie get-up. 'Justo, remember this kid did such a good job at the funeral? Russy the college boy. You got something in common, right?' He turned to me. 'Justo went to City College. World's best accountant. You know what? Justo's been doing my books since after Korea and we haven't been audited once.'

He was some sort of Latin, probably Puerto Rican, with that mixed-blood look, Spanish, Indian, black, maybe even a little Chinese, that seemed to demand the suspension of judgment of others because so much otherness was part of him. 'I hear you did good for the *shiva* too,' he said. '*Chinga* son-of-a-bitch wouldn't let me come to that. No spicks allowed.'

120

'Don't listen to him,' Shushan said. 'For the funeral and the shiva he was taking his family on vacation to Puerto Rico. I mean, scheduled for a year. What was he supposed to tell his kids – I can't go because my boss's mother passed? Anyway, spicks have to go back there once a year, just to visit the hubcaps they stole in New York.'

The street was misty from the rain, the light soft as it can be only when broken up by so many humans pulsing through the streets, the streets themselves alive with the commerce of fruit and vegetable stores open until midnight, seafood markets with the fish laid out like volunteer corpses, so pleased to greet you on their icy beds, a Chinese apothecary looking like a supermarket for clientele that was a whole other species, its dusty display window full of dried spiders, eviscerations of embalmed bats, and strange fleshy plants that seemed to be growing upside down in pots hanging from the ceiling; in a place of honor a large coiled snake, banded in black and red, moved slightly as though reacting to a dream, then settled back into mimicry of the dead. Tiny store-front restaurants were lined up like troughs on this side of the street; on the other were four-story tenements and the police station. Shushan led us to the one restaurant with the mixed menagerie turning on spits in the window where, once inside, the rotisseurs in stained white uniforms and white forage caps greeted him with a familiarity that to me was effusive, exaggerated, surreal. Shushan returned the favor by shaking hands with all three countermen, who hastily wiped their red-stained hands on their aprons – each might have been indicted on murder charges based solely on apparel. 'How you doin'?' Shushan said to each. *'Tzing-tao!'* Each in turn shouted back *'Tzing-tao!'*

'What does that mean?'

'I don't know,' Shushan said. 'But they say it all the time. Probably it's *fuck you*. Looks like we came at rush hour.'

There was not a seat in the house. All of Chinatown seemed to have been compressed into this one restaurant, whose twenty or so tables held nearly a hundred people so squeezed together that raising chopsticks could be considered an act of aggression. The waiters physically forced themselves between the backs of chairs. One of them got to the front, repeating the whole *Tzing-tao!* routine with Shushan.

'Table for four,' the waiter said. 'One minute.' He turned toward the kitchen where another waiter had already entered carrying a four-foot round table upside down on his head, followed by two more carrying a chair the same way. Our guy, obviously in charge, began barking in Chinese to the occupants of three tables in the middle of the room. They merely shook their heads. He shouted again. The waiters remained standing with the furniture over them. More shouting.

'Hey, we can wait,' Shushan said.

'You no wait. They finish. They finish, they go.'

As we watched the diners rush through their meals under the furniture poised above their heads, a bottle of Johnny Walker Black appeared in the hand of the headwaiter, who poured drinks for us as we stood. In three minutes one of the tables with two diners was abandoned, that table lifted out of the way and the larger table descended into its place with much shoving of the surrounding diners. The two new chairs were inserted at the table, a red cloth was unfurled and settled on the raw plywood top. Table settings mysteriously appeared.

'Now you eat,' the headwaiter said.

And eat we did. Despite the red-drenched meats in the window the specialty of the place turned out to be fish, plus seafood in all its bizarre variety. Everything seemed to be bathed in red sauce studded with bits of emerald green or dark brown or pink, all shimmering under the fluorescent lights.

'You know this stuff, kid? This is Hunan food. Southwest China. Think of Texas. Very spicy, but not sweet unless it's combined with something else, like salty or sour. Your American Chinese food is Guadong, which is what people call Cantonese, because Canton is where most of the immigrants from China come from. But Hunan is not just hot like Schezuan. Take fish. The idea of the sauces in Hunan food is to reveal the taste of the fish, not conceal it. And this is good fish – you can't get fresher unless you're a shark.'

'Shushan is the king of fish in New York,' Justo said. 'You want fish, you go to the Kingfish. He da Kingfish.'

'Yeah, I da Kingfish,' Shushan said. 'You like this fish, kid? Any kind of fish you like, just ask me.'

'The *chingao* Itals are waiting for Shushan to go away,' Justo said. 'They got a good feeling about what's going to happen to my man, but it's not gonna happen. Nothing gonna happen. We gonna get through the *chingao* trial and we gonna keep what we got.'

I was scooping a succulent morsel of striped bass in some sort of scallion-heavy maroon sauce that allowed the flavor of the fish through only to strike the tongue with fire, when I realized I was being invited into the conversation. 'Which is?'

'The Fulton Fish Market, kid,' Shushan said. 'Our *gavone* friends are looking to come in, maybe during my trial even, but for sure if I go away. We don't even know if they're behind the whole thing, the indictment etcetera etcetera, because one thing about the *goombah* mentality, they see something in the hands of a kike or a spick or a mick or a nigger even and they want it, so they figure out who to get on the case. They're like jackals in Africa, they lead the lion to the prey and then wait until the big cat takes it down, a wildebeest or a zebra or whatever, and then they try to get the fresh kill away from the lion. It's nature, that's all.'

'They want what we got,' Justo said.

'I make it work,' Shushan said. 'I make it friendly.

I'm like the big cop on the beat, the big mick cop who used to walk a beat in every neighborhood in the city, but now they ride around by twosies in patrol cars because they're too scared to step out. One thing about those mick cops when I was a kid, they walked the beat. You didn't fuck with them. Now there's no order in the whole city. When you get that in a place like the Fulton Fish Market, which has been supplying the city with seafood since over two hundred years, you get chaos. Somebody says, "Hey, nobody moves as much as a bay scallop until I get paid to let it happen," it causes two kinds of trouble. The first kind is bad scallops. The stuff comes in the night, it has to go out in the early morning, at the worst. Sometimes you're looking at a turnaround of twenty minutes – comes in, goes out. One minute it's on the boat, next it's on a truck, then it's at the market and bim-bam thank you sam it's out the door in somebody's pick-up truck off to some retail market in Queens or uptown to your fancy restaurants—'

'Or here,' I said, understanding.

'Or here. Funny thing, sometimes you get striper caught in the Great South Bay, out on Long Island, it goes to the market a couple hours' drive away and then somebody with a restaurant only a couple of miles from where it was boated puts it on the menu. You can't have something as delicate as this disturbed, because fish, in case you never noticed, really stinks when it's not fresh. Yeah, there are things you can do to clean up the smell, but fresh is fresh. The restaurant chefs aren't fools so they won't touch it, the neighborhood markets, they won't screw their regular customers because that's how they get regular customers. But unless there's somebody looking out for the little guy, some *gavone* is going to come in and say, "*Bona sera*, I want mine." Everywhere you look they come in for the kill on the weak and the vulnerable. It's like a nuclear bomb. You don't even have to use it – just having it is enough. They got the trash business for the same reason. You don't move the trash you got major headaches, rats, stench. Parking lots? You want the cars not broken up, pay up. Construction and demolition, don't ask. They can slow things down so much they don't have to do anything but show up and they get paid off. You know, I don't like that Bobby Kennedy, but he's right about the *goombahs*. They're out of control.'

'And you're Robin Hood, protecting the little guy.'

'Ruben Hood, yeah,' Shushan said. 'Gentlemen, listen to this kid. He's got stainless steel balls, no? Kid, you got stainless steel balls?'

'I don't know, Shushan.'

'Don't worry, you're going to know. You're going to learn more about yourself than you ever thought possible. That's why I'm introducing you to Justo here. Justo and me, Justo and I you would correct me, we go way back.'

'We go back to Korea,' Justo said, seeming slowly

126

to grow before my eyes. The light suit, dark shirt, light tie – actually some form of silver in the fluorescent light of the restaurant – the costume of the cartoon gangster, it all melted away: I saw the man. Justo's thin face was pockmarked along the two ridges that formed a vee from ear to mouth. His short hair was slicked back with enough oil to grease Shushan's Cadillac. And his dark somewhat oriental eyes were small and so close together they might have met were it not for the sliver of nose that shot directly out of the meeting of his brows. In short, no movie star. But in saying just that one word he seemed to be sitting straighter, his gaze steady, his face relaxed in appreciation. 'Korea,' he said again. 'This crazy fuck ever tell you about Korea?'

'I overheard him speaking of it to someone else.'

'Yeah,' Justo said. '*Chingao*, they didn't know whether to court-martial him or give him the Navy Cross.' He smiled happily, almost prettily. He had good teeth, big and white, that seemed to have been borrowed from someone else's face. 'So you know what, they did both.'

'Ah,' Shushan said. 'That wasn't exactly the first time I was in court.'

'Except they wanted to put you in front of a firing squad,' Justo said. 'When you was a tough kid in Brooklyn maybe you could get reform school, or even worse. But—'

'But nothing,' Shushan said. 'So what I was saying is this: The *goombahs*, their whole life is living off others. I'm not talking about your normal Italians, Sicilian, Napolida, Abruzz – I'm talking about the kind of people they're cockroaches. Their own people hate them, Russy – they suck the blood out of their own.'

'And what do you do, Shushan?'

'Me? Like I said, I'm just like the neighborhood cop, except I don't take bribes and make a better paycheck. Anybody fucks with the Fulton Fish Market, anybody even looks like it, I'm all over them before you can say scrod, not even flounder or yellow-tail but fucking scrod. No make it cod, that's even shorter. Which is why New York City gets the freshest fish, why people can go to work in the market and leave in the morning and nobody shakes them down, why the trucks roll in and out like a Swiss watch, like a Rolex or Omega.'

'So you're some kind of benevolent despot,' I said, by now wondering if I did indeed have balls of stainless steel. 'You think that's American?'

'Fuck that,' Shushan said. 'You're going to learn you can't do everything the right way, because of all the people who are ready to do it the wrong way. You're just a kid, your nose is in books, and maybe you know a lot, but what you don't know is that in the real world somebody has to make a decision every minute. Okay, sometimes you get the wrong somebody, and sometimes he doesn't have the luxury of being democratically elected, but somebody has to step up.'

'You know who else got the Navy Cross, kid?'

Justo said. 'Barney Ross the Jewish boxer from Chicago. *Semper fi* all the way. And what's his name, Sterling Hayden, the movie star? You're sitting with royalty, kid.'

'Because you shot a man?'

'Yeah, well,' Shushan said as more food appeared. It was red duck from the rotisserie in front. Shushan waved gaily to the countermen, who waved back, grinning. 'What happened was we were in a tight spot, and somebody had to make a fucking decision. So I did. That's all it was.' He looked across the table and changed the subject. 'Ira, you going to leave some of this food for other people?'

Whatever else was said over the meal remains a blur. The Scotch must have gotten to me – despite Shushan's reservations about *ganj*, I was a pot-smoker, not a drinker. Then, as we were finishing up, two elegantly dressed Chinese in metallic silk suits and white-on-white shirts came up and shook everyone's hand. Tables were again shoved aside so they could sit. Unlike the older Chinese at the graveside, these spoke perfect New York English – Jimmy was the voluble one; Tommy barely said a word – and seemed to think they had found a long-lost brother. They were obviously sports fans, immediately talking intense boxing and baseball and which college teams would make it to the National Invitational Tournament at Madison Square Garden. In something of an alcohol and Hunan haze, I pretended to be interested, perking up only when I was introduced well into the conversation, as though Shushan had abruptly realized he had left me out.

'This is Russy, my associate,' Shushan told them. 'Any time he needs a hand, I hope you'll treat him well.'

Neither Justo nor Ira was introduced, either because they were known to the visitors or because they did not matter. Why I mattered was a mystery, one which I had already come to regard with the acceptance of an orphan who is taken in by relatives he never knew he had.

When we walked outside into the November night the twenty was still on the windshield, and the car was freshly washed, its deep crimson paint glowing like a Red Delicious apple beneath the street lamps. I may actually have dozed on the trip to Brooklyn, the chattering grates of the Manhattan Bridge lulling me as the big Caddy rumbled smoothly over the metal, Symphony Sid, the jazz disk jockey, on the radio, so that when we got to my apartment house on Eastern Parkway I was still drowsy as I staggered past my wrecked Plymouth Belvedere, the poor thing stripped of its wheels like a quadruple amputee.

When I walked in the door to my apartment there was a visitor.

CHAPTER 12

In reality, I surprised Celeste more than she surprised me: As deeply asleep as she was beautifully disheveled on the mattress on the floor, when I switched on the light she leapt a foot in the air, then rubbed her eyes like a child. 'Oh,' she whispered, hoarse with slumber. 'You.'

'Yeah, well, I do pay the rent,' I said. 'Tell me, is your whole family going to show up every time I come home, Celeste? Because if so I'm going to stop coming home. And I want my key.' For some reason – aside from what was turning my pants into a tent – I was not unhappy to see her. It had been a week since I had as much as been close to a woman, not including Terri Cats, who had declared herself exempt, and the idea of getting into a warm bed with a hot woman was hardly objectionable. That was normal. To a man, especially a young man, sex trumps propriety. What was odd is that I didn't blame her for what happened. Maybe it was Shushan's sympathetic understanding of Celeste's part in the drama that had occurred in this very room only a week before, or maybe it was indeed lust, or maybe drink, or maybe I was coming to an appreciation of human frailty that was based not on morality but on empathy: in her place I would have been pissed off at me too. 'You going to be pissed off again when I don't want to see you anymore?' I said with the formality of the tipsy as I bent to hold her in my arms on the low mattress. 'I don't want to have this thing with the three Callinan brothers again. I'm running out of ribs.'

'There's a fourth,' she said. 'But he's in Vietnam.'

'Excellent,' I said. 'Did you give him a rain-check? Can I expect to see him too? *Hi, Russell. You don't know me. I'm another one of Celeste's foaming-at-the-mouth siblings. I missed the first go-round, so I hope you don't mind if I beat the shit out of you six months late.*'

'I gave them hell, Russ,' she said, her breath sweetly pungent with sleep, the must of wet flannel, a hint of cinnamon. 'I told Billy was all – a priest isn't supposed to snitch – and then he got them riled up. It wasn't my idea.'

'But you laughed when you heard the news?'

'I did not,' she said. 'Maybe smiled. But I didn't know how bad it was, not at first. Then they told me. Russ, if I can't have you the one way I don't want you the other.'

It occurred to me Father Bill might turn up with his brothers yet again to weigh in with another opinion, to say nothing of their fists, but I wasn't going to spoil the moment, or the hour if I could stay awake. 'You always feel so good,' I heard myself murmur. This in itself was strange. Celeste was mostly bones. When I mounted her her hips used to gouge me like adzes, and there was precious little padding above the waist as well. She was one of those women who believed the abominable homosexual lie, then just getting started, that equates undernourishment with beauty – no man who actually has physical sex with women wants one who doesn't have a certain softness about her, a nice round ass that raises her center up like a proffered blossom, and soft breasts to rest his head on afterward. Celeste had none of that. She was in fact an Irish-American prequivalent of Twiggy, the anorexic British model who soon would be on all the magazine covers. Celeste's was the coming look: both sensual and androgynous, eyes staring straight at you, and always the suggestion that there was not a great deal of washing going on. This was not because there wasn't. Celeste had the natural strong musk common to Irish redheads – it suffused a room when she was aroused, electric red hair that fell around her shoulders like a shimmering cape, and curiously thin lips she could hinge open like a python's to swallow mine. Also she was insatiable. Maybe by the time I was Shushan's age, which I made out to be closing on forty, I would slow down enough to be thankful for a respite now and then – so far I had never seen Shushan with a female aside from his sister and his mother's corpse – but for the moment I was grateful for a woman who could keep up with me, who wasn't a universal recipient, ever ready to be sung to but unwilling or too unsure to be part of a duet. But I was getting ahead of myself: within minutes, maybe seconds, I was asleep on her neck, her thick hair tickling my nose as I snuggled against her – for a bag of bones she was surprisingly flexible – and it wasn't until early morning, five-o-five by the loud-ticking Big Ben alarm clock on the floor, that I woke to find her astride me, which is just what I'd been dreaming. The position was natural for her, because she was almost as tall as I, with long thighs that allowed her to slide up and down the length of my cock like a violinist at full bow. This she did with real precision, because like the woman Lady Chatterley's lover complains about, who uses a man as a conveniently warm dildo, Celeste was able to bring herself off repeatedly simply by stroking and bearing down. But unlike DH Lawrence's example, Celeste was as generous about my pleasure as she was of hers. In fact, I rather doubted she could make the distinction. With her mouth sucking my lips and her hands pinning mine – a hold more erotic than real; I doubt she weighed much more than a hundred-ten – Celeste worked herself over me like a piston and each time she reached a crescendo would bite my lips with such savagery that after an hour they would have that bee-stung look of the well and aggressively kissed. But now, for the first time, while she fucked me I seemed to have flown out of myself, risen to the cracked and yellowed ceiling, and was watching and wondering what it was she felt about me that I hardly felt at all.

Certainly it was not the first time I was the object of love or at least specific lust. For all that I was young, handsome and virile, I knew that I would win no prizes as a lover. Maybe I was too handsome and certainly too young, and in an era where women had learned to become as aggressive about their sexuality as about their politics – the two already having become terminally confused – all I had to do, at base, was show up. I never chased women, merely accepted or rejected them when they chased me. I had early on come to see women as interchangeable parts, so that when I was tired of one another could be brought in like a relief pitcher, like an endless bullpen of pitchers warming up. One girl I knew complained that I was the most relaxed lover she had known – that it was almost as if I didn't care. I didn't. But now, somehow, I did. Yet this was not someone I cared for.

Celeste was just another girl. In time she would be memorable less for who she was than for what her brothers had done to me. There was nothing about her that inspired love, a fact that may or may not have had to do with what Shushan seemed to have picked up: I did not do love. I did sex. I did like. I did desire, passion, amusement, vanity, pleasure. But love was something then so far beyond me that it might as well have been another language, another culture, another species. If I cared anything about Celeste it was because she was here now, pumping me like a lubricated well-handle, writhing and moaning as if to tell me I was the one, the only one, the great and all-powerful one – but all I heard beyond the sound of her moans, my moans and air being expelled from the bellows of her cunt as she squeezed down on me was that I was the convenient one, the present one, the current one. In seeing Celeste I saw myself.

Yet Celeste had done something I would never have done: cared enough for me to try to hurt me, to get back at me, to satisfy in hate what she could not satisfy in love. Celeste was better than me: she felt. The only thing I could feel as Celeste's sweat-drenched hair leapt about her freckled bony shoulders and her eyes focused on mine as though she knew the truth but no longer cared, was that for the first time I knew something of the truth about myself: I was the invalid here, I was the wounded, the messed up, the fucked up, the heartless, the frigid, the nearly dead. And yet here she was, clutching me to her, screwing me into her as she gasped and bit and came one final time in a paroxysm that set me off, but for me the sensation was merely release, not pleasure, a kind of constricted pain, and even as she kissed my face, licking the salt off me and murmuring, I felt sickened by myself, by my unwillingness to reach out to this woman who reached out to me.

But instead I said only, 'First your brothers and now you.'

'What,' she said.

'Trying to kill me.'

'I was trying to love you.'

'Oh yeah.'

'Norman Mailer says it's the same,' she said.

She may have said more, probably did, but I was passed out under her even as she slipped off to lay beside me caressing my cheek with her freckled hands, and I didn't wake up until I dreamt someone was trying to break down the door, and woke to discover it was no dream.

CHAPTER 13

As in many New York apartments in the nineteen-sixties, the door to this one was reinforced with an iron bar braced from a hole in the floor. The rule was simple: if you lived in a place where you had to worry about making the rent every month, you needed a steel bar for the door. You lived by definition in a high-crime area. Aside from Shushan, who could afford to leave a new Cadillac with a twenty-dollar bill tucked under the windshield-wiper blade in Chinatown, everyone I knew had a barred door, a steel grill on any windows fronting a fire escape – which made escaping a fire less than likely – and a baseball bat in the entry-hall closet. I had the bat in my hand when I went to answer the door.

'It's not going to happen twice, fuckers!' I shouted. 'First one who gets in is the first one in intensive care. Come on! Come on, you two-bit Irish—'

'Federal Bureau of Investigation,' a loud, distinct and surprisingly androgynous voice came from the other side of the door. 'FBI. Open the door, please, Mr Newhouse. We need to talk to you.'

I tiptoed away from the door and to the window. There, one floor below, was a black four-door Chevrolet with some sort of gold-colored seal on the side. 'What does the FBI want with me?' I said to the door.

'We'd just like to talk with you, Mr Newhouse.'

'Well, I just don't want to talk with you. Go away.' I turned back to look at the mattress on the floor. In the excitement I had not seen Celeste leave the bed. Now, as I heard the sound of the shower, I realized I was naked. Whatever it was at the door I considered it might be better addressed with something other than a morning erection. 'Give me a minute,' I said, throwing on clothes as though I were Cinderella and the coach was leaving in seconds. I slipped my feet, sockless, into my shoes.

FBI maybe, but an unlikely pair.

The woman was about thirty, medium height, wearing the kind of outfit that would be increasingly seen as females moved into the white-collar labor force, a barely feminized take on male business attire that served the same purpose – diminishing the possibility of sartorial error by reducing all possibility of originality: white blouse, gray skirt (trousers on women were just coming to be acceptable as non-casual attire) and a double-breasted blue blazer replete with brass buttons that was not quite butch enough to conceal a solidly three-dimensional front porch. Or maybe a pair of shoulder holsters. That would make sense. An FBI agent fumbling in her purse for her gun just did not seem right, and unlike males there was no way to tuck a back-up piece in an ankle rig. No makeup, large gray eyes, and short brown hair shot prematurely with silver in a pageboy that all but concealed a deep forehead, severely cut bangs pointing down to an almost non-existent nose and a mouth that got no lipstick and hardly needed any: it was a mouth made for kissing – Jeanne Moreau's mouth in Truffaut's *Jules et Jim*, which I had just seen at the Eighth Street Cinema in the Village, broad lips, flattened as if by pressure from a lover's kiss, nothing of a smile other than availability.

These ridiculous thoughts were immediately followed by the realization that no one was about to be kissed, especially with the other fed standing right behind the first and towering over her. He must have been six-five, a bit taller than Ira-Myra's, but stick-thin, and taller and thinner for his hat, a blue felt porkpie that looked like nothing less than a continuation skyward of his angular face. His mouth was little more than a pucker. Even his tie was narrow. Only a pair of thick black glasses and a thin blond mustache broke the vertical thrust.

A woman and a scarecrow were hardly what I would have expected from America's national police force, but maybe I wasn't worth more than these.

'May we come in?' the woman said. 'Just take a minute.'

It was one of those questions that barely qualify as rhetorical. A rhetorical question speaks its own answer. This one did not require one. The two brushed by me as if I weren't there.

'Special Agent Quinones,' she said, producing a leather flap from her purse that displayed the kind of badge they used to sell in every Woolworth's in America before Woolworth's ceased to exist.

'Can I *see* that?'

'You can see this,' the scarecrow said, sticking his badge so close in front of my eyes I could barely focus. I eased his hand back gently. The truth is I knew as little of what an authentic FBI badge looked like as I did about why these two were here. 'Special Agent Mink,' he said.

'I always wanted to know,' I said. 'What makes you guys so special – are there regular agents and you're the special ones? Or is every one of you special? But that wouldn't make you particularly special, would—'

'We're all special, Mr Newhouse,' Quinones said. With her name came the recognition that she was some sort of westerner, New Mexico maybe, or Arizona. Possibly rural California. And there was just the hint of a Mexican accent in her voice, a kind of upswing at the end of each phrase. 'And you're special too.'

Celeste took this occasion to walk slowly and determinedly from the bathroom wrapped in two towels, one barely covering her from chest to pubic hair and the other making up a huge turban

141

on her head, its end trailing down her glistening backbone like the tail on a coonskin cap. When I was about nine Walt Disney had broadcast a television saga on Davy Crockett, and a whole generation of boys who had grown up in the fifties had owned polyester copies. I never had one. My friends did. But I could do a mean imitation of Fess Parker, the actor who played the so-called king of the wild frontier: 'I'm half-horse, half-alligator and a little attached with snapping turtle. I've got the fastest horse, the prettiest sister, the surest rifle and the ugliest dog in Texas. My father can lick any man in Kentucky . . . and I can lick my father!' I had to keep myself from doing it now. Celeste stooped silently to the floor at the foot of the bed, gathered up her clothes and then turned demurely back to the bathroom, her eyes unwaveringly straight ahead.

'Deaf mute,' I said. 'What can I do for you?'

'Are you Russell E. Newhouse?' Quinones asked.

'Probably.'

'And do you know a person whose name is Shushan Cats, alias Shoeshine Cats, alias Kid Yid, alias—' Quinones looked at me. 'Do you want the whole list? It's long.'

'I've met him.'

'Is that all?'

'Meaning what?'

'Meaning, is that all, that you've met him? Or is he more than someone you've met?'

'Social stuff. A drink. Meal.'

The designated bad cop now jumped in. 'Mr Newhouse, lying to a federal agent is a felony, as is conspiring to delay or hinder the apprehension of a fugitive from justice. Are you aware of this?'

'Did you two say *two minutes*?' I said. 'Because two minutes is up.'

Quinones looked peeved, as if she had been through this kind of thing before with her partner – it was hard not to like her for it. Whether real or not, she made a convincing good cop. 'Mr Newhouse, we can be out of your hair in a very short while, but we do need your cooperation.'

'Which means that if I don't cooperate you'll be in my hair for a long while, is that what you're saying?'

'Not at all,' Quinones said. 'The Bureau is interested in learning the whereabouts of Mr Cats. We'd be grateful for any assistance you can offer in this regard.'

Re-enter bad cop: 'And not happy if we feel you're attempting to—'

'Do you two always keep the same roles,' I asked as sweetly as I could. 'Or do you switch off? Personally I think the threatening female is the more effective, because it's kind of reverse casting.'

'Mr Newhouse . . .'

'Yes, Special Agent Quinones.'

'Can I call you Russell?'

'Can you call me Russell?' I let this simmer for a moment. 'Frankly, that would be a bad idea. Can you instead get to the point and then, if it's not too much trouble, leave? Maybe you haven't noticed, but I've got a guest.'

'Are you some kind of wise guy?'

'Yes, Special Agent Mink. I am. I'm also an American citizen with certain rights, the first of which is the right to ask you to leave.' I smiled. 'Special Agent Quinones can stay. I'll even give her coffee.'

Quinones flashed me a smile that was pure Jeanne Moreau, or at least Jeanne Moreau adulterated with a little Rita Moreno, who was a knock-out in the film version of *West Side Story*, which had been released the year before. 'That's a no-no, Mr Newhouse. Special agents are special because we stick together.'

'You're not missing much on the coffee,' I said, and reached for the door.

Before I could get to the knob the scarecrow's bony hand was on my arm, gripping my bicep like a plumber's wrench. 'I'm giving you fair warning, Newhouse. Screw with us and we'll screw with you. We want to know where your friend Cats has got himself to. We have reason to believe you know.'

'What reason?'

'Never mind that, kid. To date you have no criminal record. You want to keep it that way, learn to play ball.'

I peeled the man's hand from my arm. 'You won't believe this, but I really suck at sports.'

When they left – to make sure I watched the black Chevy Biscayne pull out and head down

144

Eastern Parkway – I called the Westbury. No one answered in Shushan's suite. I left my number with the desk. Beyond that, I had no idea where to look. Then I thought of someone. Information gave me an office number for Terri Cats, PhD, on East Seventy-Third. What I got was an answering service, where I convinced the operator I was a patient with an emergency. I called the new number. Silence.

'Terri,' I said as slowly and clearly as I could, 'This is Russell Newhouse. We met at your brother's. I'm calling because I just got a visit from a couple of federal agents looking for Shushan. I tried to get in touch with him to let him know but—'

A click. 'What the fuck is this?'

'I just had a visit—'

'I heard that,' Terri said. 'I am not the address you want. If you're looking for Shushan please deal with him directly. I'm his sister, not his goddamn secretary. One more thing, lover boy—'

'I really think he should—'

'You call me again at this number and I will make it my business to be very unpleasant. You think Shushan can be unpleasant?'

'I heard.'

'Don't talk, just listen. If you think Shushan can be unpleasant, he's nothing compared to me. This number is for people with real emergencies. Call it again and I can guarantee you will be even more unhappy than just knowing Shushan will make you, and if you don't know yet how bad that can be you're a fool as well as a vain young prick. Do you understand me, lover?'

'I still think—'

'You're not thinking – you're reacting. I can't help you. Where you are, no one can help you. Now leave me alone.'

The click must have been audible across the room, because Celeste started like a deer. She was fully dressed, eyes made up, and slipping into her coat, a navy pea-jacket, that year's statement of resolute androgyny. 'I really have to go,' she said. 'Whatever it is you did, I don't want to know about it. And don't call me, Russ. I'll call you.' She kissed me chastely on the cheek and left. I hadn't even had time to bar the door again when there was a knock. I looked through the peep-hole.

'Here,' she said, and handed me a key.

There it was. In the space of five minutes three females had, in one form or another, turned me down cold. The feeling of rejection was so complete I considered making it go away by lighting a huge joint and pretending to think about the meaning of it all, but I knew enough to know that this would turn into a massive giggle, a deep shrug, the munchies and then a nap. I lit a Lucky instead, then another, then a third, then walked out into the clear morning air of Eastern Parkway, the Hasidic Jews who had colonized the place since the early fifties hurrying to prayers, the Rastafarians ambling along in individual portable clouds of *ganj*, and on the way to the newsstand on the corner of Bedford Avenue managed, with absolutely no malice aforethought or after, to get arrested.

CHAPTER 14

Wherever the two characters from the FBI had disappeared to, I wasn't halfway down the block when I realized that I was being followed, by someone else.

Eastern Parkway is one of New York City's few truly beautiful boulevards. At least in conception. From its beginnings at Grand Army Plaza, where a copy of the Arc de Triomphe faces the main branch of the Brooklyn Public Library and the Brooklyn Museum (in these I had received my real education – the public schools were useless) to where it peters out after several miles into the slums of Brownsville, it is a broad tree-lined thoroughfare divided into three: four center lanes going east and west, and two parallel service roads separated from the main drag by pedestrian islands. Out of the corner of my eye I could see I was being followed by a vehicle creeping slowly down the service road as I walked east: a banged up forest-green sedan with darkened windows – an unmarked police car. To say this was eerie is a little bit like saying I had had a mildly enervating morning. Here I was, a lone pedestrian,

148

and two tons of Dodge Dart was moving just behind my left shoulder at a pace that could not have exceeded three miles an hour. I tried not to look back, figuring that if I were lucky I could duck into an apartment house, go out the back door and disappear in the alleys. This was Brooklyn, and I knew Brooklyn. But my search for an escape route was interrupted by a single baritone horn blowing somewhere behind me and then a second and then others until the noise was not so much deafening as detonating. The single lane of the service road available to traffic – on either side there were parked cars – had become a slow-motion parade with an unmarked police car leading a line of vehicles a block long and growing. But as soon as an arm came out of the cop car and fixed a magnetized gumball machine to the roof, the honking died down except for a few unaware drivers way at the end of the line. In a moment they figured it out as well. The unmarked car's siren came on and the window rolled down.

At first I didn't make the connection. Then I recognized the bald head. It was Cohen, who had appeared with his partner at the Westbury. 'Hey, kid. C'mere!'

This was not an invitation. I walked over to the car. 'Hi, detective. Nice seeing you again.' I bent to see the driver. 'You too, Detective Kennedy. What a coincidence. I live just up the street.'

'We know that, dummy,' Cohen said, not

unfriendly. 'We been tailing you since you walked out the door. Don't you notice nothing?'

'I suspected there was a parade in the neighborhood,' I said. 'How can I help you gentlemen?'

A horn sounded about six cars down. Cohen got out of the car, his bald head shining in the midmorning sun like a dented helmet, and held up a badge. The horn bleeped to an ignominious burp. 'We don't want you to take this personal, kid, but we got to do our job.'

I thought, How nice that you have one. If I had one I'd probably do it too. But the last job I'd had was emptying my semen from a condom into a specimen jar while an array of female soon-to-be strangers wondered what I was doing in the bathroom when any self-respecting male would be in just-come heaven on the way to a nap. Maybe all work was like that, less pleasant perhaps, but in the end full of adult obligation. Looked at it this way, I was merely Detective Cohen's fetid specimen.

If so, he proceeded to pour me into a jar. As a first step I had to be handcuffed, and without anyone reading me my rights. Though in the same year Ernest Miranda was arrested and convicted in the case that would three years later cause the Supreme Court to issue its Miranda decision, the only thing Detective Kennedy told me was, 'Watch your head getting in the door.'

'You gentlemen going to tell me what's going on?' I said from the back of the car. The seats were torn, the vinyl backs of the front seats scuffed, and there were brown stains on the colorless carpets that were doing a credible imitation of dried blood. If this was the vehicle, I wondered what the destination would be like. 'I thought we were friends.'

'Oh, we are,' Kennedy said from behind the wheel, fully turning around in his seat while barreling down Eastern Parkway at fifty miles an hour. 'If we weren't you'd be fucking unconscious right now.' We blew through a red light. 'Say you're some nigger,' Kennedy said conversationally. 'I never cuff a nigger without I first tune him up a little. Nothing serious. Usually body blows.'

'Unless he resists,' Cohen noted.

'That is correct. Like if he says one fucking word, like *What I do*? Or *It be raining out*.'

'Or a synonym for feces.'

'In either one or two syllables,' Kennedy said. 'But you didn't make no trouble, Russell. You're a good kid. We got a relationship.'

'These cuffs are a little tight,' I said, watching Brooklyn freely going about its business as we sailed through traffic as if there was a siren going. There wasn't. Kennedy simply drove as though there was. With nothing to hold on to but my other hand, I was being tossed around on the back seat like a steel sphere in a pinball machine. A good thing I hadn't eaten – it would have added to the decor. 'I mean, since we have a relationship.'

Cohen turned around to smile at me while I

looked past his five o'clock shadow – it would not be five o'clock for eight hours – at a tsunami of oncoming cars, trucks and scared pedestrians. 'We got a relationship, but that's different from friends. You want to be friends you got to help us find a *mutual* friend, a friend we got in common. You know who I mean.' Kennedy turned around as well, grinned, then turned back to the wheel just in time to avoid smashing into the back of a truck with a huge fish painted on its rear. Underneath was lettered: *Eat fish, live longer.*

To say that this legend was immediately engraved in my memory is to understate the case. I thought we would go through that sign and enter into an icy world of fresh fish, but instead felt my innards collapse forward as we braked. 'No,' I said. 'Who do you mean?'

Kennedy turned back again, flashing dimly vegetal teeth that seemed to have been installed to match his green eyes, a divine tic of exterior decoration. 'Don't fuck with us, kid. We're trying to help you.'

While said assistance was being executed I tried to figure out what was going on. Everybody was looking for Shushan – even I was looking for him – but why did everyone think I knew where he was? In an interrogation room in the 73rd Precinct, which looked like it had not been cleaned since the day it was built a hundred years before, I had the pleasure of discussing this with Detectives Cohen and Kennedy in considerable depth.

Kennedy was the designated bad cop – didn't police have an alternative methodology? – with Cohen the sympathetic one, probably because we were both hebes.

'Look, kid,' Cohen said. 'When my partner comes back it could get a little nasty. He had a UF-28 good to go and now because of you and that Shoeshine guy it's cancelled.' He saw the look on my face. 'UF-28. Day off. How is it you don't know that?'

'How is it I should?'

'Because your old man.'

'Because my old man what?' I said. The bastards had done their homework. 'He never brought it home. Do you?'

'I try not to,' Cohen said. 'It's hard enough being a Jew in the NYPD without bringing the NYPD into the Jews. Some is excusable. But mainly I keep it separate. If I can. A guy like Dougie, Detective Kennedy, he's third generation blue. Me, it's just a job. I'm the only one in my entire family, actually. The only one of anyone I grew up with. Mostly doctors, accountants, business.' He smiled. 'Me and your old man, good cops but abnormal hebes.'

'You knew him?'

'Heard of. We were both in the Shomrim. That's the Jewish cops' organi—'

'I know what the Shomrim is.'

'So how come you didn't follow in your father's footsteps?'

'My father's footsteps were confined to

Downtown Brooklyn,' I said. 'I wanted something more than seeing Joralemon Street all day every day.'

'A kid like you, they'd make you a dick right away.'

'No offense, but a kid like me wants to do stuff my father never did.'

'Like?'

'Travel, get into trouble, get out of it. Read books, maybe even write some. Some people are just not born to be cops.'

'Still, your old man had a good name in the department. Until he – you know.'

'I'm glad,' I said, ignoring the addendum. 'He worked hard all his life.'

'I heard your mom died.'

Shit, I thought. 'Yeah. I was little. I know her from pictures. My dad raised me.'

'So you know the drill.'

'What do you want to know?'

'It's not me wants to know and it's not Dougie. It's the Manhattan DA. They're looking for your friend.'

'An acquaintance. We're members of the same organization.'

Cohen came alert. 'What organization?'

'The Mafia,' I said. 'Sometimes called The Family. Sometimes the Cosa Nostra. You heard of it?'

Cohen was just not very bright. But he tried to be helpful. 'You know what you're saying, kid? Because you might want to think about it.'

'The Bhotke Young Men's Society,' I said. 'That's the organization, detective. Not the Mafia. It's a club for old geezers who came to this country from a place in Poland—'

'My old man's from Poland.'

'Everybody's is,' I said. 'In Brooklyn. It's just a stupid club for guys who like to talk about the old country before Hitler destroyed it. And there's burial plots in Beth David.'

'The Shomrim's plots are in Beth David.'

'Detective Cohen—'

'Stan.'

'Stan, the only connection Mr Shushan Cats and I have is through the Bhotke Young Men's. I helped with the funeral, the mourning period.'

'You can say *shiva*, kid. I'm no goy.'

'Who's no goy?' Kennedy said, walking in. He was a Kennedy in name only. Where everything about our president was elegant, understated, well-tailored, this Kennedy was so lace-curtain no amount of money would make him anything but sloppy, overblown and incredibly badly dressed, even for a cop. His rayon tie looked like it had been fished out of the East River, and his suit like what had fished it out. His shoes were unshined, but his nose made up for it. And, this close, he had had a drink, maybe in the past minutes.

As my father would have said, a disgrace to the force, but more or less standard issue. 'I was just telling Stan—'

'Stan?'

'Detective Cohen here that my only relationship with Shushan Cats is we belong to the same Jewish organization. We buried his mother.'

Kennedy crossed himself silently. 'Well, kid, if we don't find this guy you have no relationship with you're going to have another tombstone to put up.' He considered. 'Jews put up stones?'

Stan and I looked at each other.

'Yeah, we do,' he said. 'Sometimes we do that when we're not kidnapping Christian children to put their blood in matza. You know what, Doug? We been together six years day in day out, and that's what you think of Jews, that we don't properly bury our dead?'

'I didn't say that,' Kennedy said. 'It just never came up what Hebrews do.'

'You and I been to a Jewish graveyard.'

'When?'

'Moscowitz,' Cohen said. 'When that spick shot him in fifty-nine.' He turned to me. 'Big funeral. You wouldn't believe how big.'

'Huge,' Kennedy said. 'That's the kind of funeral I don't want.' He turned to me. 'That's the funeral you get when you take a bullet. Me, I plan to die on the beach in Florida on full pension.'

'Gentlemen,' I said. 'I really don't know where even to look for Shushan Cats. And to tell you the truth, I don't want to look for him. I'm a college student. My interests are women, literature and getting high, not always in that order. This whole thing with Shushan, it's an anomaly.'

'It's a what?' Kennedy asked.

'Not usual, not normal. Completely out of what anybody would expect. Like running into a street-corner Santa on Easter Sunday, or snow in July. Theoretically this kind of thing can happen, but it's unlikely. Anomalous.'

Cohen stepped in to help out. 'Like when you get a letter but it's not signed.'

'Yes,' I said. 'Exactly. Now can I please go home?'

Kennedy smiled. Under the fluorescent bulbs that lined the ceiling like railroad tracks for aliens his teeth glowed a bright chartreuse. The veins in his nose seemed to be a roadmap of a very busy city. 'Kid, we got to hold you.'

'It's not personal,' Cohen said.

'Not at all,' Kennedy said. 'Your old man and all.'

'You have to hold me. Why?'

'Because the Manhattan DA wants to talk to you.'

'About what?'

'About Shoeshine.'

'Shushan,' I said.

'You know who I mean,' Kennedy said. 'He's a popular guy right at the moment.'

I couldn't make it out. 'You know about the FBI?'

'Oh yeah,' Kennedy said.

'They try to step in,' Cohen said. 'In cases like this.'

'In cases like what?'

'We got to hold you for when Frank Hogan's office wants to see you.'

'He's the Manhattan DA.'

'I know who he is,' I said. 'I read the papers.'

The two dicks looked at each other. It was hard to believe too lumps like this had made detective. I had always thought my father's gold badge signified membership in a very exclusive club.

'We really got to hold you,' Cohen said. 'I'm sorry. It could be for a half-hour. It could be a couple of hours.'

To be precise, it was nine hours twenty-two minutes in which I sat in a five-foot square cage made of steel meshwork, and in which everything had something missing: one crippled bentwood chair minus a leg, one cement slab on which to semi-recline – it too was short by a foot – and a pile of *Playboy* magazines with the centerfolds torn out and most of the nude photos as well. I may have been one of the few college students in America who could legitimately claim to have read *Playboy* for the articles. My cage was at one end of the detective bureau, a procession of battered metal desks whose green linoleum tops were so scarred by cigarette burns there was something about them of art: Jackson Pollack might have created them on a really bad morning after.

The dicks were good to me, up to a point – outside of trips to the toilet they kept me locked up – and bought me a couple of packs of Luckies when twice mine ran out, to say nothing of meals, which they were under no obligation to provide. Lunch was all right: pizza. But dinner was spectacular: pizza with meatballs. I could hardly complain. Though they were theoretically free to come and go, neither Kennedy nor Cohen had much more freedom, in essence, than I. Whatever happened to me in the next hours and days, I did not have to return daily to this roach-infested station house in a bad neighborhood – 'One point seven miles of insanity,' in Cohen's words – where carrying a gun was as much a necessity for the citizenry as it was for the cops.

At nine-fifteen, Kennedy unlocked the cage. 'I didn't think it would take this long, but Hogan's office, they don't give a shit.'

'You on hours?' I asked, the cop's son coming out in me: overtime.

'Better believe it,' he said.

Cohen came up carrying a rolled up newspaper under his arm. 'The drill is this. We're gonna put you in the back of the car. No cuffs. When we get to within a couple blocks of the DA we're gonna put the cuffs on. This whole thing to my mind sucks. We figured an hour or two. But they been dealing with the press, the investigation, interviewing suspects. So Dougie and me we want to make sure you know we didn't mean to treat you like shit. It's just the system. So you walk out with us now, and later we'll put on the cuffs.'

'Policy,' Kennedy said. 'NYPD fucking policy. You don't need to be cuffed.'

'What press?' I asked.

The two detectives looked at each other in the dimly-lit hall.

'What investigation?' I asked. 'What suspects?'

Kennedy nodded to Cohen, who handed me the paper. It was the bulldog edition of the *Daily Mirror*, the first of several editions that would be pumped out through the night until the final edition at five AM. There on the front page was a photo from the funeral of Shushan's mother, a grainy blow-up but clear enough. It was a picture of Shushan in close conversation with a young associate – Shushan was actually clutching his arm. The associate's head was crudely circled in red, as if with a crayon. The headlines told me all I needed to know of what was.

SHOESHINE
POLISHED OFF?
CRIME BOSS VANISHES
AFTER MAFIA CONFAB
BOY-GENIUS SUCCESSOR
HELD BY COPS

But little of what would be.

CHAPTER 15

The assistant district attorney to whom I was delivered at the Manhattan DA's Office was a middle-aged woman with gray hair, gray eyes, a gray suit buttoned to the neck and sensible shoes, also gray. Even her name suggested the color – it was Grady. Her nails were bitten and her stubby fingers stained with tobacco the color of her dark gold wedding ring. Other than tiny single-pearl earrings she wore no jewelry. 'Please take a seat, Mr Newhouse.' I sat heavily on the black Naugahyde sofa at the far end of the long room from her desk. The two cops took a position by the door, as if to make sure I would not attempt an escape. They had already made a nice show of uncuffing me. Grady sat in the armchair opposite me, a yellow legal pad in her lap. If a voice could be described as gray, hers was gray. Also flat, vaguely metallic, and matter-of-fact, the voice of a teacher who had long before become disenchanted with third grade. 'You are Russell Newhouse?'

'People keep asking me that.'

Grady was uncharmed. 'Of 556 Eastern Parkway?'

'Yep.'

'Social?'

'I'm sorry?'

'Your Social Security number?'

I told her.

'Married, single, divorced?'

'Still single,' I said. 'How about you?'

'I'll ask the questions, Mr Newhouse.'

'Why am I not surprised, Mrs Grady?' In 1963 women were still addressed as Miss or Mrs Ms had not been so much as conceived, much less born.

'Call me Dolores.'

'Dolores.'

'Russell, do you know why you're here?'

'I haven't a clue.'

'Is that so?'

'Dolores, it is so.'

'Then I'll tell you,' she said. 'Do you mind if I make a record of this conversation?' She pointed down to her legal pad.

Out of the corner of my eye I could see Cohen make tiny circular motions with the index fingers of both hands. If this was good-cop, bad-cop, Cohen was up to his ears in good. For whatever reason, he was telling me what Dolores Grady was not: A hidden tape-recorder would have me on record agreeing to 'a record of this conversation.' The tape would not show Grady pointing to her legal pad. There was little I could do. Either I would not agree to the taping and set up an adversarial relationship from the get-go, or agree and know that whatever I said could become evidence in a court of law. Better to conceal what I knew. 'Sure,' I said. 'I have nothing to hide.'

'I'm sure you don't,' Grady said. 'You do know why you're here, don't you?'

'The papers have it wrong,' I said. 'I'm nobody's protégé.'

'We have Mr Shushan Cats on record as having introduced you in many venues precisely as such. Are you aware of that?'

'Dolores, do I look like anybody's idea of a gangster to you? I'm twenty years old. I'm a senior in the honors program at Brooklyn College. My biggest scrape with the law is some unpaid parking tickets which, by the way, I fully intend to pay. I don't own a gun and in the unlikely event I found one in my hand I wouldn't know what to do with it. It's not that I believe the pen is mightier than the .45 automatic, but the pen is what I'm interested in. I'm a reader, not a racketeer. If things go as planned I'll end up a college professor, or maybe a writer, or both. Okay, you could say teaching and writing are rackets, but they're legal.' I pointed to the yellow pad Grady was barely making notes on. 'Maybe one day this interview is going to end up in a book. Don't worry. I'll play it for laughs. This is a comedy of errors, Dolores. The only thing I know about criminality is that Shushan Cats is supposed to be a hood. But all I personally know about him is that as secretary of the Bhotke Young Men's Society I helped him arrange a funeral for his mother and then at his request helped him out during the *shiva*, the week of—'

'I know what it is, Russ. I was a Greenberg before I became a Grady.'

Did she mean she had de-Judaized her name, or that she had married out? I didn't bother to ask. 'When the mourning week was over I parted company from Mr Cats.'

'What's the Bhotke group?'

'A criminal enterprise in which old guys from the old country talk about how when they were young in Poland they rode horses and milked cows. It's a fraternal organization. There are hundreds like it. Now that the old country has been erased these organizations have become important to their members, because that's all that's left. They're not only legal but they're exceedingly boring, at least to me.'

'So why are you a member?'

'My late father was one, and I got drafted because they needed young blood. And very few of them write English that's grammatical. It's a job, twice a month. A volunteer job, but they throw me a couple of bucks. Anyway, considering the trouble it's caused, I may volunteer myself out of it. Dolores, if you're looking for Shushan Cats, I'm the wrong address.'

For answer she rose and came back with a thick folder from her desk.

'Is it or is it not true that your late father, Meyer B. Newhouse, was a New York City police officer?'

'Very true.'

'And that he was relieved of his badge for conduct detrimental to the NYPD?'

'He never did anything but blow the whistle on crooked cops.'

'And that a hearing was held in which he was removed from the force?'

'By the same cops he blew the whistle on.'

'And that he lost his pension along with his badge?'

'With three years to go. He had seventeen in, and they took that away. That's right.'

'And that because of this he harbored a grudge against the NYPD and against law enforcement in general?'

'What does my dead father have to do with this, Dolores?'

She looked up from her notes to peer at me over her glasses. 'Are you aware that after he was thrown off the force your father is known to have consorted with criminals?'

Oh, that. 'Dolores, my father did security for anyone who paid him. No pension, remember? He had a kid to support, and himself, and security was all he knew. You can appreciate that, can't you?'

'Did your father tell you about his criminal involvement, Russell?'

'Come on, Dolores.'

165

'Did your father ever tell you about his life after he left the force?'

'He didn't leave the force. It left him. My father barely talked to me. He was a bitter, silent man.'

'He was bitter about his treatment at the hands of the NYPD, wasn't he?'

'My father was bitter because his wife died on him. He loved her. And he was bitter that he had to raise me alone. And that every time he looked at me he saw my mom. Believe me, the NYPD was nothing compared to that.'

'Did your father carry a gun?'

'As a cop. Then when he was doing security.'

'So when you told me you are not familiar with firearms that was not exactly true, was it?'

'I know how to clean a revolver,' I said. 'I'd do that for him sometimes. And there were a number of occasions when he took me to a firing range. Maybe you'd want to know it was regularly, some-times every week. So I know how to shoot at targets. But not necessarily to hit them. Or people. And I never said I was not familiar with firearms. I said that in the unlikely event I found one in my hand I wouldn't know *what* to do with it, not how to. There, full disclosure.'

'So can we stick to the same full disclosure the first time around, Russell?'

'Absolutely. What do you want to know – where Shushan Cats is buried? I don't know. I don't know if he *is* buried, if he *is* dead, or if he just skipped out. It's a week before his trial.'

'We're aware of that, Russell.'

'Good. Then be aware as well that I'm an innocent bystander here. I've done nothing and know nothing.'

'Is this what you'd call an innocent bystander?' She handed me a stack of eight-by-ten black-and-white glossies. In each of the photos there I was, big as life. Under other circumstances I would have thought, Hey, Russ, you take a good picture. But these were not other circumstances. A half dozen photos were from the funeral: me and Shushan so tight we could have been lovers, me and Ira-Myra's, me and the Italians shaking hands, me and the Chinese shaking hands, me and Royce and the brothers shaking hands. The next batch took me by surprise: Me and Terri Cats face to face on Lexington Avenue in front of a florist and a jewelry store; further on down the street, with Terri kissing my cheek; me entering the Westbury; me, Shushan, Ira-Myra's and Justo in front of the restaurant in Chinatown. God, it looked awful. 'This means something?' I tried. 'I already told you. I helped with the *shiva*.'

For answer Grady pulled a sheaf of stapled-together sheets from her folder. If the folder didn't have my name on it, I'd be surprised. 'I have here sworn testimony from one Father William Callinan that you, Mr Shushan Cats and Mr Ira Kaminsky did threaten him with bodily harm in his church in East Harlem.'

'I never threatened anybody.'

'Were you there?'

'Yes, I was there.'

'And did you in any way protest when you witnessed Mr Cats and his criminal associate, Mr Kaminsky, threaten and intimidate a priest in his own church?'

'As a matter of fact, I did.'

'Father Callinan makes no mention of it.'

'Father Callinan and his two brothers beat the shit out of me the week before.'

Grady's eyebrows lifted. 'According to sworn testimony by Father Callinan, given today, by Mr Monroe Callinan, a New York City fireman, and by Mr Patrick Callinan, an officer of the NYPD, it was *you* who assaulted *them* and caused *them* bodily harm.'

'What is this, Russia? Yeah, I invited them to my apartment so I could wreck the place while beating the shit out of them with my face, and afterward for good measure I begged them to destroy my car. Are you for real, Dolores? Because if you are, this interview is over.' I rose.

The two detectives came alive. Each took a tentative step into the room.

'Sit down, Russell,' Grady said. 'This interview is over when I say it is.'

I sat.

'Think about this, Russell. Does it or does it not look to you like your actions, to say nothing of your background, indicate a pattern of behavior that any jury of your peers would conclude is criminal?

You have an altercation with Messrs. Callinan, and the first thing Mr Shushan Cats does when he arises from the *shiva* period is threaten vengeance on the same Messrs. Callinan?'

'Dolores, I'm a college student.'

'According to Brooklyn College, you're rarely there.'

'For crying out loud, I'm excused from classes because I'm in the honors program. I'm not supposed to go to classes. I've read all the books.' I paused, getting it. 'You're not believing any of what you're saying, are you? This is just to make me . . . uncomfortable.'

'Are you?'

'Uncomfortable? Yeah, very. You might even say scared. But I still don't know where Shushan Cats is.'

She smiled, showing small, somewhat irregular teeth, also gray. In 1963 cosmetic dentistry was in its infancy. Fluoride had only recently been introduced into New York's drinking water. Half the population had bad teeth. 'I know that,' she said. 'And probably the people who do know where Mr Cats is are never going to say. I'm afraid Mr Cats is no longer with us.'

For some reason the weight of this struck me for the first time. 'How do you know?'

She shrugged. 'After he and Mr Kaminsky delivered you to your apartment house on Eastern Parkway, Mr Kaminsky dropped Mr Cats at an Italian restaurant in East Flatbush frequented by persons associated with organized crime. The San Marco. Are you familiar with this restaurant?'

'No,' I said. 'Yeah, so?'

'Within minutes Mr Cats was seen entering an automobile with four such persons.'

'How does that—'

'The automobile was found the next morning parked with its lights flashing and its radio going on a heavily trafficked approach road to Newark Airport. Its location and the fact lights and radio were on are indications it was meant to be found. The car was of course stolen.'

'Of course.'

'Fresh bloodstains were found on the front passenger seat, along with two bullet holes in the seat itself. The bullets entered from the rear.'

I tried to imagine Shushan dead. I could barely imagine him alive. 'And you're saying it was Shushan's – Mr Cats' – blood?'

'We don't know that, at least not yet,' Grady said. 'For one-hundred-percent certainty we'd need an actual sample of Mr Cats' blood. Given his disappearance, that may be difficult. However we do know two things. One, the blood on the seat is type AB. We know from Mr Cats' military records that this matches your friend's blood type. Number two, when Mr Cats got into the car outside the restaurant in East Flatbush he was seated in the front passenger seat.'

As if to give me time to consider this fully, the phone rang on Grady's desk. 'Excuse me,' she said flatly, quite as though my not excusing her would make a difference. She nodded into the phone. 'Send him up.'

I saw the cops look at each other. Why was it everyone knew more than I did?

'You know who that is?' she asked, back in her armchair with her yellow pad on her knee. 'Downstairs?'

'Shushan Cats?'

'Russell,' Grady said. 'Shushan Cats is, as they say in the movies, sleeping with the fishes.' She looked at me with a form of drab pity, probably the best she could do. 'Or in some shallow hole in the Pine Barrens. Russell, you can forget about Shushan Cats.'

'I'd like to, Dolores, but you're not letting me, are you?'

She smiled again, but it was not pity. This smile said, *I am a fucking Assistant District Attorney, and if I wish I can crush you like a bug.* 'Mr Newhouse—'

'I thought we were Russell and Dolores.'

'Mr Newhouse, don't be insulted, but it appears you are either one of the stupidest persons on this planet or one of the cleverest. Because you are an honor student – one of your professors, a Eugene del Vecchio, went so far as to call you "a kind of genius" – and because Mr Cats, despite your denials, did indeed choose you as his successor, I am compelled to believe you are not stupid.'

'You couldn't be more mistaken,' I said.

A knock at the door interrupted what I had hoped

might be a credible claim on stupidity so profound it bordered on diagnosable mental retardation. Kennedy opened it slowly, as though unsure of what might issue forth and then, satisfied, kept opening it. Cohen stepped back. Immediately I could see why.

Our visitor filled the doorway – and more, way more. Whoever it was, he was as bizarre a creature as I had ever seen, but somehow familiar, from the long, slicked-back pale hair that ended in what appeared to be a short pony tail down to his yellow crocodile shoes. In between was a mauve three-piece suit that I understood had to be hand-made, because something that size and color did not appear on the racks at Gimbels, so beautifully cut it almost did not appear some three hundred pounds of human was tucked into it. I had read the term 'Savile Row,' and from books was familiar with the word 'bespoke,' but I had never seen such tailoring in and on the flesh. The closest I had come was the televised wardrobe of John F. Kennedy, who was regularly criticized for having his suits made abroad.

'Good evening, detectives,' the visitor said in a hoarse but plummy voice that obviously had been tuned in England but originated elsewhere. A certain Germanic glottal persevered – *evenink* – in a kind of oral palimpsest, the one accent tinting the preceding. 'I see they have you working late' – it came out *laid* – 'and I trust you will be compensated accordingly. Otherwise come to me and we shall sue for redress, no?'

With that he marched into the room, took Grady's gray talon in a paw the size of a catcher's mitt, and planted upon it a wet kiss. Grady did not look pleased. I must have looked merely puzzled. The visitor turned to me. 'So this is the famous Mr Russell Newhouse,' he said, and sat down next to me on the black Naugahyde so heavily that my sofa cushion rose up like a see-saw, levitating me with it. 'Fritz von Zeppelin,' he said, taking my hand. 'You didn't know? I have the honor to represent you.' He examined me carefully for signs of rudimentary intelligence. 'Mr Newhouse, I am your attorney.'

CHAPTER 16

Of course I knew him then. It was just that in the papers his picture was black-and-white. In the flesh his face was so florid it could have been a de Kooning canvas in dozens of shades of pink, fuchsia and red – Willem de Kooning was big then – and his eyes were a startling blue. Added to these colors his white hair gave the man an oddly patriotic look, as though made up for some pageant on the Fourth of July. Of course I knew him, but I'd hardly expected Fritz von Zeppelin to walk in the door. This was New York's premier criminal attorney – the mob's mouthpiece, as the tabloids had it. He must have seen me about to say something, because he put his spatulate fingers to his curiously thin lips – his mouth appeared in his face with no introduction, just a slit in the flesh with no transitional pink membrane – and said, 'Not a word, Mr Newhouse.' Then he turned to Grady. 'Dolores, darling, why do you have my client in your lovely clutches? Are you planning perhaps to charge him with a crime?' He smiled: the slit became vee-shaped. 'Jay-walking, perhaps?' He said it *jay-vawking*, just as Henry Kissinger, the secretary of state, might a decade later. They had the same background, except that Fritz von Zeppelin, descended from a long line of Prussian aristocrats, had left Germany of his own volition – Kissinger, descended from a long line of yids, had been forced to flee. How the disenfranchised Jew had become a Harvard professor and then secretary of state and the blueblood a mob lawyer was a mystery. Any novelist worth his salt would have had it the other way. But this was no novel. This was my life. 'Hmmm . . . ?'

I had never before known this sound to be composed of syllables. 'Mr von Zeppelin,' I said. 'I don't need a lawyer.'

He looked at me with bemused exasperation. 'Young man, do you know what they say about someone who is his own lawyer? That his client will get twelve to twenty.' He winked so hard I could feel the couch shift. 'Quietly now. And patiently, no?' He turned back to Grady. 'Unless it is the will of this distinguished office to charge Mr Newhouse, I am afraid he is late for dinner.' He turned back to me. 'Let me guess. These fine detectives last fed you – pizza, no doubt – some hours ago. No wonder you are feeling peckish.' He turned back to Grady. 'So, Dolores? Charge or no charge? I can hear the poor boy's stomach rumbling.' His lips became vee-shaped again. 'Or maybe that is my own. Good gracious, I have not eaten since dinner.'

Grady did not seem to be surprised by this display. Apparently they were old adversaries. She appeared to consider, taking off her glasses and chewing on an earpiece as though weighing the issue. 'We'll let him go, Fritz, on condition we have his word, and your word, that he stays in the five boroughs.'

The vee deepened. Von Zeppelin's tongue – it was so dark it could have been chocolate – peeped out to say hello, as though tasting the air, as though absent dinner he might suck up all the oxygen in the room and leave us all gasping. 'Do you mean, Dolores, forever?'

'For the next ten days.'

'The next ten days,' Von Zeppelin said. 'Ach, but the dear boy has plans – do you not have plans, Mr Newhouse? Do not answer – to be out of town in that period of time. Mr Newhouse, not a word, please. So, Dolores, if that is your wish I am afraid you will have to charge Mr Newhouse with a crime. Because he does not stipulate to this condition.' He turned to me. 'Or to any other.' Back to Grady. 'Dolores, how do you remain so fresh after such a long day? I must say you are ever more beautiful.'

'Fritz,' she said. 'You know I can charge him.'

'Can you? What did you have in mind?'

'Intimidation, reckless endangerment, interfering with a criminal investigation.' She paused. 'How about murder?'

'Murder?!' I must have leaped into the air, because

176

I felt von Zeppelin pulling me down. 'What the fuck are you talking about, lady?'

She shrugged. 'Complicity in murder then. How do we know Mr Newhouse here is not somehow involved in the death of Shushan Cats?' She seemed satisfied.

'How do we know, darling Dolores, that Mr Shushan Cats is dead?' von Zeppelin said calmly.

'I need a commitment your client won't travel.'

'I need a commitment there is an Easter Bunny,' von Zeppelin said. 'But no one in his right mind will give me one.' The lips went to their vee again. 'So we are both moderately disappointed, no?' With that he tugged at my elbow and stood, pulling me up with him while at the same time, because he had risen off the couch, my body was going in the other direction. For a fat man he was strong. Or maybe merely convincing. 'Okay, now, Dolores – please ask your question.'

'How did you know?' she said, curiously unperturbed. For both this was a game of chess. It was clearly not personal.

'Please, Dolores. You insult my intelligence.'

She turned to me. 'Russell. . . .'

'*Russell?*' von Zeppelin said. 'Such intimacy.'

'Mr Newhouse,' Grady said, grimacing and returning her glasses to her nose – chess might be impersonal, but it could also be unpleasant. 'Do you know who killed Shushan Cats?'

'I—'

'Be quiet, Mr Newhouse,' the lawyer said.

'Dolores, speaking for my client, I wholeheartedly assure you, in confidence and in no uncertain terms, that when Mr Newhouse wishes to communicate further on this subject you will be amongst the first persons with whom he will do so.'

CHAPTER 17

Though I had seen many limousines, and once had an interesting conversation with a limo driver – a Jamaican; I spotted him reading William Carlos Williams leaning against a long gray Cadillac; turns out he had been a teacher in Kingston – I had never before been inside one. It was easy to understand why Fritz von Zeppelin – 'You must call me Fritzi' – required this kind of ride. Aside from the pleasure of having transportation waiting at all times, his posterior amplitude required most of the back seat. New York taxis simply could not accommodate this whale. Directly in front of where he sat was a miniature Louis-the-something desk, and on the walls to either side deep gray suede pockets for files. I sat facing him precisely like a worried client in a law office, except this one was traveling uptown.

'I need to get home,' I said.

'Oh, yes,' Fritzi said. '*Marveloso*. Russ – may I call you Russ?'

'After getting me out of the lair of the evil witch Dolores, you can call me anything. Though you might remember I didn't call you. Who did?'

'Mr Ocero, Mr Cats' factotum, informed me of your predicament. As you know, I am Mr Cats' attorney. Or was.'

'It's sure then?'

'Forty to one against, dear boy. If Dolores Grady uses terms like *sleeping with the fishes*, this is a longshot against which I would not wager. Typically denizens of the office of the district attorney know more than they let on. I wouldn't doubt there exists a complete photographic record of Mr Cats entering the unfortunate vehicle.'

'But none of him exiting.'

'That would be . . . difficult,' Fritz said. 'I think though we can proceed on the assumption that two things are about to occur. The first is that you will have to come to terms with your organization—'

'My what?'

Fritz peered at me over his half-glasses. 'Come, come,' he said, as though I had declined to row for Cambridge. 'I am after all your legal counsel. You needn't be coy with me, lad. Aside from having a long history with Mr Cats, an individual whose charm was exceeded only by his integrity, there is also the matter of attorney-client privilege. You may be candid.'

'Come, come yourself. I don't have any legal counsel, nor do I need one. I appreciate Justo's helping me by bringing you in. I don't know what you cost – I probably can't even guess – but I'll figure out how to pay you. Over time. Otherwise, aside from services rendered, let's stop the clock right here.'

'Your clock, so-called, is stopped, if that is what you wish,' Fritz said with some amusement. 'Regarding services rendered, as you put it, that is taken care of.'

I didn't exactly get it, but – given that we were traveling in the wrong direction, however luxuriously – preferred just to get out. 'There's a subway on the corner. I have a train to catch.'

Fritz pulled a small phone off the wall and whispered into it. The limo pulled hard to the right and stopped. But when I moved to open the door it was locked.

'Patience, young man,' Fritzi said. 'Patience.'

I settled back in my seat, more soft gray suede. So long as we weren't moving further uptown and away from Brooklyn I could be patient, though not forever: I *was* getting hungry. 'I'm about to receive a lecture, is that it?'

'Heavens no,' Fritz said. 'It's just that it appears we may be working to cross-purposes here. Let me summarize and then I should like you to pick those elements of what I have had to say that seem to you mistaken.'

'Shoot.'

'Mr Cats is probably no longer with us. That is to say, the likelihood that he is amongst the living is not great. On that assumption we can say of the late Mr Cats that he was a prominent businessman in the City of New York whose ventures, which we need not enumerate, are at the moment leaderless. Wait, please, until I conclude. Being leaderless, these business ventures are likely to become the target of what may best be termed a hostile takeover by competing interests of a Neapolitan temperament.'

'The *gavones*.'

'Indeed.' Fritz said with some satisfaction, stretching the word into three syllables – *in-dee-eed*. Just hearing this made me agreeable – it was the mark of a natural-born litigator. I had no doubt Fritzi was great in a courtroom. A good trial lawyer has the ability to get a jury to participate, to make of the stranger an intimate and of the doubtful a distinct possibility. 'Now, your oh-so-becoming modesty notwithstanding, it appears that you are indeed Mr Cats' heir apparent, a condition whose—'

'I am nobody's heir apparent,' I said. 'First Dolores and now you. Fritzi, I am a fucking college student who owes so many term papers I simply do not have time to oversee a major criminal enterprise. Is that absurd enough? Hey, I'd love to star in this movie, but you've got the wrong actor. Wherever all you people got this cockamamie idea, please shove it back up there past the hemorrhoids, okay?'

'Mr Cats left a testament.'

'A testament?'

'A will.'

'A will?'

'*In-dee-eed*. An iron will, bullet-proof.' He smiled. 'I drew it up myself.'

I thought: Let's take this bullshit one turd at a time. 'When?'

'Friday last.'

'I was with him all day. You were nowhere near him.'

'From twelve to one-thirty, dear boy, you weren't.'

He was right. Just at noon I had gone out to get the papers – Shushan liked the *New York Post*, then the only liberal newspaper in town, and the one with the best sports section – and with them some milk chocolate from a European sweetshop on Madison at Fifty-Third, and a box of cigars from Nat Sherman's in the garment center. Because I was feeling a bit cooped up in the suite at the Westbury, I walked it both ways. It was one of those odd November days that might have passed for spring, office workers carrying their suit jackets on their arms and secretaries eating their sandwiches leaning on parked cars or tipping their faces skyward to catch the errant rays of a dimming sun. 'No accident, I suppose.'

'You suppo-ose correctly,' Fritzi said. 'Should you wish to examine the document, I'll have one messengered to the Westbury. You'll find it in order.'

'Maybe, but you won't find me at the Westbury. I'm going home to a nice hot shower in my fungal bathroom in my crummy apartment on down-market

Eastern Parkway. However up-market, the Westbury is not where I reside, counselor.'

'I understand your reluctance to return to Mr Cats' home, given the tragic circumstances – but have you considered security?'

'Security.'

'Baldly stated, the Westbury is, however discretely, the twentieth-century equivalent of a castle-keep surrounded by walls six-foot thick, themselves surrounded by a moat filled with alligators.'

'Looked like a plain old hotel to me.'

'No one gets in, son, who shouldn't.'

'Cohen and Kennedy got in.'

'Who?'

'The dicks.'

'Oh, them. Were they announced?'

'Yeah.'

'Do you think they would have been allowed up if Mr Cats deemed them inopportune visitors?' He paused. 'You needn't answer. There are always two desk clerks on duty, former NYPD. A switch at the front desk disables the elevators. Another locks the doors to the fire stairs. And the desk clerks are, however discretely, armed.'

'They looked like common, garden-variety desk clerks to me.'

'And well they should. I might add that Mr Cats' door is steel, nicely clad in mahogany, and thus impervious to all but the heaviest artillery. When you return to the suite you will no doubt be shown a number of similarly unique features.'

'I didn't see anything but a three-room hotel suite.'

'I'm sure you will be enlightened. Now, considering that a person of Mr Cats' experience and considerable abilities had taken such precautions, do you think it wise to return to your hovel in Brooklyn where you may find yourself defenseless in the event of an unscheduled visit from certain persons?'

'Certain persons.'

Fritzi seemed to grow physically, to become palpably larger in the back seat, his torso not only broadening but deepening, so that his entire being projected itself toward me like the zoomed-in image on a movie screen. 'Dear boy, do please listen carefully. In the past week your home has been invaded by three irritated brothers, on at least one occasion by their sister, by two representatives of our esteemed national police force and certainly would have been by our two friendly detectives – the delightful Kennedy and Cohen, do I have that right? – had they wished to, rather than their picking you up on the street.'

'Why do I feel like an open book?' I asked.

'Because you are a bookish sort, I should say, and that is the metaphor that would naturally come to mind, isn't it? Now tell me this. If any of these persons wished to return, could they not?'

'The sister gave me back her key.'

'*Marveloso*, Russ. And how many keys are there? And who has them? And, frankly, who needs a key? You've got windows—'

185

'With bars.'

'Yes, I'm sure you do. And a door with one of those pathetic steel braces. Do you really think either would withstand the efforts of the FBI or certain others to enter if they had it in mind to do so?'

'And why would they have it in mind?'

Fritzi let go a massive shrug that sent a mild tremor through the vehicle, like a soft wave in calm waters that makes a swimmer turn to the horizon to see what larger surprises may be in store. 'Because, my lad, your very existence is pissing a great many people off. Note how quickly the brothers Callinan contacted the district attorney's office when it became clear Shushan Cats was no longer a threat – they seem to feel aggrieved that you visited a certain church. Then there are the federal authorities. And certain persons of an Italianate persuasion. Dear boy, you have become a rather important piece in the jigsaw puzzle that is the underside of this glorious city. Did I mention the will?'

'You did, Fritzi. But a will is a one-way document, isn't it? If you died and left me this limousine, I wouldn't have to accept it, would I? In the same way, assuming there is such a will, I am not bound by it.' I looked at him. God, he was big. 'But as Shushan's lawyer *you* are bound to hand out property to those beneficiaries who are interested in receiving it. That's what an executor does, isn't it?'

'It is,' the big man said, 'But I am not.'

'You are not what?' This had become tiring. My stomach was indicating it wanted something other than pizza, and not too much later. I could get a hot dog and sauerkraut in Times Square, and a beer. The drinking age in New York was then still eighteen. I couldn't vote of course, but I could drink. Today an eighteen-year-old can vote, but can't drink.

'I am not the executor of Shushan Cats' will.'

'Who is – his sister?'

'She is a significant beneficiary.'

'Oh, no,' I said.

'Indee-eed,' Fritzi said, sighing heavily. 'The executor is one Russell Newhouse.'

'Not me.'

'Please, Russell. It hardly matters whether you honor the role or not, whether you accept the limousine as it were. The fact is, certain persons in this city would as likely accept your inheriting the mantle of Shushan Cats as they would vote Republican or eat white bread with mayonnaise. Like it or not, these people are your competitors. They may also be termed your enemies.'

'Yeah, well, I don't want the limousine. Now, if you don't mind unlocking it—'

For answer Fritzi whispered again into the tiny phone. A front door opened and slammed shut.

'This is not serious, Fritzi,' I said. 'This is a joke.'

'Indee-eed,' he said. 'But one you had best consider taking seriously. Like it or not, willy-nilly

187

you have been chosen for a role you probably do not want—'

'No fucking probably.'

'And which you almost certainly feel is not precisely your line of work.'

The street-side door opened and the chauffeur – I couldn't see his face, only the bottom two thirds of a dark-gray uniform and one gray twill sleeve – handed the attorney a copy of the *Daily Mirror*. I looked at my watch. It was just eleven. Fritzi scanned the front page. Then he handed it to me.

'You look rather good in print,' he said. 'Myself, I always come out somewhat strenuously obese.'

There I was, entering the federal building only an hour or so earlier, my hands cuffed behind me, and accompanied on either side by Kennedy and Cohen. A circular inset showed the smiling face of Fritz von Zeppelin, probably a file-photo. I hadn't seen the photographer, but probably I had missed a lot of details, having just been helped out of a police car, cuffed, and not expecting a news photographer might be tucked behind one of the massive limestone pillars that framed the entrance. From the angle that's where he would have been. I read the headline aloud:

SPRUNG BY MOB MOUTHPIECE
KID CRIME BOSS
MEETS THE LAW
DA: NEXT STOP, GANG WAR

'Fritzi,' I said, 'Would you mind dropping me at the Westbury?'

'Bright lad,' he said as we took off uptown. 'But you'll have to be brighter sooner. I know you will be. Shushan Cats would not have picked an imbecile.'

CHAPTER 18

How had I not noticed the desk clerks? Both had my father's flat, disappointed ex-copper's expression, like racehorses reduced to pulling a cart, and gray-flannel suit jackets that fit too loose on one side and too tight on the other – these were not the kind of men who had suits custom made for a shoulder holster. Both had closely cropped gray hair, one with a clipped yellow-tinged mustache that spoke of nicotine and vanity, the other half-glasses on a ribbon around a fleshy neck that spilled over the collar of his white shirt. To my surprise they greeted me like a beloved guest newly returned to take up residency. Both came out from behind the desk and pumped my hand.

'So good to see you back, Mr Newhouse,' Yellow Mustache said.

Fleshy Neck picked this up. 'Mr Newhouse, I just want you to know, on behalf of the entire staff, that anything you need, day or night, you just have to pick up the phone. We're all broke up about Mr Cats, a wonderful man and a great boss. Me personally, when I had a little trouble with alcohol,

Mr Cats himself drove me to rehab upstate, a three-hour drive, and paid for everything, and when I got out two months later he was there and drove me back and the next day I had my old job waiting and a raise if I stayed on the wagon. A prince of a human being.'

'The whole staff, everybody, it's like we lost a father.'

'He was a lot younger than you,' I said.

'So are you, sir, but irregardless he treated us like his own children,' Yellow Mustache answered. 'You can't understand how broke up we are, everybody. Always a smile, always a joke. A job like this, anywhere else you're more or less a piece of shit, excuse the language, but with Mr Cats everyone was individual.'

'I'm going to miss him too,' I said.

'You got baggage, sir?' Yellow Mustache asked.

'Mr Newhouse's things will be along later,' Fritzi said.

'Yes, sir,' Yellow Mustache said.

'We'll take good care of you, Mr Newhouse,' Fleshy Neck said. 'Don't you worry about nothing.'

If there is anything that is a cause for worry, it's the admonition not to. Riding up in the elevator with Fritzi – he took up most of the space – I had the feeling I should know more about what I shouldn't be worrying about. But I didn't ask. I figured Fritzi was doing his part of the job. And I was right, because Justo Ocero had the other part. He opened the door even before we reached it and kissed me on both cheeks. No one had done that to me before. For some reason it seemed appropriate, though this might merely have reflected my taste – and education – in films: Jean-Luc Goddard's *Breathless*, François Truffaut's *Shoot the Piano Player*, Michelangelo Antonioni's *L'Avventura* and Federico Fellini's *La Dolce Vita*. Though somehow I understood Justo's kisses were different, I wouldn't know how different – as reflected in the movies, at least – until years later, when I saw *The Godfather*. Now I was merely somewhat embarrassed and oddly comforted. Outside of sex, kisses were alien to me: I couldn't remember my mother's, and the closest my father had come to this kind of intimacy had been a firm handshake, a fake clip on the jaw and a discrete 'Attaboy.'

'Ironic,' Justo said. 'One day Shushan is mourning for his mother, now we're mourning for him.'

'We're not mourning until we know for sure,' I said.

'He's right, Ocero,' Fritzi said. 'See that. He's making decisions already.'

I looked at him. Fritzi was right, but I was only thinking of what I knew and didn't. There was no body, not yet. Maybe I'd call a rabbi and ask what to do: vaguely I recalled the case of Israeli submariners whose vessel disappeared without a trace – the rabbis had had to deal with the sticky question of whether the crewmen's wives could remarry. Here there was no wife, at least not that

I knew of, but there remained the question of status. Can we mourn when we don't know for sure? Does there come a time when death is presumed? Whatever that time, it was clearly too early. 'It's a question,' I said. 'And I don't have the answer. But we're going to look very foolish if we sit down to mourn and Shushan Cats walks in with a tray of cold cuts.'

'I'm afraid that's not going to happen, Mr Newhouse,' Fritzi said.

'Regardless, we'll wait,' I said.

'Okay,' Justo said. 'But how long?'

'I'll find out,' I said. 'Meanwhile, it looks like I'm moving in. So I'll need my stuff.'

'No prob,' Justo said. 'Ira-Myra's is already at your place getting some clothes, and I figured you'll need your school things, typewriter, books. Anything else you need, he'll call in before he leaves.'

'Ira-Myra's has a key to my apartment?'

'*Chinga*,' Justo said. 'If Ira can't get in we been paying him too much for too long. Meantime, I called Miguel and he's coming up to take measurements.'

'For what, a coffin – who's Miguel?'

'Mr Cats' tailor. Does real nice work. You ever seen Shushan Cats looking anything less than pressed? Only the best material, and class-A work. Tiny stitches. You can't even see them without a lens. Used to be with Dunhill. Also he can get any kind of fabric, stuff you don't usually see.

193

God bless his soul, Shushan liked this special kind of wool, vicuña, comes from some kind of llama? From what Shushan says, you can't even get it legally any more. Miguel has some kind of connection. Very light. You'll love the stuff. Shoes we got a guy makes them up in a week. Cordovan. It's made from a horse's beyond, if you'll believe that. Fits like a mitten and takes a great shine. Shushan, he was a dresser, God protect him.'

'I don't need shoes.'

For answer both looked down at what I was wearing, a pair of Frye boots so ancient their color was scuff.

Fritzi coughed. 'In this line of work, dress speaks for itself.'

'Yeah,' Justo said. 'Like Shushan used to say, *Think Yiddish, dress British*. A shame you're taller, otherwise you could just wear Shushan's suits. It's a fortune in suits. Only the best.'

It turns out that despite my height – at five-eleven I was four inches taller – I could indeed wear Shushan's suits. In the next half hour Miguel, a pot-bellied Dominican who arrived with a frayed yellow tape measure around his neck, a sample case of fabrics and a catalogue of suit styles, proved this to me by opening up the hems on three pair of Shushan's trousers and the sleeves on three matching jackets. Room service sent up an ironing board. The tailor went to work.

'Shirts, you're way too long for Shushan's sleeves,' Justo said. 'I'll call Brooks. White okay? Later on

Miguel can make some up that fit great, but for the moment Brooks will do, if that's okay. You got a shoe size?'

'Ten,' I said. At least I was going to get some clothes out of this. 'But it doesn't matter, because I'm just as willing to sit here in my underwear until this blows over.' Anyway, I thought, this is a great place to write four term papers back to back: One on the 'operatic structure' of *Huckleberry Finn*, one on the Polish roots of Joseph Conrad's use of the English language in *Heart of Darkness*, one on innovation in Euripedes and the only tricky one, a comparison of de Toqueville's *Democracy in America* and his later work *L'Ancien Régime et la Révolution* – I'd read neither, and the latter was in French. Almost welcoming the enforced isolation, I walked into the room I had slept in earlier. It was not the same room. There was no bed in it. It was now full of exercise equipment, the best available at the time: a treadmill, free weights and a bench, and a stationary bicycle. In the far corner were boxing gloves, a jump rope, a light bag and a big heavy one hanging like a pendulous icon from the ceiling. 'What happened to my bed?'

Justo and Fritzi had followed me in. 'You got Shushan's,' Justo said.

'No way,' I said. 'If he's dead I'm not sleeping in his bed. If he isn't I'm not sleeping in his bed. I'll take the other room.'

'That's Esther's,' Justo said.

'Esther – Terri – doesn't live here.'

195

The lawyer spoke. 'A codicil in the testament. I quote: "Esther Cats shall have her room in perpetuity."'

I considered it might be nice to have her visit. 'Isn't there some other place?'

'Shushan would *want* you to have his room,' Justo said. 'He'd also want you to have upstairs.'

'Upstairs? There's an upstairs?'

'Oh, yeah,' Justo said.

While the pot-bellied tailor reconstructed three of Shushan's suits, I followed Justo into Shushan's bedroom, the largest, a tan leather easy chair in one corner by the window but little else to indicate it was the primary residence of a human being other than a large white-porcelain ashtray by the bed that said BELMONT on it and two photos, one of which I assumed was Shushan's mother as a younger woman on a boardwalk somewhere, perhaps Atlantic City as it had been before it became Las Vegas East, and another of two children, a robust boy of nine or ten reading a picture book to a delicate girl several years younger, both seated on an old-fashioned sofa covered in clear vinyl whose surface was electric with glare from the camera flash. So this is how gangsters start out, I thought. One moment a bundle of tears and pee and the next reading picture books and the next on the front page of the *Daily Mirror*. Probably, I thought improbably, this is what someone would say about me: one day an honors student at Brooklyn College, the next on the front page of the *Daily Mirror*. At the moment I didn't want my picture on the front page of anything.

'I've seen this room, Justo.'

'Yeah,' he said. 'Have a look in the closet.'

I opened the closet door. Suits. A rack of thin ties, mostly shades of silver and gold. On the floor room on a wire rack for three pair of shoes. A pair of glowing ox-blood cordovan loafers hung neatly on one side, a second pair of impeccable blue suede oxfords on the other. In the middle, nothing. These must have been what he was wearing when he disappeared. I tried to recall it. Gray suit, white shirt, silver tie, gold links on French cuffs. I remembered: when last I'd seen him, only the night before though it seemed like weeks, Shushan had been wearing a pair of highly polished black crocodile shoes. I remember noting his belt precisely matched his footwear. I looked at the suits. If Shushan Cats was anything other than dead it made sense he would have taken a change of clothes at least. So there would be two suits missing. The suits hung on wooden hangers that fit into their own slots on the closet's metal bar. Four hangers were missing. Three suits were in the other room, being lengthened. Only one was missing. Shushan must have been wearing it when he . . . disappeared.

'Not that closet,' Justo said. He pointed across the room.

I went across and around the bed. The door wouldn't budge.

Justo went to the near side of the double bed and reached behind an end table. The closet door popped open an inch, as though a latch had been released. I pulled the door open. A staircase.

'Am I supposed to go up?'

'It's yours, boss.'

'I'm not anyone's fucking boss,' I said, but went up, contradicting in action what I had claimed in words.

Though it was close to midnight, I entered a world of light. The room at the top was enclosed in glass. Through the panes the moon shone in like a fireman's searchlight within thick smoky darkness. At the periphery I could make out stars that on a moonless night would be a shower of bright points. From the buildings on the surrounding streets more lights shown, and below on Sixty-First and Sixty-Second and on Madison and Park the lights of nighttime commerce vied with the streetlamps that from this high up seemed to march uptown and downtown, east and west, like sentinels. It was as if this building, a residential hotel in a comfortably bourgeois neighborhood, was the center of the city, and the city, whose limits I could probably see when the sun rose over Brooklyn and lit up the East River, was the center of the world. Just as my eyes became accustomed to the room, bright lights flashed on around me.

'Don't you want to see what you got?' Justo asked.

CHAPTER 19

The entire room was encased in French doors leading to a wraparound terrace that on its west side overlooked Park Avenue and beyond that Fifth and Central Park, and even further the lights of the gently winding Palisades Parkway across the Hudson in New Jersey, while to the far right could be seen the generous arch of the George Washington Bridge. In the center of the room was a square twenty feet wide, the outline of a room within a room. On the side facing me was a fireplace, split logs stacked in an alcove next to it and, surrounding that, paradise: books. And books. And books. All arrayed on thick cream-painted shelves from several inches above the parquet floor straight up to the ceiling twelve feet above. I knew it was twelve feet, because I estimated if I stood on my own shoulders the top of my head would just about reach the ceiling. In it small bright lights in regular rows were buried like jewels. I walked around the square. Each side contained . . . books. Twelve-feet tall by twenty-feet wide by four sides, with a foot between shelves. Leaving out space for the fireplace, that would be about forty shelves. I walked over to the wall and counted the number of books on what seemed to me a representative shelf. Two-hundred and forty-nine. Say two-fifty. Times forty shelves.

'Boss, let me save you the trouble,' Justo said. 'That's about ten thousand books.'

'Ten thousand books,' I repeated stupidly. 'That's what I got.' I looked at Justo. 'There's ten thousand fucking books here?'

'Shushan liked to read.'

I shuddered. 'Liked to read? A lot of people like to read. But ten thousand books is more than like to read, Justo. It's the equivalent of a public library in Queens or some state capital in the midwest or somewhere. When does he have the time to read all these?'

'Shushan, he wasn't much on sleeping,' Justo said. '*Chinga*, he'd be out at night sometimes and come back and read, get maybe four hours and do some work and then read more. You know what he used to say?'

'Surprise me,' I said, my eyes still glued to the rows of books, all in neat alphabetical order by author – Cather, Cervantes, Chaucer, Chekhov, Conrad, Dante, Darwin, Dickens, Donne, Dostoyevsky . . .

'Shushan, he used to say he didn't have the advantage of a college education, so he had to make up. He could sleep later, when he was dead, God rest his soul.'

I moved around the room to the shelves facing north. Here the titles were organized by subject.

Hundreds of books on European countries – many, many on France, some in French – and then Asia, the Middle East, Africa, South America. I took another turn and came to the west side: world history, philosophy, economics. The south side, in random order or perhaps one I could not make out, held biographies: Ghandhi, Babe Ruth, Jefferson, Henry James, the cowboy star Roy Rogers – a virtual supermarket of super names. I pulled down a biography of Sir Walter Raleigh. It opened easily. An unread book will crack. This was silent. Several pages were dog-eared. I checked one on Houdini. The same. Three dog-ears. Just as the first, it seemed to have been page-marked in doses of about a hundred pages, which probably meant that's how it was read. On the east side a curious mixture: Basic texts on real estate and the stock market, Judaica with emphasis on the Diaspora, and four shelves on crime – not murder mysteries but academic works: *The Recidivist, The Criminal Mind, American Criminal Justice, The Enemy Within.*

'Like I said, he liked to read.'

'Yeah,' I said. 'He sure did.' Then it occurred to me. 'How would we know if there are books missing?'

'You mean,' Justo asked, 'like stolen?'

'Like missing. Like . . .'

'Like maybe where he is now he took some books with him?'

'Yes.'

201

'You're real suspicious. I don't know. A public library has a catalogue. So you could match the books up with the cards in the catalogue. But Shushan, he didn't need no catalogue. He knew where all his books are. He would sometimes go in and say he needed to find a book and within seconds his hand was on it. He liked to recommend books. Sometimes when we was talking he'd go upstairs and get a book, or he'd invite me up. But it's funny. I went to college but pretty much I never read a book after, and not too many during either. I mean, I was a business major. What was I going to do, re-read *Small Enterprise Bookkeeping* for the plot? But Shushan, he always respected me for a college degree. I used to tell him, Boss, you could teach in college you got so much knowledge, but all I got is a piece of paper that says I'm a *chinga* Puerto Rican accountant. It's like he had a chip on his shoulder about the size of the Bronx. Also, you know, he put his baby sister through school. What am I saying, school? Schools. BA, MA, PhD. And he paid for her therapy. For the regular stuff, and then when she had to do it a different way to become a psychotherapist on her own. And he still takes care of her.'

'She seems pretty independent to me.'

'Oh yeah, she is. But he bought her that apartment, and a place in Key West to replace the one in Havana, and a lot more. You'll see the paper trail. He wasn't just generous with *her*. He was generous period.'

'I know, a regular Ruben Hood.' It hit me. 'What paper trail?'

'Shushan, he was very careful about documentation. Every *chinga* penny that came in and went out, there's an entry. Okay, some things we had to be a little more discrete about than others, but he liked that I kept the books tidy. More than once I had to tell him this was not exactly a great idea, because even though it's all coded a real good hand at cryptology could break it in a week at the outside. So that's dangerous, you know. But Shushan wasn't afraid. First off, the IRS – he always filed. And more or less on the up and up. He figured that was the way they would get him if they could, so it was a cost of doing business, and he gave so much away, with the foundations and the charities and all, that most years the tax burden wasn't what you'd call onerous. His word, actually. My job was to keep it less onerous. But also he was patriotic. *Semper fi* and all. Here's a guy he volunteered for the Marines in the Korean War, so he wasn't going to cheat the US government out of its share, if you know what I mean.'

'Where are the records?'

'The records?' Justo said. 'They're here.'

'Here where?'

'Here *here*,' Justo said. 'What do you think you're looking at, a *chinga* twenty-foot square bookcase with nothing in the middle?' And with that he made straight for the center of the fiction shelves, pulled back a book – appropriately it was James's

The Turn of the Screw. A wall of shelves opened inward. '*Après* you,' Justo said.

If Shushan was an onion whose layers kept revealing new layers, so was his home. The secret library hid within it a secret office, one side of which was a wall of putty-colored file cabinets and the other held a large desk with a green leather swivel chair behind it and two green-leather guest chairs facing it. To my left a door stood ajar, showing a black-marble shower, a shiny black porcelain sink and matching toilet, over which hung a small print of Georges de la Tour's *Education of the Virgin*, which I had used to look at in wonder when I came uptown to smoke a joint and visit the Frick Collection only a few blocks away. On the other side of the bathroom a small cedar-lined sauna was set into a black-marble wall unbroken but for a red terrycloth robe hung from a chromium hook like a fiery ghost. There were no windows, of course, because the office and bath were completely enclosed by the four walls of books, but above us a skylight fully the size of the room brought in enough moonglow to read by.

'In the summer you can keep it open,' Justo said. 'You can't see it so good now, but it's a glass roof with a big overhang of another glass roof, so it can stay open even when it rains. Shushan designed it himself.'

'I'm sure he did,' I said. 'In his spare time.'

'*Chinga*, he had an architect, but it was his idea. All of this, it was his idea. The architect, he was some kind of ancient French guy. And the builders he had them brought down from Quebec. Everybody who knows about this space, the library, the office, how to get up to it, they're either way out of town or dead. I know the architect died. You know what? On purpose Shushan chose an architect who was in his *chinga* eighties, so as to cut the risk. Shushan, he didn't like risk.'

'Yeah.'

'I mean, he would take chances. He never walked away when he had to step up to the plate, no matter who was pitching, but unnecessary chances never. Like with that priest.'

'What priest?'

'You know. You was there.'

'Oh,' I said. 'That priest.'

'I mean, from what I heard, this was something Ira-Myra's could have handled, or even someone else, because a thing like that could go very wrong. You're stepping on toes, if you know what I mean – the church, cops in the family, fire department – but Shushan figured it was important enough for you to see him do it personal.'

'It was an educational experience.'

'I'm sure, boss.'

'Justo. . . .'

'Yeah, boss.'

'Please don't call me that.'

'What, boss?'

'Boss. Don't call me boss. Don't do it. It's not the case and it's inappropriate. You're twice my age.'

'Shushan said.'

'Shushan?'

'Shushan, that night.'

'What night?'

'You know, when he died.'

'When people *think* he died,' I said. 'Call me cynical but I don't fucking believe it. He has a trial staring him in the face. He disappeared, that's all. It's temporary.'

'Boss, I got—'

'You got nothing. Nobody got nothing.' Had I said that? Was I already becoming someone else? 'You have zero, Justo. The DA has zero. Shushan has a trial in a week. They can't try him *in absentia.* It's against the law. Missing presumed dead is all we have, and the presumption is based on very little.'

'They found the car. His blood.'

'His blood type.'

'You're saying another guy with his blood type got knocked off in the same car he got into an hour or so earlier?'

'Maybe nobody was knocked off. So he contributed some blood.'

'That was like quarts of blood, boss.'

'Stop calling me boss.'

'Shushan said, "Anything happens to me, he's the boss." I swear on almighty Jesus.'

'Yeah, well, when it comes to Shushan Cats I think we're going to have a resurrection.'

'Nobody would like that better than me, boss.'

That was it. I'd had it. 'I'm the boss, right?'

'Yeah.'

'Follow me on this. If I'm the boss, I pay your salary – is that correct?'

'Absolutely correct.'

'And if I pay your salary I can stop paying it – is that not also correct?'

'Again correct.'

'Then, Justo, if you keep calling me boss I'm going to stop paying your fucking salary. I'm going to fire your ass.'

'For calling you boss?'

'For *anything*! For taking too long to piss. For wearing a fucking black shirt with a light tie. For being Puerto Rican.'

'I get you, b—'

'Call me Russ. Hey, it even almost rhymes with boss. Russ.'

'Okay . . . Russ.'

'And make sure no one else calls me boss, okay?'

'Okay . . . Russ.'

'Good. Now have a seat.'

Justo sat in one of the green chairs while I went around the desk and took the swivel chair. Idly I opened the top right-hand drawer of the desk. It held a box of cigars, Bolivars. Cuban. The US embargo was two years old, but I trusted Shushan not to let a little thing like a federal embargo stop him, though I'd never seen Shushan smoke anything other than cigarettes. The middle drawer held pens, paper clips, a stapler and a roll of silky thread with a red cross on it that I didn't recognize. I held it up.

'Shushan was particular about his teeth,' Justo said. 'Floss.'

'Charming.' I opened the left-hand drawer. Of course it would be there. Shushan was a lefty. It was a big Colt Combat Commander, well worn, its bluing rubbed off on the corners and on the trigger guard. It was a .45, the kind of absurdly impractical cannon, impossible to conceal, my father had had me fire many times on the range, a challenge for a kid: it kicked so hard that after firing eight rounds my wrist would be so sore for a week I couldn't throw a ball or even turn a doorknob without serious pain. The heavy steel was eerily familiar in my hand. On either side of the rubber grips was a circle with USMC in it in raised letters. 'I'm the boss, right?'

'But you don't want me to call you the—'

'That's right,' I said, liking this against my will and against all expectation. 'Don't *call* me boss. But I am the boss.'

'Shushan said so.'

'Then tell me, Justo, what precisely am I the boss of?'

CHAPTER 20

Predictably, the story of Shushan's business was the story of Shushan himself. Ever the accountant, Justo began with Shushan's return to New York after his service in the USMC or, as Justo called it, the Corps.

After his frontline duty in Korea, the Marines moved Shushan to duty instructing sharpshooters at the Marine training base at Twenty-Nine Palms, California, where he served for six months after declining a commission. In 1953 he made his way back to New York via Greyhound bus. Having been given the name of a Texan who might offer him a job, he made a stop in Dallas, where he found work providing security for a group of bar-owners, minor hoodlum-entrepreneurs, one of whom I'd met the week before in this very hotel suite, before continuing on to New York. Shushan was in a hurry to get home. He was one of those strange hybrids who could put his fist through the neck of a man twice his size but remained throughout his life, which I had to consider might very well be over, his mother's little boy. Plus his sister was still in school, and Shushan was the kind of older brother who had the need to look out for her. Without even considering the tale of how she disabled three adolescent males in an impromptu street fight, I don't believe Terri ever required protecting. Shushan's need to protect her was greater than her need for protection.

According to the tabloids, which sacrificed groves in Shushan's honor before his disappearance and whole forests after, once back in Brooklyn he fought as a welterweight for a time under the name Kid Yid – six wins, four by knock-out, one loss, two draws – and then as a middleweight under his own name – Shushan 'Shoeshine' Cats – with somewhat less success: five wins, four losses. According to the sportswriters he outmatched himself when he moved up a division – I had someone at the *Daily Mirror* morgue pull the clips. Shushan got more ink than he deserved: he was a rarity, a throwback, one of the last of the tough hebes. Jewish fighters were consistent champions through the nineteen-thirties and -forties, and Jews such big fans that at least one Italian fighter, Sammy Mandella, judaized his ring name to Mandel, and Max Baer, who fought Joe Louis, had a huge Jewish star embroidered on his trunks though he was a practicing Catholic. Shushan must have seen he'd get what he wanted faster with his head than his fists, though it's a fact he used them after he left the ring, plus baseball bats, with which weapon he was always closely associated, and – according to rumor – at least on one occasion a gun. Justo told me (a) it never happened, and (b) the other guy had it coming.

Apparently the Brooklyn bookies, most of them Jews, loved him – perhaps he'd made some money for them by intentionally dropping a bout or two – and so it was relatively easy for him to sell them his services to protect them from the Two Eyes, Brooklynese for the Eye-talian and Eye-rish hoods who preyed on them, taking as much as a quarter of their gross revenues. In any business a hit at the gross – that is, before expenses – can sink the venture: the bookies had heavy overheads, not least paying off the police, and this surcharge must have hit them hard. Shushan's pitch must have been very attractive. In return for a *fixed* weekly fee, Shushan would chase away the Two Eyes, providing protection without demanding to examine the bookmakers' books. 'Shushan,' Justo said. 'He didn't care how much the bookies made, only what he did. But you know how it is with bookies. . . .'

'No, Justo. I don't. How is it with bookies?'

'Cautious. *Chinga*, for them the odds was just as good they'd go with Shushan and then the Two Eyes would take Shushan out. The bookies wanted to see the new system work.'

'The first client is always the hardest,' I said, and as I did wondered where I'd read that. It was as though there was someone else in my head I'd never met. 'How'd he do it?'

'He waits for the Two Eyes, in this case Irish, to come to one of the bookies and collect. Then he and another guy, a cop in fact, stops the micks and collects what they collected. Of course they object. So Shushan . . .'

'So Shushan . . . ?'

'So Shushan, you know, defends himself. He and the pal beat the shit out of the micks with the old Louisville sluggers, but instead of finishing the job leaves them to go tell their boss what happened. Then he actually returns the cash to the bookie, which made an impression, I can tell you. You can figure out the rest.'

'Tell me.'

'The micks come after Shushan with a dozen hitters, but being micks they don't figure this would be expected. Somehow or other they got caught under the El on Livonia Avenue, near where the Pennsylvania Avenue IRT stop is. The thing is, no firearms. Shushan just dropped them with baseball bats and a few iron bars, you know the kind, with the twists in them. But no guns. I mean, his guys were carrying just in case, but it was a real quiet operation. Like in the Corps: never use a grenade when a bayonet will do. Maybe if they'd been killed, the micks, it would have made the papers and everyone would be excited, but this way they were just put in the hospital, absent a few teeth here and a kidney there, and when they came out they decided to leave off this particular bookie.'

'And the others?'

'Divide and conquer. All the gangs was competing

for the bookies, who were seriously exposed individuals. In that business, these guys, after all, we're talking people like me, just accountants. Shushan removed the Two Eyes from one bookie after another. He said it was like picking off bedbugs. In a year he had every bookie in Brooklyn, and Manhattan in the theater district and in East Harlem. After that he made peace with the Itals, and the micks they just moved off. Most of them their sons were in the police anyway – in one generation they went from giving bribes to taking them.'

Without the city's immigrant population, the Fulton Fish Market would not have been as big as it was. The Italians and Jews were always big seafood eaters, and all Catholics up until the Second Vatican Council, which concluded in 1966, were forbidden from eating meat on Fridays. As a result New York ate more seafood per capita than any other city in the country. Trucks brought lobsters and cod into the market from Maine and Nova Scotia and mussels and crabs from the Chesapeake Bay along with hand-size shrimp from the Gulf Coast. Lake fish came in from Canada and Minnesota. By the sixties exotics like swordfish and red snapper were being air-freighted through LaGuardia and Idylwild (soon to be renamed John F. Kennedy International), along with game fish from the Caribbean. On the Belt Parkway headed to Lower Manhattan vans carried fresh tuna from Montauk and clams and oysters

213

on ice from the Great South Bay. All of this traffic converged every night on one relatively small market on the East River. From the beginning what the papers called the mob and what young Bobby Kennedy, in the fifties counsel to the Senate Commission on Organized Crime, called 'the Maafya,' was able to control the choke points to and from the market.

To retail fish sellers in the five boroughs, this meant a hefty tax on the wholesale price of fresh fish. The truckers had to pay to reach the market, and the retail fish guys had to pay to take their fish out. And every year they paid more: the Italian families that controlled the Fulton Fish Market grew ever more greedy as demand for fresh fish declined because supermarkets now carried frozen fish. The middle and upper classes could still afford fresh, but the poor preferred fish-sticks at the supermarket for half the price. Decent restaurants demanded fresh, but luncheonettes and diners and the neighborhood chop-suey palaces were more sensitive to price than quality. It was a classic spiral. The less demand for top-quality fresh seafood the more the *goombahs* took on each truckload – they were responsible to their bosses to make sure total 'earnings' did not decline – but the more prices rose to cover these higher surcharges the less fresh fish was sold. To stay competitive with the supermarkets fresh-fish dealers would go as far as Boston and Baltimore, anything so as not to be taxed to get into the

Fulton market. With less traffic at the market, surcharges rose, which caused prices to rise, which caused demand to drop, which caused prices not to fall, as in classical economics, but to rise, as in Italian economics: the *goombahs* had to keep revenues up. One day the brother of a bookie who was enrolled with Shushan came with a proposition: for every dollar Shushan saved the wholesalers he could keep fifty cents. In the late fifties the mob was taking $5,000 a day in fees out of the Fulton Fish Market – the equivalent fifty years later of ten times that.

But the methods that had worked with the bookies would not have worked here, not least because in the Fulton Fish Market Shushan was not dealing with a dozen competing and often chaotic gangs but with one family, the Tintis, who had controlled seafood in New York for twenty years. To further complicate matters, Silvio Tinti and his son Dickie were licensees: their permit to operate in the fish market came from Vito Genovese himself, whose organization received a percentage of the Tinti take. At that time the Genovese cartel controlled the New York and New Jersey docks, a good deal of the gambling and most of the white prostitution in the metropolitan area, farming out 'properties' to under-bosses in a system so feudal it lacked only castles and moats. But in 1959 the Genovese operation lost its leader when Genovese began a fifteen-year sentence in the Federal Penitentiary at Atlanta. So Shusan went to Don

Vitone's chief executive officer, Auro Sfangiullo, a Sicilian who affected dark glasses day and night and was never seen in public attired in anything but one of two impeccably tailored double-breasted Roman suits, a black and a gray. It was known not to approach him on days when he wore the black.

Sfangiullo was so attired when Shushan went to meet him in Little Italy in the rear of a long, narrow coffee shop on Mulberry Street called Dolce Far Niente. Today the area is part of Chinatown, most of the hard-core Italians having moved to Bay Ridge in Brooklyn, to Long Island or to New Jersey. But in 1959 Mulberry Street was the heart of Little Italy. Dolce Far Niente was Sfangiullo's office. Everyone in the place was on the Genovese payroll, including the owner, the chefs, the waiters and most of the diners.

On a hot day in August Shushan entered the coffee house alone, carrying his suit jacket over his shoulders in the Italian fashion. When he got past the first tables, where Sfangiullo's bodyguards sat as motionless as the stone lions outside the New York Public Library on Fifth Avenue, he removed the jacket, hung it on a chair by an empty table to show he was unarmed and greeted his host by calling him *dottore*. Instead of kissing him on the cheeks like an Italian he took the older man's right hand in his and planted a long dry kiss on his knuckles.

'When a Jew thinks like a Sicilian it makes the

216

Sicilian think like a Jew,' Sfangiullo said, not smiling. He offered a chair. A waiter brought an espresso and a glass of cold water.

'Mediterranean people, *dottore*,' Shushan said.

'The *macedonia di frutti* here, it's good.'

'Coffee will do fine, *dottore*. I'm grateful for that.'

'For what are you not grateful?'

Shushan sipped his coffee. 'I'm given to understand the Genovese interests are troubled by conditions in the Fulton Fish Market.'

'What idiot said this?'

Shushan tapped the side of his head twice. 'Logic, *dottore*. Every year less fish arrives at the market, and less fish leaves it.'

'People are eating less fish.'

'Less fresh fish, *dottore*. Every year fresh fish becomes more expensive. Either they buy their seafood in a supermarket, which you and I know is garbage, or they eat meat, which has always been cheaper. And when they do buy fresh often now it comes from markets beyond the control of the Genovese family.'

'Even on Friday many people have stopped eating fish,' Sfangiullo said. 'It's a new time. People don't do the right way.'

'I agree.'

'So your proposal is what, to make people eat more fresh fish? To compel these ingrates, which we have loyally served with our protection for two decades, to buy fish only if it comes from the Fulton market? You are a smart boy, Shoeshine.

217

I saw you fight several times. Even when you was fighting you fight smart. A very impressive young man. So how can I assist you?'

'I've come to assist you, *dottore*.'

'Maybe you are not a Jew at all but a secret Sicilian, eh?' Sfangiullo said. 'If your tongue goes any further up my ass it will come out my mouth. Another coffee? Pastry maybe?'

'*Dottore*, I want to take over the Fulton Fish Market under the auspices of the Genovese family.'

'I want to grow hair on my penis.'

'Because I can make sure the Genovese family earns more.'

Sfangiullo tapped his left ear with his right hand.

'In the first year, *dottore*, I will raise your revenues by twenty percent.'

'How is that?'

'As you know, I provide certain services to certain people in Brooklyn and in a few spots in Manhattan.'

'As I know.'

'I am willing to turn over part of my fees from this enterprise, a going concern. The family will benefit immediately.'

'The Fulton market is not a big profit for us, and it will not be for you. The Tintis are experienced businessmen. Even under the Tintis it declines.'

'The Tintis are experienced in the business of killing the cow for meat when it can provide so much more profit in milk.'

Sfangiullo removed his glasses. His eyes were small, yellow in the whites, and unmatched – one blue, the other a soft honey brown. Maybe he wore the glasses so people would not stare. Maybe he had sensitive eyes. 'Talk in a language I can understand.'

'With your permission, *dottore*,' Shushan said, and rose and went back to pick up his jacket. Slowly he withdrew from his inside breast pocket a folded sheet of lined paper, like that torn from a school notebook. 'These are the numbers as I have understood them to be.'

Sfangiullo brought the paper close to his eyes. 'Who gave you these ridiculous figures?'

Thus began a long negotiation. Shushan had been watching the traffic to and from the Fulton Fish Market for three months. He had carefully interviewed the wholesalers. He had counted the trucks that entered and left. He had talked to the police to learn how much was being paid to keep the NYPD from disturbing the Tinti collectors who stopped the trucks. He had grown close to an associate of then Mayor Robert F. Wagner Jr. and discussed with him the decline of the market and the loss to the city. Shushan knew more in fact about the Fulton Fish Market than the Genovese family did. As feudal overlords all they cared about was earnings. They left the actual work, the details, to the Tintis. And the Tintis were not bright. 'The Tintis are running a good business into the ground, *dottore*. I am betting it can be revived.'

'And you are willing to pay twenty percent more for the privilege?'

'Absolutely.'

'Then you must be willing to pay thirty percent, if you are so certain.'

'Twenty is my limit, *dottore*. It's the first offer and the last.'

'And what is our share of the growth of this business if you are right?'

'A fixed fee, *dottore*.'

'The Genovese family does not work on a fixed anything. Except sporting events.' It was a joke.

'Think of it this way, *dottore*. Right now you have a percentage of a sum that falls every year. I am offering to pay you for the privilege of replacing the Tintis what you are getting today from the Tintis plus twenty percent.'

'To be negotiated annually.'

'Never to be negotiated again, *dottore*. And don't forget, you will never have to wake up in the middle of the night thinking, Those cheating *Napolida* Tintis are holding back. With my proposal you will have no bookkeeping, no suspicions, no anger. Every month a bag will arrive with your current take plus twenty percent.'

'No more coffee? A Coca-Cola maybe? It's a hot day.'

'You're too kind, *dottore*.'

'In one week you will have an answer.'

'Thank you, *dottore*. It has been an honor to meet you.'

'As it happens, Shoeshine, you are the first Jew I like.'

'Thank you. And one more thing, if I might.'

Sfangiullo placed his dark glasses on the bridge of his long nose and made a face like he had just stepped in shit.

'If we have an agreement, *dottore*, you must take care of the Tintis. If I so much as smell a Tinti within a mile of the Fulton Fish Market we no longer have an agreement.'

'Are you serving terms to the Genovese family, my son?'

'Not at all, *dottore*,' Shoeshine said, rising and putting on his coat. 'We are structuring a deal.' With that he took the older man's bony hand, raised it to his lips and kissed it so lightly Sfangiullo felt nothing.

At least this was Justo's take on what occurred at Dolce Far Niente. It must have been close to the truth because the next week Shushan had the license for the Fulton Fish Market. Despite all the novels and films and television shows, organized crime is not about honor or family or tradition but cash. With revenues declining the Tintis had found themselves in the same position as any corporate chief who does not produce. They had no recourse: To raise a hand against Shushan would be to challenge Auro Sfangiullo, and thus Vito Genovese. They protested, they argued, they begged. They lost.

That Justo had to explain this was proof even

to me of how little I knew about the real world. With my nose in books, I had grown up with the idea that money was something that might or might not appear as a result of work, but that the object of what one did was not money. It was pleasure, satisfaction, art. My first role model had been my father, who was a detective because he loved it, and when they took that away he did privately what he could no longer do for the NYPD. My second was Eugene del Vecchio, a poet who made his living as a professor. Neither had ever earned more than two hundred a week.

Sitting in that aerie above the suite and learning first from Justo and then from my own investigations into the files, it appeared that the world did not turn on self-image, aesthetics, eros or the odd joint. It turned on power, which could find its form as muscle or money or both. Not that I took seriously Shushan's so-called iron will, but I had to laugh that a man so much a part of the world of muscle and money could have chosen me as heir.

Two phone calls later I stopped laughing.

CHAPTER 21

Ira-Myra's had already returned when I came downstairs with Justo. Miguel the tailor was gone, three altered suits neatly arrayed on one of the two green-leather couches. Next to them was a pile of folded clothes from my apartment and on the floor a stack of books, my Olivetti portable typewriter in its sky-blue zippered case and, packed in a carton that had once held bottles of Foxx's U-bet Chocolate Syrup, all the loose sheets of paper, notebooks and scribbled-on flotsam that Ira-Myra's had been able to gather up.

'I didn't take nothing from your kitchen, boss,' Ira said.

I looked at Justo. 'More boss?'

'It's a hierarchy,' Justo said. 'You got to learn to accept it.' He turned to Ira. 'The new boss don't want to be called boss.'

Ira looked at me with the puzzled, head-cocked expression of a large confused dog.

'Forget it,' I said. 'You can call me anything you want. You too, Justo. I'm not the boss, I'm not going to be the boss, but the truth is it's just not worth the effort to fight with you two over something that's going to go away when your real boss shows up.'

'From your mouth to God's ear, boss,' Ira said.

It was midnight, but I wasn't tired. I was hungry. I'd been hungry for several hours, but in the excitement of new circumstances and in the fear that had created those circumstances I had forgotten to eat. I seemed to have become accustomed to the circumstances. But my stomach wasn't. It was audible. 'I'm going down for some deli – you two want to join me?'

Ira-Myra's shook his head.

'Justo?'

'He's not saying no to deli, boss,' Justo said. 'He's saying no to your leaving the building.'

I looked back at him. 'You're calling me boss at the same time you're telling me I'm a prisoner here, is that it?'

Poor Ira. This kind of complexity was too much for him. He retired to his seat by the door, although it was not entirely clear if he were guarding against someone coming in or someone going out.

'Boss,' Justo said. 'Maybe we should talk.'

I sat down on the green-leather couch between the two sets of clothing. Idly my left hand rested on the sleeve of one of the suits. It was some sort of light-weight wool, soft as the skin on the nape of Celeste's neck – so this was what vicuña felt like. I looked to the right: the clothes Ira had retrieved from Eastern Parkway looked like a pile of rags some medieval peasants had worn, and worn out. I realized I was hungry for more than food: soft hand-tailored wool, a hotel suite, Shushan's red Eldorado. I could get used to this. I gave Justo a smile of encouragement, and tapped my left ear with my right hand.

'For the next day or two, boss, you can't go nowhere.'

'Because Ira is going to stop me?'

'Because you are. Outside this hotel is like the Chosin Reservoir.'

I stared. 'There's armed North Koreans and Red Chinese?'

'Worse. The papers have it you're replacing Shushan. Maybe you are, maybe not. Maybe, please Jesus, Shushan will walk in here tomorrow and say April Fool! and we'll all have us a good laugh. But, *chinga,* perception rules, right? That's what Shushan liked to say. You could have nothing in your pocket but if you're dressed right and smell good you're not a beggar.' He watched my hand fingering the vicuña. 'One, you got certain Italians. Start with the Tintis. They been waiting for Shushan to fall since he displaced them. We know this. But we figured they'll wait for a conviction. The trial is next week. It could take a month, even two. Even Shushan figured he was going away. The only question is how long. We know it, they know it. It's tragic but what can you do, right? Part of the business. Like if you have a company on the New York Stock Exchange it can be worth millions

225

Monday and zip on Friday. So that's the Tintis. Definitely not divinity students.'

'There's more?'

'Good you're seated. Then you have Auro Sfangiullo. He expects people he works with to keep it zipped, and so far, with the odd exception, like that big *chinga* Joe Valachi who snitched to Congress, maybe a few more we haven't read about in the papers, they dummy up the way they should. They do their time, come out, are respected, end of story. But Auro doesn't have that feeling for non-Italians. That's why it's a closed club. The Itals don't like to do business with Irish, Puerto Ricans, Negroes, Jews. Why? Not because they're degenerate dago pricks who are prejudiced against the entire non-dago human race – which by the way they are – but because when push comes to canary, if you're not a wop you might sing. To wops, non-wops can't be trusted.'

'Which is one reason Shushan is probably alive. He faked his death to avoid trial.'

'Very good, boss. I agree. That would be the reasonable assumption. But Shushan isn't, wasn't, afraid of doing time. He wasn't afraid of it in Korea. He wasn't afraid of a firing squad, so he wouldn't be afraid of a couple of years in the can.'

'I guess you're going to tell me about Korea now.'

There was a knock at the door. Ira leapt to his feet like a drowsy sentry startled by gunshots. He checked the peephole, then let in a waiter pushing

226

a cart. If this is what it's like to be the boss, I could get used to it. I was stuffing myself with a roast-beef sandwich layered with cole-slaw when Justo picked up the story.

'Chosin, I don't have to tell you, it was so bad. We were engaged with the Red Army, not the North Koreans. They were tough but the Red Chinese was the real thing. Outgunned, outmanned, outfucked. Fox Company, 2nd Battalion, 5th Marine Regiment, 1st Marine Division. Anybody who knows about Chosin knows us. The Decoy Company. We were supposed to create the impression the entire Marine force was digging in. What a laugh. The ground was froze like rock. You know how we dug in? We pushed C-3 explosive into empty C-ration cans for a shaped charge and blew holes in the ground. It was fifteen below, though it could get to thirty-five below at night. You made coffee it froze at the top before you could drink it. C-rations was so solid you had to gnaw at them like a rat. The entire Marine deployment was shifting south-southeast to regroup. We were left behind. Started with sixty men. Two days later fifteen came out.' Justo shook his head. 'Our CO was a captain. I can't say his name. I mean I can but I won't. His family got word he was one of the casualties. He was. Shushan shot him.'

'By accident?' Even as I said it I knew.

'Annapolis graduate, can you imagine? He *got* orders to stay, create noise, action. He *gave* orders to surrender. Maybe he was right. Maybe it wasn't

227

worth forty-five Marines. But an order is an order, right?'

I didn't know how to answer.

'The captain says, "Surrender." Shushan, he's gunnery sergeant, says, "No surrender, sir." The captain raises his sidearm and tells Shushan he'll shoot the first man who doesn't follow orders. A lieutenant rushes up, steps between them and then says to Shushan, "After we finish this mission, sergeant, report to the ranking officer for arrest." Shushan says, "Oorah!" Lieutenant must have seen the future. He doesn't say *report to me*. Lost him that night. Two weeks later there's a court martial. The court doesn't know what to do. On the one hand somebody picked off the captain with a rifle. Nobody saw it, but the slug is USMC issue. That's a firing squad. On the other, if we'd surrendered it would have been all over for the retreating Marine units. We were the only thing between them and the Chinese.'

'What happened?'

'The captain is declared killed in action. Shushan makes master gunnery sergeant, that's the highest non-commissioned rank, gets the Navy Cross. Only thing higher is the Medal of Honor. What does that tell you about the USMC, boss?'

'That you must be proud to be an ex-Marine, Justo.'

'Boss, there's no such thing as ex-Marine. There's retired Marine. There's veteran Marine. But never ex-Marine. Once a Marine, boss, always a Marine.'

'I'll remember that.'

'I got out about eight months after Shushan. Found him in New York. He helped me finish college.'

'How long ago is that?'

'Nine years. Boss, Shushan says you're in command, that's good enough for me. My job is to make sure you're healthy. For a couple of days, just keep your head down, okay? You got the Tintis. You got that creepy Sfangiullo.'

'Sfangiullo doesn't even know me.'

'He might be figuring you know where Shushan is, and he'll want you to tell him.'

'According to the DA, Shushan got it in a mob car.'

'Say he didn't. We don't know for sure. If he didn't Sfangiullo wants to know where Shushan is so he doesn't cut himself a deal before the trial.'

'Unless Sfangiullo killed Shushan, or had it done.'

'Okay, say he did. Then he must figure you know things he doesn't want to get out. He probably figures if you're the designated boss then you know what there is to know. Either way, this is someone you don't want to talk to just at the moment. Then there's the cops.'

'Fritzi already handled the DA.'

'Yeah, well, I wasn't thinking of those cops. We been paying off the other cops for years. There's people out there who don't want Shushan to talk.'

'Shushan is supposed to be dead.'

'Perception rules, boss. They're in the same position as Sfangiullo. One way or the other they have an interest. Then there's the FBI.'

'I met them.'

'They're not happy the NYPD has jurisdiction. The Injustice Department. You ever hear of a little twerp name of Robert Kennedy? He's got a bug up his ass about organized crime. Maybe because his father was one of the biggest hoodlums in Boston.'

'The attorney general of the United States is trying to arrest Shushan Cats?'

'He's trying to arrest everybody. But I'm sure he's going after the non-Italians because he figures, like Sfangiullo does, they'll be the first to talk. A piece of shit like Bobby Kennedy, who was born with a silver enema up his ass, he must figure—'

The phone. 'It's for you.'

Who would call me here?

'What's up, pretty boy?'

'Terri?'

'I'm coming over,' she said. 'In an hour.'

'It's one in the morning.'

'It's not a nine-to-five job, junior. Get used to it.'

'Shushan's sister,' I said after the click.

'I figured that out, boss.'

'She's coming over.'

'It happens.'

'She didn't sound like she's in mourning, Justo.'

'So?'

'So maybe she knows what we should know.'

'Boss,' Justo said. 'I don't like to say this. I don't want to say this. I never thought I'd have to say it. Shushan, he's passed on. He's in Jewish heaven. You know what, he's been living on borrowed time since Korea, since that captain.' He paused. 'You want me to answer that?'

'Answer what?'

'The phone.'

I hadn't even heard it. 'Go ahead.'

Justo picked up the receiver and handed it to me.

'Hello?'

'Mr Newhouse?'

'Yes?'

'Eddy in the lobby, sir. I have a Mr Arnold Savory. Should I send him up?'

I covered the receiver. 'Arnold Savory. In the lobby. Is this someone we know?'

'Bookie,' Justo said. 'I was expecting this. Either him or someone else. Yeah, he's one of ours.'

'Eddy,' I said into the phone. 'Please send Mr Savory up.' I put down the receiver. 'Who is Arnold Savory?'

'A snazzier dresser than you.'

I took the hint and went into the bedroom to change into one of my three new suits, a meltingly soft number with high, notched lapels in some sort of gray hopsack. Along with a black knit shirt with an alligator on it and a pair of black shoes Ira had brought. I was just admiring myself in the mirror when Justo tapped on the door.

'It's . . . Arr-nold!'

Wow, it certainly was. I don't think I'd ever seen a man so obviously . . . Arr-nold! From the top of his champagne wig to the bottom of his creme and black shoes, Arnold Savory certainly was a snazzier dresser than I was, or most anyone I knew. In those days most gays – even the word was not in use – were closeted. It would be six years before gays rebelled against police intimidation in a riot at the Stonewall Inn on Christopher Street. It was still against the law to serve homosexuals in a premise licensed by the State Liquor Authority. Most of the bars that did have a gay clientele were in fact run by the Genovese interests, who paid off the police to look the other way, and in fact the Tintis had moved into 'licensing' gay and lesbian bars on the rebound from losing the Fulton Fish Market; they also had the wholesale flower market in Chelsea – thereby earning themselves the handle of the Pansy Gang, which they did not like. But unless you went out of your way to visit Julian's or the Creamery in the village or Hugo's uptown – a grateful Arnold Savory would give me the full tour later that year – the average New York male's chance of running into the overtly gay was as great as meeting Miss Rheingold – the monthly winner of a beauty contest sponsored by Rheingold, 'the dry beer,' whose face was all over placards on the trains: my favorite was a Brooklyn girl-next-door who reminded me of Marie-Antonetta Provenzano, whose tight sweaters and pointy bras had convinced me Italian was a language worthy of diligent study and that the female breast was cone shaped (Marie-Antonetta never removed her bra during our trysts – she said it compounded the mortal sin). I knew even less about what we used to call fags. Eugene del Vecchio was what even he called a 'homo,' but he was a poet, and had been a boxer, and presented as straight as any Kennedy brother, but beyond a few suspicious students on campus and a flamer I'd gone to high school with, my exposure to the Arnold Savorys of this world was nil.

'Mr Newhouse, I am so, so, so pleased to meet you,' Savory said, actually lisping a bit – I think he did it on purpose. 'And I am so, so, so sorry it has to be under these unfortunate circumstances.'

'We're all going to miss Shushan,' I said. It struck me maybe Shushan was unmarried for a reason I hadn't considered. Plus, Terri was bent. 'We're praying he'll turn up.'

Savory looked at Justo. 'He doesn't know?'

'Tell him,' Justo said.

'Of course we're all chagrined to hear about Mr Cats.' Savory spoke without opening his mouth beyond a crack, as though there was something in there that might leap out, or maybe enter. Later I realized it was simply vanity: the poor guy had awful teeth, yellow from nicotine, chipped and crooked. His champagne-colored mustache, which must have been dyed because the shade did not exist outside of bouffant-haired gum-chewers from Long Island, grew down over his upper lip like a veil. The total effect was that he had no mouth, only some sort of sounding device which delivered lisps and the occasional sigh. He wore a wide violet silk tie and an oatmeal-colored checked suit with brass buttons. On his cuffs were cat's-eye links of gold, or gold plate, that matched his huge tie clip, and on his fingers a set of rings that appeared to have been purchased wholesale right out of the window of one of the Eighth Avenue pawnshops. All of this paled, however, before an enormous pair of rose-colored glasses framed in heavy black plastic. These kept slipping down his nose. 'But I must admit I'm here on another errand altogether.'

Where had I heard that voice? Breathless as Judy Garland and as brassily New Yawk as Barbra Streisand, who was in the middle of a seemingly endless engagement, her debut on Broadway, of *I Can Get It For You Wholesale*.

Justo jumped in. 'Arnie has a nice little book-making operation in the theater district. He's an institution among actors.'

'And directors, and choreographers, and stage-hands, and just about anyone connected with Thespis and Terpsichore.'

'Thespis?' I said, never having heard the word used in conversation – Terpsichore the same. 'Actors bet?'

'Oh, Mr Newhouse. It's been a tradition of the

stage even before John Wilkes Booth gambled his life away at Ford's Theater.' With that he sat heavily down on the couch and, in eerie mimicry of myself only moments before, idly fingered the fabric of one of the two remaining suits.

Involuntarily I stepped back, as though his fingers might reach the third suit, on me. 'How can I help you, Mr Savory?'

'Arr-nold!'

'Arnold.'

'Well,' he said, settling into the couch and further into the role. 'As you know, Mr Cats' organization has been good enough to look after my interests over the years.'

I looked to Justo, who nodded.

'And I've always been more than satisfied. In fact, Mr Cats always said, "Arnold, you're my favorite fag bookie," so sweet he was, and he always said, further, that if at any time I wished to make other arrangements he would wish me well. In other words, our agreement was one of shall we say mutual benefit. Well . . .' His sigh filled the room with the scent of lavender, as though he had been chewing breath mints non-stop all night.

It was 1:30 in the morning. This hoodlum business was wearing. When did they sleep? 'I understand.'

'Well, Mr Newhouse . . .'

'Russ is fine.'

'Mr Russ, imagine my surprise when early this

evening two rather brutish persons – were I less civilized I would employ the term *goons* – entered my business premises and announced that they had succeeded Mr Cats, may his memory be blessed, and that—'

'We don't know he's dead.' This was getting tiresome.

'Be that as it may, Mr Russ, I'm sure you can sympathize with my shock when they said they wished to see my *books*.' Theatrical blank stare. 'My *books*? Mr Cats never asked to see my *books*. Mr Cats never so much as hinted at wishing to see my *books*.' Deeper blank. 'You do understand? These horrid people wish to charge me according to what *they* determine is my income, which I don't mind saying is not quite enough to keep me in ermines and pearls, if you get my drift. Mr Russ, please tell me you haven't turned over my account to . . .' Savory appeared unable even to speak the name. 'To such persons.'

Justo said it for him. 'The Tintis.'

'Eggs-zactly,' Savory said. 'Creatures is what they are.'

I looked to Justo. 'This something that happens a lot?'

'Never. The Tintis? The theater district is ours, half of Harlem to the east side of Fifth Avenue, and all of Brooklyn. He paused. 'For bookmaking. Other things, we don't mix in. That's the way the city is broke up.'

'So, Mr Russ,' Savory said, looking for all the

world like he might at any moment break into tears. 'What is a person to do?'

Why ask me, I wanted to say, but didn't. Instead I sucked on my tongue in imitation of thought and asked Savory if he wanted a drink. I was about to get it for him when Justo signaled with his hand palm down and went into the kitchenette. I might have sat there pretending to consider the matter forever had not the doorbell rung. Ira opened it to Terri Cats.

CHAPTER 22

If nothing else, this managed to get rid of Arnold Savory, who chugged down his vodka with a twist as though it were gasoline and he'd been running on fumes.

If Savory was all theater, Terri was all business. And, even at two in the morning, dressed for it. In fact, it appeared we had the same tailor. Both of us were wearing black knit shirts under gray suits, hers double breasted, the jacket so short my eye dropped immediately to her hips, which bloomed out from below the jacket like an upside-down question mark. There was no question mark on her face. Terri walked over to me where I stood and kissed me twice, once on each cheek, then went into the kitchen and came back with a bottle of single malt, not a common drink back then, and a brandy snifter. As she poured the scotch she began to speak, and did not pause.

'You know why I'm here, pretty boy? I'm here because we appear to be partners, and I'm looking out for my interest. Nice suit – Shushan is going to be pissed you're wearing it, but there's some doubt he's going to be back, isn't there? Don't answer.

I'm sure you've been going through this with everyone and his parakeet, so I'll make it easy for you. Whether Shushan shows up again or not, you've got a job to do and I expect you to do it with no whining, no complaints, no fucking Oh-I'm-just-a-sweet-kid-bullshit. This is all about performance, and you have to perform, not least because you are going to be someone's target whether you cop out or step up to the plate. Uh-uh, *not* a word. All I get all day is punks of all genders, all professions, all types telling me how hard it is to roll out of bed in the morning and do something without feeling sorry for themselves. You know what Shushan used to say? Life is combat. You didn't have the advantage of the Marines and Korea and everyone shouting *Semper Fi!* day and night, but you've got the next best thing, which is that if you walk away from this you're going to be Lord Jim, remember him? He walked away. You can't walk away. Aside from all the people who are going to see you as a target you're going to have me and a lot of other people seeing you as a meal ticket. In case you don't know it that includes Justo here, that lunkhead by the door and his zaftig wife, and a cast of characters you probably won't ever know exists. Listen: Every month Shushan writes checks to a couple of dozen charities, hospitals for sick kids, cancer victims, schools, plus individual people who need help in one form or another, to say nothing of researchers doing work on everything from schizophrenia to heart

239

disease. Kid, what you've inherited is a business, but it's a business that throws off enough money so that a lot of people benefit. If the wrong kind of people take over, if you allow other people to muscle you out, then you're spitting in the face of all the good my brother did, and all these people that depend on you are going to be abandoned. So when you feel sorry for yourself and want to split just think for a moment about what you don't know. People are always making decisions based on what they think they know, but they rarely consider what they don't know. Am I making myself clear, sweet pea?'

Sweet pea was apparently being given an opportunity to protest, but he couldn't. Sweet pea was smitten. 'You're saying Shushan was a kind of Robin Hood, for real, and I have to keep that going?'

'Shushan was as much Robin Hood as I suck dick,' she said. 'My brother was a tough s.o.b. who discovered he made too much money to spend and so he took care of me and his organization and enough good works so he could feel that what he did was covered by an overlay of charity and beneficence. It made him feel better than your normal garden variety snake-in-the-grass hood who doesn't see anything in the world except victims and cops. My brother saw there was something else. That doesn't mean he didn't like to bang heads or strut around like king of the hill, which he would do anyway, but he discovered he could feel really good about his crummy occupation by putting the money to use for something outside pussy and booze and cars and real estate. Net-net, sunshine, you've inherited the whole package.'

'I'm not cut out for this, Terri.'

'Probably not, but you're not going to feel good about yourself if you walk away from it either, and you might also consider that no one is really going to allow you to do so. It comes to this: *Lord Jim* or *Lord of the Flies*. Shushan says you like *The Great Gatsby* and *Huckleberry Finn*? Am I right?'

'I didn't realize you two discussed my taste in literature.'

'I'm not fucking talking about literature, moron. I'm talking about your life. *Huckleberry Finn*, the whole book is about doing something for someone else, getting a poor Negro slave out of the way of the slavers, and Gatsby, I don't have to explain that to you. It's the story of a man who had everything but love, and how love became more important to him than a million shirts. You know why people love Jack Kennedy? Because they feel in their hearts the presidency wasn't his goal but what he could do with it, that we finally have a president who cares about something outside himself and his close circle. Despite my brother's nearsighted fucking Neanderthal political opinions the truth is we do have a son-of-a-bitch president, which we will always have because that's the only way to become president, but he's a son of a bitch with a mission, which is to validate himself as a human being, probably because his father was a well-known piece of shit. You want to validate yourself as a human being?'

'I never considered it one way or another, Terri.'

She took a long tug at her drink, the kind that would have sent me into a paroxysm of coughing. 'Trust me, sweet-face, every day human beings have to make decisions that some people like to call existential, because everything hinges on their making the right choice. But some days are more important than others. Today is one of those days. Nobody can stop you from running out on yourself, but if you stick you're going to feel a lot better even if it all doesn't come out the way you'd like.'

I lit a Lucky and hoped that in doing so I would have enough time to consider.

She read my mind, the bitch. 'The thing is, my young friend, this is not a decision you can put off.' With that she stood, finished her drink on her feet, and came and sat by me.

The smell of her was overwhelming, at once vaginal and floral, with strong notes of Scotch, smoke and a heady sweet muskiness of breath that made me want to do anything to please her. 'What do you want me to do?'

'Take care of business,' she said. Her hand dropped to my knee like a soft promise. Then she squeezed it until it hurt. Like her brother she was small but intense, able to deliver power to a specific point as though all of her were concentrated on the one act. 'And don't forget that Shushan handed me cash every month so I could live way beyond my income. You fail and you let me down. You don't want to let Terri down, do you?'

'No,' I said, hoping at once that she would not see and at the same time that she would see the rising bulge in my pants. 'That's not what I want.'

CHAPTER 23

Upstairs were a number of things I had missed on first look. For starts, the reproduction of the Georges de la Tour in the bathroom was not a reproduction, or at least not a print. It was an oil, obviously old, its surface cracked, the paint chipped in the lower left-hand corner. I would have removed it from the wall to examine the back of the canvas but it was secured there, unbudgeable, a sign that it had some value at least. If this was a copy, it was an old one. De la Tour had more or less been lost to art history after his heyday in the seventeenth century – he was rediscovered only in 1915 – but as if to make up for this in his lifetime he had apparently made a number of copies of this amazing work – de la Tour's son did as well. The painting glowed. It was alive with reflected light: the virgin – ostensibly Mary but it could have been any child – receiving instruction from an older woman by candle glow, the fire itself an intrinsic component of the young girl's face. Not only was this the only painting in the top floor – a Jimmy Ernst black-on-black painting hung in the living room below,

244

though I wouldn't have known what it was but for the fact that I often saw him at Brooklyn College, where he taught – but the de la Tour was all but hidden in a private bathroom in a doubly secluded area of the suite. When I went to piss there it was, facing me as if to tell me something, but all it could tell me was: Am I a fake? I had seen the original, or perhaps just another centuries-old copy, hanging in the Frick Collection down the street – the museum was just around the corner from the Park Avenue urologist's office where so many little copies of me had been distributed to the barren suburban women who made up his hopeful clientele. Seeing it here offered all the pleasure of a private sin. If anything it was better hung and better lit in Shushan's toilet than at the Frick, four tiny but intense bulbs focused perfectly on it from the ceiling. If I were any taller I might have blocked the light as I stood before the toilet bowl, and if I stood up really straight I could cover the top of it in shadow. Clearly the painting was there for Shushan's pleasure and no one else's.

Likewise the file cabinets, which were so scrupulously organized and detailed it was difficult to believe Shushan's business affairs were illegal. From the point of view of the IRS, apparently they weren't: going back ten years, federal and New York State tax forms all listed Shushan's business as 'security consultancy.' Strictly speaking, this was not debatable. That Shushan provided security for illegal activities – protection would be the word the newspapers preferred – was not in itself illegal. True, bookies were involved in the illegal betting industry, but taking a fee from them to keep gangsters from knocking them over was totally legitimate. It came to me that this is at least one reason Shushan did not even wish to look at his client's books. Auditing their financial records in order to calculate his cut of their revenues would have involved Shushan in their business and thus complicity in an illegal activity. By taking a flat fee Shushan removed himself from intimacy with or even knowledge of what his clients did. Of course, when it came to the Fulton Fish Market, aside from the regular selling of cheap frozen pollock as expensive fresh swordfish, the market was as much on the up-and-up as any commercial institution. But even here charging his clients a flat fee kept him at arm's length from the business itself. No one could argue that he was shaking down his clients for a percentage and thus aggressively intruding in their businesses. He was simply paid a flat fee for services rendered, and all his contracts – carbon copies of the contracts were appended to each year's tax filings, as innocent as could be – could be ended by either party (on sixty days' notice) at any time. Naturally the market's wholesalers would be foolish to break off their deal with Shushan, because they'd immediately fall prey to the Tintis, to whose greedy clutches they hardly wished to return. The only variable in these simple agreements was that Shushan's fees were tied to the Consumer Price Index ('as published in the edition of the *Wall Street Journal* closest to the day scheduled for price adjustment'), a common business practice: the fish wholesalers and bookies were also charging their clients more as the cost of living rose. No less interesting was what happened to all this money.

Since it had never been earned illegally it did not have to be laundered, and so was invested in what were then considered blue-chip equities, tax-free municipal bonds and, in the main, real estate, this last such a Hebraic compulsion that 'Jewish landlord' was not only an American cliché but redundant. From the Jewish point of view, less than two decades after Europe's Jews lost their property as a precursor to losing their lives, ownership of something immoveable was almost a tactile pleasure. Perhaps Jews went into medicine, law and accounting because no matter where they were driven they could set up anew, but real estate allowed these same professionals to not even think about being driven anywhere. They were not only proud citizens of the United States, but owned a piece of same. Maybe similar desires motivated Shushan.

For all I knew he chose real estate because Justo Ocero favored it for certain tax advantages, or because Shushan loved tall buildings in Manhattan and resorts in Arizona and warehouses in the Bronx and beachfront hotels in Havana. Maybe he was some sort of architect-manqué, a frustrated master-builder who had grown up too poor to get a formal education and now was too rich to need one. As well this would explain the library and the French and Spanish learned out of a half-dozen books and a set of Berlitz teach-yourself long-playing records that I'd found in his library.

Whatever his motivation, Shushan as reader was drawn to authority. Most every section had its guidebooks. In economics were titles like *Twelve Great Economic Thinkers* and *Wampum, Gold and Greenbacks*, each a general introduction to the field that – like the university survey courses that are prerequisites for advanced study – opened the door to Adam Smith, David Ricardo, Thorstein Veblen and the dense and groundbreaking work of Fernand Braudel. In history was the same pattern, and in political science, philosophy and art as well. Literature seemed to follow no such broad outline, perhaps because the classics of fiction are themselves always on display in bookstores. No matter what today's bestseller – in 1963 the literary sensation was Philip Roth's *Goodbye, Columbus* – names like Dostoyevsky, Stendhal, Shakespeare, Twain, Conrad, Hemingway, Lawrence are virtually imprinted on our unconscious and hardly need to appear on a list of great writers. And they were all here, even such academic standbys as *The Canterbury Tales* and *Beowulf.* In poetry the selection was weak, or maybe just idiosyncratic: several collections, the best of which was John Ciardi's *How Does A Poem*

Mean, a shelf of anthologies, plus collections of Yeats, Frost, and a passel of the kind of reader-friendly poets that most English majors had been excited by in high school: ee cummings, Walt Whitman, Hart Crane. On the other hand there was everything in print by WH Auden and Allen Ginsberg, and a few bilingual editions of Rubén Dario and Pablo Neruda. These were heavily marked in pencil, as though Shushan had decided to teach himself Spanish through its greatest practitioners. The library was fascinating, but I was continually drawn back to the file cabinets.

Not least because my father's name kept appearing.

CHAPTER 24

In the meticulous folders were employment and payroll records, starting as early as 1954, one year after Shushan had completed his Marine service. A record for Newhouse began showing up in 1957, two years before my father had been cashiered from the NYPD, first as Meyer, then as Mike, which was what he was generally called. At first the sums were small, signifying I guessed part-time work, or maybe small bribes, but regular. Once a month, there it was. Then, after my father was compelled to leave the force, the payments grew. They pretty much matched what dad had been making as a detective. These were entered as salary, with deductions for income tax and social security, and went on until a month after he died, at which time a lump sum appeared: $15,000, marked *funeral expenses*.

My father's funeral had not cost him anything, but not because Shushan Cats had paid the bill. As a dues-paying member of the Bhotke Society, dad's burial, his plot and its perpetual care were taken care of. The fifteen thou I recognized right away. The sum had appeared in my father's account at the East New York Savings Bank. I hadn't thought much about it, except to think it might be some sort of error that I should not question, lest the funds disappear as abruptly as they had come to be. All I knew was that it was there. I was a grade-skipping high-school senior, sixteen years old. I had no other family. I would have to be living on my own. The money supported me for three years. In fact, as I read the entry there was still a couple of hundred bucks left.

If Shushan Cats had been to my father's funeral I had not noticed. Certainly he had not visited while I sat for the week of mourning. Was it to spare me embarrassment that a notorious gangster knew my father, employed him? I didn't know. And I didn't care. All I knew is that Shushan Cats was turning out to be some sort of iceberg in my life. I saw the glinting tip of him now, but apparently he had been a large submarinal presence all along. I considered asking Justo, but concealing what I knew would probably serve me better than revealing that I knew it. As Shushan said, 'Don't ever let the Itals know you speak dago, unless there's a good reason.' If caution made sense there, it made sense here.

My problem now was I really had to speak to the Itals. In whatever language. Maybe Fritzi the mob-mouthpiece could protect me from the district attorney, but that was not the threat that I had to keep in focus. The threat was from the people who were already moving in on Shushan's

251

clients. They wouldn't stop with a theatrical bookie in a champagne wig, big black-framed rose-colored glasses, an oatmeal suit and a lisp. They would be coming after me. If I didn't get to the Itals, I would be a prisoner in a hotel suite with ten thousand books until the money ran out. In the midst of all this I realized I had four term papers due.

CHAPTER 25

Gene del Vecchio took about an hour to arrive. He looked like he had just come from the Brooklyn College campus, all tweeds, a white shirt checked in blue and red tattersall and the kind of foulard bow tie that screamed college professor. It was a cold day in November, and he wore a coat so long it practically swept the floor. His red scarf was almost as generous. When Ira let him in he hugged me to him and said, 'How's the incipient gangster?'

'More incipient than gangster,' I said. 'Thanks for coming.'

'From what I understand coming here is the only way to see you.' He tossed a copy of the *Daily Mirror* on the coffee table. With relief I noted that the editors had been forced to look further afield than the life of Russell Newhouse for a front page.

DOGS SET ON
MARCHERS
HUNDREDS ARRESTED
IN ALABAMA PROTEST

'Yeah,' I said. 'I saw it on TV. '

'I'm going down tomorrow.'

'Where?'

'Birmingham,' he said. 'Fucking redneck cocksuckers.'

I nearly asked if these were the only cocksuckers he did not approve of, but it would have been unfair.

'You think Kennedy is going to do something about it?'

'This is a guy who didn't vote for the Civil Rights Act when he was in the Senate,' he said. 'I'd invite you to join us – three busloads from Brooklyn College, more from Hunter and CCNY and Queens – but I hear you're tied up.' He opened the paper to page three.

It appeared the *Mirror*'s editors had not totally abandoned me. There I was, in a photo they'd used before, but this time had flipped so I faced right. Opposite was another profile, facing left.

MOB BRAWL LOOMS
OVER CATS LEGACY

The man facing me was identified as Richard 'Big Dickie' Tinti. He appeared to be about forty, his hair thinning a bit in a deep widow's peak, a cigar stuck in his teeth. As though this was some prize-fight in the Eastern Parkway Arena between two relative unknowns, I had a nickname too: Russell 'Schoolboy' Newhouse. According to the *Mirror*,

I was a 'kid genius' in the 'special honors program' at Brooklyn College. It seems I could have gone to Harvard or West Point or MIT except that I preferred to stay close to my 'hoodlum associates.' According to the *Mirror*, 'Officials at Brooklyn College confided that Newhouse may be thrown out of the city school on "character issues."' According to the *Mirror*, Tinti and I had been enemies for years.

'I never met the man,' I said.

'Don't lose sleep over it,' Del said. 'And nobody is going to be throwing you out of school. That's more bullshit. But we are going to have four incompletes if you don't get me some term papers.'

By this time Ira had come in from the kitchen with a bottle of Terri's single malt and two large glasses. He poured a couple of doubles. I watched Del knock his back in one long gulp.

'You got anything to eat?' he said. 'Russ, I have been working non-stop on the Birmingham thing. I starve.'

Without a word from me Ira went back to the kitchen. In a moment he came out with a plate of cold cuts, mustard, mayonnaise, stacked slices of rye bread, half-sour dill pickles. I must have become sensitized to smell from being cooped up in the same place for so long – how long was it? Only three days, but it seemed like forever. I inhaled it all, including the poppy seeds in the bread. Del dug in.

'I'm not going to be able to give you those papers,' I said.

'We'll work something out,' Del said, his mouth stuffed. 'I've got some *mfxshehsd*.'

'Some what?'

He made an effort to get the food down. 'You guys get the best deli,' he said.

'Us guys.'

'You know.'

'No.'

He motioned quickly back and forth with his right hand, his index finger extended. 'Connected.'

'Professor del Vecchio—'

'Russ, please. Del.'

'Del, I'm not connected. I'm not anything but fucking locked up in this fucking hotel suite with fucking hot and cold running corned beef and anything else I want to order in, and you think I'm some kind of bona fide gangster? I mean, you know who and what I am. Is this a joke or what?'

I watched him put down what was left of his sandwich and pour himself another double, maybe a triple. A week before, this man was my hero. Now he was beginning to look like just another putz, a self-indulgent alcoholic who believed what he read in the papers. Worse, I was beginning to look at myself differently as well. My eyes were the same, but the mind that peered out through them seemed to have become more critical, shrewder, cooler if not simply cold. 'I didn't get what you said earlier. "We'll work something out." You've got some what?'

'I've got some old papers. We'll just put your name on them *et voilà!*'

'*Et voilà quoi?*'

'You're in a tough situation with the college poobahs, Russell. You're an A student. An A+ student. I'm not worried about you knowing the work. But enough juice from the press, given an opportunity they'll toss you out.'

'I thought you said the work was in doing the papers the best I could.'

'Consider it a favor,' he said. The scotch in his tumbler was gone. 'Maybe one day I'll need a favor back.'

At that moment any thought I'd had of showing him the secret library on the floor above evaporated like the aroma that was all that was left of his scotch. I hadn't touched mine. I realized I wouldn't, at least not until he was gone. Maybe not at all. I needed a clear head. No booze. Probably no grass. And, I realized with both a sinking feeling and a sense of relief, no sex. I could not afford distraction, not even that much.

'Thanks for coming, professor,' I said. 'I appreciate the favor and I'll remember it.' This was the man I was hoping to call on for help, for advice, for a lifeline to a vessel of sanity that was before my eyes drifting away, out of range, useless. 'You see Sheriff Bull Connor in Birmingham, give him my best.'

My guest rose somewhat unsteadily to his feet. He must have been drinking before he arrived. He must have been drinking when he used to invite me to lunch, when he lectured me on the responsibility of intellect, the value of the written line. 'Don't worry about those papers,' he said. He hugged me to him again like a beloved nephew. '*Ciao*,' he said.

The next morning I would have to make a plan. And I didn't want anyone around to bother me. Whatever I did I would have to do it on my own.

CHAPTER 26

Ira was cleaning the windshield of the Caddy in the basement when I came down. 'This car is going for a ride,' I said.

'Justo says no,' the big man said.

'Justo says no,' I said. 'That's great. You're very loyal.'

'I try to be, boss.'

'You're loyal to Justo?'

Ira appeared confused. It suited him. If you looked at his face in profile it had all the determination of a question mark, his forehead bulging over a small nose and then an abrupt chin. Only his resolute thin mustache spoiled it. Otherwise he was doubt personified. 'I'm loyal to, you know, to . . .'

'To Shushan.'

'Yeah, to Shushan. He's the boss.'

'But he may not be alive.'

'I got to have faith, boss.'

'But you call me boss.'

'I call you boss in case, you know, in case. . . .'

'In case Shushan is dead.'

'Yeah,' Ira said. He had put down his chamois rag. 'In case.'

'So if Shushan were alive you wouldn't listen to Justo, right?'

'Sure,' he said. 'Right.'

'You'd listen to the boss. What the boss told you, you'd do.'

'Sure.'

'No questions?'

'No, no questions. I mean, he's the boss.'

'And if Shushan isn't around. Say even he's not dead. Maybe he's in Las Vegas.'

'The boss never went to Vegas – he liked Havana.' Ira thought this over. 'Once or twice to Vegas, on business. We went together. But not to gamble. The boss didn't gamble.'

'Didn't.'

'You know, didn't, doesn't.'

'So maybe he's alive and is going to come back tomorrow. You don't know that one way or the other, do you, Ira?'

'I don't know it.'

'But if he's God forbid no longer with us, if Shushan is gone, then you have a new boss, right?'

Confusion is too positive a description of the feuding impulses that seemed to be caroming inside Ira's enormous head. I'd seen his hat on the chair by the door. Eight and a half. My hat size was seven and a quarter, same as Shushan's, although his head looked smaller, his hair close-cropped. You couldn't say that about me. In 1963 anyone under twenty-five carried a lot of hair. I waited while the caroming slowed. 'Who's your new boss, Ira?'

'You are, I guess.'

'And if Shushan comes back tomorrow and slaps you on the back, who's your boss?'

'Shushan?'

'Exactly. So what will Shushan say if I'm the boss and you're listening to Justo, not me?'

'He'll be pissed.'

'What's he like when he's pissed?'

Ira frowned, his mustache following the reforming line of his thin lips like a mansard roof.

'Right,' I said. 'So if he comes back tomorrow morning and he finds out you're listening to Justo and not to me, what would he say?'

Confusion.

'Would he say you did right or you did wrong?'

'Wrong,' Ira said after a moment's contemplation. 'He'd say I done wrong.'

'And if he doesn't come back, God forbid, then would you be right in following Justo's orders or mine?'

A longer pause, then the glimmer of a smile. 'Yours.'

'So either way, who should you listen to?'

No pause. No doubt. Not so much as a reflective glimmer. 'You,' he said. 'I got to follow what you say.'

'Justo might be mad.'

'Fuck Justo,' he said. 'You're the boss, boss.'

'Good,' I said. 'Now tell me, when's the last time you saw Myra?'

'Myra?'

This was like painting woodwork. 'Your wife.'

'Sure.'

'When's the last time you saw her?'

He appeared to be counting in his head. 'Four days.'

'She's a beautiful woman, isn't she?'

A flicker of suspicion. 'Gorgeous.'

'Should you leave a gorgeous woman alone four days, a gorgeous woman all alone in Brooklyn?'

'I got to be here,' he said.

'To watch me?'

'So nothing happens.'

'But you went down to clean the car, didn't you? That's what I'm looking at. You weren't watching me.'

'Wednesday.'

'It is Wednesday, Ira. So?'

'So I always give it a good going over on Wednesday.'

'Admirable,' I said. 'So you figured I was safe enough upstairs for you to leave me for an hour to clean the car?'

'I check the oil, brake fluid. It's not just cleaning. Usually I gas it up. Shushan likes it ready.'

'So you felt you could leave me alone for a few minutes, for an hour, to take care of business, right?'

'Right, sure.'

'Now I want you to listen to me, Ira. I'm telling you this for your own benefit. You love your wife?'

'Yeah, of course.'

'You don't want anyone to bother her, in Brooklyn?'

A thought, such as it was, danced slowly behind his small gray eyes, arched brown brows crinkling with the effort. 'You think I should. . . .'

'I think you should go home and sleep in your own bed with your gorgeous wife. I'm going to be fine.'

'You mean, now?'

'You can gas up the car in the morning. Just be back at eleven.'

'In the morning?'

No, dope, at night. 'Yes, eleven in the morning. See Myra, make sure she's okay.'

'I talked to her on the phone.'

'A beautiful woman like that, Ira, you can't know everything from the phone.'

'You want I should fill her with regular or high-test?'

Myra? 'What does Shushan prefer?'

'High test,' Ira says. 'That way the engine don't knock.'

'Fill her with high test,' I said. 'Go on, get out of here. I'll be fine. Nobody can get past the lobby.' But I was wrong.

CHAPTER 27

When I let myself in I found the lights turned down and music playing on the stereo: Frank Sinatra, Shushan's favorite, his voice like calming oil poured over a sea of what seemed to be a hundred storm-tossed violins, suggesting 'You'd Be So Nice To Come Home To,' complete with allusions to a fire in the hearth.

Disconcertingly, there was a fire. The fireplace was lit. I had never even considered it might be real. There was a fireplace upstairs as well, of course, with logs stacked similarly in a creche beside it. But I never considered either might actually function. I was a city boy. I had read about fires in fireplaces, but never seen one. Or smelled one. The deeply masculine aroma carried with it a lighter one, sensual, musky. It was perfume, lavender, citrus, adult. The college girls I went with were on ideological grounds dead set against perfume and makeup and anything else their mothers wore, even bras. This aroma was more than heady. It was exciting with promise.

The strings came up just as a woman's voice

cut through them. 'I hope you don't mind, Mr Newhouse. I let myself in.'

Whoever this was, she was seated demurely on the facing sofa – I could barely make her out as my eyes slowly became accustomed to the dimness.

'You let yourself in?'

'I have a key.'

I looked around. 'Are you alone?'

She laughed, her voice husky, a smoker's voice that went with the look. In 1963 platinum hair was the big thing for movie stars: Marilyn Monroe, Mamie van Doren, Jayne Mansfield, Kim Novak, Angie Dickinson, dozens more. But this was platinum with a vengeance. Piled up on her head in what was called a beehive – Jackie Kennedy used the same technique and called it *bouffant*, which apparently made it seem less cheap – the woman on the couch looked like some peculiar amalgam of all the Hollywood beauties of the day: big (very blond) hair, big (very red) lips, big (very soft) curves. The girls I knew were . . . girls. This was a woman.

'You have the advantage on me,' I said.

'How's that?' She ground out her cigarette in an ashtray that had been empty a half hour before and now held a half dozen lipstick-marked butts, and immediately stuck another into her mouth, drawing it directly out of her purse, a small beaded affair that made the woman who owned it seem even larger, monumental, iconic: Anita Ekberg in a Roman fountain courtesy of

Federico Fellini. It was as though she had stepped off the screen at the Eighth Street Cinema in the Village and found her way to this hotel, this suite, this couch. But it was no miracle. After all, she did have a key.

'You know my name, I don't know yours.'

'Darcie,' she said. 'Unless you have another you'd prefer.'

'Darcie is good.'

'Got a light?'

I sat at the other corner of the same couch, found a matchbook in my pocket, leaned across the empty cushion and lit her Parliament. In those days it was a woman's smoke. Something about the recessed filter not smearing lipstick. 'How is it, Darcie, you have a key?'

'Shushan.'

'That's a noun,' I said. 'Put a verb to it.'

She seemed unsure, then smiled to cover it. Clearly this was not someone who made her living teaching high school English.

I tried to direct her. 'I mean, Shushan what?'

'Cats.'

It was impossible not to appreciate this. Every female I knew was aggressively literate. 'Shushan Cats gave you a key?'

'Sure.'

'And why did he do that?'

'Wednesdays.'

'Wednesdays?'

'Every Wednesday Shushan liked me to be here

when he got in.' She pointed demurely to the bedroom opposite.

'And today is . . . Wednesday.'

'Til midnight,' she said.

'But you knew Shushan isn't—'

'Yeah,' she said. 'I heard.'

'But you came anyway.'

'I didn't expect Shu to be here.'

'Shu.'

'Shushan,' she explained helpfully. 'I mean, it's in the papers.'

'That and Jack Kennedy is flying to Dallas, and the sheriff in Birmingham, Alabama, one Bull Connor, is arresting hundreds of Negroes.' I watched her face, but under the smooth makeup could make out nothing. 'So why come here if Shushan is, maybe, dead?'

'He's as dead as you and me,' she said. 'I don't believe any of it. That man is tough. His muscles have muscles.'

'So you came expecting to find him. Here. Alive.'

'Nah,' she said. 'I expected to find you. I figured you're the replacement, so I ought to show.'

'The replacement.'

'If you want,' she said. 'Unless you don't find me attractive.'

What a question. After a week with no sex a guy like me, not yet twenty-one and producing so much testosterone my balls ached, would have found a bagel attractive, so long as it shifted position from time to time. And Darcie was no bagel.

'Oh yeah, I do,' I said. 'But I'm afraid I can't afford you.'

'Not to worry, Russy. That's how Shu calls you. Can I call you Russy?'

'Sure.'

'I'm on a long-term contract. Justo takes care of it.'

'How long a term?' I asked, moving closer.

'As long as you like,' she said.

For a moment there was silence. Frank was done with the first song and now had moved on to another, more up-tempo, trumpets countering the violins: 'At Long Last Love,' whose title answered the lyrics' insistent question – is this an illusion or, as Sinatra himself liked to say, for real?

Whatever it had been with Celeste and with the dozens of Celestes who had passed through my life since the day I had lost my cherry at fourteen in the basement of a tenement on Powell Street in Brownsville with the indelible Marie-Antonetta Provenzano, it was as if I had been playing sandlot ball and was now in the majors. The difference was startling, not only because Darcie was almost twice my age and her body had been lushly modified not only by emollients and powders and perfumes but gravity, and not only because Darcie knew things that my other girlfriends had expected me to teach *them*. It was that I was no longer on trial: I was not being asked to prove myself; I was asked only to show up. Darcie was doing for me what I had demanded of myself that I do for girls my own age. There was something so giving in her, so unselfish, so open and sure I could not help feeling that I was the inspiration for her soft lushness, her sweet pockets of scent, the way her hands knew where to go and her mouth what to do. Kissing her I felt I was sinking deeply into a fertile mossy earth, the taste of tobacco combining somehow with a flowery, almost funereal muskiness.

Of course she came precisely when I did, her body heaving and convulsing, her mouth making soft whimpering music as she continued to pump me, high thighs grinding slowly to a rhythm that was at once earnest and totally artificial – the best fake orgasm I had ever met, a masterful arrangement of movement, sound, scent: the best orgasm money could buy. And it worked. Because even though I had come hard and long, emptying myself like the turned out pockets of a pair of jeans, I began – almost against my will – to fuck her again.

And again.

And again.

At twenty years of age, twice was not unusual. Three times was not unknown. Four had occurred once, with Celeste in fact. And here I was going for six. Wait a minute, I thought: *she's* going for six. Darcie was the one doing it. I stopped.

'Something wrong, honey?' she asked.

'Do you get paid by the come?'

A pause. 'That's nasty,' she said.

'Because?'

'Because I get paid by the night. And if I don't like the guy I don't even show up. I'm not a whore. I'm a compensated companion.'

The distinction escaped me, but even so it was wrong to fuck a woman for an hour and a half and then insult her. This was not so much a matter of ethics – in eros there is none – as much as simple manners. Besides, I had not meant an insult, merely a clarification. I found her hand, brought it to my lips, and kissed it. 'I'm sorry,' I said quietly. 'This kind of thing is new for me.'

'What kind of thing?'

'Compensated companionship.'

'You're apologizing?'

'Yes.'

'And you think words are enough?'

'Words caused it.'

'Maybe you can think of something better.' With that she shifted her head and shoulders away from me and her bottom toward me so that my lips grazed the soft convexity of her breast. In the dimness of the room I could see nothing more than shapes. These grew more distinct as she raised her torso so as to press herself against my cheek, her nipple seeking my mouth. 'Go ahead,' she said. 'You want to. It's okay.'

It occurred to me abruptly, in the way it occurs to someone who suddenly discovers he prefers a warm climate or hates beer, that I had never been a breast man. Aesthetically, perhaps. A woman's breast could be lovely, a statement of such poignancy it could make me stop in my tracks, but as an igniter of passion it was useless. In an era when female beauty was measurable by the cup, I seemed to have been a reluctant drinker.

'Take it,' she said. 'You know you want it.'

But I didn't know anything of the sort. Until her nipple found my lips. Something old, older than memory but still fresh, a sensation of unspeakable, ineffable longing, took hold – my lips tracing the circle of her aereola, flat and smooth within and bordered in Braille around, my tongue surrendering in circles like a lost boy in search of something long misplaced – until I found it.

'Bite me,' she said quietly, firmly, decisively. 'Bite me, Russy. Go ahead. You won't hurt me.'

I sucked.

'Your teeth, Russy. I need to feel your teeth.'

I bit tentatively, then felt her hand on my head, forcing it down onto her breast, the soft flesh pillowing my face, cutting off air until I shifted a half inch.

'Like you mean it, Russy. You want me to be happy, don't you? You want me to feel it, don't you? You want – that's it. That's the way. But harder. Hard-er.'

As hard as I bit she wanted me to bite down harder, to twist her nipple in my teeth, torturing it while she moaned as she had not all night and took me half-hard in her hand and stuffed me into her, expertly, easily, efficiently. In a matter of what seemed moments she came, really came, no sham, no pretense, no script, and took me with her, after which I stayed on her breast like an infant, totally without consciousness, without identity, without shame. I had been waiting for this all my life, and had not known.

CHAPTER 28

In the morning I woke in precisely the position I was in when I fell asleep. Maybe I had never sought soft women, maybe I was afraid of what I had never had. Maybe Sigmund Freud was laughing his head off. I didn't care. I was in heaven and, to my great confusion, if not dismay, in love. Not only hadn't this happened before – even my feelings for Marie-Antonetta were no match – but the object of this passion was twice my age, bleached her hair (which was now plastered down around her face like a collapsed frame around a portrait of dissolution), rented by the night – and snored. As quietly as I could I lifted myself off her marvelously cushioned tit – the real thing: implants were not in common use – and tiptoed around the bed, Shushan's bed. According to the few words we had exchanged before we fell off together into a sleep so deep it was liquid, she had been 'seeing' Shushan for eight years – or, not to put too fine a point on it, since I was twelve. As I passed her pillow her hand snaked out and grabbed mine.

'You don't get it, do you?'

273

I sat down beside her, leaned down and pressed a long soft kiss on her brow, getting for reward a mouthful of long, straw-stiff platinum hair. 'I don't get what?'

'I'm supposed to take care of *you*, sweetie.'

'Russ or Russy.'

'Uh, uh. You're too sweet for that. I'm going to call you sweetie and if you don't like it you can jerk yourself off. You are so, so sweet.' She lay her hand in my crotch in such a way that at once she claimed ownership and let me know any such decision was mine. This kind of affection, at once possessive and liberating, was something I was not used to. It made me uneasy. Was this too part of being a compensated companion? Even more perilous, was it real? 'I need coffee,' I said. 'You want some?'

Abruptly, and with a verticular grace I could not have expected in a woman so horizontally lithe, she was instantly on her feet beside me by the bed. Even shoeless she was tall – how could I have missed that? – and so generously proportioned she seemed to overflow herself, like the head on a beer when it rises above the rim of a Pilsner glass. Her upper arms hung soft, maternal, her breasts stretched long until they rounded out perfectly like water-filled balloons, upon the face of each a distinct nearly phallic nose, itself encircled by a deep pucker like a science-fair volcano, her middle a cake fresh from the oven and partially collapsed upon itself. Supporting this architectural amplitude

274

were two impossibly slim legs, thin almost, shapely as saplings footed in nine-inch beds – we probably could wear each other's shoes – though her feet were much narrower, long toes ending in nails lacquered so brightly in red they seemed like ten tiny stop signs. On her inner thighs were tattoos in blue, though they appeared black on her pale skin: on the right *Semper*, on the left *Fidelis*, and printed upside down, either as a reminder to Darcie or a caution to anyone who might find himself so intimately positioned. 'I make *you* coffee, stud,' she said in such a way that I felt close to melting. Compensated or not, no woman had made me coffee or anything else warm since before memory. It was rare that I let a girl stay over on Eastern Parkway, rarer still for me to stay over at a girl's – most still lived with their parents. When it did occur I would take them out to breakfast at the luncheonette on the corner of Eastern Parkway and Nostrand, where the countermen, envious of what for me was a form of post-orgasmic torture, would offer me the compliment of a wink.

So it was that I remained in bed while through the wall, the one with the Jimmy Ernst black-on-black, I could hear Darcie preparing breakfast. I may have dozed off, or perhaps I was merely in that state that is somewhere between sleep and acuity, a kind of super sensitivity to what normally remains beneath the surface but upon which our lives depend. In this state it became clear to me that unless I took action I would remain a cosseted prisoner of this suite in the Hotel Westbury on Sixty-Third and Park, well-fed, well-read, well-fucked, well-loved even, but ultimately a lost soul, protected and insulated but robbed of that freedom we like to think defines humanity as both species and ideal. Resolving thus to take back my life, no one was more surprised than I when Darcie nudged me awake with a cup of fresh coffee, a glass of orange juice and an English muffin dripping with melted butter and oozing raspberry jam, to discover that in my half-sleep I had hatched a perfectly realized, highly detailed, and extremely aggressive plan.

'After you eat, sweetie,' she said, 'I'm going to eat you.'

'You are?'

'Like you've never been done before.'

I had never seen a woman leer. It was thrilling, like being smacked with something delicious, the shock mitigated by the smell, the taste, the promise. 'How's that?'

'Down to the bone.'

Darcie was as good as her word. Certainly she had a lot more experience than the girls I normally saw, who seemed to view oral sex as something between an obligation and a rite of passage, but she also loved what she did, sliding me so deep inside her I was at first afraid she might choke, and only when she kept me from withdrawing did I realize this was another league, the National Sexual League, another country, the United Sex of America, or even another sexual planet, Venus for sure. Who knew what it was – who cared? Then, when I could feel myself on the approach to orgasm, which obviously she could feel as well, she stopped, pulled away, and in one deft motion presented the full amplitude of her bottom. She was not a natural platinum blonde, but a natural coquette, wiggling her ass with such assurance, such clarity of purpose, such ease, that I moved quickly to get off my back to mount her, until I felt her hand on me, guiding me northward, and slowly insert it, corkscrewing her bottom as though it were separated from her body, a perpetual motion machine that worked while the rest of her remained perfectly still.

I'd never felt such welcome, the warmth of her drawing me slowly into her, centimeter by lubricious centimeter, and though later I compared this to the constricted butt-fucking I had engaged in with a couple of girls who pretended they liked it but needed a quarter pound of Crisco to get me half in, while it happened all I could think of was a future opening before me whose end I could not imagine but which would be wholly justified by the means. After I came Darcie allowed me, shrunken, totally spent, to ease out of her, and then, like a beneficent nurse or a mothering bitch, wrapped her lips around me and cleaned me so thoroughly I would not need to bathe. Then she cupped my chin in her hand, brought my face close to hers, and laughed.

'I'd kiss you, sweetie, but I taste like shit.'

How could I not kiss her? In a matter of moments she was dressed, and gone. Thus sorted out, every kink unbent, I went to work.

CHAPTER 29

It was Thursday, which meant I had only one full day to prepare, because I had asked Justo to let Auro Sfangiullo know I would be visiting Dolce Far Niente on Friday at two.

The accountant arrived just in time to meet Darcie walking out. I can't say who was most embarrassed: Darcie, who smiled brazenly at Justo before giving him a kiss on the forehead – she was a head taller; Justo, who looked like I had stolen something from a dead man – his eyes widened, then narrowed, then widened again; or myself, who suddenly realized, the big head seeing what the little head had ignored, that I was fucked both ways. If Shushan were by some miracle among the living, a fact against which every passing hour was proof to the contrary, I had been screwing his woman, compensated or not; if Shushan was a corpse, I was pretty close to having robbed a fresh grave. That there was uncertainty either way afforded little solace. With neither death nor life proven, I was compelled to carry both burdens. It was like being a bisexual without a date on a Saturday night: twice as lonely.

Justo sat down opposite me on one of the green-leather couches, lit a cigarette and said . . . nothing.

'I guess you're thinking ill of me,' I said, hoping at least to get this over with.

'Me?'

'No,' I said, pointing upward. *'Him.'*

'Him I don't know about,' Justo said. 'I know about me. First of all, until I learn different you're the boss. Being the boss comes with certain perks. Darcie, that's just a small one. Which, by the way, you can swap any time you want. You can have hot and cold running pussy up here, just in case you don't know. Black, white, oriental, fat, thin, young, even older. Shushan, he was kind of partial to Darcie, but she's not exactly your showroom quality late model, right? A lot of miles on that broad. But this kind of decision isn't for me. I'm just the accountant.'

'Accountants don't have opinions?'

'Not if they're smart. Shushan let me know it early. I don't buy the beans or sell the beans or even get to steal the beans, and for sure I don't spill them. I just count them. Shushan wants to know what he's got where, I tell him. Likewise, what he owes, what he's owed. There's reason in that. *Chinga,* if I'm involved in doing the business I can't watch the business. Besides which, I'm not built for busting heads. I'm built for. . . .'

'Yes?'

'For giving the boss information.'

'Because you know all the details?'

'I'm supposed to,' Justo said, grinding out his Old Gold in the ashtray already full of scarlet-tipped butts. Old Gold was a brand that had a coupon stuck to the back of every pack. When you had collected enough coupons you could redeem them for a wallet or a toaster or a radio.

In a little while a hotel maid would come in to straighten up. They always came around ten. Every day I gave the woman a fiver, which at that time was real money. You could eat a whole meal in a nice luncheonette for a buck. The money came from a big pile in my pocket that Justo had left me the first night, a thousand bucks. He called it 'walking-around money,' though there wasn't anyplace I could walk. 'Maybe you should fill me in,' I said.

'You ask, I'll answer,' he said. 'If I know.'

'What did my father do for Shushan Cats?'

No silence could have been louder than in the moments that passed while Justo lit another Old Gold, sat back on the couch, and removed his eyeglasses to wipe them with a white handkerchief from his outside breast-pocket. When he got the lenses pristine he pulled a long comb out of his inside breast-pocket and drew it methodically through his slick black hair, from forehead to the nape of his carefully barbered neck, then from each temple back around to the same spot. His hair so hugged his scalp it seemed to be painted on, and gave his beaky, angular face an eagle's look, alert, aggressive, reserved.

'Are you going to have a shave as well?' I asked. 'Because, despite what you might believe, I don't have much time.'

'Because of Arnold?'

'Because of Arnold, yes, and because probably as I sit here watching you prevaricate – you know that word? – our friends the Tintis are probably carefully dismantling the business that pays your salary, and provides me with the possibility, as you put it, of hot and cold running pussy. So say what you have to say.'

He took a breath. 'We're all concerned about the Tintis,' he said.

'All?'

He shrugged. 'Me, Ira, Mrs Ira, Terri, for sure Darcie too. And of course every bookie in Brooklyn and in the Manhattan territory, plus the brothers, and the chinks, to say nothing of everyone associated in one way or another with the fish market. It's a big problem.'

'We'll deal with it,' I said, projecting a confidence I did not precisely feel. 'But first I want to know about the little problem.'

'Meyer Newhouse.' For emphasis Justo stubbed out his second butt, half-smoked. 'A fine man, Mike. Let me start with that.'

'Thank you, though you probably know more about him than I do.'

'You know what happened with the NYPD, right?'

'I was there. My father and I lived in the same apartment.'

'I paid your rent yesterday,' Justo said. 'Just in case you're concerned.'

'I have ten days before it's due.'

'Shushan likes to pay early. Sometimes the mail to Brooklyn, it's like a foreign country. But you don't have to worry. I took care of it.'

'Thanks.'

'Not at all, boss. It's my job. What exactly do you want to know about your old man?'

'When did he start working for Shushan?'

A shrug. 'He joined the payroll in fifty-seven, March I think – I'd have to look it up – but for some time before he was more or less freelancing. Shushan needed a tough Jew, he called on your father. And he was one tough Jew.'

'To do what?'

'Sometimes just to show up.'

'To show up?'

'You know, somebody was making trouble, Mike would show up. Somebody was leaning on a friend, Shushan didn't like to have to intervene personally unless there was a real necessity. This was a time we started reducing the payroll, because we didn't need feet on the street. But it wasn't like today. We still had guys. I mean, big guys. But he'd send Mike. I mean, your father was my size. Mike would . . . show up.'

'And . . .'

'If necessary, lean back.'

'My father was an enforcer for Shushan Cats?'

'Nah,' Justo said. 'First of all, what did Shushan

have to enforce? Nobody was going to bother our bookies, not with Shushan having a writ from Auro Sfangiullo—'

'A writ.'

'A permit, like. Or a license. Maybe more like a blessing. It wasn't in writing. Just everyone knew not to even think about challenging Shushan because he was tight with Sfangiullo. They had an agreement between them. This business, Shushan used to say it should be called disorganized crime. Most of the time everyone is at everyone else's throat. They'll fight like cats over a piece of mouse you practically can't see. Who controlled what was always in flux, still is. But in some cases, like with the Fulton Fish Market and the bookies in Brooklyn and some territories in Manhattan, the boundaries of territories were as clear as on those Hammond globes. Outside of that and a few similar situations, chaos. What can I tell you? Gangsters aren't geographers or statesmen or anything rational. And the people at the top of the pile encourage it. You know why? Because if the lower levels are fighting among themselves they won't think of attacking the top layer and supplanting them. So when you hear about the so-called highly organized, super-disciplined Mafia, you're reading the usual newspaper stuff, fiction. In this business, unless you have a writ, the only thing that counts is feet on the street. Shushan had a writ. Where was I going with this?'

'My father.'

'Oh yeah. Shushan had a writ, and Mike he had a rep. First he was a tough cop – you had to be tough to be a Jew in the NYPD. Then he was a cop they threw off the force, excuse me for saying it that way, which means even the cops were scared of him, plus it was known he was alone in the world with a kid. I mean, it was common knowledge he was a desperate man. Instead of being scared something might happen to him if he got into a brawl – fists or firearms, with these guys it's always to the death – he was more scared he might lose his work if he didn't prove himself than lose his life if he backed off. Maybe Mike was no three-hundred pound gorilla, but he was all muscle and all guts. Shushan liked to say he was a World-War-II Marine, when the Marines were really Marines. You knew he was a Marine, right?'

'He always kept his dress uniform. I still have it.'

'So to protect the little he had he would rumble with the worst, which didn't happen too often because when they saw him coming they would stand clear. Personally, though, I can tell you from experience, he was a sweet man. Very friendly. Warm like. What'd I say?'

I straightened the line of my lips lest Justo think I might lose it. 'He was different with me.'

'Well, that happens. My father, he never told me once he was proud I went to college. Those old-time Puerto Ricans, for them if you didn't do manual labor you were goofing off. He still can't figure out what an accountant does. Never had a

285

checkbook in his life. Got paid in cash, paid in cash. In a couple years he goes on Social Security – I'm afraid he'll toss out the checks.'

'My father and I didn't talk,' I said. 'He never told me much.'

'Maybe he wasn't so proud.'

'I don't know one way or the other,' I said. 'And I don't care.'

'You don't sound like you don't,' Justo said. 'If you don't mind my saying.'

'Next topic,' I said.

'You're the boss.'

'Until Shushan shows up.'

'Boss,' Justo said. 'I don't think so.'

'Never mind. It doesn't matter. That's one thing I learned from my old man.'

'What's that?'

'Hope for the best. Assume the worst.'

'That's why people feared him.'

'Fear is important, I take it.'

'Oh yeah. I mean, Shushan never had to raise a hand to anyone in five years, maybe longer. Fear, it's catching. Everybody hears the stories, some of the stories even get a bit exaggerated in the retelling. People do that. So Shushan, he didn't have to work much, if you know what I mean.'

'I need to see Royce and the brothers, and Jimmy and Tommy, the Chinese guys.'

'You got it.'

'Is there someone else I haven't met?'
'You putting something together?'
'Do I have a choice?' I asked.
'Not much of one.'

CHAPTER 30

Jimmy and Tommy Wing came in first, along with two Chinese bruisers in black leather jackets who sat by the door opposite Ira like a human wall, not introduced, not even looking in my direction. I had the feeling they were not exactly English-majors. Jimmy and Tommy, however, were as American as apple dim sum, comfortably integrated into both societies, so that Tommy immediately reached out to me in the language of sports, as they had with Shushan in the restaurant, except that I knew little of professional baseball, college basketball or horse-racing, and cared less. Forgive them: they know not Wystan Hugh Auden. At four in the afternoon they put down two double shots of Old Grand-Dad like gunfighters in a movie saloon.

'You're a Jewish guy, right?' Jimmy said. He wore the kind of suit that heralded the beginning of a fashion revolution, the British assault vaulting over from Carnaby Street in London and the American front opening out of Haight-Ashbury in San Francisco. This wasn't exactly flower power, but close: Jimmy was decked out in a gray suit illuminated in thin stripes of mauve and pink,

288

framed by a high collar over four buttons, a fat mauve tie, and on his small feet peculiarly pointed dark grey jodhpurs. Tommy was just as advanced in shades of garden green. Both wore sunglasses, though the suite's curtains were drawn. 'I'm right about that, like Mr Shushan?'

'We're both Jews,' I said.

'Can you explain that?'

'The coincidence?'

'No,' Jimmy said, moving his head slightly to the left so that behind the dark lenses set in pentagonal wire frames he was probably flashing a look to Tommy. 'Jews.'

Tommy nodded. He was not a talker.

'We were discussing about it coming over,' Jimmy said. 'Jews. I mean, they tried to wipe you out and here you are and just as powerful. It's true you have a council?'

'A council?'

'That rules the world, secretly?'

'Sure,' I said. 'It's in Brooklyn. Meets every four years in the back of a kosher deli on Flatbush Avenue.'

The two Chinese were not laughing.

'That's it, only four years?' Jimmy said. 'Is that enough?'

'For most things.' I said. 'Like the color of cars. Ever notice that GM, Ford, Chrysler, they all bring out the same colors? But mostly it's political, like deciding who's going to be president. We backed Jack Kennedy, of course, because he's a Jew.'

'He's a Jew?'

'Jimmy, he *pretends* to be Irish Catholic,' I said. 'But the last lord mayor of Dublin, Bobby Briscoe, he's a Jew. So being Irish and a Jew, that happens. St. Patrick also.'

'How about that,' Jimmy said.

'Mao too.' I couldn't help it.

Justo shot me a look.

'Mao?'

'You thought only Chiang Kai-shek, right?' God help me, I couldn't stop. 'Common error.'

'Chiang?' Jimmy said.

'You know who else? Sandy Koufax.'

'Yeah, Koufax,' Jimmy added. 'Very Jewish. Fanned the first five Yankees in the first game of the series. Broke the record with fifteen strike-outs. Rubbed the Yankees into the dirt.'

'You don't like the Yanks?'

'The Yankees are basically Italian,' Jimmy said. 'Joe DiMaggio. Mickey Mantle.' In total agreement, Tommy nodded with alarming vigor. 'Yogi Berra,' Jimmy continued. 'Joe Pepitone. It's the dago club.'

I considered this for a moment while the two lit cigarettes that immediately stank up the room. *Gauloises.* Who knew Chinese hoodlums dressed English and smoked French? Still, it was a convenient opening. 'You don't like . . . Italians?'

In tandem the sunglasses came off, leaving both Jimmy and Tommy less formidable but at the same time more excitedly bright-eyed, at least visibly. Though I knew from Shushan that they stuck to their own turf, terrorizing Chinatown and a few other pockets of Chinese population in New York, I thought maybe it would be a good idea for them not to become too excited. They had a reputation for random violence. As opposed to the violence of normal hoodlums, who will gladly beat the shit out of someone on a commercial basis, Chinese gangsters might burn a fellow Chinese alive with kerosene simply because he showed too little respect. Of course they had enough business among their own. The Chinese were incorrigible gamblers, with a special affinity for blackjack, and because most had left their families behind were regular clients of the closely controlled whorehouses along Division Street. Culturally they had a predilection for hard drugs, and most of the new-style containers arriving in the Port of New York packed tight with sixty or seventy Chinese always carried enough heroin to make the shipment profitable even if the human cargo died along the way. According to Justo, if junk smelled like rotten meat, it was Chinese. 'What's to like in the dagos?' Jimmy said. 'They think Little Italy it's a state, like the Vatican or something, or Rhode Island, and God help anyone who steps inside. It's like you have to get a visa. These days, with Chinatown so crowded, when one of us buys an apartment house on the wrong street it's just not comfortable, let me put it that way. The old Italians, the plain working stiffs, they're moving out. Long Island, New Jersey, Staten Island. What are we going to do, not buy? You been on the Staten Island Ferry recently?'

'No.'

'It's like Sicily,' Jimmy said, then seemed to tire of the subject, perhaps in frustration. 'They don't like us. We don't like them.'

I smiled. 'How'd you boys like to help the Jews out with the Italians.'

'The Jews got an Italian problem?'

'A little one,' I said.

CHAPTER 31

After the Chinese left Royce and the brothers came in. Once I had the key it was easy.

'What can we do for you, Mr Russell?'

'Not a thing,' I said. 'Except maybe tell me where you get your threads.'

'You like this style?'

'The Negro is the best dressed man in America,' I said. 'You look at the television news, you see white people who couldn't dress their way out of a Klan costume. I'm not kidding you, gentlemen, clothes make the man, and your typical ofay looks like he's been dressed by somebody who normally makes flour sacks.'

'Amen to that,' Fred said. He was the tallest of the three brothers, and possibly the youngest. Ed and Ted nodded. All of them glowed metallically, the rich dark material of their suits shot through with gold thread that matched the wide bands on their porkpie hats – in 1963, unless a woman was present, men kept their hats on; when a woman entered an elevator all the hats came off, and when she got off they went right back on. Their shoes were of unusual color, brightly sueded tans and greens and blues. Each of the three brothers wore a white-on-white buttondown shirt, just coming into style. Royce's was light blue with a tab collar that pressed the knot of his silver necktie up and out like a push-up bra.

'You might appreciate fine dressage,' Royce said. 'But you telling us for a reason.'

'You can't fool a wise man,' I said.

The three brothers nodded in appreciation.

'You still be doing it,' Royce said. 'You trying to flatter us to be on your side?'

'My side?'

'Your thing with the Tintis, man, it a known conception. People be talking about it. They be saying, "Going to be blood on the street worse than Birmingham, worse than Little Rock."'

I looked at my watch. I got up and went to the 21-inch television in the corner, a top-of-the-line Zenith, the first with color and stereophonic sound, and clicked it on. Zenith had remote control for black-and-white sets, but not yet for color. There, booming out in a gravelly reassuring baritone, was Walter Cronkite.

'—while the Rev. Dr Martin Luther King told CBS News he has just begun to fight.'

And here was the man himself, dressed for societal combat in a snap-brim hat, a dark suit and a narrow two-tone silver tie that might have come out of Royce's closet. Two months before he had thrilled part of the nation and pissed off the rest with his 'I have a dream' speech during a march

294

on Washington that had brought some two-hundred thousand civil rights activists to the capital. 'That is right, because the cause of the American Negro is just and it is not going to be abandoned. The colored people of Birmingham are locked in a struggle with the forces of intolerance, injustice and plain hatred. But we will not be moved. We shall prevail.'

Cronkite's voice returned over footage of Birmingham firemen hosing down marchers, black and white, their arms locked together, as police on horseback swung in with batons from both sides. 'An epic battle is being played out on the streets of one of America's great cities,' Cronkite intoned. 'Now this.'

While a patent remedy called Serutan—' That's Nature's backwards!' — was being touted 'for the quick relief of the minor aches and pains that come with our high pressure modern life,' the brothers lit joints the size of Phillies panatellas and passed them around. I wonder if Shushan had used to smoke with them: there was so much I did not know. Had my old man smoked with them as well? The idea of my father smoking boo brought a stupid grin to my face as I took a long drag, then passed it to Justo who proceeded to suck a half inch off the joint all by himself. When Cronkite came back he was talking about a presidential trip to Texas. I got up and switched it off. 'I sure do want you on my side, gentlemen.'

'Gonna cost,' Royce said.

I looked to Justo. He shrugged. 'How can you say that if you don't know what I need?'

The three brothers grooved on that, nodding their big heads like the bobbing plastic dogs that had begun to appear in the rear windows of American cars. You never saw them in Volkswagens, the only foreign car on the roads. Nor would you ever see a big pair of fuzzy dice hanging in front. Either would block the Beetle's tiny windows.

'My man, I needs your agreeance first,' Royce said.

There was no need to look to Justo. This was a matter of someone else's pride. 'Royce, whatever you ask, you got it.'

'Mr Russ, you the right successor of Mr Shushan,' he said. 'That just the way he would do.'

'Thank you,' I said. 'I'm honored.' I was not just saying it.

'Whatever shit you be needing, we be there. Now, you know what we be requiring from you?'

I took the joint as he passed it. 'Like I said, you name it.'

'Here what it is,' Royce said. 'When this shit, whatever shit come down, be accomplished, you and me and the brothers here we going to introduce you to a little shop on Hundred Twenty-Fifth Street, and we going to buy you a pimp suit to out-pimp all pimp suits. The obscene mama of all pimp suits. And you going to accept it as our gift.'

'That's what you want?'

'Shee-it, yes.'

'Gentlemen, we got ourselves a deal.'

Between the boo and the *beau geste*, we all broke down in guffaws, and not until the four were almost out the door did we bother to discuss what I needed them for. They didn't care. Like me, they had agreed before they knew. As he grasped my hand Royce leaned close enough so that I could smell his rum cologne and, my senses heightened by the joint, even the naptholene that had been used to clean the fine wool fabric of his suit.

'Your daddy,' he said. 'One time, I was just a kid, he done beat the fecal matter out this sonbitch, not no little mo'fucker neither. Listen up, Mr Russ. You know why he did that?'

'Tell me.'

'Sonbitch called me nigger,' Royce said, the door closing with a soft click, and leaving me standing there, a bit high, a lot relieved, as though a door had not closed but opened.

CHAPTER 32

Considering that Fritzi, Justo and Terri all considered it imperative I be imprisoned in a hotel suite secured by armed ex-cops below and Ira behind a steel-reinforced door above, the drive out to Brooklyn that evening had all the tension of a day-trip up the Palisades Parkway to Bear Mountain for a bracing summertime swim in a cool lake and a barbecue of chicken and corn. My father had taken me on such a drive once, and having done so must have figured he had provided the complete filial experience and need not repeat it, though the joy of such pleasures is precisely in their repetition. Anyway, it was not daytime but early evening, not summer but late November – though it was so unseasonably warm the top would have been down on the Cadillac were it not for the light rain that had been falling intermittently since morning. Still, there was an air of recreational excitement in the big car, as though we were all going to a party. Perhaps we were.

Sitting between Ira, who drove with his customary dead-pan intensity, as if the road might disappear

298

at any time and he must be prepared to deal with such a void, and Justo, who chain-smoked Old Golds, flicking yet another butt out onto Flatbush Avenue when we came off the Manhattan Bridge as though he were laying a trail of breadcrumbs, I found myself listening with near-manic intensity to the inane lyrics coming over the Caddy's radio as the ubiquitous disc jockey Allen Freed lay down a line of self-congratulatory patter between songs that forty years later would be called 'oldies.' Apparently he was a guest on someone else's show this evening – having lost his own show in New York the inventor of the phrase 'rock and roll' was about to be indicted for taking 'payola' to plug records on air – and there was clearly an element of pathos, if not self-pity, in his rich alto as he introduced The Platters singing what was already a classic, 'The Great Pretender,' which had moved from the category of 'colored music' to just music. At least for Americans under twenty-five.

From the back seat Detective Kennedy was good enough to offer his services as music critic. Cohen at least had the sense to keep his trap shut. 'You're gonna have to pay us double if you keep playing jigaboo music.'

I turned around. 'What?'

'Must be something else on the radio, kid.'

'There is,' I said.

'Jigs is in,' Kennedy said. 'All day every day on the news, there they are, marching. What kind of world is that?'

I turned to Justo. 'What are we paying them?'

'A C each.'

I turned back. 'You want double for having to listen to jig music, is that it? Will it make you feel better if we pay you two hundred?'

'Well, I still won't love the music but, hey, hardship pay.'

Cohen remained silent.

'Makes sense. Tell me, Kennedy, what'll you do for *three* hundred?'

'What?'

'Say I give you three hundred. How about that much and The Platters can fuck you up the ass? Will three hundred be enough?'

'Dougie's just talking,' Cohen said to me, leaning forward. 'We worked a long day.'

'Nothing personal, Detective Cohen,' I said. 'But shut up.'

'Hey, I didn't—'

'Shut up,' I said. 'Now, Detective Kennedy, have you thought how much you require to be fucked up the ass by the entire membership of The Platters, which let me remind you is four gentlemen of the Negro persuasion plus one lady, who – all things being equal – may demur? Come on, pick a number.'

'I didn't mean no—'

'A number!'

'Okay, okay,' he said, a reluctant choirboy emerging from deep within the bully. 'I'm . . . sorry.'

'You're sorry for what?'

'I didn't mean nothing by it. I can stand the music.'

'You can?'

'Sure. Let's just pretend it didn't happen.'

The radio was selling Volkswagen cars. Tiny things, slow and stolid, four could fit into the footprint of Shushan's Cadillac – my Cadillac, I supposed. The people driving these two cars could have been two different species. From the perspective of many decades, it appears the *Cadillac-Magnons* of the sixties inexplicably died out, replaced by hordes of *Homo Econocar*. In those days driving a Volkswagen – Japanese vehicles were a rare sight even on the West Coast – was still eccentric behavior, like not smoking or drinking in moderation. I suppose Detective Kennedy *had* been drinking, possibly even in moderation for an Irish dick with no one looking over his shoulder. I didn't care. On my signal Ira pulled over next to a shuttered linoleum emporium that took up most of a block of Flatbush Avenue midway between the Manhattan Bridge and Grand Army Plaza, where a facsimile of the Arc de Triomphe attested to America's long on-again off-again romance with France, and with civic fickleness. Unlike the one in Paris, Brooklyn's arch – like the borough in general – was bathed in darkness. Had it been lit other than by the headlights of cars zooming around it, we could have seen it where Ira had stopped a mile or so away from where Flatbush Avenue met Eastern Parkway. That would be the preferred view, because up close we would soon see piles of garbage rotting picturesquely at its base.

'What's up?' Cohen asked, probably because he knew.

'Pay them off,' I said to Justo, who soundlessly peeled four fifties off a significant roll and passed them back over his head, not looking at the two detectives. 'Good night, gentlemen,' I said.

'What good night?' Kennedy asked, having recovered some of his native belligerence. 'We ain't even at the what-do-you-call society, much less providing security.'

'The Bhotke Young Men's Society,' I said to the windshield. 'It's a club for people with certain values.'

'Sure, sure,' Kennedy said, agreeable.

'That you don't share,' I said, still looking forward. 'So get out of the car.'

'What do you mean, Mr Newhouse?' Cohen said. 'We took your money, we're up for the job.'

I turned. 'Detective, the job was to stand by quietly in case some two-bit hoods like the Tintis try to make trouble for us sometime between when we left the hotel and when we return.'

'That's right,' Cohen said. 'No problem.'

'Yes problem,' I said. 'Now take your unquiet friend here and get out of the car. You're paid off. Leave.'

Ira walked around the car and opened the right-hand door and held it open.

Kennedy would probably die stupid. 'What, right

in the middle of nigger-heaven? How are we supposed to get out of here?'

For some reason the picture of these two white cops standing hapless in a steady drizzle on a forlorn corner at the edge of Bedford-Stuyvesant, where they had no doubt arrested hundreds, if not thousands, of blacks over a decade and a half, some of them possibly for an actual offense, caused the three of us in the front seat to start giggling like children, first myself, then Justo – as a Puerto Rican he had probably grown up in perpetual fear of the likes of Kennedy and Cohen – and then Ira, who appeared at long last to have a sense of humor, or at least an instinctive comradeship. The giggles turned to laughter, then hooting, and for emphasis Ira leaned on the horn, a monster of an instrument with a deep B-flat tone, and rode it as we circled the arch, a monument to the Union dead of the Civil War, exiting left past the main branch of the Brooklyn Public Library, built in a proto-fascist style that could have been approved by Mussolini, and then the neo-classical Brooklyn Museum. In both these fine buildings I had passed many quiet afternoons absorbing a wealth of knowledge for which, it was turning out, I had little use.

As we passed the far edge of Prospect Park our laughter subsided sufficiently for me to ask Justo, 'How would Shushan have handled that?' In ten blocks or so we would arrive at the Crown Heights Conservatory which two evenings a month sheltered the Bhotke Young Men's Society. I suppose I needed to hear the bad before I committed worse.

Justo's left hand came around to my shoulder and gave it an avuncular squeeze. 'Same way,' he said. 'Same fucking way.'

CHAPTER 33

Apparently I was in the Yiddish papers too – at that time New York had two such dailies, and a number of weeklies. In fact, I was more of a sensation in the Yiddish press than in the English: Nice Jewish boy from Brooklyn makes good in the gangster business – or bad. I should have suspected the scope of my notoriety before I entered the hall, leaving Ira outside the double doors through which Shushan had entered my life only two weeks before. Now, as Justo quietly took a seat in the last row like an impoverished Jew in a strange synagogue, everyone stood as though it really was a synagogue and the Torah scrolls had just been taken out of the ark.

Theoretically I was there to take up my pen as recording secretary, but my entrance caused the kind of uproar even Shushan's hadn't. The Bhotke members were workers in the garment center, small tradesmen, shopkeepers, salesmen, tailors, butchers, fish sellers, deli owners, more or less honest business people, with a sprinkling of accountants and dentists and lawyers, even a doctor or two, and they were applauding as if I were Sandy Koufax, another nice Jewish boy from Brooklyn whose bravura pitching had earned him the Most Valuable Player award in the recently concluded World Series, where the (formerly Brooklyn) Dodgers, defected to Los Angeles, had neatly trounced the Yankees in four straight. Hands reached out as I made my way down the center aisle to where Feivel (Franklin) Rubashkin (Robinson) opened his arms to welcome me in a hug whose aroma was purely dental, that sickeningly sweet odor overlaid with porcelain and laughing gas.

'Brothers of Bhotke,' he announced. 'He's back!'

Did they think I wouldn't be? I waved to the standing membership, many of whom I knew by name because I had recorded their ravings about misapplication of funds ('Excuse me, do we really need to pay so much to an outside attorney?' – this from an inside attorney), the suitability of Coney Island for the annual picnic ('So much crowding, so much crime – I got a bungalow colony in Parksville upstate, the society could have almost for free') and whether or not we should put up a monument at Beth David to those sons and daughters of Bhotke killed by the Nazis ('Who otherwise have no grave, no markers, no nothing – the refuse of history'). Though the membership of the Bhotke Young Men's Society held divergent views on hundreds of questions, they were clearly united on three subjects: that Walter O'Malley, who owned the Dodgers, should be hanged for removing the beloved Bums to California; that a Democrat, any Democrat, should sit in the White House; that Russell Newhouse should be loved simply for inheriting Shushan Cats' mantle as Kid Yid, the last of the fear-engendering Jews.

It amazed me how powerful the press was in fashioning this public image. Shushan had climbed, fought, gouged his way to the top of the circumcised gangster universe; I had arrived because, as with Saul and David, the departing monarch had tapped me for the job. But so far all I had done was show up. Now I would have to do something. And though I knew what to do, I did not know if it would work.

Clearly I was not expected to actually take up my role as recording secretary, a job too menial for a man wearing such a custom-made suit, and custom-made rep: the old recording secretary was back at his old post, my old post, inscribing notes in elegantly lettered Yiddish. He smiled in my direction. Feivel (Franklin) gave me a thumbs up. Though I had notes in my head for a twenty-minute speech, I decided to cut it short. This was a crowd that wanted action as much as I did.

'Brothers of Bhotke,' I said. 'I am pleased and proud to be among you this evening. Being a son of Bhotke, a grandson in fact, means more to me than being in the papers. Until recently you were the only family I had. And so I come back to you tonight to ask your help in showing respect to our perhaps departed member, Shushan Cats, a brave defender of the Jews, who has done as much with the baseball bat as Sandy Koufax has done with the ball. As we await word of Shushan's fate, and though we may fear the worst, I ask you to join with me tomorrow in a show of solidarity with Shushan, to exhibit to the world at large that though he is missing, though his fate is in doubt, we of the Bhotke Young Men's Society are solidly behind this Brooklyn hero, a Jew who took shit from nobody. Tomorrow, gentlemen, I ask that you come forward, take a long lunch break from your jobs, your shops, your practices, your day-to-day lives. Tomorrow when you join us in solidarity, holding up the symbol that made the reputation of Shushan Cats, a boxer who fought under the name of Kid Yid, a decorated Marine, a defender of his people, you yourselves will *be* Shushan Cats, as I have become Shushan Cats. Dear brothers of Bhotke, let us tomorrow show New York, America, the world, that the spirit of Shushan Cats resides in all of us. My associate will now distribute directions to and instructions for tomorrow's demonstration of solidarity. Long live Shushan Cats!'

As one the entire population of the room, some two hundred men, rose to their feet. 'Long live Shushan Cats!' they shouted. 'Long live Israel! Long live the Jews!'

Was I manipulating them or they me, *and* Shushan, *and* any symbol they could grab hold of to obliterate the obdurate memory of a Holocaust that had not only wiped out millions of Jews, including several hundred from Bhotke, but their memory. Most of the Bhotke members had emigrated in the twenties and thirties; some had sailed out of the then-free port of Danzig as late as 1939, the Hitlerites having sunk the next ship in the harbor. Some arrived in the late forties and early fifties, decorated with blue numbers on their forearms or, if they had fought as partisans in the forests, a parallel coldness of heart like that of caged animals who were now free except for the memory of the cages and of those who had put them there. Even those like my father, who had come to America as infants, carried with them the ever-present nightmare of the survivor.

Of the entire village of Bhotke, only one man had survived the initial slaughter in 1939 when an SS battalion had entered the village. According to his testimony, the village rabbi had gone out to meet the commanding officer bearing the traditional bread and salt of peaceful welcome. He was cut down on the spot, after which those too old or too young to work were herded into the synagogue to die in its flames. Deemed fit for labor, the remainder were trucked off to the Bialystok ghetto, from which they were eventually taken by rail to the death camps. Was it any wonder that a Jew who brandished a baseball bat and feared no one, and who was known to fear no one, might become a hero to the Jews who survived?

To the members of the Bhotke Young Men's Society, Shushan Cats was no criminal. The criminal statutes held no validity for those to whom the law meant only authorized starvation, torture, death. Everything done to the Jews of Europe, the Gypsies, the homosexuals, the Communists, the Socialists, the crippled, the mentally and physically retarded and the mentally and physically ill – *everything* done to these had been absolutely legal, sanctioned by legitimate courts whose judges sat in black robes and vetted each and every decree as binding, fair, in the public interest, legal. Under these circumstances, that Shushan Cats was a Jewish gangster not only could not be held against him, but was a matter for celebration.

By noon the next day the first of the Bhotke members began to appear on the fringes of Little Italy. A half-hour later there were seventy or eighty. By one a hundred fifty were gathered in the street facing Dolce Far Niente. Justo later told me that by the time I was inside sitting down with Auro Sfangiullo, the supply of baseball bats had run out and Ira had been sent off to the wholesale hardware stores on Canal Street to buy up broom sticks, ax handles and lengths of pipe.

CHAPTER 34

'You are a boy,' Sfangiullo said to me as he motioned to a third seat at the table in the rear where he was chewing on a piece of crusty Italian bread with which he'd mopped up the clam broth that was all that remained of his rigatoni. It was not difficult to understand why everyone called him *dottore*. At once diagnostic and prescriptive, he seemed to be able to reduce everything to symptoms and their cure. 'But they say you are intelligent, so maybe an old man in the body of a child, eh?' His lip curled upward on the left side, like a scimitar. It took me some time to realize it was half a smile. 'What do you say, Dickie? Boy or man?'

The other, who had shaken my hand desultorily after I had pressed my lips to Sfangiullo's, looked me up and down like a side of beef. 'Maestro, I couldn't say,' he said, saying all. 'It's hard to know what the newspapers are so wild about. Shoeshine, he was one tough kike. But this, maybe he shaves, maybe not.' The man's expression needed no translation. It was a grin of triumph.

'You're Dickie Tinti,' I said.

'You're a fucking genius,' he said.

Sfangiullo placed his bony hand on Tinti's well-tailored sleeve, out of which a French cuff peeked out enough to reveal a gold cufflink the size of a quail's egg. 'Dickie, this is a guest.'

'This guest is trying to eat my breakfast, maestro.'

It was hard to dislike Tinti. For a crook he was at least honestly what he was. I had expected him to be here: What he was was predictable.

At forty Dick Tinti had succeeded his father as head of a small but violent family dealing in fresh flowers, prostitutes and smuggled cigarettes – some said drugs too. If that last were true he could hardly be expected to sit at a table in public with Auro Sfangiullo, who drew the line at narcotics. But it was also said the good doctor had a piece of a piece of a piece of people who did. On his own account Sfangiullo was scrupulous about heroin, which was becoming a plague in New York. When eventually Auro Sfangiullo died – in bed, of a stroke – all the families without exception rushed to see how much horse they could put on the street. But while Sfangiullo ran the city for the imprisoned Vito Genovese, the white poison would not be sanctioned, at least not officially. In this Auro Sfangiullo was like some revered cardinal who managed not to notice that his priests regularly molested altar boys.

'*Dottore*, I hardly expected to come to talk to you about the Tintis and find one of them with you. Would you prefer I return another time?'

312

'My boy, if you wish to fix your situation, you should do it sooner rather than later. How many bookmakers on your list these days?'

I honestly did not know. 'One less than last week. Mr Tinti seems to believe Shushan Cats does not have an agreement with yourself, *dottore.*'

Tinti smiled genially. 'Nothing personal, but Shoeshine Cats is dead.'

'You know that for sure?'

'Kid, let's just say if he's not somebody overpaid somebody else a huge amount of money. Shoeshine is no more.'

I turned back to Sfangiullo. '*Dottore,* what if Shushan is alive?'

'What if, suppose that, let's assume this, for the sake of argument it could be . . .' The older man smiled like a grandfather, not a godfather. 'In this world we deal with the little we *do* know. What we *do* know is what we read in the papers: Got into a car with the wrong people, never seen again. For the purposes of our business there is no longer a Shoeshine Cats, a lovely man when he was with us. I mean it from the heart: a lovely, lovely man. Very trustworthy. Very . . . good. Believe me, when we get into business with a person of the desert persuasion, this means that person is on the up and up.'

'I have every reason to believe Shushan Cats is still among the living,' I said, not believing a word of it. 'Meanwhile, Shushan has asked me to hold down the fort.'

Tinti laughed out loud. 'We took over what's his name, that queer in the theater district, runs a book out of a hotel on West Forty-Sixth.'

'Arnold Savory.'

'Exactly. You aren't holding down the fort, you're holding down a fart. You know what Shushan would've done if we'd moved in on anything of his, even an old sock he was throwing out because it had a hole?' He drew his finger across his throat. 'You'd be talking to one dead Dick Tinti, kid. But as you can see, I'm very much alive.'

'Shushan's organization has a writ from you, *dottore*. I ask that you honor it.'

Sfangiullo nodded his head as though he had already thought this over. 'Young man, your boss is dead. I am informed you are the new boss. I know nothing about you other than that you are a smart Jewboy. I knew your father. Also a smart Jew. Smart is good. But you need more than smart to succeed in this business, which is to say survive. The Tintis are not my people. They are independent. So far as I am concerned, the question of the protection of the bookmakers is a territorial dispute.'

'Because the Tintis are promising you a piece of a percentage they wish to charge the bookmakers, while with Shushan you have a piece of a flat fee.'

'Economics is a significant factor in the American dream.'

'The Tintis are going to squeeze the bookies until they collapse, one by one.' I looked at Dick Tinti, then back. 'You know they're greedy.'

'Other bookmakers will arrive. Americans like to gamble. Now the state is talking about getting into the lottery business. This year you have a referendum in New York City on off-track betting. If it passes – and what do you think, it won't? – that's another nail in the coffin of the bookmakers, except there's other sports, thank Christ, so maybe, maybe not. If you look into the future maybe you want to take a bet on the future of the bookmaking business. That's not my arena. All I know is I made a deal with Shoeshine and I stand by it. But unfortunately Shoeshine is gone, so I got no deal. And you got no deal either, kid. That's the fact. I didn't make no deal with Shoeshine's heirs or appointees. Only with Shoeshine. You want to argue with the Tintis, be my guest. It's an open franchise as far as I'm concerned. Now if you'll excuse me.' A short heavy man in a blue suit and light blue silk tie had come to whisper in Sfangiullo's ear. While he did so, Sfangiullo nodded like a medical professional hearing of his patient's progress.

It came to me there was another reason Shushan may have been killed: with the future of bookmaking in New York so uncertain, Sfangiullo could have decided he wanted more cash now than in the long-term. Maybe there would be no long term. Tinti would certainly be ready to give up more of his take, and would drain the bookies unmercifully on the theory they only have a short time anyway. Maybe the gambit I had devised was academic: economics will out. From the way

Sfangiullo looked at me as the blue-suited man walked away, it did not matter. My plan was already in play.

'I am informed there is an element in the street,' Sfangiullo said, staring hard at me.

'An element?'

'Niggers.'

'Really?'

'Also chinks.'

'Also spicks and kikes, if you want to use racial slurs, *dottore*.'

'The whole street in front is full of hebes with baseball bats. At the Allen Street corner there's a gang of chinks. The other corner looks like Harlem there's so many jigs. Why are they here?'

'I don't know,' I said. 'Probably they're friends of Shushan Cats. Why don't you invite them in and ask them? I'm sure they'd like a coffee.'

'How many of these animals you got dirtying up my street?'

'I don't know.'

'You think a bunch of coloreds and chinks and lampshade people intimidates me?'

'Not at all,' I said. 'But they might intimidate Mr Tinti here.'

Tinti laughed.

I knew I had him. 'Frankly they're nonviolent, like the ones in Birmingham, Alabama.'

'They got what was coming to them,' Sfangiullo said. 'They break the law.'

'Ah,' I said. 'I'm so glad you see eye to eye with the attorney general on that.'

Sfangiullo drew his hand silently across his throat. Not his finger, his whole hand. This was not a gesture. It was language. 'The older one they should kill first,' he said. 'Because he's the president. Then the Bobby one. Both Kennedys, scum.'

'But duly elected,' I said, pushing it.

'Elected, they can be dis-elected. They hate the Italians. They hate anybody that isn't like them. Jimmy Hoffa, a legitimate labor leader, maybe with his hand in the cookie jar, maybe not, as if the Kennedys they're different, they are hounding him into a grave. Castro, he tried to bring good things to Cuba, they turned him into a Communist. Some Communist – a baseball pitcher. Batista, this son of a bitch we had to pay off every minute just to run a casino, him they protected, but when Castro came in they got scared. Maybe it's going to look bad for America if this guy, an honest leader, says okay, no more bribes, instead we got to pay taxes for casinos so he can build schools and hospitals and what not. You think anybody in the gambling business would care? You think it's pleasant to do business in a place where everybody is selling his own sister? Where you can get the clap from eating a ham sandwich? Where nobody can read and write? I'm not kidding with you. You want to run a casino you need people who can read and write and don't die on you in the middle of their shift because of some mysterious disease.

No, John F. Kennedy, he doesn't like that. Wants to replace Castro with another Batista. Let me tell you something. I'm a crook. All my friends are crooks. Every man I know practically is a crook. Everybody here, here in this room, we're all crooks. But there isn't a one of us wouldn't want to be dealing with Fidel Castro, not that crook Batista, because Batista he was a crooked crook. His word meant nothing. He stole all the money from his people and spent it on whores and drugs and who knows what filthy depravity. You think Castro would close down the casinos if John F. Kennedy he said, "Dr Castro, you're a democrat. You're for the people. You got a live-and-let-live attitude. What can we do to help?"' He took out a white handkerchief, hawked up and spat into it. 'Excuse me, but that John F. Kennedy, his brother, his other brother, the fat one that drinks too much, the whole family should rot in hell.'

Another man in blue now came up to the table and whispered into *Tinti's* ear. Apparently there was something to the blue suits, like a uniform perhaps that denoted service; I was briefly saddened that I hadn't brought such a person along. The second blue suit went away.

Tinti spoke so softly I could barely pick it up. The sound of singing was drifting in from the streets. A Yiddish melody. 'My guy says the whole street is blocked,' Tinti said. 'They got cars parked in the middle. Cars parked with nobody in them, and locked. What the fuck is that they're singing?'

'Your Yiddish a bit weak?' I said.

'What do they sing, kid?' Sfangiullo asked.

What could I do but sing it along with the people in the street, my people?

Zog nit kaynmol az du gayst dem letstn veg,
Chutch himlen bloyene farshteln bloye teg.
Kumen vet noch undzer oysgebenkte shoh,
S'vet a poyk ton undzer trut – mir zynen doh!
Kumen vet noch undzer oysgebenkte shoh,
S'vet a poyk ton undzer trut – mir zynen doh!

'Very pretty,' Tinti said. 'What does it mean in human?'

'It's the song of the Jewish fighters in the Warsaw Ghetto,' I said.

Never say that you are going your last way.
Though lead-filled skies above blot out the blue of
   day.
The hour for which we long will certainly appear.
The earth shall thunder beneath our tread – We
   are here!
The hour for which we long will certainly appear.
The earth shall thunder beneath our tread – We
   are here!

'So what does that mean?' Tinti said. 'Are we supposed to be afraid?'

'*Feccia di culo,*' I said with an even smile. '*Pisciarsi addosso dalla paura.* Ass-face, why shouldn't you

319

piss yourself from fear? I got three hundred men out there with baseball bats, and the colored guys and the Chinese are packing. If I want to I can keep you here until your *stugots*, which is your prick, turns into a *sticchio*, which is a cunt.'

'Maestro, your guest is calling me ass-facc? Do you mind if I handle this inside your place?'

'Yes, Dickie,' Sfangiullo said. 'I do mind. You want to have at him, go outside.' So the old man *could* smile with both sides of his mouth. 'Ah, you don't want to go outside, is that it?'

'They got hundreds,' Dickie said. 'What do I got, four or five here? It's a dirty trick.'

'*Troiata*, a dirty trick,' Sgfangiullo said, translating. 'Dickie, my heart bleeds marinara for you. You're an idiot, and you don't even know Italian.' The doctor turned to me. 'Tell me, kid. Where'd you learn to speak the beautiful tongue? I thought you was a Jewboy.'

'*Cette cacasenno vomitare l'anima vene finire in merda*,' I said.

Tinti's voice went up a couple of octaves. 'Speak English!'

'Some fucking Italian you are,' I said. 'Let me translate. "This shit-for-brains, who throws up his own guts, is going to end badly." Now you got it, Dickie?'

'Maestro, you going to let this Jew talk to me that way.'

'What way, you *feccia di stronzo*? *Lecceculo*, you come in here with big plans, big promises. You're going to take over the bookies, and then the fish market, and there's going to be a fortune in it, and suddenly this kid comes in and makes you *como un bello sticchio.*'

'That means, Dickie,' I said. 'Turdface, ass-licker, etcetera, etcetera, followed by "makes you look like a beautiful cunt."'

'Maestro, please, this is not right.'

'*Ruffiano siccii—*'

'Servile bootlicker,' I explained.

'Servile,' Sfangiullo said. 'That's a good translation. A good word.'

'English has a few,' I said.

'You're Italian? Where you from?'

'From Brooklyn.'

'What part?'

'Brownsville.'

'That's not an Italian neighborhood. Maybe a few. You sure you're not a Jewboy? I don't mind. Shushan, he's *Ebreo* too, and he's close to my soul.'

'A moment ago you said he was dead. Now you're speaking *nel presente teso.*'

'Newhouse. That's not an Italian name.'

'Newhouse,' I said. '*Casa, nova.*'

'Casanova?'

'Sure.'

'Casanova, where your people come from? Before Brooklyn?'

'Maestro!'

'*Uccello, tirar!*'

Poor Tinti had to turn to me.

321

'Penis, go have an erection.'

'*A un altro da tavola.*'

'At another table.'

Dick Tinti was just rising to his feet when Sfangiullo's blue-suit returned, and without so much as a pause bent to speak in the old man's hairy ear. I knew instinctively something had happened, because a moment before the singing outside – it was now 'We Shall Overcome' – slowed, faltered, stopped, voices dropping out one by one as if each had been the recipient of bad news. In the silence I understood the whispered Italian before Sfangiullo was able to repeat what he had heard. '*Il Presidente ha stato assassinato,*' he muttered, as if to himself. 'They just shot John F. Kennedy.'

CHAPTER 35

By the time I got back to the Westbury it was clear the president was dead. The newscasters working live from totally unedited reports were understandably cautious: no one wanted to speak the unspeakable. But the indications were unrelenting. Within minutes after Justo, Ira and I got back to the suite the White House made official what America feared: Kennedy was history, Lyndon Johnson having been sworn in on Air Force One as it returned to Washington as if merely being in Texas were perilous, which perhaps it was.

As the afternoon wore on the world seemed to slow down, and by evening came entirely to rest. In two years Martin Luther King would be gunned down, in seven it would be Bobby Kennedy's turn. By 1980, when a deranged Beatles fan had taken the life of John Lennon, America had become so inured to assassination that no one even thought to reflect on the obvious: a society that had sought to suppress organized crime was now functioning like organized crime writ large.

Whoever had killed John F. Kennedy – the idea

323

that it was a lone gunman remains laughable to this day – had a political agenda that could have been cooked up in eighteenth-century Sicily. The man arrested for the crime may or may not have been one of the shooters, but he could hardly have been all of them. Most likely he was the intended perpetrator, the designated assassin, the bad guy. While speculation exploded about Lee Harvey Oswald's connections with Cuba, the Soviet Union, right-wing fanatics, in that suite at the Westbury, with a tearful Walter Cronkite on the television screen and special editions of the New York papers on the coffee table, Justo and I dissected the hit from the perspective of an Auro Sfangiullo, a Royce Wilmington, a Jimmy Wing, a Shushan Cats.

'I've seen this so many times,' Justo said, pulling on a joint, its pungent fragrance filling the room like funerary incense. 'Somebody gets seriously pissed off at something someone did or is doing or maybe even intends to do. He can't do the hit himself, because number one it's dangerous, number two it's a specialist job, number three the last thing he wants to do is start a *chinga* war among the families. So he calls in a specialist.'

'Like . . .'

'Like it could be anybody. Ten, twenty years ago you had your Murder Incorporated people, Jewish hard guys from Brooklyn. They would sit by the phone, on retainer, just waiting for the call to hit somebody. I mean, this was their profession.'

324

It was Shushan's for a while as well, at least according to the newspapers. But I didn't point this out. To do so would be to besmirch the name of the dead. If anyone ever found Shushan's body and put up a stone, would it say: BELOVED SON AND BROTHER, BENEFACTOR OF CHARITIES, PROTECTOR OF THE WEAK? Maybe all that. But there would be no footnote, no asterisk leading to fine print below – AND RETIRED HITMAN. Another reason I didn't mention it: I doubted it was true. The same newspapers that painted Shushan as an former contract-killer had called me *Kid Yid Jr*, to say nothing of *Joe (Mob) College, Shoeshine Heir* and, in the *Daily Mirror*'s immortal words, *Brainiac Maniac*, replete with a list of criminal schemes some overheated flack at the Manhattan District Attorney's office had fed them as truth: Had I really put together a gang of anonymous tough-guy English-majors who for a price would threaten professors at all the city colleges to raise a specific student's grades or else? At Thomas Jefferson High School had I really bought the votes I needed to become student-body president? Was I really in charge of all the pot sold in nickel bags on all the college campuses in the Northeast? Was I really able to get a chimpanzee admitted to any medical school in New York, New Jersey and Connecticut simply by making a single whispered phone call? If the papers were so wrong about me, how much more so about Shushan?

But in a greater sense perhaps they weren't wrong about me at all. Between the tabloids, the television

325

news reports, and the subtle but pervasive word on the street, in certain circles I really was an up-and-comer. Even Auro Sfangiullo believed the hype, or pretended to. Being named heir to Shushan Cats might mean death at the hands of an angry Dick Tinti, but in quotidian terms it was nothing to be sneered at. Without even thinking about it I knew I could get a table at any restaurant in New York, the best hotel rooms, and a free pass to park on the sidewalk anywhere in town. My certainty in these matters was so great I had no need to confirm it: deference breeds confidence and that confidence inspires further deference. I now understood the meaning of Shushans leaving his Cadillac convertible totally open, vulnerable and blatantly illegally parked opposite a police precinct house in Chinatown – the twenty clipped to the windshield merely underscored Shushan's position in the hierarchy of power and influence in the city that was its capital. No one would dare take it. That's why it was there.

So it hardly surprised me the next afternoon when the three Callinan brothers arrived that I was treated like a cardinal or a fire chief or a police commissioner. What did surprise me was that I was addressed with similar deference by their sister.

CHAPTER 36

Celeste had never looked more fetching, probably because she had never looked fetching before. Something of a lace-curtain bohemian, she had never bothered when she was with me to apply makeup – excluding eye shadow – or dress to please: her appeal was direct. She offered the use of her body in exchange for her use of mine. This was a precursor to the more radical feminism that would so dominate both coasts – for reasons unknown the south and midwest remained immune to the blandishments of no blandishments. In 1963 every woman in New York and San Francisco under twenty-five with a patina of sophistication saw herself as earthy, primal, elemental. They wore pants, or dresses that showed thigh, and leather and suede. If they added jewelry – Celeste never did, not with me – it was or pretended to be African: large beads, shells, earrings that hung perilously low. Pearls didn't happen, diamonds did not make their appearance until an engagement ring changed the stakes; other- wise Mexican silver replaced the traditional delicacy of yellow and pink gold. Legs were shaved, but armpits escaped the razor. Deodorant was not abandoned, but perfume was all but unknown. Which is why my nose had not recognized Celeste even as my brain registered her presence. The smell of bergamot was not something I had ever associated with Miss Bangalot.

The woman now before me was a vision of glamour-magazine glamour: A short tan-suede coat over a tangerine sheath so richly textured it seemed burnished – I had never seen raw silk before – topped by a three-strand necklace of seed pearls, matching earrings and hair that had been worked on by someone wielding more than a rubber band. She wore heels, not clogs, and the watch on her wrist was so delicate its face may not have been readable. Hers, alight with respect, was.

'You didn't have to dress for me,' I said as she kissed me chastely on the cheek.

'No like?'

'No,' I said. 'Like. But I never thought you looked better in clothes.' Given the company, perhaps I could have worded this differently, but then again it might not have mattered.

If this disclosure pained them, or angered them, or merely embarrassed, the Callinan brothers disguised this with hearty hand-shakes, not least Father Bill, who grasped my hand in both of his long enough for the silent but heartfelt recitation of a Hail Mary. Maybe I had been sensitized to the features of our recently assassinated president, but as I looked upon the three Callinans all I could think of was loss. The Callinans were Kennedys without money, too little exercise, bad food and maybe an extra tipple with a regularity suggesting dependence. Each had the same brush-thick auburn hair, green eyes, and – especially the good padre – the tell-tale tiny explosions of burst blood vessels on the nose that speak of a natural inclination to tank up. He spoke first.

'You invited us, Mr Newhouse.'

'Russell,' I said. 'My friends call me Russell.'

'Are we your friends?' this from the fireman. I knew that because his brother was in the then tunic-topped uniform of the NYPD. I knew the uniform well. For years before my father had made detective he had used to drape the tunic over the chromed steel frame of a kitchen chair. I knew the gun he carried as well: a Smith & Wesson .38 revolver, later to be replaced in the department by the plug-ugly hard-plastic Glock semi-automatic. I had cleaned my father's gun once a week for years. He had never asked me to do it, merely showed me how. I took it from there. It was, of sorts, communication.

'Sure we are,' I said. 'We're going through a tragic period in this country, and I hardly think we can give weight to the kind of squabbles we may have enjoyed in the past.'

Father Bill crossed himself. Oddly, he was the most robust looking of the three. They were seated opposite on the green-leather couch whose back faced the door, from whose alcove Ira could watch my face for a hint of trouble before it began. This wasn't my idea, but inherited from Shushan, who had left me the fortress he had built. As Justo brought in a bottle and glasses, I could not help but notice the air in the room was still sweetly redolent of yesterday's pot, a clash of cultures if there ever was. Celeste was perched like a nervous icon at the other end of my couch.

'You need me, boss,' Justo said. 'Just call.' He disappeared into my old bedroom, probably to sit among the fitness equipment like a scholar in a gym.

Ira looked to me questioning whether he should make himself scarce as well. I shook my head so slightly only he could tell.

'Russell,' Celeste said. 'This is like a bad dream. It just got out of hand. My brothers want to apologize.'

'The fourth one too?' I said. 'I understand he's in the service.'

'Professional army,' the fireman said.

'Good for him,' I said. 'You must be proud.'

That about did it while the glasses were filled, ice plunked in, and . . . held. I supposed I was to make a toast.

I raised mine, no ice. 'Gentlemen, lady, to the memory of Jack Kennedy, a great president and a great Irishman.'

We drank. The brothers drank again. Celeste sipped. She could do that all night, eventually knocking off half a bottle. But more often she preferred grass, big Pall Mall-size joints she used to ratchet up her orgasms. After I passed out she often continued on alone. She was that kind of girl.

'So who's going to give up the first finger?' I asked.

Not so much as a clinking ice cube could be heard in the room. The three brothers looked at me, looked at each other, looked down at the plush tan and eggplant hotel carpet, past me out the windows to where neighboring rooftops neatly framed part of Central Park, then back down. The fireman looked at his hands. The cop looked blank. Father Bill pulled out his crucifix. For a moment I thought he might wave it at me, crying 'Devil, get thee away!' But nothing so dramatic transpired. I couldn't help but feel for them. Doubtless they saw themselves in the grip of the Brainiac Maniac, or Kid Yid Jr, heir to the criminal empire of the notorious Shushan Cats. I can't say I didn't enjoy it. These bozos had taken a great deal of pleasure in beating the bejesus out of me; now that they felt I had the power to do the same, and worse, I took pleasure in their fear. But there was a limit even to do that.

Celeste broke the silence. 'Russell, it was my fault.'

I turned to her. 'I've never seen you gift-wrapped. It works.'

'You do like.'

'But this is between the *brothers* Callinan and me. So please continue sitting there like a

331

sacrificial offering and let us finish this.' I turned back to the boys. 'So whose finger is it going to be? Let's see. A cop needs all his fingers – so much graft, so little time. A fire fighter probably more so – all those ropes and hoses. So who does that leave?'

Father Bill licked his lips. 'Mr Newhouse, I—'

'Russell.'

'Mr Russell, as a man of the cloth, I urge you to turn from vengeance. Vengeance is mine, saith the Lord.'

'What was He saying when you busted me up, and my apartment, and my car?'

'Two wrongs—'

'Three by my count,' I said. 'Plus bearing false witness on the part of Celeste here, which makes it four. Celeste, did I do something wrong to you other than want to stop fucking you?'

The brothers looked awful. It was hard not to feel for them. But Celeste was cooler. She always had that.

'I did wrong by you,' she said. 'As Jesus is my witness you never forced me to lie with you and commit sins. I confessed them and I've done penance.'

'And for bearing false witness?'

'Tomorrow. I'll do that tomorrow. First thing. Just understand, Russell, that my brothers meant no harm.'

'I'd hate to be in the same room when they mean it.'

'Because they believed me, because I was angry, because you. . . .'

'Wanted out.'

'I was hurt.'

'No more than I was, sweetheart. Were we counting wrongs? Isn't there a fifth? Dropping a dime on me to the district attorney when you gentlemen thought you could get away with it because Shushan is dead. Maybe he is, but his spirit liveth on. Which brings us to this evening's meat course, the little matter of whose finger is going to be sacrificed first.'

Father Bill stood up. Behind him Ira stood as well. The priest must have realized it. He sat heavily down on the green leather, resigned. 'Is there no other way?'

'Are you ready to pay the price Mr Shushan Cats demanded?'

The priest looked at his brothers. They looked at me.

I looked at Celeste. 'I still like you better without clothes,' I said.

'All right, then,' the priest said.

'You're ready?'

'Here?' he said, suddenly aware that a piece of him might suddenly disappear down a toilet, or remain locked away forever in a freezer along with the ice cubes and the silent steaks. 'Now?'

CHAPTER 37

Maybe I should have been angrier. Maybe I should have played it out further, taken the priest into the kitchen, placed his hand on the oak cutting board by the sink, brought out a cleaver – and then, only then, relented. But in the nether regions of my mind was the fear I might not relent at all. For fear of cutting off the priest's finger I cut off the game.

'Father Bill,' I said. 'Patrick, Monroe' – I wasn't precisely sure which was which – 'Celeste. We've just been through the murder of one good Irishman. I think we can do without the maiming of another.'

All at once the room was filled with expelled air – and the sour stench of stale beer. The Callinans must have fortified themselves before making their hejira to the penthouse of the Westbury Hotel. They were smiling, really smiling.

'Thank you,' Father Bill said. The other two said it together, as though in church: 'Thank you, Mr Newhouse.'

'Russell,' I said. 'But we do have some loose ends.'

The smiles drained from their faces like suds

from the bottom of a glass of Schlitz. Like Rheingold this was another brew that had over the years disappeared. *Schlitz – the beer that made Milwaukee famous*. That's how it was marketed. It was cheap. The Irish loved it.

Celeste came on again. 'Russell, please.'

'You three are going to pay for damage to my apartment. That's not much. There wasn't much to damage. Three hundred bucks. The car? After you broke it up the scavengers took the rest, so that's a total loss. Let's say twelve hundred. That's fifteen hundred bucks. Five hundred a piece. You're getting off easy.'

'No problem with that,' the fireman said. 'We can handle that.'

'Amen,' said the cop.

'But there's also that other little matter, which can't be so easily compensated. Any of you ever been beat up?' I didn't wait for an answer. They were Irish. Probably their father had been the first, then the nuns and priests. 'So you know it's not pleasant. Then there's another kind of violence in the matter of the DA, trying to hurt me by proxy when you figured I was in no position to hurt you back, or even to defend myself.'

'A big misunderstanding,' Father Bill said. 'If you'd let me explain.'

'No,' I said. 'No explanations. That would just make it worse, father. First off, I want you to come to terms with the fact that your little sister here is a woman. I don't want you ever to treat her badly because you've discovered she's not the Virgin Mary. Is that clear?'

They nodded.

'A hell of a woman, by the way. Second, I want you – all three of you – to give to charity.'

'Charity?' the priest said.

'Charity. I'll let you set the amount. But I want it to be every year for the rest of your lives. If there's a year that you don't give to charity, I'll know it, because at the end of every year, when you pay your taxes, you're going to send a note to my associate in the next room, Mr Justo Ocero, at this address, telling him how much you gave and to whom. I'll match that amount. But if I think it's too little for your income, too cheap, I'm going to go for the fingers again, with interest. Should that happen there won't be a chance to make amends. You won't be able to write another check and get out of it.'

'What kind of charity?' the fireman asked. 'Any kind?'

'Jewish?' the cop asked.

'Jewish, Catholic, Buddhist, animist. I don't care. Just so long as you do it. Think of it as penance, or absolution.'

'Only a priest may offer absolution, Mr Russell.'

'Good, then you can give them absolution, and yourself. Once a year. Can you give too much charity? No. Can you give too little? Yes. I won't accept too little.'

The fireman looked confused. 'How do we know,

if you don't mind, Mr New – Mr Russell, how much is too little?'

'You'll know when you try to pick your nose with a digit that isn't there,' I said. 'Number three.'

The brothers braced themselves. It was physical, as though they were preparing to take a blow.

'Number three is this. I'm going to forgive you for what you did, but from this day forward you owe me. Personally.'

'Owe you?' the cop said. He knew he might be called upon first. If I was the man he thought I was, he was going to be called upon. 'There's certain things, difficult. . . .'

'I don't care how difficult. You owe me. When I or a friend needs a favor, or a friends's sister's cleaning lady's lover, he needs a favor, you're there. Is that clear?'

'What kind of favor, Mr Newhouse?' the fireman asked.

'Whatever fucking favor I say,' I said. 'Are we understood, gentlemen?' Blank looks. 'You have to say it. Are we agreed on these terms, gentlemen? Yes or no?'

One by one they said it.

'Good, then we have an agreement. Now Celeste, Father Bill, Patrick, Monroe, I regret that my associates and I have an appointment in Chinatown, so as much as I'd like to sit and chat with you I've got business on Mott Street.' I stood, shook hands with each of the brothers.

Celeste kissed me, this time on the lips. 'You were great,' she said. 'You know, if ever. . . .'

'Absolutely,' I said. I put a fifty in her hand. 'Celeste, do me a favor and take your fine brothers out for a drink. My treat.'

Father Bill turned back at the door. '*Any* charity?'

'Any charity. Just make sure.'

'You're going to want a receipt?'

'I trust you, Father Bill,' I said. 'I trust you all.'

CHAPTER 38

Despite the chill I had Ira put the top down on the Caddy as we sailed downtown in traffic abnormally light for a Saturday night. The assassination seemed to have altered the face of the city. Few people were on the streets. Still, the movies on Forty-Second Street and in Times Square remained open: *The Ugly American, Charade, From Russia With Love, The Great Escape, Hud* and (with a block-long line) *PT-109,* starring Cliff Robertson as a wartime JFK; for those who didn't wish to be reminded of the news there was *Irma La Douce, Tom Jones, Bye-Bye Birdie, Flipper* and *Lassie's Great Adventure,* to say nothing of *King Kong vs Godzilla, The Slime People* and *It Happened At The World's Fair* with none other than Elvis Presley, plus Jerry Lewis in *The Nutty Professor.* Yet the streets that met Broadway were filling with theater-goers prepared to be delighted by Richard Burton in *Camelot* and to split a gut with Zero Mostel in *A Funny Thing Happened On The Way To The Forum,* along with less-certain results at *Stop The World – I Want to Get Off, Brigadoon* and *Oliver.* But beyond these pockets the streets themselves seemed somber, or perhaps only less frivolous. Even the panhandlers had disappeared. The murder of a president is not something people are prepared for, and Kennedy's successor, despite his decades in Congress, or because of them, was not a known quantity to the average New Yorker. Then there was the all but unspoken question: Who was behind it? Had Oswald acted alone? Was a foreign power involved, as the network television news anchors passively suggested with each new disclosure of the unbelievable details of Oswald's life – Marine, defector to Moscow, supporter of Fidel Castro – or was it all a right-wing conspiracy cooked up by the proto-fascist wizards of Dallas, or the Mafia, or. . . . No one knew. The shadow hanging over the city was not mourning. It was the uneasiness of the uninformed: uncertainty, doubt, suspicion, palpable fear.

As we drove down Fifth Avenue into the Village the normally buzzing streets were all but unpopulated save for a handful of young couples scurrying down the pavements outside the Church of the Ascension at Tenth Street and lonely young men carrying guitar cases strapped to their backs like centurions retreating behind their shields. A few disconsolate transvestites stood chattering in the cold at the corner of Eighth Street, the Village's main drag in both senses. At Sixth a squadron of Hell's Angels revved their Harleys. Further down an interracial couple, arm in arm, turned into the doorway of the massive apartment house at One

Fifth Avenue, the doorman showering spit on the pavement as he closed the glass door behind them.

'I was listening through the door,' Justo said practically under his breath from where he sat between Ira and me. 'Shushan, he would be proud. *Chinga*, you did it beautiful.'

'Yeah, yeah,' I said. 'Ira, if the president's dead or not we should have some music, right?'

The big man turned on the radio, which took a moment to warm up. This was pretty much the last of the tube radios. Micro-electronics were coming in. The remorseless march of technology would soon become the dominant factor of American life, ultimately to become a fetish whose roots lay in the space race with the Soviet Union, which the year before had beat the US to the moon. It was the dawn of a new age. I hardly noticed.

Hello mudda, hello fadda

'What the fuck music is that?' I said. We were coming to Washington Square, on the edges spilling with people who, from the way they clumped together, had probably gathered spontaneously. Over the gag song on the radio I could now hear the cacaphony of plucked strings and plaintive strummed chords that was the feeble public mourning of the young and the would-be young. Though I didn't quite share the views of Shushan Cats and Auro Sfangiullo regarding the now slain

341

president, neither had I cared much for the man. There was something wrong there that a glamorous wife and well-cut suits could not quite hide.

'That's Allan Sherman – it's a funny song about summer camp.'

'I've never been,' I said.

'Yeah, but it's funny,' Ira said. 'The kid is—'

'Change it back,' I said.

'But boss—'

'But boss nothing. It's not music.'

By this time the Miracles had disappeared from WABC and the Crystals were into their sweet driving lyrics, senseless drivel and pure longing at the same time. I suppose the song was about desire. No one who heard it, loved it and sung along really knew or cared. It was the nature of doo-wop: the lyrics could be in Estonian. Whatever 'Da Doo Ron Ron' was intended to signify, in 1963 its very meaninglessness was part of the secret handshake of a distinct and unfettered generation. Of course, we didn't know that – then.

'Boss,' Ira said as we stopped at the light.

'Listen to this guy, Justo. He's growing a mouth.'

'I'm entitled to my own opinion, ain't I?'

'Not while I'm in the car, Ira.'

'But . . .'

'Who's the boss, Ira?'

'You are, boss.'

'So suffer,' I said.

As we turned the corner I could see the park

was packed, maybe more than a thousand people, most of whom seemed to be armed with instruments: guitars, mandolins, banjos, zithers, harmonicas, concertinas, bongo drums. At school I'd mostly just tolerated the folk scene, flannel shirts, carefully torn jeans, bad haircuts, no haircuts. Now I felt an odd kinship with these lost souls who had seized upon a dying tradition – in 1963 rock was ascendant, jazz still hip, but folk was just plain goofy – to create a bridge to a simpler past.

These were the sons and daughters, grandsons and granddaughters of the Bhotke Society, of the Knights of Columbus, the Ancient Order of Hibernians and every other immigrant group in the city, the native-born generation having turned its collective back on the discredited culture of their parents – except for food, because tastes formed in childhood could not so easily be negated – to become *un*-hyphenated Americans. City of immigrants, New York was the center of the folk music renaissance, where a Robert Zimmerman become Bob Dylan, and where countless Goldmans and Manellis and O'Keefes identified not with the old country but with the makers of Appalachian ballads, Texas cowboy serenades and the labor hymns of Colorado miners.

'What are they so *chinga* sad about?' Justo asked no one.

'They lost a hero.'

'But he was a shit.'

343

'They don't know that,' I said. 'It's all image. We know only what we think we know.'

'*Chinga*,' Justo said. 'I hope Shushan ain't dead.'

A moment of silence while the Crystals rounded on. 'Me too,' I said, but for the first time wondered if I meant it. Uncertainty, doubt, not knowing what I knew or didn't – I had been living with this for a week.

But by the time we pulled up to the restaurant with the chickens and geese and who knows what other creatures hanging in the steamy window like crimson mummies, I realized that it didn't matter. Shushan Cats could be sitting at a table inside waiting for me, smiling, laughing, taking everything back, and I would still never know certainty again. One way or the other, I had busted out of my cocoon. I was in the world. Nothing would be as it was. I was coming to like it.

The three countermen greeted me with raised meat-cleavers, grinning over uniformly crooked brown teeth; it was clear I had replaced Shushan in their eyes. Yet if they had even noticed me before it was fleeting, just another face in Shushan's entourage – did everyone in New York now know who I was, and how did they know when I was just finding out?

Except for one large table in the rear hidden by a screen, where I could just about make out a small party sitting at a large round table, the restaurant was empty. Four waiters stood like a frieze at the rear wall, napkins on their sleeves,

344

smiling in welcome beneath an enormous Chinese poster celebrating a hydroelectric dam. It was eight-thirty on a Saturday night. Why was the restaurant empty? Were all lovers of Hunan cuisine in mourning for Shushan Cats?

Then Jimmy Wing came up, thin and durable as only an ascetic Chinese can be in a Carnaby Street suit, and ushered me to the table behind the screen, where Royce and the brothers were already settled down with an open bottle of Johnnie Walker Black, with them Jimmy's mute companion, Tommy, and an older Chinese who sat almost motionless, as though waiting for food to be brought to his lips.

'We took over the place for the evening,' Jimmy said, winking. 'Otherwise too noisy.'

CHAPTER 39

It was time to repay a debt, of course, which is why I had brought these two groups together, the yellow and the black, so they would get the bad news at the same time, lest they convince themselves – gangsters are no less paranoid than anyone else – that the other was receiving the long end of the stick. Immediately Jimmy Wing presented me in what I assumed to be Mandarin to the elderly gentlemen, who was introduced as Mr Sue. He may have been one of the Chinese at the funeral, or not.

'Mr Sue is my godfather,' Jimmy said.

'You mean . . .'

'No, I mean *my* godfather. As in godfather, not . . .'

'Not *godfather*,' I said.

'Yeah. Godfather, not *godfather*.' Jimmy released a sidelong smile. 'But, as it happens, Mr Sue is also not without a certain status in the Chinese community.'

'I understand.' I turned to Mr Sue. 'I'm honored to be in your presence, father.' I seem to have been using that word all day. But this father was no priest.

Not by accident do priests dress in black and white. Mr Sue's habit was a continuum, with no absolutes. His hair was a cloud of silvery wisps, his lips thin and dry under a salt-and-pepper mustache that gave him a slightly Latin American look, and his suit, shirt and tie were in various shades of grey, so that his pale face looked like it had been mounted on a granite plinth. His eyeglasses were silver, the lenses tinted with a touch of lead.

Jimmy translated. 'Son Wing – that would be me – has explained your situation, which is very difficult. In a few words, let me say that I and my associates will be pleased to see you in Chinatown, and to offer any assistance necessary should you require it. Or even wish for it. An old man like me can not last forever. I live in the hope the people whom I represent and your people will continue to share a common interest. Especially in these times, when nothing is certain even about what is certain, friendship is to be cherished.' After the translation – for all I know Mr Sue had expressed his opinion about the tripe-in-duck's-web soup – the gentleman gave his hand to the nonsyllabic Tommy, who pulled him slowly to his feet and walked him out the door, possibly to a waiting sedan chair.

'More food for us,' Jimmy said.

'You finished kissing up?' Royce said, apparently unhappy to be left in the back of the bus. 'We here to eat and talk, not to see no fucking Chinese movie.'

347

The food began to arrive, coming in stages, unordered, a series of gentle waves washing up intense Hunanese tastes, long smoking and simmering having electrified the flavors, all of them in calibrated degree and in bizarre combination sour, sweet, salty, bitter and hot – this at a time when Chinese cuisine even in New York was mostly chop suey. If last week's dinner was superb, this evening's was a feast of rolling flavors, one uncovering the next. The talk was less subtle. Royce had an agenda, and he was as candid about it as the Hunanese were in naming their signature dish *chou dofu*, which translates to 'stinking tofu.'

'I'd love to help you, man,' I said. 'But what you're asking for is not mine to share.'

'Mr Shushan ain't returning to the land of the living no time soon,' Royce said. 'You the heir.'

'Apparent. We don't even know if Shushan is . . . wherever. But I can make it easy for you, gentlemen. Say Shushan *is* alive. He could be, right?'

'Then where he be?'

'For the sake of argument say he is.'

'For the sake of argument,' Royce said with his mouth turned so far down his lips could have been a mustache.

'If so,' I said, 'then giving up any of *his* territory, even the small bit you ask for, is not mine to do. I can't hand over what isn't mine.'

'Assuming he alive.'

'Okay, now – once again for the sake of argument

348

– let's assume Mr Shushan Cats is no longer among the living. Let's just speculate.'

'Then you *would* be able to help us out, help an ally out,' Royce said. 'I mean, you don't help your friends, who you help? All we talking about is six blocks in Harlem. It's rightly ours. Power to the people and all that. We don't come into where white people live. You got to let us have what's ours. Specially if Mr Cats he dead.'

I thought: No, dummy, it's *Mistah Kurtz – he dead*. But there was no sense saying it. Shushan was probably the only gangster in New York who had ever been in a library, much less owned one. 'Eloquently spoken, Royce. But assuming Mr Cats *is* dead, then responsibility for these six blocks – fourteen actually, but who's counting? – would fall to me. They'd be mine.'

'Right on.'

'And I'd be a fool to give them up.'

The ensuing silence could be pierced with a chopstick.

'You saying you going to give our Chinee friend what he want but because we just a lot of uptown Negroes we in line for turd steak with pee gravy?'

I could feel Jimmy Wing's narrow eyes on me. 'When did I say I was parting with territory, either to benefit you or Jimmy or anyone else?'

'Everybody expect that, as a gesture,' Royce said.

I couldn't help but laugh. 'Doesn't it seem to you a gesture is just that? I don't mind making a gesture, Royce, but the nature of a gesture is that it isn't corporal' – I saw the doubt in his eyes – 'that it isn't something you can take to a bank or hide under a mattress. It's a display. It's like a mother's caress. It doesn't mean she wants to fuck you. It means that you're dear to her.'

'Why you on about mothers?' He looked to the three brothers for affirmation, and got it in three dull nods. 'Is you going to share the wealth with us Negroes or just with this greaseball chink here.'

The greaseball chink did not so much as lower an eyelid.

'Royce, my man,' I said. 'Jimmy likes that about as much as you like being called nigger.'

'I don't give a whore's pussy what he like.' If it wasn't real anger it was a good imitation.

Out of the corner of my eye I could see Ira, seated by the door, tensing. A big man like that, he moves in a room it's felt. Next to me Justo silently sucked his way through a pile of soft-shell crabs with honey-walnut sauce. I allowed myself a sigh. 'Tell me, Royce. You and the brothers, would you talk this way to Shushan Cats?'

He didn't like where this was going. 'If necessary.'

'But did you ever?'

'You not Mr Shushan.'

'Fucking right I'm not, and fucking lucky for you,' I said as quietly and slowly as I could. 'Shushan would have you belly up on the table in the time it takes to whistle the first bars of 'Take

These Chains From My Heart And Set Me Free.'
You know that?'

'You ain't Mr Shushan.'

'No, I'm more generous. Here's what's not going
to happen. In return for doing me a favor yesterday
in Little Italy I'm not going to move into your
operation in Harlem. I'm going to let you continue.
I'm also not going to be more angry than necessary regarding your little display of greed here.
What you did for me yesterday, and what Jimmy
here did, and what the members of a certain Jewish
society you never heard of did, those are in the
way of favors that friends do for friends. In case
you don't know it, Royce, friends don't charge
their friends for favors, because the moment they
do they cease being friends and all you have is a
business relationship. You know how things are in
business. They're not as gentle as they could be.
In the words of Auro Sfangiullo, what we would
have is disorganized crime. Lucky for me it's still
organized enough so that I could have sixty of
Auro's best *goombahs* in front of the Apollo Theater
in an hour. How much grass you going to sell
under those conditions? How many women are
going to be on the street? I'll fucking collapse every
business you have. Pass the noodles.'

It is amazing how much noise a group of men can
make simply eating. The verbal silence was subsumed
in a symphony of slurping, swallowing, chewing and
bumping into things reaching across the table. Beer
was poured, bottles clinking on glasses. The only

351

words we heard were Chinese: Jimmy Wing ordering the waiters to bring more.

'You a mean mo-fucker,' Royce said finally.

I smiled. 'It's for your own good. When you need a favor you know where to turn. Believe me, you want Shushan Cats for a friend.'

'Shushan? Man, he—'

'Royce, he could walk in the door any minute.'

'You sure of that?'

'Yes,' I lied. 'Absolutely.'

'How you know?'

'Think about it, you big buffalo. Day after tomorrow he's supposed to show up in court. If he doesn't show the district attorney himself is on record saying the defendant is buried somewhere in the pine barrens of New Jersey, or dumped out at sea off Montauk. In ten minutes the judge is going to dismiss the charges.'

'What happen he do come back?'

'I haven't the slightest idea, Royce. They may have to start the whole process again, or maybe they'll just pretend it never happened. I don't know. I do know that no one even looking like Mr Shushan Cats is going to be in that courtroom on Monday.'

'That be cool.'

'You know what else be cool?'

'What that?'

I signalled Justo, who wiped the anise sauce on his hands on a linen napkin and reached delicately into his shirt pocket, carefully avoiding contact with the lapel of his silk suit. He gave a check to Royce, who unfolded it.

'This be twenty-five gees.'

'Yeah, so?'

'Intense green, my man.'

It certainly was. In 1963 twenty-five thousand was roughly equivalent to a quarter million today.

'For a good cause.'

'But this much? Why you don't just give it to the man youself?'

I smiled as I thought Shushan might, a broad tooth-baring grin. Probably I failed. Shushan had large teeth, several of his molars capped with gold, giving his laughter added sparkle. 'Because I want *you* to give it to him. I want it to come from you.'

The brothers looked at one another, waiting for more. Finally Royce let it out. 'What the catch, man?'

'The catch is I want you guys to take part in this,' I said. 'I want you to be there when those redneck assholes try to bust up some little piccaninny trying to go to the wrong school in Selma, Alabama or people trying to register to vote in Philadelphia, Mississisippi, which activity you probably don't bother with up here – which is okay, because the right to vote also means the right not to, except that you probably voted for that schmuck Kennedy – or trying to get a tuna on toast at any drug store below the Mason-Dixon Line. I want you and the brothers to *be* down there, because with guys like you down there the heads going to be busted won't just be nappy ones.'

'I don't get it, Mr Russell.'

'You just got it. Now give it forward. In person.'

'How I going to find Dr Martin Luther King?' he asked.

It made me laugh. 'I think his current address is the Birmingham city jail.'

On the way out Jimmy Wing took my arm and whispered, 'You know, Mr Newhouse, the last thing on my mind would have been to ask anything for our help yesterday.'

The man fibbed well. 'Of course,' I said.

'Only if you could help us with Mr Sfangiullo. . . .'

'Of course.'

'There are issues. Sometimes Chinatown and Little Italy, they encroach. You know, issues of territory, accommodation. Good relations.'

'I'll see what I can do.'

'Mr Sue, he knew your dad.'

Did everyone know my father but me? 'How so?'

'Mr Sue has long been a major figure in Chinatown.'

'So you said.'

'In a case of mistaken identity – you know all Chinese look alike, right? – Mr Sue was arrested in a minor matter having to do with gambling.'

'How minor?'

'Major.'

'Where does my father come in?'

'Detective Newhouse, he sprung him.'

'Just like that?'

'Mr Cats asked him to see what he could do.'

Idly I wondered what else my father had done for Shushan in the years before he was kicked off the force. 'And Mr Sue remembers?'

'Mr Sue forgets nothing. Not to the bad, not to the good. And he remembers the sons of those who were kind to him.'

'He seems like a fine man.'

'In his time he was the most feared man in Chinatown,' Jimmy said. 'Now he is among the most respected. Maybe next year he will graduate to most loved.'

I clasped Jimmy's hand as we stepped outside. From within I could see Royce and the brothers still socking it away. 'Which I take it is your goal as well?'

'A long life opens the door to possibility.'

Inside the Cadillac Ira started the engine. Justo was already in the middle seat, the wide red door of the boat open in invitation. I removed the twenty still clipped by the wiper blade to the windshield. A night in November, it had grown cold. We put the top down, turned on the heat.

'Whatever you want on the radio, Ira,' I said.

He smiled under his thin mustache and leaned forward to turn it on. It took a moment to warm up.

'*¡El presidente está muerto. Viva el presidente!*'

As with the radio, a few seconds would pass before I realized Justo was not talking about

Lyndon Baines Johnson. With the sound of Ned Miller singing 'From A Jack To A King,' a country song that unexpectedly had crossed into pop, it came to me what I would lose if Shushan returned. I'm ashamed to say it but as the big Caddy sailed uptown I hoped he *was* dead. By noon the next day I would have my corpse, but it would not be that of Shushan Cats.

CHAPTER 40

As usual Ira preceded me into the suite to tuck me in. This was what he called it. He just wanted to make sure, he had been trained to make sure, there would be no surprises for his boss when he opened the door. That night there was, but it was pleasant. A woman's black lace bra and panties, both generously sized, lay on the green couch opposite the door. Ira took one look and decamped.

When I awoke the next morning Darcie was serving me breakfast on a tray. Never in my life had I eaten a complete Ozzie-and-Harriet breakfast. Now I was having it in bed.

'You sleep well, honey?'

'Um.'

'It's after ten,' she said, a gentle tone of maternal reproach in her voice. I suppose men who had mothers never need to hear that, never need to take a nipple between their lips – maybe they did or didn't do it, but they didn't *need* it – never took pleasure in the yielding flesh of a woman old enough to be their mother. 'I bought orange marmalade, or you could have raspberry jam, or both. You want another cup of coffee, Russy?'

While I sat up against the pillows happily munching I heard the doorbell ring. Half asleep, it meant nothing. Then, half-awake, everything. Who was this woman lulling me into a sense of well-being? For all that I had fucked her she was a stranger about whom I knew little and, it shocked me to realize, trusted less. Why had the doorbell rung without a call from the desk clerks below to ask if someone could come up? Was it some neighbor asking to borrow a cup of sugar? Bullshit it was. I was out of bed in an instant, looking for something, anything. There was a gun and a collection of baseball bats upstairs, but I had depended on Ira for protection. For all I knew the entire Tinti clan was in the next room, and the closest thing I had to a weapon was my dick.

Quietly I approached the door and tried to hear over the sound of the television who it was. Ever since the assassination televisions remained on all over the city, probably all over the country. At night from my window the surrounding apartment house windows radiated an eerie blue-white. Now, straining to hear who the bitch had let in all I could hear was a young newscaster named Dan Rather telling us that Lee Harvey Oswald would soon be transferred from the basement of a Dallas police station to county jail. Killing a president got you only county jail? I wondered what killing the heir to Shushan Cats would get you. But it soon became clear that I was not going to be the victim that day.

It was not the Tintis who had gotten past the security downstairs but Terri Cats. Of course. Why should they even bother to call to say she was coming up? She had a key. She knew all the desk clerks, had for years. Hurriedly I got into a red silk robe from Shushan's closet and stepped out into the living room.

'Well, well,' Terri said. 'The young lion.'

'Just the zoo kind.'

'Not from what I hear,' she said, rising to kiss me on both cheeks like a French sister-in-law in those movies I loved at the Eighth Street Cinema. 'God, Russell, you smell like pussy.'

'There may be a reason for that,' I said.

The reason reentered from the kitchen with a cup of coffee and handed it to Terri. I had almost reached for it.

'I'll get yours, sweetheart,' Darcie said, then turned to Terri. 'The tough guy here takes it black.'

It occurred to me Darcie had not asked how our guest wanted hers. 'You okay?' I asked.

'Compared to what?'

'Compared to a couple of days ago. The whole country's in sackcloth and ashes.' I pointed to the television, where a crowd of reporters was waiting to shout questions at Lee Harvey Oswald in what would go down in history as the world's most viewed perp walk. 'In case you didn't notice.'

'You know what?' Terri said, shrugging her

delicate shoulders for emphasis. 'Every day half a million people die in this country alone, a good many of them in agony. Do you really think I'm going to sweat the death of a fucking politician?'

Although I'd felt much the same, the harshness of its expression was not so much unpleasant as personal: I was being reprimanded for a softy. 'A death's a death.'

'He fucking had it coming,' she said. 'I told you he wanted to do good. He just never got around to it. Kennedy was a fraud.'

'Aren't we all?'

'Oh, for crying out loud, Russell,' she said. 'Yes, we all create illusions for other people to believe, and for us as well. But when it comes to serious stuff – love, hate, work, things that matter – it helps when we know the difference. In my professional opinion, kid, the man didn't even know he was a fraud. The new president, that's a whole different story. He's the most real president since Truman. You're going to see things happen, not just talked about.'

'Like.'

'War, peace, that kind of thing. He's going to do things, some good, some bad, maybe even tragic. But he's not the kind of jerk-off that invades Cuba with three CIA guys and two hundred pissed off out-of-shape ex-country club types who want their cigars back. If we have a war, Johnson is the kind of guy who is going to unleash the dogs. And I wouldn't be surprised if he's the president that changes the black-white equation in this country.'

'He's a Texan.'

'Exactly,' Terri said. 'You think a Yankee is going to get in there and bang heads in the South? No, Johnson is going to prove himself by out civil-rightsing the civil rightsers. It's the way of the world. Look at you. Last week you were a kid who lived in books. Now you have one of the world's biggest private libraries upstairs and I'll bet you haven't cracked one book in it.'

My God, I thought. She's right. 'I've been busy.'

'Yeah,' she said, winking. 'I heard.'

Darcie handed me a fresh cup of coffee, then sat close to Terri and put her head on her shoulder. Terri reached around and began stroking Darcie's back under her robe. Darcie made a noise I had not heard. It wasn't a loud shudder or the muted orgasmic scream that went off like a distant siren, growing louder as she grew closer. It was a purr.

'What the fuck is that, Russell?'

'What the fuck is what?'

Darcie shifted to look as Terri pointed.

This was worse than junior high. From under the soft folds of Shushan's red silk robe a part of me was pointing back.

'Tsk, tsk,' Terri said.

If she was going to say something to further humiliate me I'll never know what it was, because just at that moment a muffled shot exploded softly in the room, like a gun fired under a down pillow, followed by sounds of a struggle, men hollering, and Dan Rather shouting in excitement, 'This is unbelievable. It appears Lee Harvey Oswald has been shot. I repeat. Lee Harvey Oswald, accused assassin of President Kennedy, has been shot live on tv.'

Probably every conversation in America stopped at that moment, as ours did, but mixed with the shock I shared in seeing a second murder of national proportions only two days after the first was my own special shock – of recognition. 'My God,' I said aloud to myself. 'I know that man. That's Jack—' I searched my memory for the name. 'That's Jack Ruby!'

'Who's Jack Ruby?' Terri asked.

Fear flushed through me. 'Shushan's friend,' I said. 'He was just here.'

CHAPTER 41

With serpentine grace Terri extricated herself from Darcie, rose silently from the couch and switched off the set. Standing there she seemed to replace Dan Rather, Lee Oswald, Jack Ruby, everything. 'Shushan *knew* this guy?'

'Knew?'

'Knew, knows. I'm asking you a direct question, sweet-face. I'm his sister. I want to know.'

I looked to Darcie. She took the hint and went straight to the bedroom and shut the door. 'It could be his double.'

'With the same name? They just said it. Jack Ruby.'

'I don't know.'

Terri came and sat beside me so that I could smell more than her perfume – which was, however inappropriately, *Joy*. It could just as well have been *Fear*. Her face an inch from mine, she fixed me with her eyes. I could hear her swallow, almost feel it. 'Russell, listen to me. Listen carefully. This is trouble.'

'It doesn't have to be,' I said, not believing it.

'This guy Jack Ruby, he probably knows two thousand people. Think about it. Even the Dallas cops knew him, know him. They let him get into the room. They let him get close enough to shoot. Not everybody he knows, who knows him, is going to be implica– '

Terri raised her finger to my mouth.

Despite my fear I wanted to feel it *in* my mouth. 'It means nothing,' I said.

She pressed her finger hard on my lips. 'We don't know what it means. We probably can't know. Not all of it. But believe me, sweet-face, this is not good.' Although it seemed impossible, she drew closer. I could see the fine peach fuzz on her cheek, the smudge of mascara where she had been a bit less than exact, the flecks of gold in her brown eyes. 'What the fuck do you know about this?'

'Nothing, I swear.'

'Where's my brother?' she said. It was not a question but a threat. Then a cry of desperation: *'Where's Shushan?'*

'I don't know,' I whispered. 'Maybe dead.'

'Maybe,' she said slowly, 'not.'

'I just don't know.'

With that the toughest woman I had ever met dissolved onto my shoulder in tears. They poured down her face and onto my neck, then darkened the red silk of my robe – Shushan's robe. She wept for what seemed like an hour. Probably it was only minutes. Eventually Darcie came out – she must have heard the sobbing – and took up a position on Terri's other side, hugging her until they wept together, all three of us a human sandwich of confusion, doubt, fear, despair. We might have remained that way all afternoon but for the phone.

It was the front desk. 'Mr Newhouse, sorry to disturb you, but there's a man downstairs wants to come up.'

'Does he have a name?'

'A lot of names. Says you know him. He's a dentist.'

CHAPTER 42

This was expected, but not so soon, not mere moments after the assassin of John F. Kennedy – the alleged assassin: we would never know – was himself murdered on network television by a man I had met. I had thought him a clown. Maybe he was. But unlike Oswald, who was declared dead at the same hospital Kennedy's lifeless body had been delivered to two days earlier, there was no doubt of Jack Ruby's guilt. We had all seen him do it.

Or heard. 'On the radio as I was parking,' Feivel (Franklin) said, sweat beading on his brow and dripping into his big eyes so that he had to remove his rimless glasses and mop them with the white handkerchief that always stood like a ready flag of surrender in his breast pocket. Probably he had never thought of it as anything other than decoration, as though any of us was immune to tears. 'There's parking on the street. Sunday. The only day, aside from holidays, you can park free. I'm just backing in, I heard it. The man who killed the president is killed.'

'A tragedy,' I said.

'A big mess,' he said. He sat where I pointed, on the green couch whose back was to the door, his long frame folding in slow-motion like a mournful concertina. He wore a brown suit, a figured tan tie of some sort of artificial silk, and between his brown shoes and the one-inch cuff of his trousers thin brown socks with white clocks embossed on them.

After Darcie, dressed only in a shimmering silver robe – apparently compensated companions traveled prepared – served him a cup of coffee, I signaled her to join Terri in the bedroom. I could still hear sobbing through the door. Certainly Feivel (Franklin) could as well. He had the good sense not to ask. Maybe he thought I was twice the man I was. One bedroom, two women. I caught him peering at the other doors – who knew how many women I had in the place? 'Nice digs,' he said.

'Digs?'

'You know—'

'Yeah, dat's da way gangstahs tawk, eh?'

'I mean no disrespect.'

'None taken,' I said. 'Coffee just right?'

He probably would have nodded in satisfaction to a cup full of hot piss. He sipped. 'This Jack Ruby, you don't think he's . . .'

'Oh, he is.'

'He doesn't have to be. What kind of name is Ruby?'

'Made up,' I said.

'Made up?'

'Shortened from Rubinstein probably,' I said. 'That's just a guess.'

'I was thinking the same, Mr Newhouse.'

'I was Russell two weeks ago.'

'Time changes people.'

'So which is it, Feivel or Franklin?'

'Whatever you like.'

'Rubashkin or Robinson?'

'It's legally changed,' he said, still sweating. He must have had glands like sacks. 'Cost three hundred and seventy-five smackers.' He reconsidered. 'Dollars. People call me what they like. I can't get a court order against that. Legally is one thing.' He sipped again. There couldn't be much left in the cup. 'So you think, you're sure—'

'He's a Jew, Feivel.'

'He doesn't have to be.'

'Did you see his face?'

'I heard it on the radio.'

'I could turn on the television,' I said with no such intention. If I never saw Jack Ruby's face again I would be content. All I could do was see it, without a television. 'He's a Jew, trust me.'

'What do you think? It's bad, right?'

'For the Jews?'

'For the Jews.'

'It was pretty bad for Lee Harvey Oswald.' My visitor didn't react. 'That was a joke.'

He nodded avidly. 'I get it.'

'You worry about bad for the Jews, good for the Jews?'

'Doesn't everyone? I mean, every Jew?'

'I don't know, Feivel. But I know why you're here.'

'You said to come. If it's the wrong time – my God it's probably the wrong time.' His eyes went to the bedroom door. 'I mean, with the killing, and the president, and . . .'

'Feivel, stop sweating,' I said. 'You're among friends. I'm a paid up member of the Bhotke Society, isn't that right?'

'Absolutely. Mr Shushan Cats too.'

'Be that as it may, Feivel, you have nothing to fear. You brought out half the society to Mulberry Street on Friday. You did good.'

'The others, some of them had to work. And some are religious – on a Friday, before the Sabbath. It's hard for them.'

'You did good. Don't worry about it.'

'The important thing is we demonstrated our support for a fellow member.'

'Believe me, Feivel, if Shushan himself had been there he would have been impressed.'

'Any time,' he said. 'Any place. Whatever you need, the Bhotke Young Men's Society is with you. Like we say, from birth to death.' His face dropped. 'Not that I'm suggesting. . . .'

'Don't sweat it,' I said.

'It's a chronic condition, Mr Newhouse. In the summer I'm like a bathhouse. Even in November I can't stop my body from—'

I left him to go into the bedroom to get my wallet. Both women were stretched out on the sheets I had so recently stained with Darcie. Now the big blonde held Terri in her arms as she continued to sob, softly now, almost beyond hearing, her chest heaving but making little sound. I left the wallet and came back to see Feivel standing, looking at the Jimmy Ernst on the wall.

'It's a black painting,' he said. 'All in black. Different colors of black.'

'We pride ourselves on the appropriate art for every occasion,' I said. 'Feival, on your way out, I want you to have this check.'

'Oh, there's no need for that. I did what I could. As president of the society that's my job.'

'It's not for you, dummy. It's for the society. I want you to arrange a memorial for Shushan.'

'He's dead then?'

'I haven't the slightest idea, but since we may never know it seemed to me only right that we should somehow mark his presence among us with a stone. I checked – there's nothing in Jewish law that says we can't. We just shouldn't carve on it *in memorium* or put on a date of death, because maybe he's not.'

'Maybe he's not?'

'Nobody knows,' I said.

Feival unfolded the check. 'This is one big stone. I don't know if they have a stone this big, or if Beth David would allow it.'

'Feivel, remind me not to let you work on my teeth. Twenty-five thousand dollars is not what I

370

want you to spend on the stone. I don't know. Spend five hundred. The rest I want you and the Bhotke Society to find a charity, something worthwhile, where it will do good. Tell whoever it is if they use it well there will be more every year on the anniversary of Shushan's disappearance. Plenty more. But it has to be a good cause.'

'A yeshiva?'

'What else you got?'

'Hospitals, libraries.'

'More personal.'

'I'd have to think,' he said, looking again down at the check. As with the check for Dr King, it was a serious sum of money in 1963. 'Maybe we could plant a grove in Israel. For those from Bhotke who died in the camps.'

'They're dead.'

'They should be remembered. It could be a whole forest. Something substantial.'

I'd hoped the dentist would bring it up, so I wouldn't have to reveal an emotion I took care to conceal. 'An orphanage,' I said. 'Something for kids who are alone.'

'An orphanage.'

'That's a good idea, Feivel. I'm glad you thought of it.'

After pushing him out the door I went through the bedroom – both women were sleeping now, Darcie snoring softly like a slipper dragged rhythmically across a sandy floor – and climbed to the silence of Shushan's penthouse, then entered his

371

office. I opened the file cabinet where I had discovered my father's employment record, the drawer containing Shushan's arsenal of Louisville Sluggers. They seemed to be dozing there, waiting for their owner to take them out. In the toilet I opened my red robe and pissed for what seemed like an eternity into the spotless black porcelain bowl as I re-examined the brightly lit painting opposite that I had seen – whether copy or original – so many times at the Frick down the street. I flushed and left Georges de la Tour to return downstairs. Exhausted, I lay beside the two women, Terri again the meat in a human sandwich, and joined them in the surcease of sleep.

At some point – it was dark – I woke to the sound of subtle activity beside me, and opened my eyes. I had always been curious about what lesbians did. It was beautiful in its way, lyrical almost, a velvety sliding, totally muliebricious, uncompromised by the requirements of an architecture God or nature had designed. It seemed so much more intimate than anything I had ever done with a woman, trust replacing thrust, a purity of endless moaning. Though I understood I might be more than a spectator – Darcie proffered a smiling glance of welcome while Terri's face was hidden between her thighs – I was emotionally unable. Having dreamed of Terri Cats for two weeks, shuddered at her touch, I could not bring myself to make a move in her direction: circumstance had knocked the testosterone clear out of me.

When the phone rang I grabbed at it, the two women ignoring the interruption as they were content to ignore me.

It was Fritzi. 'Russell?'

'The same.'

'What are you doing tomorrow morning, my boy?'

'I don't know,' I said. 'Depends who gets killed next.'

'What?'

'Kennedy, Oswald. Maybe they'll take out Jack Ruby. Who knows?'

'Who cares? Tomorrow Shushan's trial opens.'

'Shushan who?'

'Don't play with me, Russell.'

'How can they have a trial if he's . . . gone?'

'They can't,' Fritzi said with some finality. 'That's why I need you there.'

The women were writhing beside me like fecund snakes, the high smell of female lust filling the room like an acidulous cloud. 'Fritzi, I have to take Shushan's place in jail as well – is that what you're telling me?'

He laughed. 'Russell, listen to me. Are you alone?'

'More than I've ever been.'

'What am I hearing?'

'Hamsters,' I said. 'I always wanted some as a kid.'

'Good, good,' Fritzi said. 'I'll pick you up, tomorrow morning at eight. Wear a dark suit, dark tie, white shirt. Shave.'

'I don't have to be there.'

'My boy, listen. The judge will note there is no defendant. She—'

'It's a lady judge?'

'It's 1963. They can vote too.'

'Hell of a year so far. Go on.'

'Her honor will note there is no defendant, and may make any number of decisions. She can vacate the indictment. I'll motion for that. *Hopt v. Utah 110 US 574, 28 L Ed 262, 4 S Ct 202 (1884)*. She may go for it. There is such a thing as the Fourteenth Amendment. No defendant, no due process. But considering the newspaper interest – there will be reporters, a lot of them – it's likely she'll adjourn for a month, two if we're lucky. She can't adjourn indefinitely, of course. But that will take the pressure off for a while.'

'What pressure, Fritzi? The man is either dead or disappeared.'

'Listen to me, legal eagle. Assume that some time in the future Shushan *re*-appears. Should this trial be concluded it can not be reopened.'

The thought chilled me. I had handed out Shushan's money like sticks of gum, sat in his place with Auro Sfangiullo, fucked his mistress – and almost fucked his sister. 'You're telling me Shushan is alive?'

Silence. 'My boy, I honestly don't know. My job, one way or another, is to defend my client. I'm on retainer. If Shushan should come back some time in the future he will have beaten the district attorney. The feds may go after him, of course, but we'll blow up that bridge when we come to it. Of course, if he never comes back, nothing is lost but my fees which, considerable as they are, are not much to a man of Shushan's wealth – of your wealth, Russell.'

'Tell me again why I have to show up at the courthouse?'

'It looks better. Here before the judge is the very man who as Shushan's designated heir is already running the family business, as it were. I can call you to the stand and ask you to state if you have spent Shushan's money, if you have taken steps – we need not specify – to run his business. If the judge asks if you consider Shushan to be alive, what will you say?'

'That I don't know one way or the other.'

'But that you are working on the assumption he is not among the living.'

'I just paid for a monument at Beth David.'

'Beth David?'

'It's a cemetery. Just a monument, no date of death.'

'Excellent, excellent,' Fritzi said. It was as though he had just bit into an especially tender and flavorful piece of meat.

I could almost hear him salivate. 'And if I don't come? If I don't want to be in the papers more than I have to? Fritzi, believe it or not, some of us don't want to be on the front page of the *Daily Mirror*. You know what, I've been called Maniac Brainiac once too often.'

'Believe me, the reporters *will* be there, because that's what they do. But the timing couldn't be more favorable. It couldn't be better if we'd planned it. Lad, this whole week every paper in New York, hell, in the world, will be exclusively devoted to Kennedy, Johnson, Oswald and what's-his-face.'

'Jack Ruby,' I said.

CHAPTER 43

Terri had zero interest in being in court; Darcie less. I felt the same, but considering that Fritzi had been there for me, springing me from the clutches of an assistant district attorney who did not have my best interests at heart, I would be there for him. And perhaps for Shushan. Dead, alive or simply unclassifiable, Shushan Cats had changed my life. Terri was right: books, which had been all, were now merely a pleasant memory, a backdrop, a frame of reference. My adventures in literature could not hold a candle to my adventures in Little Italy, in Chinatown, at the Westbury. Whether purposely or not, I had read to experience the world through the eyes of others. I was now experiencing it through my own, to say nothing of other parts of my anatomy. Thus it was with some reluctance that I rose from what had become a triple bed, washed, shaved, put on a fresh white shirt still in its wrapper – monogrammed at the right cuff *RN* – a dark tie, and a charcoal-gray cashmere suit from Shushan's closet that Miguel has magically altered to fit. I could not however walk even a yard in Shushan's shoes. I had my own, a full complement of them, in black and russet and gray suede. Thus attired for court I slipped a brown crocodile wallet filled with cash – there was a mountain of it in the safe upstairs – into the inside breast pocket of my suit, picked up my key and – for the first time unaccompanied by either Justo or Ira, whose day off it was, stepped into the brass-lined elevator, greeted the two desk clerks and burst from my cocoon onto East Sixty-Third Street. Alone.

Though I had been on my own all my life, being alone was something else. After being accompanied, protected, part of something, solitude was a heady experience. The day was clear, but not this clear: I had never seen so clearly. Every dot of color, every freshet of aroma, every note of traffic came to me as a gift.

At just before eight in the morning the Upper East Side was the picture of probity, civility, order. Norman Rockwell, whose cover illustrations defined the character of the *Saturday Evening Post*, would have painted the neighborhood as a crisply fashionable utopia – urbane, moderate, calm – where all the doormen saluted and all the children were safe, and everyone was so damn good-looking. A few leaves remained on the slender gingko trees planted every twenty feet or so, tiny older women in tailored coats walked their tiny older dogs in tailored coats, dark nannies pushed prams carrying pale infants, and bankers and admen, editors and lawyers stepped gingerly out of the brownstones that adjoined the Westbury and waved down cabs – a good many in those days still roomy eighteen-foot Checkers – or made for the subway on Lexington a block east. Here and there a school child could be seen waiting with his tall, impossibly thin mother for a tiny yellow van, and a bluff cop would pass on foot patrol, a rarity in the city but mandated here in its richest neighborhood. It was almost forty degrees, warm this early in the morning for November, but I would have been coatless in a snowstorm: other than the ratty leather jacket – it had been well used when I acquired it at a thrift shop – that I had worn when first I had come to reside at the Westbury – had it been only days? – I owned no coat. Because I normally went from the hotel garage to the Eldorado and then only a step from the car to my destination – we parked where we wished – I'd never needed one. I made a note to stop at Trippler after court. According to Justo, Shushan liked their winter coats, traditional and warm, better than Brooks. Madison at Forty-Sixth, a stroll from Nat Sherman's where I might buy a cigar, or a box. It was all so easy. *An overcoat, sir? Something in cashmere to go with the gentleman's suit? Will that be check or charge, sir? Cash? Certainly, sir. Will the gentleman be wearing the item, or shall we have it wrapped?* Hand-stitching every millimeter, Miguel would take weeks making a coat. The unseasonably warm weather couldn't last that long. While at Trippler

I might get a tie for Justo, something a bit less flashy than the white silk ribbons he wore habitually with his dark shirts. And at Nat Sherman's a box of Churchills for Ira. Maybe a box of candy for Myra. Flying down Madison in the Cadillac I had noticed tiny shops with *chocolatière* in their names. And jewelers, of course. Maybe something for Darcie who, compensated or not, gave me such pleasure, and for Terri, who gave me such delicious pain. Celeste deserved something too. And I did as well: I didn't own a watch. I was wearing one of Shushan's. I looked down at it now – 8:01. Gold, Audemars Piguet. Probably a good one. But not my taste exactly. Maybe I would pick out a watch too. Hell, after the brief session at court maybe I would walk all the way uptown, window shopping, or actually shopping. I hadn't taken a long walk in weeks. I didn't miss the subway, but those long walks had always made me feel on the edge of something exciting. I wanted that again. Who knows whom I would meet, what I would see, consider, buy. According to Justo if I wished I could write a check for a three-story brownstone just like that. I could fly south to Florida or the Caribbean – but since Kennedy's embargo not to Cuba, although Justo explained this might be achieved through Mexico, my passport unstamped. I'd need a passport though. There was a passport office at Radio City. I wondered what was playing at the Music Hall, probably still *It's a Mad Mad Mad Mad World*, and the floorshow with all those long-legged dancers. Two weeks before I made it a point to see only European films – Truffault, and Antonioni, that crowd – and now I was considering sitting through a kitschy Hollywood comedy in garish color on a screen as big as my ego. Of course two weeks ago it was critical that I present myself to the world, and to myself, as a bona fide intellectual. Now I had nothing to prove, neither to the world nor myself. Two young women passed, models maybe, or stewardesses – we didn't call them flight attendants then – or maybe call girls; one looked back. I gave her a wink, and knew I could have her, or a hundred like her, and I considered calling to her – 'Hey, miss! Did you drop this?' – but I didn't need to remove my handkerchief from my breast pocket and wave it. I didn't need to chase after skirts. I didn't need to –

A long blast of automobile horn brought me to earth.

It was Fritzi's limousine. I had never seen it in the light of day, and assumed it was his. What I had thought was black was deep blue, its top sheathed in crenellated black vinyl, a luxury treatment just beginning to appear. For all I knew this was not Fritzi's limo at all. Hadn't Shushan stepped into a car and vanished from the face of the earth? I hesitated, pulling a cigarette out of my pocket – I had learned from Shushan never to expose the pack unless you were offering them around – and lit it with a gold Zippo marked USMC under an embossed globe and anchor that had been in the top drawer of Shushan's bedside bureau, along with a couple of cartons of Luckies, an assortment of Havanas and an unframed photo of Shushan as a young boy. Idly I wondered why the picture was inside the drawer rather than on the dresser with the others, where it could be viewed. The horn sounded again.

The limo's rear door opened.

If I had any questions regarding why Shushan did things one way or the other, I could have had my answers on the spot. 'Hey, Russy, you want an engraved invitation?' Shushan said loudly and too casually as he leaned out the open door. 'Wait much longer you'll miss seeing me convicted.'

CHAPTER 44

With Fritzi taking up the entire back seat I perched opposite Shushan and said . . . nothing. Of substance Shushan said as little. He commented on my suit – 'We got the same taste, I got one just like it,' to which I replied, 'Not any more' – and on how much I'd 'filled out' (how much could that have been in a week?) and what was I reading, to which all I could manage was a shrug. Shushan had been busier, having used his 'time at airports' (he left it at that) to plow through Philip Roth's *Goodbye, Columbus*, *The Stranger* 'by that French guy, and partways through a book by JD Salinger called *Franny and Zooey*, very talented but tied up in himself, self-indulgent like Esther would say. I liked the Kaymus more. Very serious.'

'Cahmuh,' I said.

'Gezundheit.'

'It's pronounced—'

'You know, kid, I got such good reports about you, and then you go and act like you're twenty years old and correcting your uneducated old man.'

'I never did.'

'I don't mean about him. Let me tell you something, kid. Never correct somebody while wearing his suit.'

'It's not your suit,' I said. 'It's my suit. It doesn't fit Shushan Cats anymore. It fits Russell Newhouse.'

'Yeah, Russell Casanova.'

'You've been talking to Justo *and* Auro Sfangiullo. I've been under observation for a week, is that it?'

He laughed. 'Not exactly. The earth doesn't go in an orbit around you, you know. Nah, I spoke to Justo yesterday around seven on the business picture. *Il dottore*, he was kind enough to visit me later the same night.'

'Where?'

'The Sherry-Netherland. It's a hotel.'

'I know it's a hotel.'

'I didn't want to bomb in on you unannounced. Maybe for you Darcie would be a problem. Me, I'm comfortable.'

'You don't call this bombing in?'

'Auro says you are one impressive little gangster.'

'I'm as much a gangster as you are a. . . .'

'A what?'

I had almost said *intellectual*. What was I so angry about, that Shushan Cats was alive and still reading books? That I was alive and wasn't? This man had changed my life, probably for the better. And even if the change were not permanent, as if anything could be – things seemed to moving pretty fast in

November of 1963 – resenting Shushan's return was tantamount to wishing him dead. Dead, I realized, was the key. I wasn't angry at his return. I was angry at his departure. 'You know how many people cried that you were . . . gone?'

He laughed. 'Fewer than those who celebrated.'

'Where the hell were you?'

He laughed again, deeper, a rolling chuckle. 'My mother, of blessed memory, she liked to use that tone. *Shushi, darling boy, I was all night up with worrying.* She got used to it. Maybe you should too.'

'You plan on doing this a lot?'

'I don't do much in the way of planning,' he said, serious now. 'But if it should happen, let's say if Fritzi fucks up in court, I might be gone for a while.'

Fritzi took the floor with a stage cough. 'I absolutely guarantee that will not be the case,' he said, full of himself as ever. 'Ninety-three percent.'

Both Shushan and I looked at him.

'That is, better than ninety percent, but not quite one hundred. For one hundred I'd have to bribe the judge.'

'*Nu?*' Shushan said.

'Her Honor Myrtle Went—'

'Went?'

'That is her name, lad. Judge Went, I am afraid, is not susceptible to the usual blandishments.'

'You tried the *un*usual?' Shushan asked, his brows arching.

'An individual close to her honor touched on the subject of a federal judgeship. Judge Went let it be known she was happy in the Supreme Court of the State of New York. She's due a federal position anyway. She knows it. I suppose she can wait.'

'While Shushan rots in prison?' I said. 'What about the jurors?' Was this me? What next, threatening witnesses? How far had I come in a week? 'Ninety-three percent, Fritzi, is not very solid.'

'Whoa, kid,' Shushan said. 'Before you go and start shooting up the courtroom, I'm satisfied with fifty percent. For a lawyer, that's a good number. And even if we lose we got an appeal. This is America, not Russia. Despite the Kennedys – good news, there's only Bobby left – who have zero respect for the Bill of Rights, we have an independent judiciary and I have friends in . . . all kinds of places. Besides, nobody's rotting in jail. Hey, how much can they sock me for, with good behavior?'

'Seventeen months,' Fritzi said. 'Max.'

'Believe me, Russy, I'm touched by your concern, but frankly I could use a vacation. I go away you can send me five hardbound books a week – that's state regulation, right Fritzi?'

'Plus no limit on paperbacks and magazines.'

'So I can catch up. For instance, I could read everything by Monsieur Kaymus – right, kid?'

'Point made. I apologize.'

'What do you think, I'm back so you're going to return to that shit-hole apartment on Eastern Parkway – by the way, one day that's going to be prime real estate; we should probably buy there, especially near the museum and the library. You know where I mean, a left off Flatbush Avenue when you come to the arch?'

'I was just there.'

'Terrific old apartment houses, as good as Park Avenue. Really worth a shot. Collect rent for thirty years and then take them condo. Where was I? Oh yeah, you being thrown out in the cold. Look, kid, I wouldn't do that to a stranger. You're like my own blood.'

'Thank you, Shushan. I don't know what I was thinking.'

'You were thinking you like cashmere, you like Darcie – she's something, that broad – and you like long red Eldorado convertibles. Hey, I don't blame you. But nobody's taking that away. Wherever I am, Shushan Cats will make sure you're okay. You did fantastic. I'm proud of you.' He turned away. 'Fritzi. . . .'

'Tell him after court,' the lawyer said. 'You do not want an emotional scene in a public forum.'

'I think he should know now.'

'Trust me, Shushan,' Fritzi said. 'This waited a long time. It can wait another hour.'

'Tell me what?'

'Be patient, lad,' Fritzi said, his German consonants nearly overcoming his British vowels.

'*Pee bayshent, glaad* yourself. What's the big secret?'

'Fritzi is right,' Shushan said. 'Anyway, we're here.'

387

Outside the courthouse – it was the same building to which two NYPD detectives had escorted me only days before – stood a small mob of photographers, some still armed with the ancient Speed Graphics that would soon be replaced by downsized .35 mm single-lens reflex cameras and these by digital gizmos the size of a pack of cards. Though it was broad daylight enough flashes went off to illuminate a movie set as Fritzi and I walked tight on either side of Shushan. In the brightness I now noticed that Shushan had acquired a tan. It seemed even deeper set off by his pale blue silk tie and light gray suit. Like me he was coatless. Fritzi on the other hand was layered in vest, suit and topcoat replete with velvet collar, all topped by a dove-gray Homburg that must have been custom made for his swollen head. In his hand he carried a briefcase so small compared to his considerable bulk it was hard to believe these were all the papers necessary to Shushan's defense. Under his other arm was a tightly rolled umbrella – was he planning to use *that* in court? As we got past the photographers, Shushan walking as tall as his five-seven could manage and smiling like a bronzed Montgomery Clift about to receive an award, a confetti of questions flew up out of the compact mob of reporters behind the lensmen:

'Hey, Shoeshine – you carrying a toothbrush?'

'Mr Cats, are you innocent again?'

'Fritzi, can you stop the parade a minute so we can ask some—'

Shushan stopped, we with him. 'Gentlemen,' he said slowly and clearly, and almost in a whisper – the actor's trick of compelling an audience to pipe down lest they miss something. 'The district attorney thinks he can stop an individual from providing security for another individual, or individuals. Maybe as a young man I skated a little bit too close to the edge, but in today's case what we have is the authorities have a hard-on – if you need another word, try erection – to nail me for doing for people what the same authorities should be doing, which is protect them. Write it down, gentlemen: This case is as much an issue of civil rights as our colored brothers and sisters are bravely facing in Alabama. Now if you'll excuse us, we have an unjust accusation to defend.'

I flinched. No matter how many books Shushan read, he would always be a high-school drop out, product of the Brownsville streets. In point of fact, we were fellow alumni of Thomas Jefferson High School, and had even suffered some of the same teachers. But I went to class. He should have added 'against' to the end of his final sentence, which could have been improved further by a complete overhaul: *We have to defend ourselves* – who was this *we*; was I included? – *against an unjust accusation*. But rewriting Shushan was as vain as it was unnecessary. He had made his point, giving the press what it needed and in so doing framing the story that would be in the afternoon papers in a matter of hours.

After posing for the photographers once more, we were suddenly inside an overheated courtroom, rising when the judge entered, a stern-looking woman with straightened gray hair done in a kind of African pageboy, the white collar bordering the neckline of her black robe a bright demarcation between dark and dark. She did not sit.

'Ladies and gentlemen,' she said in a voice like paper being slowly and deliberately torn, 'It is fitting that we stand for one minute of silence to honor the memory of our slain president.'

I looked sideways to Shushan, but he betrayed no emotion at the suggestion that John F. Kennedy was worth this.

When the minute was up Judge Went merely said, 'You may be seated. Counsel for the defense, you have a motion, do you not?'

Fritzi stood. I could see why he won cases. He looked for all the world as though he could effort-lessly *sit* on an opposing argument until it expired by suffocation. The level of the courtroom itself seemed to shift as Fritzi took three balletic steps forward (like most big men, he had early learned to move with grace) enough to take control of the real estate between the judge and jury, twelve of the most innocuous faces I had ever seen, or not seen in the way the drab and affectless pass us every day in the subway or on the street – but not so close to the bench to challenge the authority of the judge by moving into her immediate space.

'*Good* morning, your honor,' he said brightly, as

though they were merely passing on the stairs. 'If it please the court, a family matter of the utmost delicacy and urgency has arisen, as I noted in my informal communication with your honor late last night, and I therefore ask that this trial be adjourned forty-eight hours, in order that my client make the proper arrangements.'

What fiction was this? I knew as little as the grinning reporters seated opposite the jury and scribbling notes – doubtless they had seen Fritzi in action before. The 'mob mouthpiece' was known for his ability to delay proceedings, dragging them out until a jury member grew ill or a prosecutor apoplectic, or the judge up and died. While her honor made a brief note, I considered what this family matter of the utmost delicacy and urgency might be. A birth, a wedding, a bar mitzvah? An appointment to be fitted by Miguel for a new suit?

'Both counsel in my chambers,' the judge said. 'Bailiffs will instruct those having business before this court as well as members of the public to remain patiently where they are. This court is in recess for six minutes.'

With a start I realized who the prosecuting attorney was. I had sat in her office and been grilled until Fritzi had sprung me: the same man's cut gray suit, the same gray hair, the same dry efficiency. She followed the judge through a door at the front of the court and Fritzi followed after, pausing only long enough to throw a sad-clown's face of resignation in the direction of the jury.

'That bitch has been after me for years,' Shushan said.

'Yeah,' I said. 'Me too.'

He looked at me. 'For years?'

'Days,' I said. 'What's the secret?'

'Secret?'

'The family matter of the utmost delicacy and urgency.'

'Yeah, well,' Shushan said.

'Yeah, well?'

'I was hoping we could talk before the trial. Maybe after, when we have a little privacy.'

'This is private,' I whispered. 'You could write it in a note.'

'A death,' Shushan said.

Abruptly I envisioned Terri, her wrists slit, then her throat. Projection, I thought. Some part of me would probably like her dead. 'Justo? Ira?'

'They're fine.'

'Okay, so who's the fictional corpse?'

Shushan leaned closer. 'I'm sorry we have to do this, here. We should have more time.'

'We have six whole minutes.'

'Your mother died,' he said.

Big news. 'When I was a kid.'

'No,' he said. 'I mean, your mother is dead.'

I considered. Was this a puzzle, a distinction with a hidden difference? 'Okay, and my father too. I'm a fucking orphan. Is that what you're saying? I know that. It's not very interesting. Just what is.'

Shushan looked pained, as though he had tasted

something unreasonably bitter. 'You know the truth about language?' he said. 'It's no way to communicate.'

'Shoosh, I'm listening, but not getting it.'

'I mean to say, I'm trying to tell you. . . .' He seemed to be on the brink of abandoning the attempt altogether, then plunged on. 'Your mother died.'

'I *know* that.'

He put his hand on my shoulder, tightening his grip. 'Yesterday,' he said.

CHAPTER 45

How long does it take to discover your life is a lie? Most people take forever, if they discover it at all. Me, I was luckier. It took all of six minutes, five minutes actually and one of silence until Dolores Grady reentered, glaring at me as she took her place at the table to the left, where she busied herself zipping up her briefcase. Then came Fritzi, looking like he'd scored a hole-in-one and nodding to the jury like Arnold Palmer acknowledging the gallery's awe. After a moment Judge Went climbed back on the bench, the court-room standing. When she sat, we sat. She banged her gavel three times. 'This court is adjourned until Wednesday at 9 AM. Members of the jury may go home but are advised not to read news-papers or watch television news or hear news on the radio. You may not speak of this trial to anyone, not even to a fellow member of the jury. In the event you are contacted by persons known or unknown you should (a) decline to carry on any conversation bearing on this trial and (b) imme-diately contact the bailiff with full information on said contact.' She turned to Fritzi. 'Mr von

Zeppelin, we have here the final adjournment of this trial – is that clear?'

Fritzi stood. 'It certainly is, your honor.'

'My condolences to the family,' she said. 'This court is adjourned.'

After we rose for the judge to exit, I continued standing, staring into the middle distance, trying to comprehend what I had just been told. A strange arithmetic had entered my life: what I had thought was real was now proved unreal. Facts could no longer be depended upon. Everything added up, but differently. *X* now meant something else entirely; thus *Y* was different. What I knew about myself was the same, but rearranged like a room full of furniture that I stumbled into as I tried to navigate in the dark. In a daze I watched Fritzi climb into his huge belted topcoat, blonde cashmere so soft it hung in gentle folds like drapes framing a large window. The jury emptied out, looking puzzled, disappointed. To my left Dolores Grady and her prosecutorial team wheeled out their files – who knew what was in them that Fritzi intended to defend against with a briefcase so small it could not have held more than thirty sheets?

'Mr Shushan Cats?'

I heard the voice, recognized it, but couldn't place it.

'Such police work,' I heard Shushan say. 'You eye-deed me out of this huge crowd? What's up?'

'I'm Special Agent Quinones of the Federal

Bureau of Investigation. This is Special Agent Mink. Would you mind if we asked you a few questions? It won't take long.'

'Fritzi?'

I turned to see the lawyer place the pearl-gray Homburg on his head, where it sat so lightly, tipped a bit to the right, it seemed a breeze might blow it off. 'My dear, we're in the middle of a criminal trial,' Fritzi said. 'Why don't we all wait until it's over? Fair play and all that. Please do take a number.'

'I'm afraid that's not possible,' Quinones said. She'd done something to her hair, dying out the bit of premature gray so that it was uniformly brown. Curiously, it made her look older. 'There are two ways we can do this, Mr Cats.'

'Yeah, I know,' Shushan said. 'The hard way or your way. Just tell me what it's about.'

Quinones looked at Shushan, then at Fritzi, then at me, finally back to Shushan, who seemed suddenly combat-ready, as if waiting for a punch so he could deflect it and go in underneath for the kill. His legs moderately spread, his arms hanging loose, beneath the relaxed demeanor he looked vaguely dangerous. Probably he looked that way to a lot of people. 'Mr Cats, we'd like to talk to you about where you were on the twenty-second of November.'

'That would be, what—'

'Friday, sir.' This was Mink of the short fuse.

'Friday the twenty-second of November? I was in Texas.'

'Houston?' Quinones asked. 'El Paso? Fort Worth?'

'Dallas,' Shushan said. 'Is there a law against that?'

Special Agent Mink put his hand on his ear and turned away, facing the entrance to the courtroom. I followed his gaze. There on either side of the double doors were two more poorly dressed federal specimens – unmistakable: it was as if they had had to pass a bad-suit exam to get the job.

'Sir, there is at this time no law against being in Dallas the day the president was shot,' Special Agent Quinones said. 'But there might be. Is there someplace nearby we can talk?'

Shushan laughed. 'Spend a lot of time at the movies, Miss Quinones? Yeah, there's someplace nearby we can talk. You like Italian food?'

CHAPTER 46

Dolce Far Niente seemed deserted without the slight figure but large presence of Auro Sfangiullo. At this hour, barely eleven, it was devoid of diners except for a few individuals, all men, all excessively well-barbered, who sat one to a table drinking espresso and reading the racing sections of the *Mirror*, the *Post* and the *Daily News*.

We had pulled up in front on Mulberry Street, parking directly beneath a sign reading NO STANDING/TOW-AWAY ZONE. Two carloads of FBI agents tucked in right behind us. It seemed only people like Shushan and those who pursued him could be assured of a place to park in this city – both groups clearly above the law. Fritzi's uniformed chauffeur sat in the limo, its motor running, while on either side drivers sat in the two FBI cars, miserable black Chevy Biscaynes, bottom of the line, occasionally pressing their ears to get better reception.

At the round table we were shown to in the back, Shushan ordered a bottle of Montepulciano Soriano 1955, and told the waiter to bring only three glasses. 'The FBI is not allowed to drink, gamble or enjoy the pleasures of the flesh while on duty,' he said pointedly to the waiter, then winked before turning back to the table at large. 'Or any other time. Except for J. Edgar Hoover, and that's limited to dressing like a lady and taking it up the. . . . You know why we're here?'

Not only wouldn't Quinones and Mink drink, they wouldn't eat either. Except for a cup of instant coffee – the waiter said he would search the kitchen for this exotic substance – they sat and watched while Shushan ordered and, as the fragrant food was brought out on heavy white dishes, seemed to grow visibly more glum, like vegetarians at a pig roast.

'Sir, we're here to ask you some questions about your activities over the past week,' Quinones said.

'No, no,' Shushan said. 'It's clear why you want to talk to me – what I'm asking is do you know why we're talking *here*, in this place?'

'You like the food?'

'The food is good. Try a little *bruschett'* at least. It's with the table. It's not like anybody's paying for it. It just comes when you sit down. No? Why we're in this place is some people are very sensitive about secret meetings with the FBI. You have this Bobby Kennedy still around – your boss? Nobody knocked him off yet, but we can hope. Seems like the little prick has a perverse interest in organized crime, which by the way doesn't exist. It's more like restrained anarchy. Never mind. So if it got out I was having a secret meeting

399

with you two very nice individuals suspicion would enter the picture like cockroaches in a new chop-suey joint. Here, nothing is secret. There's no suspicion because it's all out in the open. Of course either way I'd never tell a thing about certain people and their activities, but it's better not to tell in public. You sure about the *bruschett'*? The *mozarell'* is something else, if you like that. Made in the back. You ever think maybe you're on the wrong side of the law? We eat better.'

'When did you arrive in Dallas, Mr Cats?'

'Last week sometime.'

'Sir, I'll make it easy for you,' Quinones said. 'You flew out of Idlewild last Monday at five-twenty PM on Pan Am flight forty-one, stopping in Dallas, continuing on to Mexico City, where you stayed at the Reforma Inter-Continental. Three days later you returned via Dallas, where you stayed at the Hilton, returning yesterday afternoon at six-fifteen PM, after which you checked into the Sherry-Netherland.'

'Sounds about right.'

'Sir, why did you fly to Mexico City?'

'Because I can't fly to Cuba anymore, that's why. I got prime real estate in Havana I can't even visit. I suppose you know that.'

'A hotel and casino,' Quinones said.

'El Flamboyan – people here think it means the flamboyant. Which it does. But it's a tree, *delonix regia*. The Royal Poinciana. Got them all over the property. If I could I'd invite you down. I can't.

400

Cuba was raped for centuries, mostly by us, and now we're upset they put in socialism? Tell me something, what's so evil about socialism? You don't like socialism, send in the Peace Corps. Build schools, hospitals. Don't make the Cubans the enemy. For crying out loud, their national sport is baseball. We used to buy their sugar, now you can't even get a legal cigar. Sure sometimes you have to use force, but setting up Fidel Castro as David with us as Goliath, how does that make sense? How does that make things better? This entire country has communism on the brain, like a disease. Let me tell you something, Special Agents Quinones and – remind me.'

'Mink.'

'Mink. You know what the antidote for communism is? *Food*. Medicine. Schools. Hollywood movies. Schwinn bikes. Jazz. Tourism. Jobs. What a fucked-up situation. We have these Kennedys, they're like some form of perverse American royalty. They look like movie stars, they fuck movie stars – Jack Kennedy's father used to fuck Gloria Swanson, among others, and both sons fucked Marilyn Monroe, probably your boss Bobby would still be fucking her – you didn't know that, but it's true. I know people who know. And not just Marilyn Monroe, about as ditzy a specimen of the female mammal as you'd want to avoid in a closed room, didn't even wash for crying out loud. I could give you a list. So instead of picking up what that Eisenhower did, which was send troops into Little

Rock to protect little colored kids, the Kennedys they're blowing a fuse about organized crime, about the Teamsters union, about Fidel Castro, about some country in Asia nobody but the French ever heard of, and they're sorry they did. Let me tell you. Like a lot of guys, I fought in Korea. Did I go there because of some political ideology? Absolutely not. I went because I was a kid and thought being in a war would be the coolest thing since fast cars and slow women. But when I got there I realized, you know what, this isn't our war. This is about some kind of religious fervor called anti-communism. You think there's a difference between the North Koreans and the South Koreans? They both stink of *kimchee*, they both speak a language related only to Hungarian and Basque – that's actually a fact – and they both hate the Japs and the Japs hate them. So forty-five thousand Americans ended up dead or missing in action. You know how we could've avoided that? Give the poor slobs something to eat. And you know why we won't? Because there's no damned money in it. You ever hear of the military-industrial complex? Even Dwight Eisenhower was warning us against it, and he's not exactly Karl Marx. So who did we have sitting in the White House? The military-industrial complex with well-cut clothes and great hair. Since 1960 every time I talked to somebody in my business who isn't a complete moron, the first thing they would say is somebody should put a bullet through that asshole Jack

Kennedy's head and his brother too, because they don't provide anything for this country other than bullshit, image, style. The perception of leadership. Between you and me, I'm surprised somebody didn't take the shit out months ago.' He looked to Fritzi, who had put down his fork, a rare occurrence. The look on the lawyer's face was: Please, please, *please* shut up. Shushan ignored him. 'You know every morning at eleven the prick went for a swim in the White House pool and then some poor White House college-girl intern blows him. One of them should have bit off his dick.'

Quinones must have wished she was wearing a wire. Maybe she was, or Mink. 'I take it you didn't care for the president, Mr Cats.'

Shushan shook his head.

'What were you doing in Dallas, Mr Cats?'

'I'd been there after Korea. Knocked around, worked for some people. So I went back for a visit.'

'Went back for a visit. Was that a general visit, see the sights – what are the sights in Dallas, Mr Cats?'

'Damned if I know. Just hung out with friends.'

'Mr Cats,' she said. 'Is one of those friends a Mr Jack Ruby?'

In the silence I could hear ice cubes rattle in a pitcher on the bar fifty feet away. '*Mr* Jack Ruby?'

'Mr Jack Ruby,' Quinones said.

Shushan removed a Lucky from his jacket pocket and lit it in one motion with a silver Zippo embossed in gold with the Marine Corps eagle, globe and anchor. 'I know Jack.'

'Did you see him,' Quinones asked. 'In Dallas?'

'I did.'

'Is Mr Jack Ruby the reason you went to Dallas?'

Shushan scratched his ear. 'Absolutely.'

'Absolutely?'

Shushan stubbed out his Lucky. Normally he smoked them till they turned his fingers brown. 'I know this is going to sound . . . weird. Jack is one fucked-up guy. Excuse my language. I mean, he's been fucked-up forever, since he was an embryo. Mother was nuts. Crazy violent old man. Grew up in foster homes. Never had a chance. Also, not so bright. I mean, bright enough to work for the FBI, but for normal life he has problems. That's a joke.' No one laughed. 'Unfortunately, as you may have noticed, he has a temper, which is never good. But also a big heart, emotional. I mean, what could be more emotional than knocking off the guy who knocked off the president? So what happened is this. My mother died a couple of weeks back, God bless her. I'm actually just out of the mourning period. I don't suppose you're Jewish?'

'Christian Scientist,' Quinones said.

Fritzi stopped shoveling mozzarella. 'They save on doctor bills,' he said. He was speaking directly to Shushan: be cautious.

'Methodist,' Mink said. 'Why does that matter, sir?'

404

'I don't suppose it does,' Shushan said. 'Where were we?'

Watching him I realized he was now running the conversation, asking the questions, setting the agenda. I still had a lot to learn.

'The mourning period,' Quinones said.

'Thanks,' Shushan said. 'A rough week, as you can imagine. So what happened? Much to my surprise, who comes to the mourning period, aside from people I know and see all the time, business associates, people from my Jewish society, but one Jack Ruby. I don't even know how he heard my mom was . . . deceased. Maybe an associate of an associate. Something like that. Suddenly Jack shows up. He's wearing boots, you know, cowboy style, with eagles, and a Stetson – that's a hat . . .'

'I know what a Stetson is, Mr Cats.'

'Well, it really stood out. I mean, you're supposed to cover your head, the men, at a Jewish mourning, but that hat, that was . . . it stood out is how I'd put it. Look, I worked for the man ten, eleven years ago, when I got out of the Marine Corps—'

'We're aware you're an ex-Marine, Mr Cats,' Mink said.

'I'm not,' Shushan said. 'There's no such animal as an ex-Marine. Once a Marine, always a Marine.' He smiled. 'You're not.'

'Army,' Mink said. '101st Airborne.'

'Not a bad outfit,' Shushan said. 'Anyway, Jack comes to the funeral, visits me at my place for the mourning period, stays about two hours, two very

405

long hours. You know how it is with people from the past. Sometimes you're more important to them than they are to you. I worked for him, Shorty Farber, Ralph Silverstein, Lew Cobb, Big John Albright – they had the main bars on the same strip, two blocks more or less. I got hired by all four of them.'

'Five names, four bars, sir,' Quinones said.

'Nice catch. Lew and Big John were partners. Yeah, I worked for five guys, but in four bars.'

'How did you do that, Mr Cats?' Quinones asked. 'Typically.'

'Every night I'd stroll from bar to bar, making sure things were quiet. People got drunk. In Texas they like to fight. You had to calm them down. Not real hard work. I probably would have stayed who knows how long, but Jack got into a pissing match with Shorty and Ralph, small-time stuff, arguing about stealing talent from each other – strippers. What they had was strip clubs with pretensions: a magician, a country singer, sometimes a really bad comedian but basically the clients were there for the flesh. The other acts just covered the clubs in the eyes of the law, not legal exactly but the cops never bothered except for free drinks. Jack is one of those small-time guys who actually like cops. And then because the four clubs couldn't get along, the bar-owners each decided to hire their own security, not share me. So that's when I came back to New York, which I probably would have anyway. My mom was here, my late mom, bless her, and

I have a sister. Hometown stuff. You want to hear this?'

'Please,' Quinones said.

Shushan lit another Lucky, this time offering them around. I took one – in 1963 not only was smoking normal in a restaurant but we smoked in the *middle* of a meal. The FBI declined. 'Next thing I know, last week after my mom's mourning, I get a call from Jack in Dallas.'

'A call?'

'A phone call. Aside from his visiting for the mourning, understand this is somebody I haven't seen since 1953. On the phone it's like we're best friends, having coffee every other day. "Shushan, it's Jack. Can you come down?" I tell him I'm a little busy now, he knows my mother just died, I haven't even looked at my business for a week, that kind of thing. Between you and me, to avoid further involvement with Jack I would have told him I was having an operation to remove my gentiles. I mean, it's like some girl you *didn't* screw in high school calls and says she needs you to fly a couple thousand miles because she's dreaming about you. As if it's bad enough you didn't have much in common in high school, now you have to get involved with them years later.'

'But you did.'

'The man was crying on the phone. I went down, held his hand. I think he was having what they call a breakdown. He was a wreck. His business

407

wasn't doing too well. There was trouble with one of the strippers he was dating. She walked out on him. Men get to a certain age, things don't work out, they can get . . . desperate.'

'You went to Dallas to spend time, three days in fact, with someone you'd prefer not to know?'

'Jack Ruby gave me my first job when I got out of the service.'

'Ten years ago.'

'Yeah.'

'And that obligated you—'

'Sure. I don't forget when people are nice. Now, you know, they're all nice. Uniformly. But then, what was I, a punk kid with not even a suit of clothes? Jack Ruby bought me my first suit that wasn't khaki.'

'Mr Cats.'

'What?'

'I understand you served with distinction in the United States Marine Corps.'

'They give you medals for just showing up.'

'The Navy Cross?'

'I got lucky.'

'I don't believe that, Mr Cats. It's clear you were a hero.'

'A long time ago, so what?'

'You're a marksman.'

'In the Marines. I haven't shot at a target in years.'

'At a target?' Quinones asked. She was good.

'At a target, at a person, at anything.'

'Mr Cats, did you have anything to do with the assassination of President John F. Kennedy?'

Fritzi tapped his wine glass three times with his fork. Everyone in the restaurant looked up. Our waiter started to come over, but must have read the faces at the table. He stopped. 'Don't answer that question, Shushan. It's an insult to you as a peace-loving person and as an American. Miss Quinones—'

'Special Agent Quinones,' she said.

'Of course. Special Agent Quinones' – he said this so slowly you could have finished the soup of the day (lentil, with olive oil and rosemary) between syllables – 'Not only will my client cease answering your questions, but I believe he is owed an apology.'

'It's only a question, counselor.'

'Shushan, button up. You've talked enough for one day.'

Shushan stifled a laugh. 'You know why I'm talking, Fritz?'

'Because you're not as smart as I think you are?'

'Tell me, Fritzi, do I sound like I got anything to hide? I don't, which is a fact. A person with something to hide, he wouldn't admit to not particularly caring for John F. Kennedy, he wouldn't volunteer that he knows Jack Ruby, he wouldn't even mention Cuba. Fritzi, I got nothing to hide. So I can talk freely. It's still America.' He turned to Quinones. 'You want to arrest me on what I said?'

'No,' she said. 'Not today.'

'Not never,' Shushan said. 'If you arrested me for what I said you'd have to arrest a million people, because we got the same story.'

'A million people don't know Jack Ruby, Mr Cats. Not before Sunday.'

'Yeah, that's right. Only maybe ten thousand. He owned a bar, for Pete's sake. He still does. How do you think he got into that basement in a police station when they're transferring Lee Harvey Oswald? He knew all the cops and they knew him. Do I look like the kind of guy who goes around assassinating presidents? I mean, really?'

'I don't know how such a man looks,' Quinones said.

'According to your people, he looks like Lee Harvey Oswald.'

'As a marksman, Mr Cats—'

'A former marksman.'

'A former marksman who, when he was rotated out of combat duty in Korea, was an instructor in marksmanship at the United States Marine Corps training facility at Twenty-Nine Palms, California—'

'For six months, until my tour was up.'

'As an expert marksman, would you say one man could have fired the bullets that killed President Kennedy, and wounded Governor John Connelly, from that distance and angle?'

Shushan didn't pause. 'Absolutely not.'

'Because?'

'Number one, the Mannlicher Carcano. If that was the gun, it's a shitty gun. Hey, this is a rifle you can buy mail order for twelve bucks, sometimes less. Number two, reload time. This gun, it's famous for a really bad action. And in Dallas it all had to happen in seconds. I don't know about Lee Harvey Oswald, but I was good with a rifle, and I couldn't do it.'

'You don't know about Lee Harvey Oswald?'

Shushan stubbed out his cigarette and motioned for the waiter. 'Espresso all around,' he said. 'And the bill.'

Mink broke in. 'Not for us, sir. It's against regulations to take favors of any kind from a suspect in a criminal investigation.'

'A *suspect?*' Fritzi pushed his chair back from the table. The sound of metal scraping against the marble floor with three hundred pounds on it was like an animal in pain. 'My client is a *suspect* in a criminal investigation? This interview is over, o-v-e-r. Over. Shushan, don't say another word.'

'Why not?'

'Because I'm your attorney and I'm telling you not to. Special Agent Quinones, do you intend now or at any time in the future to charge my client with a federal crime?'

'Not at the moment, counselor.'

'Good. When you change your mind, do let me know.' He stood. Shushan remained seated. Slowly Fritzi sat back down, glaring at his client.

'Mr Cats,' Quinones said. 'First of all I want to

thank you for your cooperation, and your frankness.'

'Like I say, I got nothing to hide.'

'Is there anything else you might wish to tell me?'

Shushan shrugged, almost petulantly.

'Especially your views on whether or not Lee Harvey Oswald acted alone.'

'If he acted at all,' Shushan said. 'In my opinion it was two guys, minimum. And one of those guys was not Lee Oswald.'

'I appreciate your candor, Mr Cats.'

He smiled.

The waiter came up, standing at Shushan's right side. There wasn't a bill. There never was. Shushan took a crisp hundred out of his pocket and passed it to the waiter, who took it and the hint and disappeared.

'And I appreciate your homework,' Shushan said. 'You know I *know* Lee Oswald couldn't hit the Camel billboard from across the street in Times Square.'

Fritzi just shook his massive head.

I hadn't said a word throughout the meal. Now I wanted to say something, but I didn't know what.

'Then why as his instructor in the USMC marksmanship course at Twenty-Nine Palms did you pass him with the grade of marksman?'

I looked at Fritzi. Sweat was pouring off his forehead. Shushan's was dry, his tan merely giving off an oily sheen of confidence and good health.

'He was kind of a lost soul.'

'You passed him even though he couldn't hit the—'

'No, of course not. I had a responsibility to the Corps. Technically he passed. Like in high school, he had the equivalent of a sixty-five. Passing, but just. The Corps gives instructors a little leeway in these matters. I could have failed him, made him repeat, and probably he would have failed again. And that would have been it. But he was . . . I don't know. A kind of sad sack, a lost soul like I said. I knew he wouldn't last long in the Marines anyhow. It's not like he was a lifer. How much damage could he do? Maybe I was wrong. I had just come out of combat. I'd seen the best-trained men fall apart – my own captain was one of them – and I'd seen fuck-ups who stepped up and became heroes. Maybe this kid would do that. He was a real fuck-up too, not even at the level of a Jack Ruby, who could at least run a bar. Badly, but he could. Let me tell you something. I was a good shot, and I couldn't have carried off what Lee Oswald is supposed to have done, for sure not with that rifle. You know what they call that gun in Italy? The humanitarian. I doubt it could be done with a Marine-issue sniper's rifle like the M-2b, and that is a good gun.'

'But you did know Lee Harvey Oswald.'

'You know that. I was his range instructor a long time ago.'

'And Jack Ruby.'

'And I think the Kennedys are full of shit.'

'Therefore you had a grudge against the President and his family.'

'Grudge? Let me draw you a picture. When Shushan Cats has a grudge against you, you know it. I didn't have no grudge. I just think he was a shitty president, just like his brother is a shitty attorney general. Does that mean I'm going to pop them? Listen, the number of people I don't care for you can count in the thousands. I don't go shooting them. In case you don't know it, murder is a crime. Knocking off the president is a federal one. And also it's a waste. You take out one asshole and another pops up. You could spend your life at it and there'd be no change. You think I'm ever going to get back El Flamboyan? In a word, never. Some things you got to live with.'

'Mr Cats, do you have an opinion, a view, a guess even, regarding who was behind the assassination of the president?'

'Sure.'

'Mr Cats, in your opinion who would that be?'

'Probably somebody who was very pissed off.'

'It wasn't you?'

Shushan rose from the table, I with him, then Fritzi. 'Of course not.'

'Even though you have a record of acting for others in such matters?'

'When I was doing what I did, when I was just starting out, it was stuff within a certain circle. I don't do that any more, and if you ask me officially I never did.'

'But someone did it to President Kennedy.'

'Rightfully, so far as I'm concerned.'

'Mr Cats, are you defending the assassination of a sitting president?'

'I'm not defending it,' he said. 'It's a crime, isn't it? But I'm not crying about it either.'

'Do you know or suspect a specific party to have been involved in the assassination? Do you know who that was?'

'Somebody.'

'Can you give us more?'

'Let's see,' Shushan said. 'Who would want to put John F. Kennedy out of our misery? Look at the number of people he upset. Screwed the coloreds, screwed the Cubans, and he's drafting people for a war in a shit-hole called Vietnam that is going to make Korea look like *The Ed Sullivan Show*. Also he was not so popular with the lunatic fringe on the right either. The John Birch Society, those people, they didn't like what he said. Or that he's Catholic. The criminals didn't like him or his brother for business reasons, and he fucked every woman for miles, so his wife probably wouldn't mind if someone knocked him off either. Guy like Dwight Eisenhower, head general in World War II, big-time golfer, grandfather type, what's to hate? You know why Ike was so popular? He didn't make promises he didn't keep. People feel let down by idealists who aren't. Lyndon Johnson, you know he's a scheming bum from the outset, so you're cool with that. Kennedy, it's like you take home the most beautiful girl at the party, and comes a certain moment you find out she has a dick. Man, that's not just uncomfortable. Somebody got angry.'

'Somebody,' Quinones said.

'Somebody,' Shushan said. 'But it wasn't me.' He offered his hand to Quinones, who took it, and to Mink, who didn't.

'Don't feel bad, special agent. Not everybody can be a Marine.'

Quinones stifled a smile. 'If we need you tomorrow, Mr Cats, where can we find you?'

'At a funeral,' he said.

We walked out, Shushan and I and Fritzi, followed by the two FBI agents, and behind them the two earphones who had stood for an hour just inside the entrance to Dolce Far Niente. The smell of basil and clam sauce and fresh espresso must have driven them nuts.

'One last question, Mr Cats.'

'I don't date cops.'

Quinones ignored it. 'Mr Cats, have you ever met, personally I mean, President Fidel Castro of Cuba?'

Fritzi's chauffeur was holding open the door of the limo.

'Of course not,' Shushan said, and got in, I after him.

CHAPTER 47

This time Shushan made the funeral arrangements, and he was good at it. I hadn't thought of limousines and masses of flowers; Shushan laid them on. At my request the service was at the graveside. Shushan found a new rabbi, who carefully tore the collar of my beautiful black mohair suit along the seam; still it took Miguel the tailor two days to repair. It was a proper funeral. Shushan made sure all was done by the book as, he assumed, my mother in her right mind would have wished.

From the little my father had talked about her – mostly all he said was: 'Russ, your mother was a wonderful woman' – in her better days she was the spiritual leader of our household, very concerned – perhaps rigorously so, though I will never know if at some point she crossed the line into obsession – with keeping a kosher kitchen and with the overarching Jewish questions of the day: the violent birth of the State of Israel, the welfare of the surviving remnant of Jewish victims of the Nazis in Europe, and the mass resettlement in Israel of close to a million Jewish refugees who had been booted out of the Moslem nations of the Middle East. As in Shushan's home, a blue-and-white Jewish National Fund tin box had a prominent place in our kitchen, and as a child every day I would make sure to drop in a penny or two because 'mommy believed in charity.' Every so often an emissary from the JNF would come around to collect the proceeds, never more than five or six dollars in coins, and after counting it would carefully inscribe a receipt in my mother's name. Neither my father nor I ever bothered to correct the record. Somehow it sounded crude, arrogant, final: 'Mrs Newhouse is dead.'

Besides, my father knew it was a lie.

According to Terri, who had visited her at Shushan's request, my mother was a manic depressive with paranoid delusions that neither drugs nor shock therapy would ameliorate. Shushan suspected my father had removed her from our home because he no longer trusted her with his son. Was there cause? Had he found me somehow brutalized, or was my mother's growing paranoia threat enough, a radical form of post-post-partum depression that would only eventually have placed me in peril? I spent a solid hour talking to Terri about this, becoming intimate with Shushan's sister in a way I had never imagined.

'Bottom line,' she told me, 'Your father had to send his beloved wife away to save his son. He never forgave you for it.'

'Wouldn't you say that was unfair?'

'What I'd say has no bearing. It's what happened. Must have really fucked you up.'

'I love it when you talk all clinical,' I said. 'Let me put it this way: it was like being locked away in a benign prison, where you got three square meals but your jailer never talked to you.'

'Never?'

'Seldom.'

'Seldom isn't never, Russ. Self-pity doesn't become the new you.'

I sighed. 'I rarely get a chance to wallow in it.'

'Do I look like someone who gives a shit?' she said. 'In fact, if you want to talk further, and you should, I'll have to refer you.'

She gave me a piece of paper with a name on it. I tossed it in a municipal wastebasket on the way home.

This remained the Westbury, where I spent long hours talking with Shushan and hearing his plans. For me. He knew people who could open the door to the Naval Academy, after which he thought I might want to make a career of the Marines. Marine Aviation, that interested him. Also intelligence. He thought intelligence was right up my alley. It was eerie to get all this fathering from a man who had avoided even the risk of creating a family. All the women he went with were paid for.

'My sister says I won't accept a broad to replace my mom,' he said. 'So that's why my love life is limited to whores. Can you believe? Typical Esther psycho-bullshit.'

419

As if to prove he had no feelings in the matter, he dropped Darcie, and let me know he had no problem with my continuing in his stead. For a while I did, but between her former relationship with Shushan and the ongoing affair with Terri, several weeks after the funeral I ended it. Predictably she did not hold it against me. That she did not I held against her. In terms that Terri would understand, Darcie had simply become another woman who had let me down.

As with most of the people who turned up at the funeral, I kept tabs on her over the years. She continued on with Terri even after marrying a widower with three children who had started out as her client. She gave up being a paid companion to become, as she proudly told anyone who would listen, a real mom. As Mrs Franklin Robinson she lived a stable and satisfying life in a house on Kings Highway in Brooklyn, and so far as I know never called her husband Feivel, which must have made him happy. Feivel/Franklin's practice was so-so, but he eventually made a small fortune from the invention of a chemical compound that restored the whiteness of teeth stained by coffee, tobacco and time. One of his patients was Arnold Savory, who learned to smile again after having his mouth redone at a Manhattan clinic licensed to apply Rubashkin/Robinson's product. Like the actors and directors who remained Arnold's clients as betting on football and basketball replaced the horse-racing business that was taken over by state-run off-track betting, he was not shy in declaring that his mouth had been Franklinized, a life-altering event.

Auro Sfangiullo had been right about the state's entry into legalized gambling, but he lived barely long enough to see it happen. When he died – the *Daily Mirror* gave him a front-page send-off: R.I.P. DOCTOR RESPECT – Dickie Tinti replaced him as managing director of what Shushan and *il dottore* both liked to call 'disorganized crime.' This was almost inevitable. With Sfangiullo's passing went all constraints on drugs. The Tintis became the major player in cocaine – both the refined white-collar variety and the crack that would decimate Harlem and other black areas of New York, including my own home turf of Brownsville. They turned over billions, left a lot of headless bodies scattered around the metropolitan area – a trademark of sorts – and eventually became such a public menace that Dickie was convicted of conspiracy to obstruct justice (in this particular instance on dubious evidence). He was put away for twelve years. The prosecutor in his case – in the words of the *Daily Mirror*, which often seemed to have more sympathy for the hoodlums than for their hunters – was 'anti-mob mom Dolores Grady,' who had borne twins late in life and took time out from the trial to express breast-milk in the judge's chambers. Though there were whispers about such a close relationship between lawyer and judge, there was nothing sexually inappropriate. The judge was a woman.

Her Honor Myrtle Went *was* criticized however for instructing the jury to 'destroy the vermin that infects this city,' just as she had been similarly criticized for her instructions to an earlier jury in the case of Shushan Cats. Though the same prosecutor was in place and the district attorney's office mounted a strong prosecution – things came out in the trial that made me shudder – Judge Went told the jury to 'deliberate on the facts in context. Many times in American history individuals have been compelled to act when the authorities refuse to. I share with you the concept of the Underground Railway, when Harriett Tubman acted outside the law to free Negro-Americans from the shackles of slavery, and I also note the work of Dr Martin Luther King and his followers, who even today are beaten and jailed by the authorities for attempting to secure and protect the rights of their fellow Americans. Defense of the fearful and downtrodden is in itself not a crime but a virtuous act.' All but one of the jury members were hyphenated Americans: four Afro-, three Latino-, one Chinese-, an Italian- and two Jewish-. They deliberated all of three minutes. Shushan walked.

Went became a federal judge in the Northern District of New York, where her decisions opposing school-busing, affirmative action and racial preferences were so regularly and predictably overturned that she became known in legal circles as Judge

422

Went That-a-Way. When it became public knowledge that she headed a charitable foundation funded by Shushan Cats – a profile in the *New Yorker* brought the connection to light – she managed to avoid the formal censure that would have struck down a white judge in the same circumstance, a clear case of the racial preference she otherwise opposed.

Fritzi died of a massive heart attack in 1982 while at a weight-loss spa in Utah. This may have been for the best: as he grew slimmer the less he succeeded in court. It was as if his physical presence had been his trade secret. When he ceased appearing to be a force that could squash the opposition, the opposition squashed him. It was Fritzi who so unsuccessfully defended Dickie Tinti, and it was in the midst of a final appeal that someone put Tinti out of New York's misery with a crude blade in a shower at the New York State Correctional Facility at Otisville.

Justo stuck with Shushan until the day of his sixtieth birthday, when he retired to Puerto Rico, where he had been buying up beachfront property for years in Vieques, site of a former naval bombing range.

Ira and Myra finally had a baby – apparently they had been trying for years. In respect of this, Shushan fired Ira as his wingman and set him up running a limo company, where his hours were strictly nine-to-five. In gratitude the couple named their daughter Shushana, and in reciprocal

423

gratitude her namesake visited her once a month bringing so many toys Myra had to put her foot down. It was not a light foot. She had grown obese – Ira remained besotted – but now she could enter a room knowing men could gaze upon her because they were no longer smitten.

Miguel the tailor, so self-effacing it was hard to know he was in the room, was struck by a bus on Madison Avenue and, though doctors could find nothing seriously wrong, declared he was unable to stitch again. Shushan provided for Miguel and his family for the next forty years.

Recruited with a full professorship to Columbia, Eugene del Vecchio grew increasingly radical. When the civil rights struggle transmogrified into nationwide rioting after the murder of Martin Luther King, Del moved on to become one of the major tacticians of the Gay Liberation Movement – in his memoir, *Mauve,* he claimed to have invented the word 'gay' itself – and was a leader of the crowd that had fought a police invasion of the Stone Wall Inn, a homosexual bar in Greenwich Village, the Boston Tea Party of the gay movement. He became known as a kind of left-wing gun for hire. In 1964, he came to prominence as the principal faculty backer of the Columbia Free Speech Movement, in which students took over the chancellor's office and trashed it; eventually they were expelled by police, Del with them. At some point he gave up poetry entirely, but wrote regularly for radical publications. By the turn of the century he had become a resident talking-head on cable news, and for a period of months engaged in a rancorous but ratings-positive debate on 'permissiveness' that covered everything from politics to parenting.

In all the flash and fire, no one pointed out that neither Del nor his right-wing opponent, a pop psychologist named Dr Terri Cats, was an actual parent. Terri's first book, *Stop Acting Like A Child!*, had been a bestseller. Despite one critic calling it 'Dr Spock for Republicans,' or because of that and similar pans by the liberal press, Terri became a fixture on television and eventually host of her own advice show on cable.

Everything in the years since 1963 seemed to move to the margins. It wasn't so much that the center would not hold – no one knew where it was.

Celeste began studying to become a nun, then reversed course, had her lovely apple breasts augmented to melonic proportion and for over a decade under the name Cin More made dozens of adult films. When the Internet got going she leveraged her following and her cleavage into digitized erotica, eventually running several companies catering to a menu of well-defined pornographic tastes. According to *Time,* which did a cover story called *Naked Internet,* 'Ms More is to the incest taboo what Washington was to the Delaware and to jingoism what John Wayne is to the Green Berets.' Though Celeste was estranged from them after her descent into porn, all the Callinans must have shared a moment of deep unease at the comparison. Their baby brother, Duncan, was among the first Special Forces personnel to die in Vietnam.

The three surviving brothers became known in their respective professions for their charitable endeavors. Patrick the cop rose to captain and spent most of his spare time and money on expanding the Police Athletic League, which offered sports as a hopeful antidote to such inner-city standbys as drugs, impersonal violence and casual sex. Monroe the fireman was lost in 9-11 a month before his scheduled retirement – he and his wife had adopted twelve children, most of them in some way deformed, crippled, retarded or all three: one daughter was deaf, dumb, blind and autistic. Father Bill was involved peripherally in the church child-abuse scandal when, as executive assistant to the bishop of Garden City on Long Island, he was discovered to have serially trans-ferred abusive priests. Embarrassed in the press, he remained in the church. What the journalists did not know, because Father Bill did not disclose it, was that for forty years he had dedicated himself – raising money from wealthy laymen – to a private effort to force out errant clergy, sometimes with bribes, sometimes with threats, while at the same offering counsel and aid to their victims.

Royce Wilmington was for a time Dick Tinti's man in Harlem, but on an evening at Palm Gardens in New York in 1964 Royce met a charming ex-con called Malcolm X who convinced him to examine his soul in the light of salvation in Islam. As Ahmed 24X, Royce became a power in Harlem politics and a force to be reckoned with by his former associates in the drug trade. Ever the smooth operator, Jimmy Wing left crime as well. With his silent partner Tommy he opened high-end Hunan-style restaurants in New York and Los Angeles, then sold these to open the immensely successful chain of fast Chinese food places known as ChopStix. Pepsi owns them now.

Jack Ruby's conviction on 'murder with malice' of Lee Harvey Oswald was overturned in 1966 on the grounds he could not have gotten a fair trial in Dallas. Shortly after a new trial date was set, he died of cancer in Parkland Hospital, where John F. Kennedy had been declared dead three years earlier and where Oswald himself died after the shooting. All through his incarceration he claimed there was a conspiracy he could not talk about because even in prison he was not safe. 'Everything pertaining to what's happening has never come to the surface,' he declared in a televised interview. 'The world will never know the true facts of what occurred, my motives. The people who had so much to gain, and had such an ulterior motive for putting me in the position I'm in, will never let the true facts come aboveboard to the world.' Yet on his deathbed he seemed to recant. A shrunken hulk, he was barely able to gum the words, 'There is nothing to hide – there was no one else.'

The assassination of John F. Kennedy and its aftermath remained an open sore in America for decades. Fidel Castro categorically denied he had anything to do with it. Dozens of books were written pointing the finger at one or more of the usual suspects – organized crime, the CIA, right-wing loonies, the National Rifle Association, Aristotle Onassis (he is said to have lusted that much after Jacqueline Kennedy, who became his bride) and that ever-present bugaboo of the twentieth century, the Soviet Union. As with Ruby, nothing would ever be known for sure. Even after the fall of the Berlin Wall, when documents in the newly opened KGB archives unquestionably proved the Soviets had had no part in either the murder of the president or of his alleged assassin, experts immediately came forward to call the documents faked.

After the tide of conspiracy books came an antithetical bulkhead of print claiming to demonstrate beyond a doubt that Lee Harvey Oswald had acted alone and that Jack Ruby was an unconnected nut case. Yet polls continued to show that most Americans believed something larger, better equipped and smarter than Oswald had killed the president, and that Jack Ruby's murder of Oswald was proof.

Though it was he who had gotten the nation involved in a land war in Vietnam, the cult of John F. Kennedy as a great president continued to grow, especially in light of the dismal record of his successors: JFK's war, pursued with fatalistic resolve by Lyndon Johnson, made the Texan so unpopular he declined to run for a second term; a documented racist paranoid, Richard Nixon was forced to resign the presidency to escape criminal charges; Jimmy Carter proved himself not only incompetent but a self-righteous prig; by his own admission a lying adulterer, Bill Clinton became the first modern American president to be impeached. Though Ronald Reagan was widely respected, the two Bushes who claimed his legacy were and are widely considered to be moronic. Excluding Reagan, who was considered a light-weight when elected and left office in a halo, not one ended his term of office with his reputation intact.

Shushan Cats remained Shushan Cats, though he mellowed over time. At my mother's funeral he bonded with the officiating rabbi and gradually became involved with the religion he had all but ignored. To his library he added hundreds of books on Judaism – I know he never shelved a book without reading it – and from time to time even attended synagogue, always on the anniversary of his mother's death. He became an easy touch for Jewish charities, and began supporting various causes in Israel, especially orphanages. After the Six-Day War he flew to Tel Aviv where he was gratified to discover that Israel Defense Forces training was based almost to the letter on United States Marine Corps doctrine. In 1970 he took me with him for the dedication in the resort town of Netanya of the Goldie Cats Center for Lone Soldiers, a residence for Israeli conscripts who had no homes to return to on leave.

As though it were no longer worth doing because the challenge was gone, when Shushan was declared not guilty of providing legal protection to illegal businesses he seemed to lose interest in his core enterprise. The Fulton Fish Market remained lucrative, but he had grown out of it. Eventually Shushan set up a security firm manned by ex-cops (among them a couple of retired NYPD detectives who had once fed me pizza) and hired an ex-FBI special agent to run it. He knew how to pick people. Anita Quinones aggressively expanded the business with security contracts for Kennedy Airport, the Port of New York Authority and Amtrak. By now a mere passive investor, twice a year Shushan showed up for board meetings, but that was all.

Of course he continued to make money, the losses in Cuba covered handily by shrewd purchases of huge tracts in Orlando, Las Vegas and the Dominican Republic. He spent an hour each day investigating opportunities in the stock market, early on diversifying to foreign shares because he suspected, rightly, the dollar would fall. Most of his time was devoted to charity.

He supported reading programs in the public schools and backed politicians in both parties who agreed to promote laws providing grants for underprivileged university students. He wrote checks with a consistency that was unique even then, thoroughly researching each field. But he was also a soft touch – according to Terri, an easy mark – who could never turn away a panhandler or a former colleague down on his luck or a medical researcher with a sure cure for cancer, heart disease, diabetes or even illnesses of which Shushan had never heard. When Jack Ruby died it was Shushan who paid for his stone at Westlawn Cemetery in Chicago.

He paid for the alteration of my mother's monument as well, thus obliterating the engraved lie I had lived with since I was five. All remained the same but for a single date: my mother died the day John F. Kennedy was assassinated.

'I didn't hear of it,' Shushan told me on the way to the cemetery in the back of a long slate-gray limo, Ira following in the Eldorado with Myra, Justo, Terri and Darcie. 'I was in Dallas. The people from the place, the private hospital whatever, upstate, they were under orders never to talk to anyone but me. Not even Ira. Justo knew, but Justo is a one-way sponge. Justo wouldn't tell your friend Professor del Vecchio the guy himself was a fag if I told Justo it was a secret. Your mom's thing, it was confidential. I probably wouldn't have known for a while except that when it happened I called Justo from Dallas. We were both shocked, Justo that I was alive and kicking and me that your mom, you know, she wasn't. I'll tell you, your mom was put away for fifteen years. Every month after your old man died I paid the bill, and every month they'd give the same report, word for word: Sheila is in excellent health. You know, except for being not right in the head. So I never expected she'd just . . . die.'

'How not right?'

'It's like she was burned out in the brain. Sealed up. You could talk to her and she wouldn't answer. Then when you were in the middle of something, tipping a nurse to take special care of her or just getting ready to leave, she'd start talking a mile a minute.'

'You went up to see her?'

'Twice a year. Maybe I should have gone more. But that was your father's schedule. I kept to it.'

'He went hunting.'

'Is that what he said?'

'Twice a year. But he never bagged anything. Never caught as much as a rabbit. I always thought it was odd, because he was a good shot. A terrific shot. Very steady hand. When I got older I figured it was some woman. Officially he never dated. I figured he didn't want me to know.'

'He had a date with your mom.'

'Some date, Shushan.'

'Yeah, she wasn't exactly a live wire.'

'You said she talked.'

'Nobody could ever figure it out. It was all unconnected words, like she went into a dictionary at random and picked out unrelated words. I knew when she got worse because after a while it wasn't even words, just syllables like, then just sounds, not speech at all.' He looked away. 'She used profanity. In the midst of all these nonsense sounds you'd hear *fuck* and *bullshit* and *cocksucker*. I'm no nun, but it was unsettling.'

'Tell me about my father.'

'What do you want to know? He was a good man.'

'Was he on the take?'

'You have to understand the circumstances.'

'You're saying they were right, that he *was* crooked?'

'Crooked, shmooked,' Shushan said, suddenly interested in something outside the car, then turning back. 'Your mom was sick.'

'That's a very intimate word, *mom*.'

'Your mother was sick. He couldn't leave her alone, not with a little kid. He put her in Bellevue, it's a public hospital, but when he went in there he knew he had to get her out. He found this place upstate. They have deer that come right up to the porch to eat out of your hand. The people up there they don't even talk about unemployment – there's no jobs period, no industry, no business to be unemployed from. Believe me, they get a paycheck at this hospital they stick. They'd be crazy to be anything but wonderful to the patients. They call them guests, if you can believe. A solid move on your father's part. But it wasn't free. Suddenly your father, as straight a shooter as there ever was, he finds himself all jammed up for cash. Monthly. For a civil servant, this was a heavy nut. He did what he had to do.'

'He came to you.'

'A good thing. I mean, he could have gone to the Tintis, or worse. I heard him out and told him, Mike, I got a little foundation that can help out. He tells me, Mr Cats, with all respect for your generosity, I don't take charity. It was a Mexican stand-off for a while, like two guys arguing over a restaurant check. In the end what could I do? I put him to work.'

'As?'

'Whatever came up.'

'For instance.'

'For instance if somebody got out of line.'

'My father was five-five in his elevator shoes.'

'I'm five-seven. So what. You think people are more scared of me or Ira? Ira is a bruiser. Us little guys, we compensate.'

'What else?'

'What else what?'

'What else did my father do for you?'

'This and that, no special thing. Whatever came up. I trusted him pretty much from the start.'

'You don't want to tell me.'

'Details? Kid, it's ancient history. I can't even remember myself. Nothing bad. Just normal activities. When your father passed, I kind of took over the responsibility upstate.'

'You took over.'

'What was I going to do, look away? They would have dumped her out to a state institution. You don't want to know about places like that. People laying in their own filth. It was nothing for me. I mean, what am I supposed to do with all this money, buy more cars? I got a dozen suits.' He looked down at mine. 'Well, minus three. How many do I need? I live in a fucking hotel for crying out loud. Top-of-the-line Caddy. Eat in the best places. Vacation wherever I like. I want a book I buy it. I even got the best lawyer, or at least the most expensive.'

'But you went up twice a year.'

'A drive in the country. Nothing strenuous. Anyway, Ira did all the work.'

'But he doesn't know.'

'Ira knows what he's supposed to know. Justo knew because he paid the bills. Terri, I talked about it with her. But outside of that, zip. What am I supposed to do, take out an ad in the *New York Times?* Let me tell you something, kid. There's some things I did, in my early days especially, I'm not so proud of. That's when I made my reputation as someone not to fool with. So those things I'm not so proud of, I figure they actually put me in a position to help other people, maybe they didn't have the advantages I had, like it says in that book when you made fun of me, *The Great Gatsby.* But from the beginning I realized that if I did good things and told people I was doing them it wasn't pure. It was advertising myself. Promotion.

Believe me, I know that when you're in the same position, and I expect you may be because you're smart and ambitious and people trust you, then you'll probably do the same.'

'Thank you,' I said.

'For what?'

'Taking care of my . . . mom.'

He waved it off, then let out a long, slow sigh.

'You knew it was me,' I said.

'Hmmm?'

'At the Bhotke Society. You knew it was me.'

'Maybe,' he said.

'But you never made contact before that. You didn't come to my father's funeral, or visit me during the *shiva*.'

'What was I going to do, show up at the cemetery? Hello, kid. I'm a friend of your father's. All that stuff he told you, that they threw him off the force because he was too straight, that the cops on the take wanted him out, all that was a lie? Your father's friend turns out to be the so-called notorious Shoeshine Cats.' He lit a Lucky out of his pocket. 'You want one?'

'No.'

'Better you didn't know. I'll tell you. Like you never had a mother I never had a father. So like all kids in that kind of situation I made stuff up. I said my father was the bravest, strongest, best father before God took him away. You know who took him away? I found out in my mother's things. She kept a diary on paper scraps. In Yiddish. I got it translated. I went to this stranger, a rabbi in Jersey I never met before in my life, and said here's my mother's diary. I'll give a contribution to anything you name, but if you tell anyone what's in it I'll cut your dick off and stuff it in your mouth and they'll find you that way on the street in front of your synagogue. God didn't take my father. A broad did. Some whore. Or maybe not. Maybe she was the image of virtue. For me the same. Anyway, I heard he died out west, Albuquerque or something.' He rolled down the window and tossed out the butt. 'So what was I going to do, spoil your dreams? What kind of man would do that to a . . . ?'

'To an orphan.'

'Yeah, so what. We're all orphans, eventually.'

We rode in silence for a while until we reached the gates of Beth David. In a matter of moments I would once again stand before the conjoined graves of my parents. I considered not asking, then did. 'A question. It's . . . serious.'

'About Dallas?'

'No,' I said. 'I'm not interested in Dallas.'

He smiled, a wan almost bitter smile, part appreciation, part regret. 'Okay,' he said. 'Fire away.'

'Why does someone fake his own kidnapping, his own apparent murder? The blood on the seat. The bullet holes. You were coming back, so why do that?'

He laughed so hard the limo driver turned around, hearing it even through the glass partition.

'You got a good head on your shoulders, kid. I'll say that.'

'It just doesn't make sense.'

He looked past me to the orderly ranks of the dead as the limo made its way slowly to the Bhotke plots, reached into his pocket, pulled out another Lucky, stuck it resolutely into his mouth, then removed it. He rolled down the window and tossed it out. 'I didn't expect to come back,' he said quietly. 'I probably wouldn't have. I got some property in Mexico, beachfront. Some time I'll take you down. Cuba I like better. But Mexico, I could live there quietly. I got a Mexican passport even. You can just buy them. And I was tired. Really tired, kid. Money, I got plenty. I'm forty-two years old. I could be your father. I didn't want to die doing what I was doing. I wanted a fresh start. Very few men can have that. But I could. What do I have? Friends? Justo could live without me. Ira the same. Professional associates? Don't make me laugh. No wife, no kids. Just Terri. And I'll tell you, I didn't even know if I'd let her know. Maybe yes, maybe no. Then I got word.'

I saw it in his eyes. 'My mother died.'

'Yeah,' Shushan Cats said. 'She sure did.'

'You came back for me.'

'Look at that crowd. Must be everybody we know. Plus the press. One thing I wouldn't miss, the press.'

'You came back for me.'

438

'Russy,' he said, looking out through the limousine's tinted windows at the small piece of real estate that was all that remained of Bhotke, where my family and Shushan's had originated – Floris in his case, but close enough. Through the glass I could see the society members, Shushan's professional associates, maybe three hundred people. Behind us the Eldorado pulled up, its wide doors opening to let out Justo and Terri and Darcie and Myra and Ira. 'Russy, I was alone in this world a long time,' he said finally. 'Nobody should be alone.'

The rest of that morning had all the implausible clarity of a dream, and as with a dream its details faded fast while its effect managed to be both imponderable and clear, something lost that remains forever, its absence more permanent than its presence – tactile, palpable, real. I can recall every face, even those who are now themselves passed on, but nothing of what was said, by me or by anyone else, remains. Except this.

At the end of the service, after I had shoveled in the first spade of dirt and stood aside to watch the others as they filled the raw pit, a young woman approached. She was wheeling a baby in a small carriage on the grassy, uneven ground. Short, dark and full-breasted, she reached out and touched my sleeve. 'You don't know me?' she said, not a question but a fact.

'I. . . .'

'Marie-Antonetta Provenzano,' she said shyly. 'Bork now. We sort of dated, in high school.'

So she was. The Italian goddess of my youth who had moved away, leaving me with adolescent heartbreak, unmitigated longing and a solid appreciation for the language that may have saved my life. 'Wow,' I said.

'Yeah,' she said, rocking the carriage. 'Wow.'

'And you have a kid.'

'Three,' she said. 'Actually.'

'You've been busy.'

'Eddie, my husband, he's watching Eddie Jr. and little Anthony. I saw about the funeral on TV. I've been following your career. Actually.'

'Career?'

'You know, what you've been doing. How you became a gangster and all.'

I gave her a smile, the best I could do. 'It's nice of you to come.'

'I don't live far,' she said.

'It's been great seeing you, Marie-Antonetta.' Then I compounded the lie. 'You haven't changed at all.'

'You neither,' she said, drifting off into the crowd as though she had never lived, while I remained my past transmuted, my future marvelous, unwritten, my present turbulent, uncertain, yet for all of that rock-steady, anchored, secure. The first twenty years of our lives shape who and what we are. Call me lucky: these were mine.